PRAISE FOR CHRISTIE CRAIG AND
DIVORCED, DESPERATE AND DELICIOUS:

"Christie Craig delivers humor, heat, and suspense in addictive doses. She's the newest addition to my list of have-to-read authors....Funny, hot, and suspenseful. Christie Craig's writing has it all. Warning: definitely addictive."

—*New York Times* Bestselling Author Nina Bangs

"Readers who enjoy Jennie Crusie and Janet Evanovich will fall head over heels for *Divorced, Desperate and Delicious*, a witty romantic adventure by debut author Christie Craig....A page-turner filled with humorous wit, sexy romance and just enough danger to keep you up long past midnight."

—RITA Award-winning Author Dianna Love Snell

"Suspense and romance that keeps you on the edge of your seat...until you fall off laughing....Christie Craig writes a book you can't put down."

—RITA Finalist Gemma Halliday

"An exceptionally funny, fast paced, snappy read with unusual humor that will make you laugh."

—Huntress Reviews

DANGER

"We've been trapped in a freezing room by a killer. I'm wearing a fuc—friggin' pink scarf." Carl took a step closer. "I'm about to crawl in bed with a gorgeous redhead but there's not a chance in hell I'm going to get lucky." He paused and his right eyebrow arched. His eyes twinkled. "Is there?"

"No," Katie insisted, but dang it if she didn't feel the thrill of knowing he wanted her. "We're just sharing body heat."

The truth started perking deep down. She would love to share more, but admitting that to herself was dangerous; admitting that to him could prove fatal. Not *deadly* fatal, but fatal to her relationship with her fiancé. A relationship that already had issues. Her stomach wiggled in a bad way.

Carl stepped closer, his eyes carrying a leftover smile. "You know, for it to really work, we should take off our clothes."

The idea sent fantasies upon fantasies doing sexy little dances through her mind. "I think we can skip that part."

CHRISTIE CRAIG

Weddings Can Be Murder

LOVE SPELL NEW YORK CITY

LOVE SPELL®

June 2008

Published by

Dorchester Publishing Co., Inc.
200 Madison Avenue
New York, NY 10016

ISBN 10: 0-505-52731-6
ISBN 13: 978-0-505-52731-8

The name "Love Spell" and its logo are trademarks of Dorchester Publishing Co., Inc.

Printed in the United States of America.

10 9 8 7 6 5 4 3 2 1

Visit us on the web at www.dorchesterpub.com.

This is dedicated to my husband whose endless support and encouragement have been the springboard to my achieving my dreams of publication. Steve, I love you the whole world. (Did I mention you enough this time?)

ACKNOWLEDGMENTS

I'd like to thank:

My agent, Kim Lionetti, who tolerates my wacky sense of humor and says yes to my crazy ideas, even if it means being tied up and videotaped. (You can see what I mean on my website, www.Christie-Craig.com.)

My editor, Chris Keeslar, who allows me just enough rope to swing on, but never enough to hang myself. (But save that rope, Chris, I might be making another video.)

Faye Hughes, my friend and writing partner on my nonfiction books. (Even though she insists I need a limit on the number of bathroom scenes in my books.)

Lieutenant D. R. "Duke" Atkins, Jr., with the Houston Police Department, who still talks to me even though I misspelled his name on my last acknowledgement page. (But honestly, if it bothered him so much, he could have his name changed.)

All my writing buddies, who are the glue that keeps this writer together and sane…well, mostly sane.

My daughter, Nina Craig Makepeace, whose wedding (though not one person was killed and no ring was ever flushed down the john) inspired this book.

And my son, Steven Craig Jr., whose skill at humorous banter is mirrored in all my heroes.

Weddings Can Be Murder

Chapter One

Yesterday, Carl Hades had been shot at by a man wearing a black thong and a pink silk nightie. Even in his line of work, that was hard for a devout heterosexual male to digest.

Carl dropped his Glock and gun oil on the kitchen table beside his bag of worms. He needed a down day. No headaches, no pressures, no—

A sharp jingle rang from his phone.

No friggin' calls.

So, who the hell was ringing on a Sunday morning?

He dropped into a kitchen chair. Ignoring his Verizon special telephone, he stared at a stack of last week's mail and popped a worm into his mouth. A gummy worm. The sour flavor brought his taste buds to full alert. His six-year-old nephew had gotten him hooked. He doubted the candy was on the surgeon general's list for healthy living, but then, neither was getting shot at, and he hadn't broken that habit, either.

A second ring? Let the voice mail catch it. Carl bet it was his dad, anyway. Who else would be calling now?

Stretching his legs, Carl bumped Precious, a silver poodle too damn prissy for any man to own. Not that

Carl owned the dog. His ex-girlfriend did, but she'd neglected to take the animal when she'd left a year ago. Just as he'd neglected to take the fuzzy mutt to the shelter as he'd threatened to do.

A third ring.

He dropped a worm to his unwanted foot warmer. Leaning over, Carl counted three green worms and one sissy dog. Precious looked up—beady eyes, black nose, and gray fur.

"You don't like the green ones either, huh?"

Fourth ring.

He eyed the stack of mail. His gaze hit a Victoria's Secret catalog. "Nice."

Even more than worms, Carl liked what was inside the blue bra and matching panties. How Vicki had got him on her mailing list, he didn't know, but he wasn't complaining. The near-naked cover girl had potential. But on second thought—nah, he didn't do redheads, not even in his fantasies. Too difficult. Too much like Amy.

He flipped the page to a brunette. *Oh yeah*.

Fifth ring.

Carl eyed the ringing phone again as Precious rested a snout on his foot. What if his dad really needed something? He reached for the phone—without shifting his foot—and checked the number displayed on the small screen. It was for a neighboring Houston area code—his brother's new area code. His brother he could deal with.

Answering the phone, he grunted, "I already helped you lug moving boxes Friday night." He waited for Ben to sweeten the deal with an offer of his wife's apple pie. His mouth watered at the thought. When there came no reply, he added, "Okay, but only after my morning constitutional."

"Mr. Hades?" a feminine voice queried. "Carl Hades?"

Carl paused. "Sorry. I thought you were someone else." Of course he had. He wouldn't be telling a woman he was about to go take a—

"Obviously," she snapped. "My name's Tabitha Jones. You might have heard of me via my business. Tabitha's Weddings."

"Weddings?" Maybe his morning constitutional was a better topic. He rolled his shoulder. His left rotator cuff pinched—the pain due to a bullet he had taken last year. Yeah, he really did need to stop getting shot at.

He picked up his bills with his left hand. The gas bill landed in the gotta-pay stack.

"I'm a wedding planner," came the voice on the other end of the line.

"That's nice."

"The best in Texas." Ms. Jones sounded annoyed that Carl hadn't admitted that he'd heard of her. "I got your number from Mr. Logan. You helped him with a situation."

The "situation" had been a six-foot-plus forty-year-old who had a hard-on for Mr. Logan's thirteen-year-old daughter. Catching that damn pedophile had felt good, too.

"I did." Carl squared his shoulders and brushed his heel against the dog resting at his feet, waited for the woman to continue.

"I've got a situation and hoped you might help me."

Carl dropped his handful of mail. "What kind of situation?"

"I'd rather discuss this in person," she said. "How about four? No. Four thirty."

"Today?"

"There's a problem with today?"

Her tone was haughty. He never dealt with haughty too well. "It's Sunday." *And I've got a date with a model.* His gaze shifted to the catalog.

"I'll pay you time and a half," she snipped.

"Maybe you should fill me in on what this is all about."

"I'd feel more comfortable talking in person. Please?"

Was that fear in her voice? "If things are that bad, maybe you should call the police." There was a line between what he did now and what he'd done when he'd carried a badge. She needed to know that.

"I did call them, but I don't think they took it seriously."

"Took what seriously?" When she didn't answer, he clarified, "Look, Ms. Jones, I prefer not to waste my time or yours. Give me some details, and I'll tell you if I can help you." *And no more cases that involve armed men wearing thongs.*

Her pause hung heavy. "I think someone is killing my brides. And I think I know who it is. Or at least it's got to be one of four people."

Well, hell. He'd spoken too soon. If he had to choose between getting shot at by a cross-dresser or hanging around a bunch of bridezillas, bring on the cross-dresser.

"Please. I really, *really* need your help."

Chapter Two

"It's normal." On her knees, Katie Ray stared at the porcelain throne and fought the nausea that threatened to erupt every time she thought about the wedding.

"Normal?" Leslie Grayson, her best friend, back in town for the first time in a year, stalked into the bathroom. "Oh, gawd, you're pregnant."

"No." Katie shoved her mane of hair from her face and watched Les grab a washcloth from the cabinet and dampen it. "I've got a nervous stomach, remember? I barfed before every big final exam. Before every big job interview." *Before the big funeral.* She shoved that thought away. "Well, this wedding is big." And it was happening so fast. Two weeks and counting.

Les handed her the wet cloth. "Are you sure you're not pregnant? Accidents happen."

"Between Joe's engineering job, my job at the gallery, and planning the wedding, we've hardly had the opportunity to have an accident."

Les's frown told Katie she'd just given her friend more Joe's-not-right-for-you ammunition. "And what does that tell you?" her friend said, rolling her green eyes.

"It tells me we've been busy." Katie twisted the diamond on her finger. Actually, Les had a knack for knowing how men rated in the world of Katie Ray. She'd pegged Rick Baker as a dweeb in junior high, Jason Tanner as a pervert in college, and a slew of others. *Don't go out with him. You'll be sorry*, Les would say, and dang it, if she hadn't been right most of the time. But how could Katie listen to Les now, when . . .

She blinked. "You've never even *met* Joe."

"But I've heard you talk about him three times a week for almost a year. And I know what I hear."

"What do you hear?" Katie asked, unsure she wanted to know.

"I hear a friend who's still trying to deal with losing her entire family and so worried about turning twenty-nine that she'll marry the first Tom, Dick, or Joe who comes along."

The engagement ring received another twist, up and over the knuckle, as a new wave of nausea threatened. Katie edged closer to the toilet and tried to control her stomach. "You would love Joe if you met him." The two not having met was a failing Katie planned to remedy tonight.

Not that she was telling Les. Why give her friend time to prepare a list of are-you-good-enough-for-my-best-friend questions? As an ex–investigative reporter, Les excelled at putting people in the hot seat. Better to surprise both Joe and Les. And they would love each other. How could they not? Les was smart, gorgeous, and now one of Boston's most popular restaurant reviewers. Joe was a sweet, handsome man, who was . . . was going to be Katie's husband.

Husband. Nausea hit hard, and Katie promptly threw up.

"Gross." Les swung around. "You know, I haven't missed seeing you do this."

"Sorry." Katie released her hold on the throne and ran the wet washcloth over her mouth. Feeling better, she stood up and flushed. "It's just wedding jitters."

Les turned around. "The idea of getting married

shouldn't make you puke. You should be happy and . . . glowing." Les's brow puckered. "Not green and wearing a dribble of something unidentifiable on your chin."

"Sorry." Katie ran the cloth over her face. And that's when she noticed it. "Fudge!" She dropped to her knees and started doing the pat-and-crawl shuffle across the tile floor.

"Fudge what?" Les asked. "And you know, you really should just say 'fuck.' Everyone knows you mean 'fuck.' "

Katie swept her hands and gaze on both sides of the porcelain bowl. Once. Twice.

"My ring." Katie held up her naked left hand and stared at the still-swirling water in the john. "I think . . ." A sob left her throat. "I think I just flushed it."

She promptly puked again.

Several hours later, Katie studied the maps she'd printed off the computer to help her find Tabitha's new place.

"I wish you'd postpone things until tomorrow," Les said. "Today's my grandma's birthday. Everyone's coming over for cake and ice cream. Mom will kill me if I don't make it."

Katie glanced up. "You're not missing anything with me. I'll get the cake samples and we'll taste them later. All Tabitha wants today is a check. I'm meeting her at four, swinging by the jewelry store to pick up my new ring, and meeting you at five at Dave's Place. Tight, but doable."

"You're not telling Joe about the ring, are you?" Les asked.

Katie sighed. How did you tell your fiancé that you'd flushed his eight-thousand-dollar engagement ring down the toilet? "Why? I'm replacing it." All three plumbers she'd called had assured her that as soon as she'd hit the flusher, her ring had taken the fast track to the city's sewers.

Frowning, Katie checked her purse to make sure she had the checkbook to her new account. This would be the first time she'd used the money left to her by her parents' insurance policies. Oddly, it hit her that she was using money gained through the loss of her family for the sole purpose of starting her own family—with Joe. *Happily ever after, here I come.* So, why wasn't she tossing emotional confetti around instead of tossing her breakfast?

She met Les's suspicious gaze. "Joe doesn't have to know."

"Already keeping secrets from him, huh? I don't suppose you'd listen if I said flushing your ring down the toilet was your subconscious trying to tell you something."

"No, I won't listen." But the thought kept running circles in Katie's head. Hence, the decision *not* to tell Joe about the little incident.

They stepped outside; the November wind sent goose bumps chasing hairs across Katie's skin. She considered going in and grabbing another sweater. But hey, the Rays were tough.

Les yanked her jacket over her breasts. "Dang. It's colder here than in Boston." She paused. "When will I meet this man who can't find time to make love to his bride-to-be?"

Katie turned to lock the door—and to hide her white lie. "Soon." And she hoped that after meeting Joe tonight, Les would drop the call-off-the-wedding rally. "Remember, five at Dave's Place. Oh, and here's a key to my house in case the party ends early."

"Key. Dave's Place." Pocketing the key, Les took two steps toward her car, then swung around. A cold breeze scattered her blonde, wispy hair across her face. "I know I sound like a broken record, but I think you're rushing into this."

Katie pulled her blue cardigan closer. "We've dated a year, and Joe's great." She said it as much for herself as she did for Les's benefit. "You know how I know he's great?" she went on. "Because the first time I met him, I thought, 'Wow, Les would totally love this man.' Can't you be happy for me, just a little bit?"

Les swept back her hair. "Maybe I haven't been here to watch love happen. But I haven't heard love happening in your phone calls either." She sighed. "Tell me you love this guy, really love him, and I'll totally get off your back."

Katie looked at her best friend since kindergarten, and while the words lay on the tip of her tongue, they were held back by another wave of nausea. "I love him," she finally spat out, and didn't want to think about why those words had felt forced.

"Could you say that with more conviction and without turning green?" Les frowned and leaned close. "I don't see 'happy' in your eyes, Katie. I don't even see 'I've had great sex' in your eyes."

"I'm happy." Katie, not wanting Les to look any closer, dug into her purse for her Tums. "Be at Dave's at five."

"Right." Les huffed. Les's huff always meant something. Sure enough, Katie's friend was studying her. "You still aren't painting, are you? You were happy when you were painting."

Katie cut Les a don't-go-there look. "I manage a gallery. I get my art fix there."

"You loved painting," Les said. "You were happy when—"

"I sucked at painting." Katie shivered.

"So said your parents."

"And the critics," Katie reminded her, thrilled when her ringing cell phone put an end to the subject. When her parents were alive, Katie didn't mind bitching about them. Everyone bitched about their parents, didn't they? But somewhere in life's rule book it stated you shouldn't speak ill of the dead. Katie, like all the Rays before her, followed the rules. Plus, everything bad she'd ever said now haunted her. Losing loved ones did that.

She grabbed her phone from her purse. The call registered as out of the area. "Hello?" Steam floated from her breath and warmed the tip of her nose. "Hello?"

Nothing.

"Hello?" She heard a faint sound—of music?—"The Wedding March." "Tabitha?" The line went dead.

"Your wedding planner?" Les pulled her suede jacket sleeves over her hands and did the I'm-cold shimmy.

"They didn't answer." Katie snapped her phone closed. In spite of the cold, she and Les stood in the middle of her front yard, studying each other the way friends do after not seeing each other for a long time. "I'm so glad you're here," Katie admitted, and gave her friend a hug.

"Liar." Les hugged her back. "I've been a pain in your ass."

"True." Katie chuckled. "But puking alone isn't fun." And she had been alone—and lonely—for too long. Going from being a part of a family of four to being a party of one had taken its toll. Then, six months after the accident, Les got a job in Boston. The combination had resulted in a hard year and a half.

But what about Joe? Shouldn't he have taken the edge off the loneliness? The question ran laps around Katie's mind. She answered it by telling herself that nothing took the place of a best friend.

"Speaking of asses," Katie said, "do these jeans make my butt look big?" She turned and gave her friend the back view.

"Your size-six ass never looks big," Les said. "If you weren't my friend, I'd hate you."

Katie swung around. "And I'd trade this freckled package for yours any day of the week. Men love blondes."

"As long as a sexy redhead isn't around." Les eyed Katie's hair. "Plus, I've gained ten pounds. Occupational hazard."

"And it all went to your boobs." Katie pointed to the evidence. They both chuckled as Katie glanced at her watch. Obviously, six hours wasn't enough time to play catch-up with a friend you hadn't seen in a year. "I have to go or I'll be late to the cake maker."

"Go." Les started to her car. "But bring some chocolate samples."

Recalling Les's chocolate-is-the-substitute-for-sex theory, Katie yelled out, "Wait! What happened Thursday night on the date with Mr. Sexy Voice?"

"Oh, gawd, I haven't told you." They met halfway and huddled for warmth. "When the waiter brought our check after dinner, Mr. Sexy Voice looked me right in the eyes and said, 'I hope you're going to be worth the price of your steak.'"

"Get out of here. *No*." Katie giggled.

"Honestly. And when I gave him the evil eye, he had the nerve to ask if I was jealous that he had a penis and I didn't."

Katie rubbed her hands together for warmth and anticipation. Les always had great comebacks. "And what did you tell him?"

"That with what I have under my skirt, I can get all the penises I want. Then I paid for my dinner and left. Frankly, those Yankee men just don't do it for me."

Katie laughed, but she knew it wasn't any Yankee persona or penis envy keeping her friend celibate. Les had loved Katie's brother as much as she had. Katie would bet Les's engagement ring still hung from its chain and lay hidden under her tan turtleneck. Sometimes life was so unfair. But Katie refused to crater. Cratering just wasn't in the Ray bloodline. Rays were strong and successful. That was why Katie's dreams of being an artist had been so un-Ray-like. If a Ray couldn't do it perfectly, they simply didn't do it.

Les hugged her again. "I'll see you tonight. After dinner, we'll paint our toenails. At least I'll get you painting something."

As Katie crawled into her Honda, her phone rang again.

"Hello?" Another musical snippet of "The Wedding March."

"Tabitha?" The connection died.

"Strange," Katie mumbled. "Very strange."

Chapter Three

Joe Lyon stepped out of the dressing room and onto the platform to let the tailor mark the hem on his tux. And he hoped like hell the man would hurry. The damn thing fit like a life jacket: cumbersome, heavy.

"You look good." Harry, one of his groomsmen, had followed him to get his tux.

"I look like a hotel doorman." Joe pulled at the choking collar. Button-downs and Dockers were work attire. He hadn't worn a suit in ages, and had only donned a tux twice.

"Hey, you want to go out for a beer tonight?" Harry asked.

"Can't. I'm meeting Katie." Was that at four or five? Oh, hell, he couldn't remember.

"So, the ball-and-chain dance begins," Harry said. "How you guys can give up the single life is beyond me. Did you see our waitress at lunch? She was hot and I got her number. Variety. Staying single means you get to sample them all."

Joe ignored Harry. Truth was, he'd hardly spent any time sampling Katie these last few weeks, which partially explained why he had these antsy feelings. Could distance cause cold feet? But damn, it didn't make sense. Katie was sexy, smart, funny, and good-hearted. She was everything a man could want. Even his mom agreed. And he and his mom didn't agree on much. So why had he practically avoided Katie these last two weeks? Why wasn't he aching to be with her 24-7? What did it mean?

"You done?" he asked the man who had been chalking his pants and now stood on the other side of the room staring at him. Joe glanced around. Harry had disappeared, too.

"Been done." The man laughed. "Got cold feet, do ya?"

Joe stepped down from the platform and went to get his clothes back on. *It will go away*, he told himself. The anxiety. The doubt. It would go away. Before the wedding, he hoped.

And if it didn't? Hell. What would he do?

About four that afternoon, Carl watched a guy pay for a pack of thirty-six lubricated condoms in neon colors and wondered how long it would be before he trusted himself enough to start tapping the well again, trusting himself to separate the physical from the emotional.

He waited until the man left before plunking down the bag of gummy worms on the store counter. The lady there scanned his worms and grinned.

"Looks like he's going to have a better day than you or I," she said with a laugh.

Carl didn't need to be reminded. His cell phone rang, and this time he carefully read the number of the caller. No more daily-constitutional talks with strangers. "Hey, Dad. How's Austin?"

"Good. I'm thinking of staying for a few more days. It depends if Jessie can get off Monday. We don't have anything that can't wait, do we?"

We? Carl frowned. After giving his dad a few jobs, his old man believed they had a regular gig. It wasn't that Carl thought his dad, two years retired from Houston

PD, couldn't do the job; Carl just didn't want to spend his every working hour with the old man telling him how to run his business and his life.

He pulled out his wallet. "Stay and have a good time."

"Did you get the pictures to Mrs. Davis?"

"Yeah." Carl dropped a few bills beside the worms on the sales counter.

"Did she like the one of her husband dressed in that pink silk gown with the slits cut plum up to his wing-wanger?"

Carl could tell his dad's girlfriend wasn't around now. Buck Hades had a way with words, like a hung-over sailor on a more colorful day, except in the presence of a lady.

"I think she picked that one to show the judge."

His dad laughed. "Gotta love this job."

Love it? Photographing cross-dressers and cheating spouses didn't fit Carl's idea of love. He longed for a real case.

"Is that all?" the woman behind the counter asked. Carl sent her a nod.

"Where are you?" his dad asked. "Tell me you called that friend of Jessie's cousin and took her out. She had a nice rack on her."

Dropping a few bills, Carl frowned. "What part of 'when you get your ass tattooed with a pink butterfly' didn't you understand?" Okay, so he might have inherited his dad's colorful language problem. But the old man's interference had gone too far.

"You gotta move on. I know Amy did a number on you, but it's not healthy for your prostate to go a year without—"

"My prostate is fine." Carl spotted the cashier's grin, and his frown deepened.

"Waxing your own candle isn't the same thing," his dad said.

Okay, Carl wasn't going to get into a conversation about waxing his candle or prostate cleansing with his dad. He'd rather talk about his daily constitutional with Tabitha Jones.

"Enjoy Austin," he said. He grabbed his worms, left his change, and had almost shut his phone when he heard his dad's voice.

"Are you going to your brother's to help him finish moving?"

He raised the phone back to his ear. "I helped Friday night, but I may drop by if my meeting doesn't go too long." He ducked into the cold and headed for his car. While it rarely happened, the forecast had Houston hitting the single digits tomorrow, and it felt like the front had jumped the gun.

"What meeting?" his dad asked.

Carl crawled into his car. "It's about a case."

"What kind of case?"

"Don't have the details yet. We'll talk later."

"Son, about your women issues . . ."

"I told you, Dad, I don't have women issues."

"If it's about your mom, you need to know—"

"Gotta go." One button push ended the conversation. Some subjects were delicate, such as candle waxing and his prostate. Others were downright barred. He pocketed his worms, tossed his phone into the passenger seat, and drove off to talk to Ms. Jones about her missing brides.

Katie dropped her keys and checkbook into her bag with the ten Styrofoam boxes of cake, and left her purse behind to lighten her load. Todd Sweet's assistant had given her extra samples.

As Katie moved up to the porch, she glanced around the wedding planner's new place. The silver maples fronting the house stood naked and almost ghostlike; their dead brown leaves scuttled across the lawn in the icy wind. A shiver, and not just from the cold, hopscotched up Katie's spine. The place looked like a fortress—*or a prison*. She noted the bars on the windows.

Tabitha's praise of her new home as Katie remembered it stood at odds with its ambience. *It's six times bigger than my old house. And with five acres, I'll start throwing weddings here next spring.* Katie wasn't so sure she shared Tabitha's feelings for the property.

Not that Katie's feelings on the subject mattered much to Tabitha Jones. They weren't exactly friends. Tabitha was simply a rich patron who frequented the gallery Katie managed. So when Joe had asked her to marry him and wanted it to happen ASAP, before his mother's illness took a turn for the worse, Katie had gone straight to Tabitha for advice. And because Katie had offered the wedding planner a few discounts on artwork, Tabitha had felt compelled to do the same—even when it was last-minute planning.

No complaints from Katie. It felt nice knowing she had professional help. Her mom, the professional type, would have approved.

As Katie knocked, she looked down at her ringless left hand. She was amazed she didn't feel naked without it. Probably because she'd only worn the ring for eight weeks.

Already keeping secrets from him, huh? Les's question tiptoed across Katie's mind. Happily, she didn't have time to ponder it because the door swung open.

"Hey," Tabitha oozed. In her late forties, the woman breathed out words more than she spoke them. "How's my latest bride?"

"A little nervous," Katie admitted. "Hey, I brought some extra wedding cake samples in case you wanted to try them."

"I never sample," Tabitha snapped. She ran a hand over her white suit as if to emphasize her slim shape. "Plus, you're not using Todd Sweet for the cake. And I just hired you a different DJ, florist, and photographer."

"But you . . . recommended them. And—"

"Trust me." Worry flashed across Tabitha's face, but

then she smiled. The worried look left so fast that Katie wondered if she'd imagined it.

"Come in!" Tabitha said. "Why don't we head to my office?" She swept out her arm as if to show off her place.

"It's really big," Katie said, not wanting to lie, and still worried about the sudden change in her wedding plans.

"I know," Tabitha said. "I'm lucky to have gotten this place. I just had the carpet installed. Don't you love it?"

"Umm," was all Katie said as she looked. White. Startling white. Hurts-to-look-at-it-too-long white.

They walked down the hall and into an office where, in the blink of an eye, Tabitha, the patron who bought lots of art, morphed into the Nazi wedding planner from hell.

Poised like a matronly high school teacher behind her large mahogany desk, Tabitha commenced to ream Katie out for waiting so long to organize the grand event. Never mind that Tabitha was the one changing things midstream. Then, typing on her keyboard, Tabitha switched from reaming to spouting orders. Katie had to:

Go to the new florist to pick out her flowers. Today.

Get new samples and make an immediate decision on the cakes. Today.

Have the wedding dress fitting by . . . last week.

And drag her "one" bridesmaid, Les, to be fitted for her dress by . . . today.

And if it didn't get done? The big, black, slimy, hideously ugly wedding monster would rise from the earth and gobble Katie's head off, and the whole wedding would be a big freaking joke. Which *wouldn't, couldn't,* happen because Tabitha Jones didn't throw bad weddings.

Okay, Tabitha hadn't said the monster stuff, but it had been implied. When had the wedding become more about the wedding planner than the bride? Since when did a wedding planner have the right to make changes without consulting the bride? Katie started to ask. "I—"

"You got all that?" Tabitha barked.

Truth be told, Katie wasn't a pushover. She faced disgruntled artists, dissatisfied art dealers, and idiot art critics at her job on a regular basis. She could hold her own pretty darn well. But some people scared her. And right now, Tabitha Jones was one of those people.

"I got it." Katie tapped her notebook with her pen.

A ringing doorbell interrupted the tense silence and Tabitha's white-suited body rose from her white leather chair. The woman liked white.

"It's probably . . . my next appointment. Give me a sec, sweetie," Tabitha said.

Sweetie? Had she said "sweetie"? Yup. And now the Nazi wedding planner from hell was patting Katie on the arm.

"Just relax." Tabitha's words once again oozed out rather than being barked. "Weddings can be murder, but we have to stay calm." She started to the door. "I'll have him wait in my second office."

Wanting to get out of there ASAP—before Tabitha's bipolar personality did more morphing—Katie pulled out her checkbook and wrote Tabitha a check for the agreed-upon amount. Which, all of a sudden, seemed to be a lot more than Tabitha was worth. Not that it mattered. Katie had hired her, and paying her now was only fair. Well, maybe not really fair, but it went back to the fear factor, and more importantly to Tabitha being a regular gallery patron. Ticking her off wouldn't be good for business.

Katie signed her last name on the check and paused when she realized it would probably be one of the last times she wrote Katie *Ray*, because she'd soon become Katie *Lyon*.

"Katie Lyon." She said the name aloud and . . . bam! Her stomach went from okay to sour in zero flat. Her gaze shot around for a trash can. None.

"Oh, fudge." Cupping her hand over her mouth, she realized she couldn't give up her last name any more than she could puke on Tabitha's new white carpet. The Ray name was one of the last ties she had to her family. Instant tears clouded her vision. Why did her family have to die, leaving her all alone?

She was still fighting the nausea and cloudy vision when she heard a scream. And not just any scream, but an oh-shit-I'm-screwed kind of scream. And not the good kind of screwed, either.

Jumping up, Katie shot to the door and peeped through the open slit. She could see the screaming Tabitha, but not the person being screamed at.

While eavesdropping on private screaming matches wasn't Katie's thing, she couldn't help but try to make sense of the jumble of words.

"You! Brides. Can't do this. Psycho freak. Murderer!"

All of a sudden, the words weren't important. Not when the loud pop sounded. And once again, it wasn't a *good* kind of pop.

With her nose poked through the small opening of the door, Katie watched Tabitha Jones, bipolar wedding planner extraordinaire, fall to the floor. Something bright red flowed out the front of Tabitha's white dress and trickled down onto her brand-new, white—startling white, hurts-to-look-at-it-too-long white—carpet.

"Fudge." *Oh, hell.* Les was right. This deserved the real word. "Fuck!" Then, unable to help herself, she barfed.

Staring at the mess—which looked like a bad abstract painting in shades of mauve against the white carpet—Katie lost her ability for rational thought. Time seemed to stand still. She vaguely recalled looking for a phone to dial 911 and not finding one. The next thing she knew, she had her bag, which held her cake samples, her keys, and her checkbook, and was hotfooting it down the hall.

Down the hall.

Away from the front door.

Away from a bleeding Tabitha.

Away from the person who had made Tabitha bleed.

And deeper into the house that looked *way* too much like a prison.

She'd only made it a couple feet when she heard them: footsteps. She screamed and took off at a dead run.

Chapter Four

Carl parked behind a silver Honda that was parked in front of a white elephant of a house.

He let his motor continue to run while he listened to his CD. From the conversation he'd had with Ms. Jones, he figured he might need a bit of Zeppelin before facing both her and her story of missing brides-to-be. He wasn't sure if he bought into her concerns, either. From what she'd said, the cops hadn't given her story any weight. But he'd learned the hard way not to discount anything too quickly. Discounting things had gotten him shot.

When the song finished, he forced himself out of his car and studied the house. Having grown up only a few miles down the road, he'd heard the rumors about this place. Supposedly, the guy who'd had the home built was a rich paranoid schizophrenic who'd believed the government was out to get him. Carl chuckled. A home with so much prison emphasis was going to house a wedding planner? What irony, seeing that marriage was the social equivalent.

To some people. Carl admitted that his older brother seemed happy locked up in his jubilant little life with a doting, pie-baking wife, cute kid, and a fetching *manly* dog. *To each his own.*

His humor vanished when he heard a scream. Grabbing his gun, he edged up to the door, which stood ajar. Thrown subconsciously into his police training, he backed up against the wall and became acutely aware of his surroundings. The cold. The wind. The sudden silence.

And the coppery scent.

Counting to three, he shifted to peer inside. His gaze lit on a woman lying faceup on the carpet. Blood. It was everywhere. "Ah, shit."

Was it Tabitha? Was she the one who'd just screamed?

As if in answer, another scream sounded. And not from the lady in white.

The urgency in the shrill voice echoing from deeper inside the house put Carl on automatic. "Police!" he called out. "Throw down your weapons!"

He'd surged into the room before he realized what he'd said. He wasn't with the police anymore. Not that he missed it.

Like hell you don't. He hadn't stopped loving this: the excitement, the rush that came with catching the bad guys. He gave his once-injured shoulder a good roll.

Moving in a little more, his gaze cut back to the victim on the carpet. He started to check for a pulse, but the blank stare in her eyes told him not to waste his time. Dead. She was dead. This part of police work he didn't miss.

A banging noise from the back of the house sent another shot of adrenaline down his spine. He reached for his phone to call for backup, but then remembered he'd left his phone in his car. "Shit!"

Choices flipped through his mind: grab his cell, wait for backup, or rush in like a fearless hero. He hated making quick decisions. Particularly those that involved life and death. Especially when it involved *his* life and death.

He'd taken two steps toward the door to grab his phone when another scream split the silence. "Fuck!" He always had to be the hero, didn't he? He swung around and took off down the hall, his gun held tight.

The deeper he got inside the house, the creepier the place felt. Most of the windows were covered with plywood. The doors were metal and had the old-fashioned bar-across-the-door lock. The hall dumped him out into one big room, with only one window, then spidered off in several directions. The outlying halls were darker and colder.

He chose one to follow.

"Police!" he called out again. "Throw down your weapons."

This time, he'd purposely said the words. Yeah, he could be arrested for impersonating an officer, but something told him the person he was after wouldn't have the authority to make the arrest. Besides, *Police!* sounded better than *PI—I don't have a right to be here, but I am anyway.*

Okay, maybe he had *some* right. Tabitha Jones had been about to hire him to protect her and investigate her bride situation. And if it wasn't Ms. Jones dead on the living room floor, then she might be the one screaming, needing protection.

Carl moved with his back against the wall, almost blinded by the surrounding darkness. Another crash echoed close by. The hall ended at a heavy metal door that stood ajar. He gave the dark room a quick overview, tightened his grip on his gun, then stepped inside.

Raspy breaths filled the darkness. Feminine breaths. Not that being female made a villain less vicious. Carl believed in equal opportunity. Hell, he'd been confronted by some pretty scary broads. And he wasn't just referring to Mr. Logan in that pink nightgown.

Sucking air into his tight lungs, he listened, hoping to

get a fix on the person in the room, hoping even more they didn't have a fix on him.

After blinking, his eyes became a tad more accustomed to the darkness. He made out what he thought was a woman crouched beside a table. The sounds of her breathing grew intense—hyperventilating intense. Following the raspy sounds came whimpers, soft crying. He inched in. Smelled a flowery scent. *Nice.* His gut told him this wasn't a villain, but another victim.

Which meant someone else could be in the room.

He shifted his gaze around. Too dark, so he depended on hearing. Finally, semi-satisfied he was alone with only a crying, perfumed female, he knelt in front of her. "Ma'am, I—"

She charged him, and her head slammed into his abdomen. Like most of her gender, she was a hardheaded little twit. Carl landed with a thump on his back. The hyperventilating, sweet-smelling individual—definitely a woman—fell right on top of him. Soft curves and breasts pressed against him. For just a second, he let himself enjoy it.

But all good things must end, and this one did as soon as all that softness started hitting, kicking, and clawing. Fingernails raked his jaw. Her knee shot up between his legs. Thankfully, she missed his balls and only connected with his thigh.

He caught her by one shoulder. "Stop! I'm the poli— I'm here to protect you."

She stopped. He heard her inhale, backed by a sighlike whimper. But then came a scuffle from behind them and a loud squeak of metal on metal, followed by an even louder clank. It took Carl about two seconds to realize what had happened.

Someone else *had* been in the room.

That someone had shut the heavy metal door.

That someone had set the bar on that fucking heavy metal door.

"Shit!" He pushed the woman off. On his feet, he felt his way to the door, and sure enough, it was shut.

Sure enough. It was locked.

Sure enough. They were royally screwed.

Chapter Five

As soon as he set the lock, Tabitha's murderer took off down the hall. He didn't breathe until he got to the front room, until he left the darkness and saw the blood. Lots of blood. His heart continued to race. His mind, however, calmed.

He walked by Tabitha's body, loving how the red appeared against all that white. White carpet. White suit. She wasn't wearing a wedding dress, but the color was right. He loved how red looked against that pristine brightness. Blood against virgin white. A shame he hadn't brought his camera, or a bouquet of flowers to set beside her.

He circled the wedding planner's body, humming "The Wedding March" to keep the laughter from echoing in his head. Tabitha wasn't a bride. He hadn't wanted to kill her, hadn't *needed* to kill her the way he needed to kill the others. Just as he hadn't needed to kill the other one. But . . .

His gaze shot down the hall. It had been too dark to recognize her, but he'd checked her hand. No ring. She wasn't one of his brides. But had she seen him shoot Tabitha?

Probably. That meant he needed to kill her, as he'd

killed Tabitha, because Tabitha knew or thought she knew. She hadn't figured out who was doing all the killing, but she'd told him her suspicions. He was proud of how he'd scoffed. Sometimes he really fooled people. They thought he was normal. Tabitha had thought he was normal. She'd even slept with him . . . but she'd have slept with anyone.

He stared down the hall, humming. He would pretend she was a bride. Too bad he hadn't brought his knife.

Suddenly he remembered: she wasn't alone. *Police.* He recalled the man yelling that out. He gripped his hand tight around his gun. How could he have forgotten? He couldn't start messing up, losing focus. They'd send him back, back to that hospital where his mother had sent him so many times. He had to act normal. They had to believe he was normal. He couldn't make mistakes.

Think. Think. Think. Why had the police come? His pulse thundered through his body. He rocked back and forth on his heels. Back. Forth. Back. Forth. Had Tabitha been telling the truth when she'd said she called them?

What was he going to do? Should he take Tabitha's body with him? No. She wasn't his bride. She didn't belong with the others.

His gaze shot from the hall to the front door. Run. Should he run? Maybe the woman he'd chased hadn't seen him. Maybe she wouldn't be able to identify him. Or maybe he just needed to finish it. Maybe he needed to kill them both.

The laughter in his head echoed louder, and he started humming again. "Here comes the bride, all dressed in white." He gripped his gun tighter in his hand and started down the hall.

The party had bottomed out, and Les Grayson's mom had walked her two sisters to their car. Les's brother had been given "Mimi duty." At age ninety, Les's grand-mother always had someone assigned to her, just in case.

Les's gaze moved around her mom's kitchen. It felt weird being back home. Nothing had changed. Her dad still hid behind the shed to smoke cigars, as if her mom didn't know, and her mom still compulsively clipped coupons. Tim, her twin brother, still searched for the perfect woman, and if given half a chance would probably skip out of helping her with the dishes, even when it had been *their* chore for as long as Les could remember.

And everywhere she looked, she saw Mike: sitting at the kitchen table helping her mom organize coupons, slipping out the back door to talk to her dad while he poisoned his lungs.

Les had left Piper, Texas, to forget, but someone had forgotten to tell her hometown it was supposed to forget, too.

"You okay, sis?"

Les turned to face her twin brother, the dish-washing escape artist. "Don't I look okay?" She feigned a smile.

"You look like you did the day Mom's cat invited your gerbil to lunch." His gaze moved to her hand where she toyed with the ring that lay beneath her shirt.

She dropped her hand. "I'm tough."

"I'll bet the cat thought your gerbil was tough, too." He shot her a grin. "Are you dating yet?"

Les raised an eyebrow, proud of this much at least. "Yes."

"Anyone I need to go beat up?" That was Tim's way of asking if she'd had sex.

"My last date asked if I had penis envy. You could beat him up."

Her brother smiled. "Give me his address." He glanced back into the living room. "Oh, crap. Mimi's taking her clothes off again."

"Stop her," Les insisted. "Mom left you in charge."

Tim snickered. "I'm a guy. I'm morally opposed to stopping any woman from taking her clothes off."

Les scowled at him. "Even when it's your grand-mother?"

"You've got a point." Tim poked his head out the door. "Stop that, Mimi. It's not bedtime yet." He glanced at Les. "Are we sure she wasn't a stripper back in the day?"

Les laughed. "Oh, yeah. I can see her pole dancing."

Tim studied her. "I've missed you, sis."

"Me, too," she admitted. They'd already done the hug thing when she'd come in, or she would have given him another. Tim pretty much had a one-hug rule.

"Then move back home. Boston's bad on Texas girls. I've heard you say 'you guys.' Twice. Hurt my ears and everything."

Grinning, she studied her Diet Coke. "I'll move back soon."

"You've got to get over it, you know?"

"I'm working on it." Les didn't attempt to lie. Not to Tim. "I'm making progress. Seriously, I've had three dates in the last month."

"And I'm assuming none of them cut the mustard." He pulled a soda for himself from the fridge. "Maybe you're too picky." He popped the top. "Like you accuse me of being."

"I'm not picky. I just want . . ."

"What?" he asked.

"The spark. That little voice in my head that says, 'Wow.' "

"You haven't felt 'wow' about any of the guys you dated?"

"Not even a baby wow," Les admitted. Then she met her brother's eyes, the exact same bright green as her own. "It's as if my wow voice box is broken. I want it to work. I want to feel wow. But I don't." Her throat tight-ened.

"Maybe you just haven't met the right guy."

Maybe the only "right" guy for me died.

The thought ran a circle around her heart. Of all Les's most recent fears—yes, she had a few—this one plagued her the most. Because while she still missed Mike so much her fingernails hurt, she wanted to get past the hollowness living in her chest. She wanted to know the thrill of flirting again, of being flirted with, of sharing secret smiles. She wanted another first kiss, first touch. She wanted wow. And some really hot sex, too.

Tim set his drink on the counter. "Mom said that Katie is getting married."

"I'm afraid so."

"You don't like the guy?"

"Haven't met him." And bam, just like that, the thought slammed into Les's scruples. Could she be jealous that Katie had found a wow and she hadn't? Oh, crap. Nothing like realizing you're a jealous bitch. Add fear of unfair jealousy to her phobia list.

"Woohoo!" Mimi's voice came from the living room. Tim took one step out the door, put it in reverse, and came back.

"'Fraid you're going to have to handle this one," he said. "Damn, I'm never going to be able to look at a pair of boobs the same way."

Before Les could ask, Mimi came strolling into the kitchen. The only thing she wore was a smile and the new hot-pink tennis shoes Les had brought her from Boston.

Les glanced away from Mimi's naked, wrinkled body to Tim's panicked look. "Darn," she said. "I've gotta run or I'll be late meeting Katie." She shot her brother another smile, kissed Mimi's cheek, and walked out, leaving Tim to contend with their naked grandmother.

"Poetic justice!" she called out and chuckled. "How many times did you leave me to deal with the dishes?"

Katie heard the tap-tap of angry pacing and occasional curse words. Shaking so badly she also heard her own teeth chatter, she scooted across the cold concrete floor to the even colder stone wall and curled up into a ball. The chill that shot through her didn't feel real. Maybe it wasn't real, but her buns sure felt frozen.

"Shit. Fuck!"

This had to be a bad dream. She couldn't have seen someone get shot. Couldn't just have been chased through a dark, dungeonlike passageway and had a gun jammed into her ear.

More pacing. "Shit. Fuck."

Or was it all real? Her stomach hurt and rumbled, but Katie was too scared to throw up.

Hiccup.

She was too scared to think.

Hiccup.

Too scared to . . . *God, let this just be a dream.*

"It's going to be okay," a deep voice said.

Had she spoken aloud? She stared into the darkness and tried to make out her companion, but only a dark shape loomed over her. Letting out a slow breath, she pushed the nails of her index fingers into her thumbs. She'd read that could prevent a person from having a panic attack, and while she'd never been plagued with panic attacks, just nervous puking, if there were ever a time she'd be close to panicking, it was now. Right now.

Her breath hitched again. She heard a little whimper escape her throat. Crying had never been a big recourse for her, either. Sure, she'd spilled her share of tears— mostly over boys. Later in life, she'd cried over men, over the art critics' reviews of her work, and she'd cried for a week after she'd gotten the dark news about her family. Sometimes she still cried about that, but most of the time she could control it. Right now wasn't one of those times.

More whimpers escaped her throat, and she cupped a hand over her mouth.

Hiccup.

She heard the footsteps move closer.

"It's okay," the masculine voice said again.

This man obviously didn't know what she knew. He didn't know Tabitha had been shot, that Katie had almost been shot, that she, along with this stranger who said *fuck* and *shit* way too much, was apparently locked in a dark prisonlike room.

"Oh, God!" The words escaped her tight throat as tears started rolling down her face.

She heard him kneel down. She saw the dark figure looming over her, and like lightning, her thoughts flashed back to the other person who'd chased her. Before she knew she'd done it, she kicked the hell out of the looming stranger.

He let out an *oomph* of air and then spoke. "Damn it, lady, I was . . . just trying to help."

Okay, she was definitely having a panic attack. Why else would she have kicked him when she really didn't think he was a bad guy? She couldn't remember why she felt that way, but it had been something he'd said. Hadn't it?

She drew in another shaky breath and dug her nails deeper into her fingers. "Sorry." She pulled her knees tighter to her body.

A lengthy pause passed before he spoke. "Are you hurt?"

She did a quick mental assessment of her body. She remembered being tossed against a wall, feeling something cold and metallic press against the side of her face while . . . while that creep had started running his hands down her left arm and feeling her hand, her fingers. Feeling, as if . . . as if looking for a ring. He'd probably meant to rob her.

But she didn't have a ring.

The thought slammed against her brain. She'd flushed her eight-thousand-dollar ring down the toilet this morning.

Okay, she was clearly getting less scared, because the urge to throw up hit her hard. She cupped a hand over her mouth, but it was too late. She lost the rest of her lunch on the floor.

Immediately, she heard another gagging sound. She wiped the back of her hand over her mouth. The silence played Russian roulette with her sanity and she spoke before she thought.

"Nervous puker," she muttered.

"Sympathy puker," he muttered back.

It was so inappropriate, so insane—laughing at a time like this—but it happened. The sound of his chuckle followed hers: a deep, husky, pleasant sound. Her head instantly cleared of what she'd assumed was panic. Or at least she felt more in control of her thoughts and breathing. However, her butt, plastered to the floor, was frozen for good now.

She leaned her head back. They both laughed for several minutes. Then there came a silence. She wasn't sure how much time had passed—maybe five minutes, maybe more.

"Are you okay?" he asked again.

"I think so." She moved several feet away from the mess she'd left. As she scooted, her brain scooched closer to the reality of what had happened. She remembered seeing Tabitha fall to the carpet. She remembered the blood.

"Someone shot Tabitha." Sudden fear settled in her stomach. Her heart raced. Her mind zipped back to the wedding planner. "I tried to call for help, but there wasn't a phone. She needs an ambulance."

Her companion inhaled. "I . . . don't think that will help now."

Katie closed her eyes—not that the blackness behind her lids was any darker than the blackness in the room. "Is she dead?"

"It appeared that way," came the reply, sounding as if the man had gotten closer. "So, I'm assuming you don't have a cell phone."

"Left it in my car." Why hadn't she brought it in?

Another pause. "Can you tell me what happened?"

She took a deep breath. "Someone shot Tabitha."

"I know." He didn't say it sarcastically, but calmly. "Did you see it happen?"

His voice was deep, solid, and comforting. She let herself soak up that sound before answering.

"No. From the office, all I could see was Tabitha. But he chased me in here. He grabbed me and slammed me into a wall." Her mind replayed the scene in her head like some low-budget movie. "He held the gun to my ear." She hated low-budget movies.

"Did you see him at all, enough to give a description?"

Right then, Katie remembered another reason why she trusted this man. He was police. Yes, she'd heard him tell her that.

No wonder he made her feel safe. No wonder he wasn't too worried. Police never worked alone, did they? Surely, he had a partner who would let them out. And if he didn't have a partner, he would have radioed in his location.

Hearing the man move, she recalled he'd asked her a question. Oh, yeah: he wanted a description.

"He was taller than me. But it was so dark, I didn't make out his features. I'm sorry."

"Considering what you've been through, you're doing good."

She rocked back against the wall, tightened the blue cardigan around her, and hugged herself against the cold. She wished rescuers would hurry up and let them out. Not that she was looking forward to seeing Tabitha. Maybe there was a back door. Katie inhaled and tried to keep her teeth from chattering. But they chattered anyway, like a windup toy that wouldn't stop. *Click. Click.*

Her companion shuffled around. "The heat's not on in this part of the house." He inhaled, the sound of his breath filling the darkness. "Here. Take my coat."

"No, I'm fine," she lied. "I've got a sweater."

"It's thin."

"How . . ." Could he see that well in the dark?

"I felt it," he said, as if reading her mind. "Take this."

The *whish* of material dancing in the air filled the room.

"Here." He had one of those deep voices that demanded obedience. Probably learned it in the police academy.

"Only for a few minutes."

She reached out in the darkness until she touched something leathery and soft. She threw the worn material around her, where it melted against her shoulders like a hug. The warm scent of leather, along with a masculine spicy smell, floated up and brought on images of a rough-around-the-edges cop type to go with the voice. She found herself squinting, trying to make him out. While she could almost see a shadow, she couldn't identify his features or figure out his size. He could be short and round or tall and lean. Then, for a flicker of a second, she remembered landing on top of him. Nothing too soft or paunchy, he'd been hard and—

"Better?" he asked.

"Yes, thank you." She inhaled, and let his scent fill her senses. "But aren't you cold?"

"Nah, I'm thick-skinned. What's your name?"

"Katie Ray. And yours?"

"Carl Hades."

Silence crawled back into the room like an unwanted guest. She listened to see if she could hear anything happening in other parts of the house. Not a sound, not even a murmur of voices. "Why aren't they letting us out?"

"Who?" he asked.

"The other police."

His pause lingered like a fog. "I . . . I'm not the police."

"You said you were." She scooted closer to the wall. Okay, the man's unexplainable, I'm-Mr.-Safe presence started to fade.

He shifted. "Yeah, I did sort of say that, didn't I?" She waited for him to offer an explanation. He didn't.

"So, you just lied?" Her teeth started to chatter again. She couldn't feel her butt or thighs at all now.

"Sort of." His footsteps padded across the floor.

"Sort of? How do you 'sort of' lie?"

"It sounds as if you're getting nervous of me again."

"Well, yeah. After witnessing a murder and being chased by the murderer, I'm locked in a dungeon with a man who tells me he's a cop and then tells me he's *not* a cop. I thought I was being rescued. Now I'm back to just being locked up with a guy who cusses too much."

He chuckled.

"I'm not trying to be funny."

"Sorry," he said.

Sorry? She'd bet he wore a smirk on his handsome face. Not that she knew he was handsome. He could be hideously ugly. Not that she cared how he looked. Beggars couldn't be choosers, and cop or no cop, she was begging him to get her out of here. He could be bow-legged and missing his front teeth for all she cared. She ran her thumb over her left ring finger and a hint of nausea tightened her throat.

After several calming breaths, she raised her shoulder and inhaled from his jacket. Carl Hades didn't smell ugly. No. He smelled like one of those kinds of guy so good-looking that they were stuck on themselves. Then again, he had been nice enough to lend her his coat. And she didn't care how thick-skinned he was, he had to be freezing.

A clatter echoed, and her heart jumped into her throat. "What was that?"

"I knocked something over. I'm looking for a light switch."

"Oh." She shook from the cold—or was it from the panic? Her teeth chattered again.

"You know, we've been in here for . . . a while, and the only one who's sustained any bodily injuries is me. If one of us should be nervous of the other, I got dibs."

She recalled kicking him and maybe more. "I was scared."

"Which is why I'm working on forgiving you, but by now I'd hoped you'd learned that I wasn't out to hurt you."

"I have, sort of, but when people lie, trusting them is hard."

"I used to be a cop." His footsteps filled the dark. "Now I do PI work. Sometimes I forget and say 'police.' Sometimes I say it because it gets people's attention." His dark shadow moved in a circle around the room. "Ms. Jones wanted to hire me."

"Hire you to do what?" Her teeth clicked together.

"To . . . She didn't give me . . . details."

His pause said a lot. It said *big fat lie* is what it said. Oh, she believed him about being a PI; it was the not knowing the details he lied about. So he cussed and lied.

"What were you doing here?" he asked.

"Tabitha is . . ." Nausea pulled at her stomach. "Was planning my wedding." She took deep breaths through her nose.

"You okay?"

"Just my stomach."

"Not again," he groaned.

In spite of the nausea, she smiled. "I think it will pass."

"Good." Relief echoed in his voice. "Is it something you ate, or are you pregnant?"

So, the guy cussed, lied, and asked inappropriate questions. "No! Neither!"

"Sorry. It's just . . . you're getting married."

"People don't have to be pregnant to get married."

"No. Just crazy." His shuffling footsteps sounded.

"Well, I'm not crazy."

"Good. I'd hate to be locked up with a psycho."

"You got something in particular against marriage?" she asked, just because talking felt better than the silence.

"Nothing in particular. It's pretty much everything about it."

She didn't offer a comeback. Why should she? She didn't care how this man felt about marriage. She switched topics. "No light switch?"

"Not so far, but I can't get to all the walls. There are boxes everywhere."

She glanced in the direction of the door, and her heart picked up its pace. "Do you think he's still out there?"

"Nah. He ran the moment he locked us in." But her companion's voice lacked its earlier confidence. She could have used that confidence right now.

"What if he wants to get rid of us first?"

"He would have done something by now."

"What if he thinks I can identify him? What if—"

"Don't work yourself up," the man said. "You're going to start your teeth chattering again. And that makes me nervous."

She closed her eyes and concentrated on breathing and not chattering. In her mind's eye, she envisioned painting slow, easy strokes. "How long before you think someone will find us?"

"Soon," he said. "Will someone miss you this afternoon?"

"I was supposed to meet Joe and Les at five."

"Joe and Les?" He continued making padding sounds.

"My fiancé and my best friend. Oh, shoot. They don't

even know the other is showing up. They probably won't even—"

Another clatter sounded. But this one didn't come from inside the room. "He's still out there!" she said. Her insides commenced to quiver, followed by the chattering of her teeth.

Chapter Six

Les walked into Dave's Place, trading the thick, cold smell of the storm outside for the restaurant's warmth and aroma of grilled meat. Too much garlic, she knew immediately. Luckily, she liked garlic. She scanned the restaurant for Katie. Then she walked into the bar and did a visual rundown. No Katie.

She almost turned to ask for a table, but spotted two empty stools at the bar. Three men sat there with their backs to her. Two watched the TV, which hung from the ceiling; the other read the paper.

Reaching up, Les fingered the ring resting between her breasts and remembered what she'd told her brother only a few minutes ago: She was moving on. Getting past losing Mike. But was she really?

If she were trying, wouldn't she want to practice flirting instead of slinking back into the restaurant and waiting alone? Yeah, she would, but right now Les didn't feel like faking it. God knew she'd faked being interested with all three of her dates.

She had her foot poised to swing around when the guy reading the paper swung first. He had an eager expression on his face, as if he expected her to be someone else. Their eyes met. Locked. He had dark, straight hair and amazing eyes. Bedroom eyes. A deep blue. Then his mouth, also pretty amazing, turned up in a smile. At her. A secret smile. Right then, and for the first time in eighteen months, Les heard it. That little voice. Her wow voice.

Returning his smile, Les hitched her purse up on her shoulder and moved to the empty stool next to him. Maybe, just maybe, there was hope for her after all.

Another big boom sounded, and Katie jumped an inch off the floor. "I hadn't planned on dying today," she squealed. And she really did like sticking to her plans. The Ray family always stayed on course.

"It's just thunder," her companion said. "Take some deep breaths."

Katie counted to ten to keep her mind from flashing to the other bang she'd heard. She tried to keep the image of Tabitha hitting the carpet from replaying in her head, and she turned back toward the voice of the man named Carl.

"Your best friend and fiancé don't get along?" he asked, believing she needed to talk.

He was right, and she answered. "They've never met before. She's been living out of town."

Another pause. "Do they know where you are?"

"Les does."

"Will she be worried enough to come looking for you?"

Katie considered the question. "Yeah, but I don't think she knows where to look."

"Maybe she'll call your parents?"

It had been months since the mention of her parents brought on that stabbing grief. But she supposed that, after today's events, she was vulnerable. "They died." Her eyes stung.

"Sorry." His feet moved, followed by a slight popping

of his knees as if he was lowering himself down again. "How long ago?"

His question told her he'd probably heard the emotion in her voice. "A year and a half." *Tomorrow.* Crazy how the mind kept up with those things, even when you didn't want it to.

"Accident?" he asked.

"Yeah," Katie answered, and tried not to sniffle.

"What happened?"

"An 18-wheeler happened."

"Damn."

"Yeah. Damn." Katie pulled her knees to her chest and wiped her wet cheeks on her pants.

Neither of them spoke for a long time. Then his voice filled the room. "I lost my mom when I was fifteen." His words sounded as if they had lingered on his tongue, as if he'd had to force them out.

And she heard a lot in the deep timbre of his voice. He didn't talk about the loss of his mom, but was offering her a glimpse at his own pain to let her know he understood.

"I'm sorry," she answered. "What happened?"

"Cancer happened," he said.

"It must have been hard."

"It wasn't easy. But it hurts less as time passes."

"Yeah." *But it still hurts too much.* Silence took another lap around the room. Katie's thoughts tried to return to Tabitha. Not wanting to go there, she reached for another topic of conversation. "What about your dad?"

"He lives a few miles from me. Does some odd jobs for me, with my business. But he thinks he has all the answers and doesn't mind sharing. He's a pain in the ass."

"But you love him a lot." She got that from the softening in his voice.

"He's an okay guy." Even more softening.

She stretched out her legs. Her foot bumped up against his. They both pulled back at the same time.

"Will someone come looking for you?" She waited for him to answer, wondering if he had a wife. Sure, he'd practically told her he didn't believe in marriage, but that could mean he felt shackled in one now. "Your dad, or . . . anyone?"

"Dad's in Austin. My dog will miss me when he doesn't get fed. But I haven't trained him to call 911 yet."

The mention of 911 made her recall how she'd looked for a phone in Tabitha's office. Fighting off those thoughts, she tried to envision Carl dishing out food to his dog. "What kind of dog is it?"

He paused. "A big one." His whole tone had changed. He'd lied again—though why he'd lie about having a dog was beyond her.

"How big?" The coldness of the floor continued to seep through her thin jeans and into her butt.

"*Big*-big. There has to be a light in here," he said.

Was he a compulsive liar? If so, he needed practice. Or maybe he wasn't that bad at lying, but there was something about how a person spoke and listened in complete darkness that made lies more apparent. Maybe she and Joe should try it. Cut off the lights and just talk one night. What would she hear in Joe's tone? What would he hear in hers? Would he explain why these last two weeks he'd been too busy for her? Would she understand why it hadn't bothered her that he'd been too busy? Her stomach trembled, and she decided not to think about that.

The sound of Carl moving again brought Katie's gaze up. "What are you doing?"

"I'm going to move some of these boxes so I can find a light switch."

Was he just trying to stay warm? "You should take your jacket back." She pulled from the wall and slipped it off.

"No. Keep it."

"I'm warm now," she lied, and held it out.

"Well, I'm practically sweating," he insisted.

Another lie. Determined to win this argument, she stood, and took a step. Her foot hit something and she tripped. The jacket fell and she followed it. Fortunately, instead of hitting the floor, she hit him. He caught her around her waist. Since she was a good eight inches shorter than him, her head rested against his chest. A solid, hard, masculine chest.

"You okay?" His breath brushed across her temple.

His touch was so warm, she didn't pull away. "I'm scared." She hadn't meant to say that, but something about being near him made her want to confess.

"Don't be. Someone will find us." His hand eased up her waist to her back.

She let herself soak up his body heat. She got this fluttery feeling in her stomach, and she hoped he wasn't going to pull away. It wasn't the masculine appeal that she longed for, she told herself, it was . . . safety. He felt so safe.

He cleared his throat. "You should put my coat back on."

Inhaling, she caught that spicy scent, the fresh woodsy smell that had clung to his jacket. It smelled better on him than it did on the leather. "How do you know?"

"Because I can *feel* you're cold." His hand whispered up her back to touch her hair.

Okay, she had a nipple alert going on strong and he'd noticed, but she chose to ignore his comment and her nipples. "No, how do you know someone will find us?" She stayed where she was, the side of her face resting lightly against his chest, feeling warmer than she had since this whole thing started.

"Ms. Jones sounded as if she worked around the clock. Someone is going to come for an appointment and they'll see . . . her body and call the police."

Katie remembered something about Tabitha and groaned the words aloud. "But Tabitha doesn't work on

Mondays. And we were probably her last appointments today."

"Shit." His body tensed against hers.

"Yeah." She raised her cheek off his chest to look at him. This close, she could make out some of his features. He was . . . he was as good-looking as he was good-smelling. Right then, something familiar tickled her mind. Not as if she knew him. But as if she knew someone who looked like him.

Her gaze moved over his face. Big eyes—brown, she thought—a wide forehead, thick lashes beneath dark eyebrows. Straight nose, angular face, cheeks . . . One of his cheeks had scratches. Vaguely, she recalled fighting him.

She touched his chin. The stubble of his five o'clock shadow teased her fingers. "Did I do that?"

"Yeah." He caught her hand in his.

"Sorry," she whispered.

"I've just about decided to forgive you," he whispered back, his tone teasing, yet soft and comforting.

They stood there staring at each other. Bodies touching.

His warm hands moved back to her waist. "Hello, Katie Ray," he said as if he were seeing her for the first time, too.

"Hi," she managed to say, but her mouth had gone dry.

His head lowered. The soft touch of his breath warmed her cheek and caressed her senses. "Green or blue?" he asked.

"Huh?"

"Your eyes, are they green or blue?"

"Blue," she said. "Yours?"

"Brown."

Like his hair. Or was it black? With so little light, distinguishing color was impossible. Her gaze moved to his mouth. Full lips, with a bowlike top.

Then the most inappropriate thought flipped through

her brain. She wanted to kiss him. Or him to kiss her. Either one would work. *Not!*

She flew out of his arms so fast she tripped again. Only he wasn't there to catch her this time. Landing with a thump on some boxes, Katie went one way, sending the boxes another. She landed on her butt and it may have hurt. She wasn't sure; that was one of the advantages of having a frozen tush.

"Are you okay?" he asked, his voice tight. Tense.

"Yeah." *Hell no!* How could she be okay when she had almost kissed a stranger, when she was getting married in two weeks? Married to wonderful, nice, sweet, handsome Joe.

It was the darkness. The dark created an intimate setting. That's all. That's all it could be. Because she loved Joe. She did.

Oh, God, her stomach hurt again. She rose, placed one hand on the wall and . . . and she felt . . . Thank God!

"Watch your eyes." She flipped the switch.

Light. Glorious, beautiful light filled the room. She blinked. No more intimacy issues. Now she would see things clearly. The brightness burned her corneas. She blinked again. Then she focused on the man standing a foot in front of her. All six feet plus of . . . of a body double for Antonio Banderas. Not good! Not when Antonio had starred in all her sexual fantasies since . . . well, for as long as she'd been having sexual fantasies. There was only one thing she could do.

She turned the light back off.

Les sipped at her glass of merlot, a good wine from California's Napa Valley region, and tried to see, without being caught trying to see, if the man sitting to her left wore a wedding ring. That would explain why, other than one quick nod and the shadow of a smile, he'd gone back to reading the paper. Just her luck, the first guy who sparked her wow voice and he'd rather read about—she followed his bedroom eyes to the paper—earthworm farming. Great!

She hadn't been so lucky with the man sitting three stools down. Oh, no. Brad, as he'd introduced himself, moved to the empty stool beside her and started sending her come-on-baby smiles and telling her all about his big new car, his big new job, his big boat, and his big bank account.

The only thing he hadn't bragged about was his big penis. Which meant he had a little bitty one. Probably no bigger than the tan line he had around his left finger where, obviously, he'd taken off his wedding band. Ugh. She hated cheaters.

Which was one of the many things she'd loved about Mike. He would never have cheated on her. He had been, without a doubt, the most loyal, honest, caring person she'd ever known. She touched the ring between her breasts.

"So, how about it?" Mr. Cheater's question brought her out of her reverie. "You game?"

"Game for what?" She twirled her glass in her hands.

"Dinner. And wherever that leads us, sweetcakes."

Sweetcakes? She counted to three, glaring daggers.

"Bartender," Brad hollered so loud she flinched. "Get this lady another drink. She needs to mellow out a little."

She gritted her teeth. "Sweetcakes doesn't *need* another drink. Sweetcakes isn't feeling—"

"Oh, yes you do. I can tell when a woman needs a drink, and you need one." He leaned in. His breath smelled like a blue-cheese burger with onions and a side of stale beer.

Suddenly, the guy to her left dropped his paper. He stared dead-on—as in *you could be dead soon*—at the man needing a breath mint and crowding Les's breathing room. "Did it ever occur to you that she was with me?"

Brad's mouth dropped open. "But you two didn't . . .

Sorry!" He dug money from his pocket, dropped it on the bar, and left.

Les didn't watch him leave. She was too busy studying her potential worm farmer, who she'd just noticed didn't wear a ring or have a cheater's band. Interesting. Very interesting.

"Thanks," she said. And again she heard it.

Wow.

"Tell me you just cut that light off, and it didn't blow!" Carl tried to control the emotion in his voice, but on the inside all he could think was, *Fuck!* It was bad enough he was trapped with any woman when he really wanted to stay a hundred feet away from them all, but no, he had to be stuck with—

"I cut it off."

"Why?" He'd been squinting, trying to make her out, praying she didn't look as good as she sounded or smelled. Yet here he was, with a redhead who'd upstage that auburn-haired underwear model from the Victoria's Secret catalog. Oh, he'd felt her when she'd been close and knew she had potential, but face it, men were visual creatures.

"Because it hurt my eyes."

It had hurt his eyes, too. Not the light, but seeing her. His mind had photographed the image of her standing there looking a lot scared and even more beautiful. And seeing a scared, beautiful woman had thrown his want-to-be-a-hero instinct into high gear. Ah, but it had been that instinct that had gotten him so deeply in trouble with Amy.

He inhaled and let it out slowly as Katie Ray's image flashed in his mind again. He couldn't recall exactly what she'd been wearing or what color it was, but damn, if he couldn't recall that the body beneath her clothes was curvy in all the right places. So curvy that in that flicker of a second, he'd re-dressed her in a few of Victoria's little outfits. The green, sheer one. Or blue, to match her eyes.

Not that the color of her outfit or her eyes mattered. It was the color of her hair that did him in. And it was long. God, he loved long, red hair. Especially the dark auburn shade. He remembered its texture. Silky soft, sweeping down her back. So exquisite it'd taken major willpower not to run his hands through it. To bury his nose in the strands and breathe.

He shook his head to clear the images from his mind. "Fine," he growled. "Leave it off for a minute, but then it's got to come back on."

He had to find a way out of here. No way in hell did he want to spend the next thirty-six hours with a soft-feeling, sweet-smelling female who'd already managed to get under his skin. One who evoked his want-to-be-a-hero instinct.

Why the hell had he told her about his mother? Okay, he knew why. Because he'd heard a familiar pang of grief in her voice. Because . . . their throwing-up adventure had thrown him back to the chemo days.

You don't have to come in here, his mom would say. But he hadn't been able to stay away . . . not when he knew she needed him. So they would sit on the john floor, take turns throwing up and laughing about it. Fuck, it hurt to remember. So he pushed those thoughts back into the darkness where they belonged. Thoughts of Red stormed in and took their place. Of how she'd smelled, of how soft—

He blamed this on the be-a-gentleman gene that he'd inherited from his dad—the one he wished he could get surgically removed.

Not that the gentleman gene was as dangerous as the hero instinct. He'd wanted to be Amy's hero. To save her. He'd failed. Just as he'd failed to save his mom.

No! He'd already shut down those thoughts.

"Are you ready?" he asked.

"Ready for what?" Her soft reply whispered over him. Damn, even her voice made his jeans feel tight. Of course, it probably wasn't just her, but the fact that he hadn't buried himself inside a woman in over a year. Damn he missed that, too.

"Turn the light back on, Red."

Chapter Seven

Les smiled up at her hero of the hour. "I appreciate your getting rid of him."

"My pleasure." His bedroom eyes twinkled.

Pleasure. *Remember that?* She did remember . . . vaguely.

"I'm Leslie." She extended her hand. His warm palm melted against hers, and she saw a flash of brightness and heard a big . . . crash of thunder. Just a storm outside—not emotional fireworks. Then came another lightning flash, but she barely noticed.

She barely noticed that the bar went utterly dark, that the electronic hum of the heater, the TV, and the ovens in the kitchen all stopped. Ah, but she noticed how his palm fit against hers, how his musky, masculine scent filled her lungs. The silence hung, but only for a flicker of a second, because the groans and moans of people wanting their dinner chased it away.

"I think the storm has finally arrived," Les said, feeling jumpy, not from the weather, not from the darkness, but from a closeness and sexual awareness she hadn't felt in ages.

"Yeah." The man's voice rang deep, husky, close. He continued to hold her hand. "Are you scared of storms?"

"No." The whisper of his breath caressed her cheek.

"Are you sure?" His thumb passed over the back of her hand. "Because you're trembling."

Air caught in her throat. His touch, so simple, sent messages throughout her body. Messages that said she'd gone too long without feeling this. Feeling alive.

"Maybe I'm a little scared," she lied. Or was it a lie? What was the emotion dancing in her stomach if it wasn't fear? And just what was she afraid of now?

The lights flickered back on. The crowd in the restaurant cheered and the magic of the moment evaporated like a drop of water on a hot, sunbaked sidewalk. But in spite of the cold and storm outside, Les felt hot. Not sexually hot. Okay, maybe she did feel that way a little. But mostly the heat was like . . . like she stood too close to a flame. And who wanted to get burned?

The hero holding her hand pulled away. Almost too fast. Les tucked her hand in her lap and the diamond ring between her breasts felt colder than before.

She glanced at her watch and fiddled with the band. Five thirty. Where was Katie? She didn't look up but felt the man staring. "My friend's late."

"Mine, too," he said, and just like that he poked his nose back into the paper. Something about his fast retreat told her that, while they might have had a moment, even a magical one, he wasn't interested in taking it any further. And while she hated admitting it, further didn't interest her, either.

"Thanks again." She butt-scooted off the chair and went to wait in the crowded restaurant. Crowded—lots of people, where she waited alone, where she realized how lonely she really felt.

After trying to call Katie and getting no answer, Les wondered if she should just go to Katie's house and wait. It wasn't like her to be late. Katie was . . . well, a bit of a perfectionist. Not that she expected so much from other people, but just from herself.

A trickle of uneasiness slid down her spine.

"Where are you, Katie?"

Katie hit the switch and the light flooded the room again. She blinked. Carl blinked. They stared at each other like strangers. And they were strangers, but not really.

For the last—she checked her watch—hour, they'd been together in the dark. She'd hit him, scratched him, kicked him. They'd shared memories about the death of a parent, or in her case, parents. And, oh yeah, they'd thrown up together. Not that it meant anything, but oddly, it did. Les was the only other person alive who even knew about her nervous-stomach situation.

Funny how being trapped in the dark with a stranger could seem so, well, intimate. She felt herself blush.

The silence grew awkward. Carl's gaze shifted around the room. "Pay dirt!"

"What?" Katie folded her arms over her chest, hoping to snatch a bit of warmth.

"There's a door behind this stack of boxes." He pushed the stack away far enough for him to slip between them and the wall. The sound of a doorknob turning filled the room.

"Is it locked?" Katie moved in and peered through the crack. What she saw made her take a quick step back. Carl held a gun in his hands.

"I didn't know you had a gun," she accused, remembering the feel of that cold metal against her ear earlier.

His brown-gold eyes cut to her. "You're not going to freak out on me again, are you?"

"I didn't 'freak out.'" The Rays didn't freak.

"Yeah?" He touched his scratched face. "How did I get these?"

Well, if they did freak, they apologized. "I already said I was sorry."

"Yeah, you did. Go stand over there." His voice lowered, and her heart skipped a beat.

"Why? Did you hear something?" Her words seemed to ring too loud. While the room rang too quiet.

"Just do it." He breathed the words like an order.

"You're a tad bossy," she muttered, but moved back. Hands clenched, she listened. The click of a knob filled the silence. The sound of a metal door squeaking open came next. Followed by the sound of footsteps—Carl's footsteps. His footsteps walking away, while her size sevens were left behind. Alone. And alone sucked. Bossy or not, she wanted him back.

"Carl?" she whispered.

Carl didn't answer.

From his car, parked down the street, Tabitha's murderer stared at the dark house and remembered two people were still in there. Panic started to drum through his chest. Closing his eyes, he banged his head on the steering wheel. What should he do? What should he do? If they had cell phones, the police would already have arrived. Then again, he remembered Tabitha complaining about no cell phone service on her block. Maybe they were really trapped. He still needed to take care of them. But maybe not just now.

He had time. Time to think straight. Time so he could focus. Time to make the laughing stop, because the laughing always messed with his thoughts and he didn't want to make a mistake. He couldn't make a mistake.

Time to check on his next bride. He picked up his phone and dialed her cell number. It rang . . . and rang twice more before going over to voice mail. He punched in her home number.

No one was there, either. Where was she? Her answering machine picked up. "Hi, you've reached Katie. I'm sorry I'm not home right now, but leave a message and I'll get back to you."

Hearing her voice made him remember seeing her for the first time. She had sat across his desk and smiled at him so prettily. Just remembering made his body tighten with need. Need to see her in her dress, to see the fear in her eyes, to control her, to hear her cry and beg him to forgive her.

Did he have time?

Les checked the time again. Katie was more than an hour late. Where was she? She tried Katie's home phone again. No answer. Snagging her purse, she walked out of the restaurant, giving the man still waiting at the bar a quick glance.

Then, remembering Katie's key, she checked her pocket to make sure she hadn't lost it. It was still there. Pulling her jacket closer, she walked out of the restaurant and took off for her car.

"Carl?" Katie called out his name again and held her breath and waited, praying she wouldn't hear shots being fired or him screaming out. She counted to ten and then couldn't stand it anymore. "Carl?" She called louder.

"Yeah." Footsteps echoed. "Good news. Bad news." He walked out from the small opening between the boxes and the wall.

"What?" she asked, and noticed he'd put away the gun.

"The good news is, if you have to p . . . use the bathroom, you can go. The sink's not working but the toilet is. Bad news is there isn't a way out."

"Not even a window?" She wrapped her arms around herself to ward off another chill. That's when she noticed all he wore was a black, short-sleeved polo shirt and jeans. He had to be cold.

"Afraid not." He ran his hand across his chin, where his five o'clock shadow seemed to have gotten a couple hours' head start. A rasping sound filled the room.

"So we're stuck in here," she muttered, and had one of those I'm-going-to-cry moments. Of course, she wasn't really going to cry. Or at least she was going to try really hard not to.

He studied her. "I'm not giving up yet."

"Aren't you cold?" Her words created a puff of vapor.

"Where's my coat?" He looked at her with a pinched brow.

Turning around, she grabbed his coat from the floor and handed it to him.

"Not for me. Put it on. You're freezing."

"I'm not that cold," she lied.

His gaze lowered to her breasts. "Could have fooled me."

Vaguely remembering he'd already pointed this out, she went on instant nipple alert and pulled the ends of her sweater over her breasts. "That's rude."

"But true." He took the jacket from her. "A damn shame your wedding planner was too cheap to heat the whole house."

"Probably would cost a fortune to heat all of it," Katie defended Tabitha because . . . because it felt wrong not to.

With the coat still in his hands, he stepped closer. But instead of donning the coat himself, he slung it over her shoulders and gave it a quick tug to cover her breasts.

She stood there trying to decide whether she should argue about accepting it. A firm believer in picking her battles, she decided this wasn't worthy. The fact that the jacket felt so good had nothing to do with it, either. Well, almost nothing. She snuggled deeper into the coat's warmth and tried not to think about how good that masculine warmth had felt to lean against.

Carl walked over to the door that led to the hall and studied the doorknob. Kneeling, he checked out the lower door hinges.

"If I had the right tools, I might be able to take the damn thing apart." He glanced over his shoulder at her.

She had slipped her arms into his jacket and it now hung open. Noticing his gaze fall to her breasts, she zipped it up.

"Thank you," he muttered, and refocused on the door.

"You know," she said, "we might find some tools in these boxes." And something to wear, so he would wear his coat. At least then she wouldn't have to smell him all around her. "We should go through them."

Her attention shifted to him again. Still kneeling, with his back to her, he wore his dark brown hair combed straight back. It was thick and hung to the back of his collar, the edges flipping up. His shoulders were wide and his torso tapered into a thinner waist.

He glanced up and his thick eyebrows arched. "Good idea, Red."

Holy Monet. He really did look like Banderas. Enough like him that the sexual fantasies Katie had woven over the years started playing again in her mind. His taking his shirt off. His taking her shirt off. His doing more than looking at her breasts. His hands . . . his mouth . . .

His brows pinched. "You okay?"

"Yes. Why?" she managed to squeak out.

"You got a really strange look on your face. You're not going to puke again, are you?"

"No." Oh, great. So her turned-on look resembled a throw-up look. Not what any girl really wanted to know. Guilt and embarrassment had her nipping at her bottom lip.

He continued to study her. "Let's do it."

"Do what?" she asked, still chasing a few of those sexual images from her mind.

"Search the boxes. I'll unstack. You start going through them."

While waiting for him to hand her the first box, she struggled to find a safe mental, and verbal, topic. Her gaze caught on the prisonlike walls. "Who would build a house like this?"

"He was a nut job—thought the government was out to get him, built it to keep people out."

"How do you know?"

"I grew up close to here. Rumor was the place was haunted."

She glanced at him again. "Oh, that makes me feel good."

"Scared of ghosts?" He set a box by her feet and smiled. His smile was near perfect.

"Ghosts, I can handle. Real people scare me." Along with sexy men who had her forgetting she was engaged. That in less than two weeks—Right then her stomach soured. She almost suggested he look at her face again so he might know one look from the other.

"Me, too," he said.

"It looks like a prison on the inside."

"Maybe he thought he might have to take prisoners."

"I can't believe Tabitha likes, *liked* this place." Her breath hitched. She'd rather think about sexy smiles than remember that Tabitha was dead. That the wedding planner's body lay out there covered in blood. That the guy who did it might still be out there.

"Here, start on this box," he said, as if he understood her situation. He scooted the box with his foot.

Katie got down on her knees and opened it. She found a few silk plants and some hand-painted ceramic planters. While she repacked the items, Carl pulled down the other boxes.

Katie's mind went back to Tabitha and she felt guilty for being upset with the woman right before, before . . . *Think about the good stuff.* Closing her eyes, she remembered how Tabitha always lit up when she saw a piece of art that she loved.

She opened her eyes and sensed Carl looking at her.

"You okay?" Concern flickered in his golden brown gaze.

"Yeah." She felt caught by his regard. Warmed by it. And at this room's temperature, it took a lot to be warmed.

He nodded. "What do you do for a living, Red?"

"I manage an art gallery in Houston."

"Are you an artist, too?" He set another box down.

"No." The one-word answer came too quickly, too boldly.

He chuckled. "So what kind of art do you do?"

She frowned. "I tried to paint, but I sucked at it."

"Well, I see a lot of sucky paintings in museums. Once, at a street fair in Mexico, they had an elephant doing paintings. He wasn't perfect, mind you, but good enough that I actually bought one."

"So you're a true connoisseur, are you?" she asked.

"I know what I like." His gaze roamed her.

His blatant innuendo had her feeling jittery. But a part of her sang. *Antonio likes me. He really likes me.* Not that it changed anything, because she loved Joe. She did. Besides, if she allowed herself to get anything close to turned on, he would probably accuse her of preparing to throw up.

After a few minutes, Carl added, "I can't see you *not* being good at whatever you put your mind to, Red."

"Which is exactly why I gave it up." She took a deep breath. "The Rays don't fail at things. Rule number one. Actually, rule number one was to keep your pants on, but 'Thou shalt not fail' came right after that."

He lowered a box. "Hard rule to follow, isn't it?"

"I didn't set it. My parents did." She stared at the boxes. "My dad was a doctor. My mom was a lawyer. High achievers. Being successful was important."

"I meant the keep-your-pants-on rule." He chuckled.

She looked up and offered him a grin but no comment. But she thought about it. Because in her fantasies, Banderas had—

"So your parents were hard-asses, huh?"

"No," she said, a little firmer than she intended. "They . . . loved me. Wanted me to be successful, hence the rules."

"And did you always follow your parents' rules?"

"Don't we all?" she asked, mustering her defenses.

"No, I piss my father off every chance I get. When I was young, I would actually go out of my way to piss him off."

"I guess we're different." But she hadn't forgotten the love she'd heard in his voice when he'd spoken about his dad.

"Yeah. I'd agree on that one." He went back to the boxes.

"It's not like I miss painting. I get to be around art all day. I sell art. I manage the gallery. I don't even miss it."

"Right," he said, but his tone scoffed.

They worked in silence for the next few minutes. The second box contained some books. "That's how I met Tabitha," Katie said, wanting to think positive thoughts about her wedding planner. "Tabitha loved art." She eyed Carl. "She loved contemporary, mostly. Anything in a Picasso style turned her on. But she also loved some traditional pieces, those with a Postimpressionistic feel."

He pulled another box down. His expression, and a completely glazed-over look, told her he seriously didn't have a clue what Postimpressionism was, and he probably couldn't distinguish a Picasso from a Norman Rockwell. Of course he couldn't. He'd bought a painting that an elephant had done at a fair.

It still felt good to talk about Tabitha, so she continued. "She also had a thing for sculptures. Mostly bronzes, anything to do with the human figure."

Glancing up, Katie saw the bottom of the box he held was about to burst open. "Watch out!" Not wanting to break any of Tabitha's things, even if she was dead, or maybe because she was dead, Katie popped up, hoping to hold the bottom together—but it was too late. The bottom of the box gave way and its contents spilled out. Operating on instinct, she'd caught one item—a hair dryer, maybe, she wasn't sure—before a book, clothing, and other paraphernalia rained down to the floor by her shoes. Then she got a good look at the paraphernalia.

A pair of fur-lined handcuffs.

A whip.

A black bustier, complete with garters and fishnet panty hose.

Oh, and she hadn't imagined the book. Its title was something like *Positions You've Never Tried*.

That wasn't all.

There was also a pack of never-before-opened edible panties—in wild strawberry flavor.

And last, floating down and landing on the toe of Katie's two-inch heels, was a pair of fire engine–red crotchless panties.

A deep husky laugh exploded. That's when Katie noticed that the "hair dryer" she thought she'd been holding was actually a very big penis-shaped vibrator, complete with an electrical cord.

"Oh, yuck!" She dropped the vibrator. It rolled to her shoe and she kicked it away.

His laughter slacked off just enough for him to speak. "Looks like art wasn't the only thing that turned Tabitha on."

Chapter Eight

The house was dark, as if his sweet Katie wasn't home. And that was okay. He'd be waiting for her. Tabitha's killer parked down the street and moved quietly. The bitter cold ate through his black jacket, but the temperature kept everyone inside—which would make it easier.

No one to hear her pretty cries.

"Poor little Katie Ray."

He checked again to make sure there wasn't a car parked out front. No more mistakes. He closed his eyes and hummed to keep the laughter from ringing in his head.

He remembered her. She was beautiful. Red hair. Of course, he liked brunettes best. It was easier to pretend they were Maria.

Normally, he didn't feel the urge so soon. It had only been a couple of weeks since he'd taken his last bride. But the whole thing with Tabitha getting suspicious had made him antsy. And when he got antsy, he remembered. Remembered how beautiful Maria had looked in her wedding dress. Remembered how she'd walked down the aisle. How she'd stood in front of everyone he knew and started laughing. Then, trying to control herself, she'd leaned in and said, "I can't do this."

He'd known she laughed when she got nervous, but right then it had felt so personal. No one at the church could have heard what she'd said to him; they'd only heard her laughter. And before long someone else was laughing. And he had stood there humiliated in front of everyone, listening to them laugh. Just as they'd laughed when he was a kid.

Then Maria had run out of the church.

Fighting off the past, Tabitha's killer shook from the cold. He pushed open the wooden gate that led to Katie's backyard. He needed a bride. Needed to hear them cry the way Maria should have cried. He closed his eyes and took deep breaths before he started humming again.

"Here comes the bride, all dressed in white."

In the distance, a dog barked. Then a spray of headlights danced through the slats of the wooden fence. Was that her? "Welcome home," he whispered, and went to hide in the shadows. As he leaned against the house, he smelled smoke from the neighbor's fireplace. That's when he realized what he'd do with the cop and woman locked in at Tabitha's place.

He'd always been fond of fires.

Settled in, he pulled out his cell phone and a small tape recorder. He always liked to let them hear the music before he moved in. It was, after all, their song.

Les parked in front of Katie's patio and frowned when she didn't see any lights on in the house. Where was Katie? Les had waited another half hour at the restaurant and had called her cell phone and her home phone, but had only gotten voice mail and the message machine.

Still sitting in her car, Les noticed the storm had passed, but tiny balls of sleet clicked against the windshield. Had Katie gotten caught in the storm and held up by traffic?

Finding the key, Les darted for the front door. The cold sent shivers down her back, and she wished she'd brought some real winter clothes with her. But Houston wasn't supposed to get this cold. Freak of nature, the news had called it.

She stepped into the dark entryway. The heater kicked in, groaning like an old house. Katie's place was too young to groan. But it still groaned. A spooky kind of groan, too.

Locking the door, she scanned the darkness for a light switch. Her mind shot to the stranger who'd held her hand when the lights had gone out. A simple touch, but she'd had sex that felt less intimate. Which meant one thing.

She needed to get laid.

Her mind accepted the idea, but her heart rolled over laughing that she even thought she was ready. Her hormones and heart didn't see eye to eye.

She found the switch. Light flooded the room at the same time as the phone rang. *Katie?* She darted into the dark living room.

She found the receiver. "Hello?" No one answered. "Katie?"

Still nothing, but she could hear someone breathing. "I'm wearing a red bra and a thong. What are you wearing?" she snapped. Short intakes of air filled the line and then she heard . . . music. "Hello?" The line clicked off.

Les collapsed on the sofa. Wrapping her arms around herself, she stared at the ceiling. What if Katie had been in an accident?

No. Not Katie, too.

Her chest tightened.

Looking at the phone she still held, she dialed Katie's cell number again. It rang, then went to the recording. "Katie, I'm getting worried. Call me. I'm back at your house. I'm . . ."

The heater clicked off, replaced by a scary-movie kind of silence. "I'm sure you're fine. Traffic, right?" Les popped up and went to the back door to make sure it was locked. It was. "I'm going to shower—a long hot shower—and we'll have a pajama party when you get home. And I'll tell you about this hot guy I met tonight. He made my wow voice go off, Katie. Of course, I'm not ready yet. Okay, call me."

She had no sooner hung up when a sudden clatter came from outside. Swinging back to the door, she hit the light switches. Light flooded both the living room and outside on the patio.

With her nose pressed to the cold, glass panel of the back door, she cut her eyes left. Nothing.

Right. Nothing.

Of course, nothing. Just the wind.

Telling herself Katie was fine and it was only the storm outside, Les went into the bedroom. Yep, a hot shower sounded good. She turned on the radio so she wouldn't have to hear the heater bitch about spewing warmth. Her clothes came off, landing here and there. Yeah, she was a bit of a slob. A slob compared to Katie, who was, well . . . perfect.

Naked, but realizing Katie might call, she did the streak into the living room and grabbed her cell phone to take with her into the bathroom. Katie would call or come home soon. Surely.

Katie reached for a new box. She'd confiscated some packing paper to clean up the mess they had both left on the floor. Just like a man, Carl hadn't offered to help, but at least he'd said thank you.

So far they'd found books and dishes. And in a big box, she'd found a foldout bed—just one—and oh yeah, that one box of sex toys. Which Carl, aka Mr. Banderas, hadn't stopped snickering over.

He let out another chuckle.

"You can stop laughing now," Katie snapped. "It's rude to laugh at someone who—"

"Whoa!" He held up his hands. "I'm not laughing at Tabitha. I'm laughing at *you*."

"Me?" she asked. *Well, that's much better then. Not!*

"Yeah. The look on your face was pretty funny."

"It's still rude. They were her things." She didn't want to get into her feelings about him laughing at her.

"And I don't see a thing wrong with them either," he said. "I mean . . ." One of his eyebrows shot up. "I figure most of you women have toys. All the girls I hang out with do."

"And what kind of girls do you hang out with?" She opened another box and feigned disinterest in his answer. But actually, she waited with an on-the-edge-of-your-seat anticipation.

"No, this isn't about me. I simply wonder if you have toys."

She could feel his gaze, could feel her cheeks brighten. Of course she had toys. Okay, a toy. She was almost twenty-nine and she wasn't a prude. But her toy wasn't penis shaped. She'd bought the kind over which, if she accidentally died, whoever cleaned out her things and stumbled upon it wouldn't have a heart attack. Her battery-operated device could be used as a foot massager, or to soothe aching necks.

However, she was not going to start talking sex toys with Carl. Not when every time she'd used the uh . . . foot massager, the imaginary lover had been a man who looked just like him.

She stiffened. "I think we need to change the subject."

"And just when it was getting interesting, too," he said. There was a pause, some rattling of paper, then he spoke again. "So, what do you want to talk about?"

"Why do we have to talk at all?" She looked up.

"Because you get nervous when it gets quiet."

Okay, it was true, but she didn't like him pointing it out. "Oh, I know a subject. How about the dog you lied about?"

The look on his face made her laugh.

"How do you know I lied?" His dark brow creased.

"I heard it in your voice. Like you heard it in mine, when I said I didn't paint." She glanced down at the array of dishes in the box. "You don't even have a dog, do you?"

"I have a dog," he said indignantly.

She tried to remember what he'd said about the dog that made her think it was a lie. "But it isn't a big dog, is it?"

The surprise lit his eyes and she chuckled. "What? He's not a manly dog? Is that why you lied?"

When he didn't answer, she laughed harder. "What is it? A little Yorkshire terrier?"

He stared at her, then answered. "A poodle."

Oh, this was too rich. "That tells me a lot about you, Carl."

"It tells you what?" His eyes stayed on her.

"It tells me that you're the macho kind of guy who thinks he has to have macho things or he's embarrassed." She leaned against the wall and watched him watch her. "So, what happened? Some girlfriend stick you with the dog?" She laughed again.

The sound of her laugher washed over Carl. Never had he heard a more beautiful sound. He didn't give a rat's ass that he was the cause of her laughter. She could poke fun at him all day because . . . Damn, but she was beautiful when she laughed. Her eyes lit up and her mouth—a full mouth perfect for all sorts of bedroom things—melted into the most beautiful smile.

"Well?" she asked. "Is that it? A girlfriend left the dog?"

"Yeah." He didn't try to lie. Her comment about old girlfriends should have had him laying bricks to rebuild his guard. Should have had him backing away from this playful place they'd arrived at. But blast it if he didn't like this place.

"So you think I'm macho, huh?" He grinned.

"Yeah. So much that owning a poodle offends you enough that you lie about it." She made another cute face.

"I'm not offended. It's just not the kind of dog I'd get if I went to get one. Besides, I don't own it. He was abandoned. I'm probably going to take him to the shelter."

"Bull. You love the dog. You just won't admit it."

"Why wouldn't I admit it?"

"Because you're macho," she repeated with a smirk.

It was the smirk that clued him in. What a second ago had sounded like a compliment, now didn't ring that way anymore. "And macho doesn't do it for you, huh?"

Okay, he should cut this crap out. He was flirting, flirting with danger and with a woman so unlike his type. Hell, the type of woman he'd dated, before he'd stopped dating, didn't blush, didn't hesitate to fill him in on their do-it-yourself toys. The women he'd dated hadn't been engaged to someone else.

Plain and simply, he didn't date the marrying kind. And perhaps that was why she intrigued him. She was just so damn refreshing. And he was having more fun right now than he'd had in years. Never mind that they were locked up in a room cold enough to be a morgue and, appropriately enough, that there was a dead body a few rooms away. Fun, in spite of the cold that dug into his gut.

"Macho isn't *in* anymore," she answered.

"What's in?" He forced his attention to the box's contents. Doodads. He picked up a figurine. Dust catchers. And women wanted to set them all around a house for *what* reason? He had a box in the attic that Amy had left along with her dog.

"Women want metro men," she said.

"Metro?" He looked up and watched her shiver. "Men who use public transportation?"

She grinned again. "Metrosexual men aren't afraid to be in touch with their feminine side."

He closed the box. "So women want gay men? When did this happen? Don't tell me, it was the movie. *Broken Mountain*."

"*Brokeback Mountain*."

"Well, something was broken for someone to make that film. Not that I got anything against it."

Her sexy mouth twisted into another smile. "Metro isn't gay. Just men who aren't afraid of being sensitive. Men who aren't afraid to cry, or admit they like quiche. They may even know how to cook it. Men who put up with overbearing moms. Or"—she pointed at him—"who admit they could like a poodle."

He set another box down beside her. "I'm not afraid of being sensitive. Hey, I donate blood." Her expression drew his gaze and kept him talking. "I didn't actually cry, but giving blood almost brought a tear to my eye."

She laughed again and he wanted to lose himself in that sound. "I wouldn't know how to cook quiche—not sure I'd know a quiche if I ran over one—but I'll eat just about anything that doesn't bite back. And not to brag, but I cook a mean scrambled egg and can grill burgers and steaks better than any man this side of the Houston Ship Channel."

Lifting the box lid, he discovered more knickknacks, but his eye quickly went back to her. "I'll admit I'm not proud of having a sissy dog following me around, but I haven't used his fuzzy butt for target practice. Doesn't that make me part metro?"

She studied him. "You can't admit you like him, can you?"

"I don't hate him. And hey, I feel bad when I step on him. Which I don't do on purpose. The damn thing has a foot fetish."

She shook her head and her red hair shimmered. He let his mind drift to what it would be like to feel it on his naked chest. To feel that mouth moving south. His gaze cut to the door. They were locked up, it was colder than a witch's tit, what better way to stay warm than have a few rounds of hot sex?

She brushed her hair back. "Poor dog."

His dick started reacting to his wayward thoughts. Then he remembered all the reasons getting it on with her wouldn't be smart. Ahh, but he'd always been more brawn than brains.

Silence fell, and he let it linger before asking, "Your fiancé, is he metro?"

Her attention lifted from the box, and he could swear he spotted half of a frown. "Joe's a very nice man."

"But does he cry, cook you quiche, and own a sissy dog and admit to the world that he loves it?"

"He doesn't cry."

She pulled the jacket tighter. Carl liked seeing her in it. He'd love seeing her out of it, too. "Does he cook?" The cold made his shoulder ache.

"No." A puff of vapor left her lips. "And he doesn't have a dog, but he's very sensitive to my needs."

Only a real queer wouldn't give his left nut for the opportunity to be sensitive to your needs. The crude remark almost slipped from his mouth, but he bit it back. He tried to justify his sudden dislike for her fiancé, but couldn't think of a good reason. "What does Mr. Sensitive do for a living?"

"He's an engineer. And his name is Joe Lyon."

He stared at her left hand, and while he'd noticed it earlier and hadn't asked, now his curiosity bit harder. "Why aren't you wearing an engagement ring?"

Her gaze shot up. "I . . . I don't want to talk about it."

"Trouble in paradise?" Why did that thought make him happy?

"No." She opened a new box and her eyes widened. "Yes! Finally. I think I just found something we can use."

Tools? Relief swept over him. Every instinct Carl

owned told him the sooner he got away from Red, the better.

After hitting another ice patch, Joe pulled up to the curb and dialed Katie's cell again. It wasn't like her to not show up. He'd been worried about her all evening.

Yeah, when you weren't too busy flirting with sexy blondes.

He thumped his hand on the steering wheel. What the hell had he been doing? Okay, he knew he hadn't done anything that constituted cheating. But damn if he hadn't wanted to.

Taking a deep breath, he ran his hands through his hair. Wanting to do something wasn't a crime. But was it a sign? A sign that he was making the biggest fucking mistake of his life?

The sound of BB-sized hail pelting his windshield drew his attention to the bad driving conditions. Had Katie been in an accident? Or had he gotten the time wrong? Was she ticked at him? That would explain why she wasn't answering his calls.

"Oh, hell!" He deserved Katie's anger. Not for getting the times mixed up, if that was what had happened, and maybe not even for being attracted to the blonde, because he hadn't done anything, but he deserved shit for ignoring Katie these past few weeks. He was one lucky bastard to have found her. To have someone as good-natured, as loyal, and as breathtakingly sexy, who wanted the same things out of life that he did. A woman who could tolerate his mom. A woman whom his mom approved of. Marrying Katie made sense. Perfect sense.

So why the fuck didn't he feel lucky?

Chapter Nine

"Tools?" Carl jumped up to see for himself.

"Not tools," Katie said. "Clothes."

He stared at her. "Clothes?"

She stood and unzipped his coat. "Yeah. Now you can quit pretending you aren't cold and have your jacket back."

Okay, he had to admit that he was freezing his ass off, but he felt positive he hadn't shown that bit of weakness.

"Clothes," he repeated, with about as much enthusiasm as he'd say *tax audit*. But then she stripped off his jacket and he got to see what he'd been missing since she'd zipped the thing up.

And he had missed it, too. She tossed his jacket at him. He caught it before it hit his face and obstructed his view. His gaze whispered over the soft mounds of flesh filling out her thin, sexy-as-hell pale blue sweater and matching top. Then his focus moved down to the same-color jeans, which fit like a glove, showcasing every dip and curve. He loved dips and curves.

She pulled something bright yellow from the box. It looked like a bulky ski jacket. Which was going to cover up more of that curvy body than his own jacket had.

When she slipped one arm in, the hem of her sweater

rose and gave him a peek at the skin of her flat belly. Yes, he liked skin. His gaze stayed riveted to the spot, hoping for another flash. It had been too damn long since he'd seen feminine belly skin. Touched skin. Tasted skin.

His mouth watered. Then it was gone.

She pulled the thick ski jacket closed in front and zipped. Reaching down, she brought out a matching scarf. She wrapped it around her neck twice, and it even covered up the bottom of her face—which cheated him out of seeing her mouth. That hurt, because he'd really enjoyed looking at her mouth.

Then came the gloves. He hadn't thought about her hands being sexy, but he knew he was going to miss seeing them, too.

"Here." She reached back into the box and tossed a scarf at him. "Put this on."

He caught the fuzzy and glittery pink strip of fabric. "Red, you're nuts if you think I'm going to wear this."

"Oh, yeah," she said, the tease in her voice muffled by the scarf. "I forgot. You're macho."

"And proud of it," he snapped. "And to prove it, I'm going to go pee standing up, something I bet metro men don't do anymore." He tossed the scarf back into the box. But he did slip his jacket back on and cast her a quick glance.

"All I need is hot cocoa and something to eat," she said.

The mention of food had his own stomach growling, and he remembered. He pulled the bag out of his coat pocket.

"Here, have some worms." He tossed them to her and took off to the head.

While lathering soap over her body, Les thought she heard something. Then she thought she saw something. Okay, she did see something. A shadow on the other side of the shower curtain.

Katie? She'd started to call out when a leg, a *masculine, hairy, naked* leg, slipped from behind the drape of plastic and moved inside the shower. Inside. Inside the shower.

Inside the shower with her.

Following the leg was . . . Yes, it had been a while, but she still recognized a half-aroused penis when she saw one.

Her first reaction wasn't fear. More like shock. More like *incredible* shock. Astonishment, even. But forcing her eyes from the impressive male package to the man's face, all her stunned emotions were yesterday's news and fear jumped into the driver seat.

Him!

The guy from the bar. The one she'd thought was a hero. He'd followed her.

Heroes didn't follow girls from bars. Freaks followed girls from bars. As an ex-investigative reporter she knew what freaks did to their victims, too.

Her lungs gave up every bit of air she had to make sure her scream could be heard on the other side of China. Then, realizing screaming might not be enough, she started fighting. Fighting mean. Fighting dirty.

She kicked. She curled her hands into tight fists and punched.

The intruder stood frozen, staring at her with eyes wider than Ping-Pong balls. So she uncurled her fist and fought like a real girl. She ran her fingernails down the side of his face so hard she knew she'd drawn blood. That at least got a reaction from him. He backed up.

"Stop," he spat out.

Oh, yeah. As if she was calmly going to let him rape and possibly kill her. Panic jolted through her. She tried to lunge out, but her foot slipped and she tumbled full force into him. They fell, or rather slid, down into the tub. They went down really smooth, him on the bottom, her on top. The soap she'd slathered on her body made for some serious slipping and sliding. Her naked body slipping all over his naked body. The feel of his arousal, now more than half-mast and positioned between her thighs, sent her panic roaring to new levels.

He grabbed her arm. Trying to grab the edge of the tub, she knocked off the dandruff shampoo. Knowing a weapon when she knocked one over, she snatched it up and squeezed like her life depended on it—which it probably did—until the whole bottle emptied into his eyes.

"Damn!"

While he frantically wiped at his face, she jackknifed up, stepping on his face in the process, and hurdled out of the shower. But the moment her wet, shampoo-laden foot hit the tile, she went down, and her hand landed on the floor by the phone. She snatched it up.

Flipping the phone open, crawling toward the door, she dialed 911 and started screaming, "Help me!" The shower curtain rustled behind her. Breath held, phone to ear, she bounced to her feet and flew out the door.

Obscenities spouted out from the bathroom. Yeah, it always did take a few minutes for the shampoo to start stinging.

Les tore out into the hall. "Help me," she screamed again into the phone, and tripped again.

"Hey." The man appeared at the bedroom door.

Les scrambled up. Afraid she'd never outrun him, she darted into Katie's study, slammed the door, and locked it. She flung herself against it. Her heart throbbed against her chest bone. Oh, God, she couldn't breathe.

A voice came out of her phone. A woman's voice. The 911 operator. "Are you okay? Talk to me!"

"Help!" Les squeezed the words out. "He followed me."

"Where are you? Give me your address."

"I didn't follow you!" a masculine voice boomed from the other side of the door.

Les spouted out Katie's address. "Please hurry."

"Don't hang up!" the 911 operator insisted. "Do you hear me? Stay on the line. The police are on their way."

"The police are coming," Les yelled at the intruder. "Get out of here!" She glanced around the study for something she could use as a weapon. She grabbed an umbrella. Phone in one hand, umbrella in the other.

"I don't know who the hell you are," the man said, "or how you got here, but I did *not* follow you."

Les's heart hammered as she stared at the door. Cold air stirred across her naked butt, reminding her that she was wet and naked and she'd come within a hair of being raped. Another frigid blast of wind made her skin prickle. She turned around and saw the broken window. Glass lay scattered on the carpet. Was that how he'd gotten in?

"If you're calling the police, you'd better tell them that I didn't lay a finger on you," the intruder yelled from the hall.

She heard his footsteps. What if he went around and tried to come in through the window? Her heart thumped harder.

"Are you still with me?" the 911 operator asked.

"Yes." And Les pressed her other ear to the door to listen. Nothing. Had he left?

"Are you safe right now?" the voice asked.

"I don't know," Les whimpered, and thought she heard a door.

"Is he still there?" she asked.

"I think he might have left." Les forced herself to breathe.

"Can you get out of the house to go to a neighbor's?"

Les's gaze shot back to the window—where she swore she saw a shadow. Then she saw it again. Did he plan to come in through the window for her? She unlocked the study door and tore out into the hall.

"Worms?" Katie flung the bag to the floor.

"Sour gummy worms." Carl laughed and grabbed

them and handed them to her. "Oh, the green ones suck. Even Precious says so." He disappeared into the bathroom.

She saw him start to close the door. Her gaze flew back to the other door leading in from the hall. "Wait," she said.

He stuck his head back out. "What?"

"Nothing," she said, feeling ridiculous. The man deserved some privacy, and she just needed to toughen up. For God's sake, she was a Ray.

He stared at her, then at his hand on the door. When he stepped back in, he left the door ajar.

Okay, so he'd guessed she was afraid. She should be embarrassed. And she was, when she heard the sound of him emptying his bladder.

When had she become a wimpy woman?

Since you saw a woman killed a couple of hours ago.

True, she had good reasons to be a little nervous.

Silence fell. A slight bump sounded against the door. And not the door to the bathroom, either. *Oh, Lord.*

Was she so nervous that she would imagine noises? It came again. A tap. Her breath hitched. She hadn't imagined that.

"Carl!" she screamed.

The naked woman slammed right into Joe. Of course, he was assuming it was the same woman. He couldn't see shit. He'd barely managed to find his jeans. The blonde had squirted him right in the eyes with Katie's dandruff shampoo. And he'd let her—he'd lain there with her soapy body slipping and sliding on top of him and let her squeeze the entire bottle into his baby blues. And he'd fucking kept his eyes open, too.

Normally, he wasn't so passive, but he'd been beyond stunned when he'd stepped in the shower—expecting to see Katie all naked and hopefully willing, hoping to reconnect with his fiancée, praying some hot sex would chase away his doubts. Instead, for a second there, he'd thought he was hallucinating. Yeah, he'd been stunned all right.

He'd moved past stunned now, because when she started to fight again, he started to stop her. Hurting her wasn't his objective—protecting himself was.

She swung her knee up. He caught it. She went to whack him in the face with her phone. He ducked. She swung an umbrella at his head and he snagged it and tossed it away. Then he caught her wrists. Her phone fell to the carpet.

"Stop it," he screamed. Holding her wrists in his hands, he moved her against the wall to prevent her knee from taking out his family jewels.

"I'm not going to hurt you." He knew he'd scared her, but he had to get her calmed down. Calm enough so when the police arrived, they didn't shoot first and ask questions later. Questions, as in *does the dead guy have any identification on him?*

But, damn, this didn't make sense. What was this blonde doing in Katie's shower? Who the hell was—*Oh crap!*

Katie's friend who lived in Boston was supposed to be here that week. He remembered this woman telling him she'd been waiting for a friend at the bar. She could have been waiting for Katie, too.

The blonde continued to struggle. Her breasts brushed against him. He ignored his body's response to her tight nipples and focused on crucial shit. As in *the police are on their way here now*. The police whom she'd told that he was a freak who'd followed her home.

What had Katie told him her friend's name was? He clawed at his memory. "Les? You're Les, aren't you? I'm Joe Lyon, Katie's fiancé."

Les heard the words, but they hung somewhere between her hearing and believing. Closer to hearing than believing.

Her basic instincts still screamed *fight*. She gave her knee another upward thrust before his words really registered.

He was . . . "You're *Joe*?" It didn't make sense. "No, you broke in through the window."

"I did not!" he growled. "I used my key."

"You're hurting me." She tried to yank free.

"If you promise not to attack me, I'll go get my driver's license for you to see."

Les relaxed—well, as relaxed as you get when you were naked, and up until about a second ago, damn certain the man pressing you against the wall was a murdering rapist. Oh yeah, she was calm all right. Her heart hadn't had this kind of workout in years.

"Can I get my wallet?" His hold on her wrists loosened.

"Are you there? The police are on the street," a voice echoed from Les's phone.

Joe released her, slowly backed away, knelt, and handed her the phone. "Take this if it makes you feel safer. But when you see my license, I want you to call off the troops. Got it?"

When she nodded, he shuffled back two steps. Much to his credit, he never let his gaze travel down her body. Her very naked body. If he were a rapist/murderer, would he have given her the phone, and would he have been polite enough not to look? Did rapists offer their IDs?

But why had he broken . . . ?

I'm Katie's fiancé. I didn't break in. I used my key.

Trying to breathe, she felt his words vibrate in her head as she watched his bare shoulders and jean-covered butt move toward the bedroom. He'd put on his pants. Which was a heck of a lot more than she wore.

"Ma'am? Are you there?" the voice came again from the line.

"Yes," she managed to say.

Looking toward the living room, she saw Katie's chenille Mickey Mouse throw tossed across a chair. She ran and snatched it up, and wrapped herself in it like it was a beach towel. When Les looked up, Joe—or the man who had almost convinced her he was Joe—was walking down the hall with his wallet in his hand. He handed her his license.

Les turned on the light. Her gaze shot to the open back door. Who had opened it? Who had broken the window? Her heart raced.

She turned the light on and studied the license. *Joe Lyon.* Swallowing, she put the phone back to her ear. "Is . . . is it too late to tell the police that I made a mistake?"

Carl had barely had time to get his dick back in his shorts when he heard Katie scream.

He stormed out of the bathroom, his gun drawn. "What?"

Red stood pressed against the wall, pointing at the door. He'd seen dead people with more color in their faces. He moved in front of her, his gaze and gun now aimed at the door.

He heard it. Someone was out there. He motioned for her to move into the bathroom.

Of course, she didn't.

Forced into action, he caught her arm and growled, "Go. Lock it. Don't open it unless I tell you to. Got it?"

She looked up at him, all desperate-like. She leaned in, so close her lips pressed against his ear. "You come, too."

"No." He caught her by the elbow and moved her into the bathroom. When she didn't close the door, he did. He backed against the wall. "Lock it, Red." He didn't move until he heard the click.

He took a deep breath and waited, preparing himself for the inevitable. If this was the same person who'd shot Tabitha, Carl didn't question his intentions in coming back. Red had pegged it earlier. Murderers didn't like leaving witnesses.

Sirens echoed and blue flashes flickered in through the front window. Les's gaze shot to Joe. Right then she noticed the red, angry scratches across his jaw. She'd done that.

She'd also flirted with her best friend's fiancé. And he'd flirted back. Okay, not much, but he had flirted. Oh, and she'd seen him naked. He'd seen her naked. He'd made her wow voice go off. Oh, hell, why couldn't he have just been an ordinary rapist/killer.

"The police are there," the woman on the line said. "You can explain it to them."

Explain? Oh, that would be really easy, considering Les didn't have a fucking clue what had happened. She recalled the broken window in Katie's study and the open back door.

And Katie being MIA.

Joe met her in the entryway just as the knock sounded.

"Piper Police," a voice called out.

"Just a second," Les answered. Opening the door, Joe and she came face-to-face with two cops, pistols drawn.

Their eyes went from her, elegantly dressed in a Mickey Mouse throw, to the shirtless, red-eyed Joe with a bleeding face.

The guns quickly turned on Joe. "Step back," one of the officers yelled.

"Wait," Les said, and held up her hand. "It's a mistake."

"A mistake?" the shorter of the two officers asked.

"Yes," Les said. "A big one."

Carl heard the thump again. He waited to hear the bar being removed. His finger tightened on the trigger; then a whimper and a sniffing noise rang in his ears. He stood frozen, listening, wanting to be sure. The tip of something white appeared under the door. A paw . . . a paw with its nails painted pink. Then came the all-telling bark.

Carl released the expired air held in his lungs and tried to slow the adrenaline pumping through his veins. *A dog.* And from the looks of the painted nails, another sissy mongrel.

"Red." He knocked on the bathroom door. "You can come out."

The door swung open. "He left?" she asked breathlessly.

Carl reached under his jacket and holstered his gun. "It's a dog." The bark came again.

Fear still masked her expression, and he saw she was trembling.

"It's okay now," he said, purposely keeping his voice calm.

"I want this to be over." She blinked, and a few unshed tears webbed in her lashes. "No more dead people, no more guns. I want to be warm."

Her scarf had come untwisted and hung loose around her neck. The lack of color on her face brought new meaning to the word *pale.*

"I know." He took the steps separating them and pulled her against him. She buried her face against his chest and wrapped her arms around him. Tight. Tight, as if she didn't ever want to let go. All her softness fit against him, reminding him that in addition to her being scared, she was also female.

He lowered his face in her hair. God, she smelled good. He breathed in and tried not to let his body respond to her scent, or to the fact that he hadn't held a woman in months. He told himself she needed to be held, not laid.

Unfortunately, he had the opposite problem. He needed to be laid, not held. The situation wouldn't have been so pressing if he'd kept his date with the model this morning. But no, Ms. Jones and her talk of brides had ruined the mood. Realizing his "situation" grew harder, he pulled away before she felt it. Crazily enough, he literally had to pry her arms from around him. It was obvious to him she didn't have a clue how hard it was to walk away. And he meant that literally.

Sighing, he went and unfolded the cot that had been pushed against the wall. "Why don't you sit down before you fall down?"

"I'm not going to faint," she said, as if insulted—or maybe just mad he'd pushed her away.

"I said 'fall,' not 'faint.' "

She moved to the cot. "I'm not normally such a girly-girl."

"I like girly-girls." He smiled, not wanting to offend her.

"You know what I mean. I can usually handle—"

"Don't beat yourself up. You're doing better than I expected." He meant it, too. "The first time I saw someone get killed, I lost it. You're doing better than I did."

She drew her legs on the cot, huddled for warmth. "What happened?"

He hadn't planned to give details, but if it helped her— "It was a domestic dispute. I'd only been on the job a couple of months. The husband pulled a gun."

"Did you . . ."

"No, my partner shot him."

"That must have been hard." The color was back in her face.

"It wasn't easy. But my point is that you're actually holding together pretty good. For a girl." He winked at her.

She scooted back until she leaned against the wall. Then she pulled her knees up to her chest. "Thank you," she said.

"Just doing my job, Red." And as long as he could remember that, he'd be okay. Despite his actually liking Red—his flirting, and wanting to do more than flirt— he'd come here because Ms. Jones was going to hire him.

This was a job. The rules, his rules, were written in stone: catch the bad guys, be someone's hero, and then get out. A *temporary* hero. The one time he'd let his emotions get caught up, he'd got burned and stuck with a damn poodle with a foot fetish.

Frustrated, he backed against the cold wall and let his eyes move around the room. It was time for him to face it. They really were going to be stuck here. And since Ms. Jones didn't work on Mondays, they actually could be in here until Tuesday.

Buck Hades used his key to get into his son's place. "Carl?" he called out. "We decided to come on back." His son didn't answer, but his son's floppy-eared dog yapped its way around the corner.

The dog raised up and put tiny paws on Buck's knee, which caused Buck to say, "Don't even start pretending you like me. And you know I don't like you." He said it in case his son was listening. After giving the room another look-see, Buck gave the animal his customary rub behind the ear. Truth was, he was a sucker for the dog just like his son. Though neither one of them would admit it.

"Where's your master?" Buck walked toward the bedroom. Maybe his son wised up and had a woman here? He stopped. Hoped.

"Carl?" He knocked on the half-opened door. "Son?"

When there weren't any bumping sounds or a *get the hell out of here, Dad*, he poked his head in. Nothing.

He glanced at his watch. Almost ten. Lately, his son kept kindergarten hours. He turned around. Precious met him in the living room carrying his food bowl in his mouth. The dog dropped the dish at Buck's feet.

"Carl didn't feed you?"

Buck grabbed the bowl and went and filled it with Kibbles 'n Bits. Then placed the food on the floor. The dog hung back.

"Well, you gonna eat or not?" Turning around, Buck saw his son's answering machine on the cabinet. The light was flashing. He hit the button to listen to the messages.

"Hey, Carl. It's me, Ben. Where are you?"

Buck frowned. Why hadn't Carl shown up at Ben's? You could set your clock by Carl. Though his younger son had a knack of being a nonconformist—hence his early retirement from the force—the boy didn't let people down.

Yeah, Buck was damn proud of both his boys. Well, he would be proud as soon as he got Carl hitched to a good woman. A man needed a woman. Without one, he was only half-human. And Buck himself had been half-human for too long. Which was why Buck had come by to tell Carl that he and Jessie were planning on tying the knot.

His son Ben would be thrilled. Carl would be the difficult one. He'd taken his mother's death the hardest. And part of Buck knew that Carl wouldn't be dancing a jig at the idea of this marriage.

The dog standing by Buck's feet crunched on a nugget of food and looked up with appreciation. "You're welcome," Buck mumbled. Barking, the canine ran back to get more. "You really haven't been fed, have you, big guy?"

Carl took his responsibilities seriously. He wouldn't have left the dog without feeding him if he'd expected to be out this late. A bad feeling stirred in the pit of Buck's stomach. The feeling parents get when they're worried about their kids. Carl wasn't a kid, but sometimes even a man needed a hand. And as long as Buck was alive, he'd be there, his two hands ready.

He picked up the phone and dialed *69. A recording came on. "Congratulations. You're probably getting married. You've reached Tabitha's Weddings. . . ."

Buck hung up and eyed the canine. "Why would a wedding planner be calling my son?" Buck asked the dog. "And why do I have this feeling my boy is up to his ying-yang in trouble?"

The dog tilted his head to the side and eyed him, and the feeling in Buck's gut bit harder. It was, in fact, the same feeling he'd had right before he'd gotten the call that Carl and his partner had been shot.

Chapter Ten

"Why the hell would I break the window when I have a key?" Joe curled his hand into a fist, growing more annoyed at the cops who tried to make him look guilty when even the woman who'd originally called them seemed to believe him now. Not that she was being friendly. Those glares she shot him every few minutes had him on his last nerve.

He reached up and touched the scratches, studied her through stinging eyes. She shot him another look that said she didn't appreciate sharing the same air with him. He still didn't quite get why she got to be the one pissed off here. Wasn't he the one who'd had the first layer of his corneas burned off with dandruff shampoo, had a goose egg on his shin, busted gums, and four claw marks across his chin?

She shoved one sleeve of her sweatshirt up to her elbow. She'd gotten dressed right after the cops arrived, and had even brought him his shirt from the bedroom. Folding her arms around her middle, her sweatshirt fell off one shoulder and he got a glimpse of her red bra strap. For a second, the memory of her nakedness appeared in his mind.

"Are you sure you trust this guy?" the smaller of the

cops asked, and his voice brought Joe back to the moment. And a damn good thing, too. He had no business thinking about Katie's friend naked.

"Trust him? No." There she went with the go-to-hell looks again. "But I don't think he was the one who broke in."

The bigger cop crossed his arms. "So you think someone broke in while you were fighting with your friend's fiancé, who you thought had broken in. A little far-fetched, isn't it?"

Joe closed his eyes. It was hard even for him to believe.

"Yeah," Les said. "And the back door was open, too."

Joe remembered stepping inside the house and feeling the draft. "It might have been open when I came in," he said. "I remember turning up the heater because it felt cold."

"So you think someone was in here and they heard you opening the door and they took off."

Joe cut his eyes to the cops. "I know it sounds crazy." The older cop took off outside.

Then another thought struck Joe. "Oh, shit. Katie?"

"Excuse me?" The younger cop asked.

Les's gaze met Joe's. They shared the same concerned look.

"Katie's missing," Joe said. "My fiancée. She was supposed to meet us at the restaurant. What if . . ." He couldn't say it. He didn't want to imagine anything happening to Katie.

"Is her car here?" the cop asked.

"No, it's not," Les said. "And neither is her purse or keys. I don't think she's been home."

Joe raked another hand through his hair. "It's not like Katie not to show up."

The cop frowned. "Has she been okay lately?"

"Okay?" Joe asked.

The cop shrugged. "Is she nervous about the wedding?"

"No," he said, the same time Les spouted out, "Yes."

"She isn't . . . nervous," Joe insisted, not wanting to believe it. Or maybe what he didn't want to believe was that he hadn't paid enough attention to Katie to know how she felt.

"But," Les added, "he's right. This isn't like Katie."

The cop arched his brow. "You remember the bride who disappeared from Georgia? She created a whole story about a kidnapper. Getting married makes people do crazy things."

"Katie wouldn't do that," he and Les said at the same time.

The bigger cop came back in. He shivered and looked at his partner. "There's a tree limb lying by the window. Lots of ice. It could have broken the window when it snapped and fell."

"What about the door?" Les asked, looking worried.

"Maybe it blew open," the bigger cop said. "We've had forty-mile-an-hour wind gusts tonight."

Even Joe had to admit the cop's theory made more sense. What didn't make sense was Katie's disappearance. Even if she was nervous about getting married, he didn't see her running away. Oh, no, that was *his* MO. He'd been the one running for the last month.

Les wrapped her arms around herself, sending the sweatshirt slipping off her shoulder again. "I thought I checked it before I went to take a shower."

"Sometimes we forget," the officer said.

From the way the two of them inched closer to the door, Joe knew they were finished. "Wait a minute," Joe said. "What are you going to do about Katie?"

The officer cut him a stern look. "Call around and check with some of her other friends. She's probably waiting out the storm somewhere. If you don't hear from her in twenty-four hours, give me a call, or make a report to Missing Persons."

Les turned around and glared at Joe as if he knew the

magic words to make the cops do something. But as frustrating as it was, he didn't know any magic words.

"This one is white cake with strawberry filling," Katie told Carl, and passed him the Styrofoam plate.

He sat on the floor beside the cot. She'd told him he could sit beside her, but he'd refused, almost as if he thought it might lead to something. Of course, it wouldn't have. She wouldn't let it. She wouldn't cheat on Joe, not even with Antonio Banderas. And that was about the fifth time she'd told herself that in the last five minutes.

After spending too long in total silence, her bladder had forced her to go check out the bathroom. While in there, Katie saw Carl's gummy worms, which she'd left on the bathroom counter. Her stomach had growled with hunger, and that's when she remembered she had brought her bag in here with her wedding cake samples. So here they were, feasting on worms and wedding cake.

He scooped up a bite with his fingers. She watched him close his eyes and savor the cake. "Damn, this is good. Even better than the last. You have to go with this one."

Katie frowned, remembering Tabitha telling her she shouldn't use Todd's cakes. Then she frowned deeper when she remembered, due to Tabitha's most recent situation—being dead—she wouldn't be helping Katie with the wedding at all. Katie's stomach roiled. She wasn't sure if it was the thoughts of Tabitha being dead or the thought of the wedding that caused it. Then it occurred to Katie that due to the circumstances, maybe she and Joe should postpone the wedding. The thought sent a shiver of relief through her that left her shaken. Why would she feel relief?

"Try the red worm." Carl smiled and pointed.

Katie looked at the bag and frowned. "I've had enough." Then she remembered something he'd said before he'd gone into the bathroom. "Precious?" Katie grinned. "You dog's name is *Precious*?" She took the next sample out of the bag.

"Hey, I didn't name him." Carl held up his hands. "I tried changing his name. I even explained to him that no respectable male poodle would go by that name, but it was useless, he refused to answer to any other."

"And he doesn't like the green worms either?" she asked.

"He won't touch them," Carl explained, and he took the Styrofoam container she handed him. "You didn't try it. You okay?"

"Yeah." Glancing down into the bag, she said, "I think that one is white cake with buttercream icing."

He continued to stare. "You sure you're okay?"

"Yeah." Leaning over, she looked in the bag. "We still have four more to try." She met his gaze.

His tongue swiped across his bottom lip, and he held up his hand. "Actually, we probably should save some for later."

Mesmerized by his tongue, a few of those Banderas fantasies came back to play with her sanity. But she didn't look away from him. He didn't look away from her. Suddenly, she was glad he wasn't sitting next to her on the cot. Glad her parents had instilled the "keep your pants on" rule.

The whimpering sound came at the door again. "I remember Tabitha's dog's name is Baby," she said, hoping to break the awkward moment. "You think it's hungry?"

"I don't know, but if you even try to give Baby some of that cake I'll have to arrest you. That's breakfast."

The idea that they would be spending the night together made her nervous. "Arrest me? You're not a cop. Remember?"

"I'll make a citizen's arrest," he teased.

Their gazes met and held again. She looked away and tried to think of a safe subject. "I'm sure it has some food set out for him, don't you think?"

"Yeah." He cupped his hands together and breathed into them for warmth. The dog whined again.

"It sounds scared." Katie went and sat down beside the door and wiggled her fingers under it. "It's licking my fingers."

"Lucky dog," he said.

She cut her gaze back to him and saw the heat in his eyes. Heat she could use right now. His breath caused a puff of steam. She pulled her knees up to her chest and decided it was best to ignore his statement. She wished she could ignore the chill seeping into the butt of her jeans and the thrill his flirtatious remark had caused.

She wiggled her butt to keep the cold from freezing her buns. "Is it getting colder or is it my imagination?"

"Definitely getting colder," he said.

Neither of them spoke for several moments. She got up from the cold concrete and went back to the cot.

"Why did you stop being a cop?" She tried not to shiver.

He stood up and paced across the room—a man who didn't want to be here. "I tell you what: you tell me why you aren't wearing an engagement ring, and I'll tell you why I gave up my badge."

The moment the police walked out the door, Les glared at Joe. There were a thousand different emotions running marathons inside her, tangling up her thoughts, playing mind games. Anger. Fear. Helplessness. Worry. Anger. And, oh yeah, anger.

She drew in a breath. "You're not going to do anything?"

"Do what?" He backed up as if he was afraid of her.

"Anything to convince them to find Katie."

"I think I pretty much lost my credibility with them when you called and said I was a serial murderer/rapist."

"Like that was my fault." She stared at him.

"If you'd listened instead of coming at me like a wildcat with its tail on fire, I would have told you who I was."

"Listen to a naked guy who stepped in the shower with me? Well, excuse me—my bad!"

"I thought you were Katie."

"Not at the bar you didn't. Or are you blind?"

"Almost, thanks to you." He pulled at the bottom of his eyelids and showed her his red eyes. "Or do they just feel like they're the color of blood?"

"You know what I mean," she said. He'd *flirted* with her. Maybe it had only been very light flirting, but—

"Right now the only thing I know is—"

The phone rang, and they both ran for it. She got there first and snagged it up. "Hello?"

Nothing.

"Hello?" She pressed her ear closer to the receiver and heard music. Just like the phone call earlier.

Katie watched Carl pace around the room. Every breath he took left a wisp of fog.

She hadn't answered the question about her engagement ring. Not only because she didn't want to talk about it, but because thinking about it made her stomach quiver. After only having a few bites of cake and two worms for dinner, she didn't want to lose it.

Slipping the gloves back on, she wrapped the scarf back around her neck and face. She tightened her legs together, seeking warmth. "The news said the cold front wasn't supposed to arrive until tomorrow."

"Well, they lied," he said, sounding annoyed. At her or the situation, she didn't know, but suspected both. Then, all of a sudden, she remembered the rest of the broadcast, about how four people had frozen to death in Dallas as a result of this front. Surely, it wouldn't get that cold here.

She looked at Carl, who'd ripped off a few box tops and was placing them on the floor to sit on. Steam continually rose from his lips. The floor was like ice; her own butt hadn't warmed yet.

"Your ears are red from the cold," she said. "You should wear the scarf." She picked it up where she'd set it beside the cot and tossed it to him.

"And with my luck we'll freeze to death and I'll be found dead wearing a pink, glittery, fuzzy scarf. I'd rather chance losing an ear to frostbite."

"Are you that unsure of your masculinity?"

"My masculinity is doing just fine, thank you," he growled.

"Then put it on!" she challenged.

Frowning, he snatched up the scarf and wrapped it around his neck. "Happy?"

"Doesn't it feel better?" If she didn't think he'd take it off, she would have laughed at how the pink scarf looked on him.

Then his words *freeze to death* rang in her ears. "You don't think we could really die from the cold, do you?"

The phone went dead. Les stood there, fighting the sense that something wasn't right.

"Was that Katie?" Joe asked, his tone impatient.

"No. It was . . . They played music."

"Probably the wrong number," he said.

"Maybe." An unnatural chill climbed her spine. "But . . ."

"But what?" he snapped.

His tone sent her mood plummeting down a level. She considered insisting he leave, but remembered Katie was missing. So maybe he had just as much a right to be here at Katie's as she did. "That's the second time I've gotten a call with someone playing music."

"And you think that has something to do with Katie being missing?"

"I don't know, I just think it's strange."

"Everything is strange." He took the phone from her hands and started dialing.

"Who are you calling?" she asked.

"Katie's cell phone again." He punched in the number, listened, then dropped the phone back on the charger.

"Anything?"

"Voice mail."

"Something's wrong." Les forced the words out.

"I know." He did another pace around the room. "Do you know where she was going today?"

"Yeah. She was going to the cake maker, the wedding planner, and then—"

Les bit off her words. *To pick up the new ring.*

"Then to where?" he asked.

"Nowhere." Lying had never been her specialty, but this time she knew she'd failed at it miserably.

Suspicion twinkled in his blue, bloodshot eyes, confirming she'd been right. "It doesn't sound like nothing," he said, and took a step closer. "What are you not telling me?"

Tabitha's killer dropped the phone and listened to the wedding music. The laughter echoing in his mind caused his head to pound. *Ha, ha. Throb, throb.* He started to rock. Back. Forth. Back. Forth. When things went bad, his migraines got worse.

He'd almost had Katie Ray. He'd been inside her house, on his way to her bedroom where the shower had been running, when he'd heard someone at the door. He'd barely managed to get out the back in time. Panicked, he'd driven by his other brides' graves and left flowers. Then he'd come home, but nothing felt good. Nothing felt right. He went into his closet, all the way to the back, and pulled out the wedding album where he kept pictures of his brides.

Oh, his beautiful brides. Four of them. Sometimes, looking at the pictures was all he needed. He'd gone years without needing to find a new one. But then the laughter had come back. Tabitha's fault. She'd begged him. He hadn't done a wedding in three years, but six months ago she'd come calling. She'd been desperate, someone had canceled, and she'd begged.

His head kept pounding. Something tickled his mind as if he'd forgotten something. When the migraines hit, he had to work hard to stay focused. To act normal. What had he forgotten?

Then he remembered. Remembered the girl and the cop back at Tabitha's. He'd had a plan for dealing with them. What had the plan been?

Oh yeah, he'd been going to burn it down.

He had to do it. Looking at his watch—almost eleven—he should do that soon. But when everyone was asleep. Midnight.

If only his head would quit shooting that blinding pain. If only that man hadn't walked into Katie's house and stopped him from claiming his bride. He could have added her picture to the others. Setting the album on the floor, he pulled out his digital camera from his coat pocket and set it beside his recorder. Then he set his alarm to go off at midnight.

Chapter Eleven

Les walked to the kitchen, more to escape Joe than from needing anything. Unfortunately, he wasn't the type to let people escape easily. He followed her into the kitchen and pinned her with another accusing look. Les grabbed a diet soda from the fridge and pretended she wasn't bothered by his look, or by him. But the truth was, Joe Lyon bothered her.

Bothered her plenty.

He gripped the back of a wooden kitchen chair. "You said Katie was nervous about the wedding."

"Yeah." She popped the can top and took a sip. The carbonation burned her throat. She swallowed.

"How was she nervous?"

"Wedding jitters. No biggy."

"That's all?" He slapped her with another look.

"Yeah." Not that Les had believed it then . . . or now.

Joe took a deep breath and studied her harder, and she didn't like the way he looked at her. "Do you think she ran away?"

"Oh, hell no! Katie would *not* run away." Les remembered how Joe had flirted with her. "Even if she should."

He stepped forward, so close she could count his eyelashes. "If you know where she is and you're not—"

Les slammed her soda down and poked him in his chest. "If I knew where she was." *Poke.* "I'd be with her and not here." *Poke.* "Katie is my best friend." *Poke.* "Since kindergarten." *Poke.* "And—"

He grabbed her wrist. The memory of him holding her hand in the bar hit hard. And her stupid wow voice spoke again. Damn the voice. And damn her for wanting it to come back.

"Then what are you not telling me?" he asked.

She snatched her hand back. This was crazy. So freaking crazy. She could not be feeling even the slightest spark for this man. This was Katie's fiancé. So why had he even given her the time of day at the bar? If he'd ignored her as an engaged man should have done, then none of this would have happened.

"I'm her fiancé." His eyes flashed blue fire.

"Exactly!" she said. "You're her fiancé. Why did you . . . ?"

"Why did I what?" he asked, when she couldn't finish it.

"You smiled at me." Oh, God, that sounded so lame.

"And since when is smiling a crime?" he asked, *not smiling*.

"You told that guy hitting on me that I was with you."

"Because I thought you wanted to get rid of him."

"I could have gotten rid of him myself."

"What? You keep a bottle of dandruff shampoo in your purse?"

For some crazy, unknown reason she wanted him to admit it. Admit that he'd flirted with her. "You held my hand when the lights went out."

"You seemed scared." His voice held a ribbon of guilt.

Guilt was good. *No.* Guilt was bad. Guilt had been bouncing around her chest since he'd told her who he was. "You ran your thumb over my hand," she said before she could stop herself. *You made my wow voice speak for the first time in eighteen months.*

Neither of them said a word for a few minutes. Then

he spoke. "Instead of accusing each other right now, we should be trying to figure out how to help Katie."

The truth of his words sank in. She hated being wrong, but wasn't above admitting it. "You're right." She inhaled. "I'm just . . . scared."

He blinked. "Me, too."

She nodded. Their eyes met. "I'm sorry," she said. *Sorry for ever going and sitting beside you. Sorry for the scratches and for squirting you with dandruff shampoo. Sorry for bringing up the fact that we flirted.*

Yep. She was really sorry for bringing up the flirting issue. They were adults, after all. And nothing had happened. Seeing each other naked in the shower had been an accident. Obviously, she was blowing this whole wow-voice thing out of proportion.

His shoulders fell. And Lord help her, she couldn't help but notice they were nice shoulders.

"What are you not telling me, Les?"

That getting married upset Katie so much that she threw up and accidentally flushed your engagement ring down the john. Les almost told him that, then recalled how determined Katie had been to keep it from Joe. If Les thought she could lie convincingly enough, she'd do it, but she didn't feel convincing. So she opted for the truth—the truth about not telling the truth.

"If I'm not telling you something, it's because Katie wouldn't want me to. It has nothing to do with her not being here. Nothing to do with how she feels about you or about any other man." Les threw in the *other man* part just in case he was the jealous type.

Not that he needed to worry. Katie, like her brother, was loyal to the core. She would never consider letting a man touch her as long as she belonged to Joe. Never.

"Just get in bed with me." Katie watched Carl rip off more box tops to lay on. She remembered how cold the floor was.

His gaze shot up and he studied her as if contemplating her offer. "Better not."

She was freezing. The ski jacket kept her top half warm, a lot warmer than his leather jacket had, which meant he was probably even colder than she was right now. In spite of having pulled the sheet off the mattress and draping it over her legs, everything below and above the ski jacket had passed the cold stage and headed to the numb level. She remembered her father talking about a couple who'd been caught in the snow in Colorado and how they'd stayed alive by sharing body heat. "Look—"

He held up one hand. "Tempting offer, and believe me, I don't usually tell women no, but I'd better not."

"Oh, puh-leeze. It's for body warmth."

"Red, I'm totally aware of how hot your body is. I don't need to get any closer."

She rolled her eyes and, yes, his comment made her happy, but now wasn't the time to . . . "We're adults."

"That's part of the problem. I'm an adult male and you're an adult female. Did you miss that class in high school?"

"Nothing is going to happen," she insisted. "Just come get in the bed. How hard can that be?"

He shook his head. "That's the problem, it can get—"

"Stop that." She slapped her hand over her ears, but it hurt to touch them, so she pulled away.

"Stop what?" he asked, and stood up, rubbing his hands together for warmth.

"Stop talking dirty."

"I'm not talking dirty. I'm talking facts."

"Facts I don't need or want to know about," she lied, and felt slightly disturbed that his dilemma made her want to smile.

"Which is exactly why this isn't a good idea. Because if I crawl in that bed with you, you're going to know."

"Are you telling me you have no control over . . . over *it*?" Oh goodness, she couldn't help herself, her eyes lowered. She snapped her gaze up and hoped he hadn't noticed. But from the smirk in his eyes, she knew he had.

"Nope." He grinned and stood a little taller. "It pretty much has a mind of its own."

She rolled her eyes. "Then we'll ignore it."

"Easier said than done."

"We're in trouble here and you're thinking about sex," she accused, and then silently slung the accusation right back at herself.

"I'm a man, that's pretty much what we do," he snapped. "At least the macho types do. The sensitive ones may be different."

"So you'd rather die than share your body heat." Her teeth chattered, and just like that, she wanted to cry.

The look on his face softened. "We're not going to die."

"The tops of your ears are redder than blood." Emotion rose in her throat again. "I've never been this cold."

He studied her. "Ah, fuck it!"

She had to clinch her jaw to keep her teeth from chattering. "Do you really have to say that so much?"

"Say what?"

"Fuck."

"You don't say it?" His brow pinched. "What, another rule?"

Her teeth chattered. "I say it, but only if the situation is f-word worthy."

"I'm wearing a fuc—friggin' pink scarf." He took a step closer. "I'm about to crawl in bed with a gorgeous redhead but there's not a chance in hell I'm going to get lucky." He paused and his right eyebrow arched. His eyes twinkled. "Is there?"

"No," she insisted, but dang it if she didn't feel the thrill of knowing he wanted her. "We're just sharing body heat."

The truth started perking deep down. She'd have loved

to share more, but admitting that to herself was dangerous; admitting that to him could prove fatal. Not *deadly* fatal, but fatal to her relationship with Joe. Her stomach wiggled in a bad way.

He stepped closer, his eyes carrying a leftover smile. "You know, for it to really work, we should take off our clothes."

The idea sent fantasies upon fantasies doing sexy little dances through her mind. "I think we can skip that part."

"See. Definitely f-word worthy." He took another step closer and shrugged his shoulders. "Well?"

"Well, what?" She barely managed to find her voice, her mind stuck on the fantasy of seeing him take off his clothes.

"You gonna scoot over, or do you want me to crawl on top?"

Now came another fantasy. Him on top. Her on top.

Oh, hell, he was right. This was f-word worthy. And she'd been fucking stupid to make this suggestion. "Forget I asked. You were completely right. You should sleep on the floor."

He frowned and waved his hand at her. "Scoot over, Red."

When she didn't do so immediately, he exhaled. "I'm not going to try anything. I swear."

Yeah, but I might. She shivered, but not from the cold.

He pulled back the sheet, crawled in beside her, and drew her against him. And there was a lot of him to be against. Every inch of her that touched inches of him became sensitive and alive.

Neither of them spoke for the next few minutes. Then his voice came at her ear. "Breathe, Red."

She inhaled.

"Better. Now, try to sleep."

Sleep? How? When every nerve ending she owned was doing a happy dance—including nerve endings she didn't know she owned?

He raised her wrist and glanced at her watch. "It's eleven o'clock. Morning will be here before you know it."

Tabitha's killer put the photo album of his brides back in the closet and tucked the images away in his mind. Midnight approached, and he needed to finish what he'd left undone.

He remembered the empty gas cans stored in the garage. Walking into the kitchen, he found matches tucked in a drawer.

Realizing he hadn't eaten, he cut himself a big slice of chocolate cake. As he slowly took bites, he fought the panic looming too close to the surface.

He checked his watch again. Almost time. All he had to do was set a fire in the back of the house so Tabitha's two guests would be dead before the fire trucks arrived.

Chapter Twelve

Les watched Joe rake his fingers through his hair. Again. Obviously a nervous habit. A habit that made his hair stand up in a little-boy cowlick kind of way. She had the oddest desire to lick her hand and run it over Joe's bad do, the way her mom had done to her brother's hair all those years ago. Of course, she didn't dare touch him.

With hair sticking up at weird angles, he kept staring at her. No doubt he thought she was hiding something important.

While a flushed engagement ring might be important, it wasn't her news to tell. "Girls keep secrets from guys," she said. "And that's all I'm saying."

"It has nothing to do with where she's at?" he asked.

"Nothing." Les hoped he heard the honesty in her voice.

He frowned. "I guess I have to trust you."

She let her shoulders relax. With this issue behind them, now they could . . . "What are we going to do?"

He looked around. "Katie has a notebook with all her wedding stuff. I thought I could call everyone she saw today." He eyed the countertops. "It's usually lying around."

"I think it's in the bedroom."

Les took off to get it. When she got back, he had a phone book spread open on the kitchen table. He took the notebook from her.

"While I call them," he said, "why don't you call the hospitals? See if there have been any accidents."

Memories slammed into her and pushed her right into a world of pain.

Joe continued, "We can use our phones and leave Katie's home line open in case she calls."

Les's lungs refused the air she offered them.

"I got the phone book out." He motioned toward the table.

Les's gaze shot to the opened page. *H* for hospitals. And there were the doodles and checkmarks on the page. Her doodles. Her checks. The memories grew closer.

She'd sat right here in Katie's kitchen eighteen months ago, used the same phone book, and called the hospitals. She'd been the one to learn that there had been an accident. She'd been the one to talk to the ER nurse. She'd been the one to know by the nurse's tone that Katie's brother, the man Les loved, was gone, and wasn't ever coming home—no one was. No survivors.

Les reached up and twisted the engagement ring that hung around her neck. One day her life had been fairy tale perfect. Engaged to marry her best friend's brother on whom she'd had a crush since third grade. Then an 18-wheeler shattered all her dreams and burned them to ashes.

Oh, God. Tears stung her eyes and she closed them. She wanted Katie to walk through that door. To say something lame about traffic or how her wedding planner had kept her late.

"You okay?" Joe's voice sounded too distant, his touch on her shoulder too close.

She opened her eyes; his concerned bloodshot eyes stared down at her. "Fine. I'm fine." Forcing herself to move, she went to find her cell phone. She couldn't fall apart. She had to find Katie.

Please, God, let Katie be okay.

Katie felt Carl's warm breath stir against her hair. She wasn't sure how long they'd lain there. Thirty minutes? Maybe more. She'd checked her watch once: a few minutes past midnight. She should be sleepy. But no.

He'd left the light on. Thank goodness for small favors. The darkness would have made it even more intimate.

His chest melted against her back, and he had one arm tucked around her waist. The front of his knees pressed against the back of hers. This was for warmth, she reminded herself. Oh yes, his heat wrapped around her, seeped through the thin jeans and warmed her down to her very core. Warmed her in ways an engaged woman shouldn't be warmed by a man who wasn't her fiancé. Warm like she hadn't felt warm in a very, very long time.

Every place their bodies met tingled, and she ached to get closer still. She longed to roll over and slip her hands under his jacket, under his shirt, to feel skin. Naked skin. To press her mouth to his, to taste him. She wanted all of him against all of her.

Guilt swarmed her like fruit flies on an expired banana.

She shut her eyes and reminded herself she wasn't doing anything wrong. Just staying warm. Being attracted to someone wasn't a sin, acting on it was. And she wasn't acting. No, she'd never act. She loved Joe. *Yes, think about Joe.*

"You stopped breathing again, Red." Carl's words came so close to her ear that goose bumps played hopscotch on her neck.

"I'm breathing." She took in a mouthful of air.

Another pause came and went. "Are you warmer?" he asked.

"Yes." She heard the dog whimper at the door.

"Good." His arm curled tighter around her.

Another minute passed, and she heard his stomach growl. "You want some more cake?"

"Nah. We'll save that for breakfast. Then we'll have worms for lunch. It's what you call living large."

The tease in his voice made her smile. "I'm not eating the green ones." She rolled over and his scent and smile filled her senses.

"What do you really have against marriage?" She wasn't sure why the question popped out. Maybe she wanted to remind him and herself that she was engaged. Or maybe when you snuggled with a guy and listened to his stomach growl, you wanted to know a little about him. While she felt she did know him, she'd really only begun to scratch the surface. Carl Hades, aka Antonio Banderas, fascinated her. He had a crusty side, a side she wanted to brush off to get to the good stuff. She knew that good stuff existed, like his love for his dad, like his giving up his coat, like his telling her about his mom.

"Why do you think only crazy people get married? Did someone hurt you?"

He arched one of his brows. "You gonna tell me why you aren't wearing a ring?"

She almost considered rolling over, but then she didn't want to go back to the silence. "I lost it. I lost my ring."

"Here?" he asked, as if he might help search.

"Not here."

He studied her as if he could see she was holding something back. And this close, there was no telling what he saw.

She knew what *she* saw: warm, golden brown eyes that laughed a lot. Tenderness, and someone who didn't want anyone to get too close.

"Where? Where did you lose it?"

She spat out the truth. "I was throwing up and it fell . . . in, and I . . . accidentally flushed."

"In the john?" He laughed. "You flushed your engagement ring down the john?"

"It isn't funny." She fought the wave of nausea.

"Oh, yes it is, Red." The cot shook with his laughter.

Katie's stomach shook with it. She gave him a stab in his ribs with her elbow. He grabbed her arm, but didn't stop laughing.

"Now answer my question," she insisted. "Why do you not want to share your life with someone?"

His lips tilted to the left in a sexy smile. "I share myself when I'm in the mood."

"So you're the type of guy who uses women for sex and runs out when things start getting serious."

His smile faded and his brow tightened. "I don't use women. But just for the record, using people isn't gender specific."

"So you . . . do what?" she asked, annoyed and not totally understanding why, except she didn't like men who thought of women as bang toys. "Go up to a woman and say, 'hey, let's dirty up my sheets, but don't plan on hanging around long enough to change them?' God . . . you remind me of someone in high school!"

"Believe it or not, Red, some women don't want commitment any more than some men do."

"No, all they want to do is get screwed by some selfish guy whose only goal is to get between their legs and squirt them with a little of his DNA." The moment the crude words were out, she regretted them. "I shouldn't have said that." Embarrassed and annoyed, she rolled over and gave him her back.

This time he didn't put his arm around her. And as much as she hated admitting it, she missed it. And it wasn't about being cold, but about being close. It was about feeling less alone. And he did that—made her feel less alone.

She counted the gray specks on the gray wall and finally relented and rolled over. "I just can't imagine why anyone would choose to be alone. Alone sucks. Hurts. We weren't created to be alone. Did you know that a newborn baby left without human contact is less likely to live than one that is being held on a regular basis? We are supposed to be with our families—to be loved, held. And families aren't supposed to die and leave one member behind. They—" Her chest tightened and she realized what she'd said.

"Is that why you're getting married, Red? Because you lost your parents? Because you don't want to be alone?"

Immediately, she remembered Les's words from today. *I hear a friend who's still trying to deal with losing her entire family and so worried about turning twenty-nine that she'll marry the first Tom, Dick, or Joe who comes along.*

Katie wasn't stupid; she knew part of the reason she wanted to get married was so she wouldn't be alone. But it wasn't the only reason. And even if it played a big part, was it really a bad reason?

And she did love Joe.

Didn't she?

The question rolled around her heart and butted heads with a thousand other questions floating around in there that she'd refused to answer lately. Like why had Joe been distant for the past few weeks? Like why did she feel certain a piece of paper claiming that she was Joe's wife was going to chase away the loneliness when being his girlfriend and then his fiancée hadn't done the trick.

Oh, God. Were Les and Carl right? Was this whole wedding a big mistake?

Her stomach churned. Seriously this time. She lunged up, crawling over him, one hand over her mouth, and barely made it to the bathroom in time.

Right after she let go, she heard, "Ahh, Red, not again." And he threw up, too.

Les and Joe had been at it for about twenty minutes. Joe had dialed every number in Katie's wedding book and gotten nowhere. Not surprising for twelve thirty in the morning, but still. He left five messages: one for Tabitha Jones, the wedding planner, and one each for the florist, the DJ, the minister who was to marry them, and the photographer.

He slammed the phone down, and was about to call the local police station when his gaze caught on Les. Her hands shook. She was talking to the fourth hospital.

"Yes, I'll hold."

She reached for the pen and started doodling in the corner of the phone book, and a wet drop appeared beside where the pen met the paper. The ink became blotchy.

Joe looked up and saw her tears. His gaze went from the doodles that had been on the phone book earlier to the ones she drew now. Matching doodles.

Just like that, he remembered Katie telling him about the night her family was killed. Her parents had been driving in from Austin with her brother, but they hadn't shown up. Les had been here, too. While Katie had called some of her brother's friends, Les had called the hospitals. And he remembered something else, too. Les had been engaged to Katie's brother.

Damn! How hard was it for her to make these calls again?

He took the phone from her. "I got this. Why don't you make us some coffee?"

She wiped her face, stood, and went to the kitchen cabinets.

A voice came on the line. "No one fits . . ."

"Thank you," he said, and closed Les's cell phone.

"What did they say?" Les asked from behind him.

He turned around. "She isn't there."

Les slumped back on the counter, and Joe wondered whether, if the counter hadn't caught her, she would have fallen over.

"I'm sorry. I just remembered that you did this before."

She swiped at her tears. "It can't happen twice," she said. "That's what I keep telling myself."

He went to her and folded her into his arms. She gripped two handfuls of his shirt and buried her head in the crook of his shoulder. He pressed his face into the soft wispy feel of her blond hair and just held her while she cried.

Five minutes later, they were still standing in the kitchen holding onto each other. For comfort. For human contact. And it felt good and right. Like holding her hand earlier had felt right. Right now, the feel of her breasts against his chest sent other feel-good messages spiraling through his body.

Her scent, a vanilla musk, filled his nose. The visual of her naked in the shower replayed in his mind. He had a flashback of how her bare breasts had felt against him when he'd held her against the wall in the hallway.

She raised her face; their gazes met and held. He leaned in just a breath, their lips almost touched. Almost.

Guilt slammed into him. He dropped his hands.

As if she read his mind, she jumped back. "You said we'd try the police one more time."

"Yeah." He walked to the table and picked up his phone.

"Don't touch me again." Her voice boomed behind him.

His first impulse was to insist it had been innocent. And it had started out like that, but it hadn't ended that way. He still almost said it, but he simply wasn't fond of lying. "I won't." He looked back, expecting to see fury in her eyes.

However, the same emotion bouncing around his chest was expressed all over her face. Guilt. It should have made him feel better to know she wasn't holding him solely responsible, but it didn't.

"We haven't done anything," he said, more for her benefit than his.

"I love Katie," she said.

"Me, too." And it was true. He loved Katie, but he

was through lying to himself, too. He didn't love Katie the way he should love her. He loved her as . . . as everyone loved Katie. She was just too good a person not to love. She was the type who bought all her lightbulbs from the disabled. Who gave up one Saturday morning a month to hold premature babies. She was smart, could talk about art until the cows came home, and she had a way with people. She could make them laugh, make them open up. She saw the best in everyone and it just made a person want to be that best.

So yeah, he admired Katie, he respected Katie. He loved who he was when he was around Katie. And she was too damn beautiful for him not to respond to her sexually. She had every trait and quality he'd been looking for in a wife. And at thirty-four years old, he'd been looking for someone to marry for the last two years. But for the last month, he'd found himself wondering if the respect-and-admiration kind of love was enough. He kept waiting for the emotion to kick in, the one that made good sex mind-blowing sex, the one that told him she was the one.

It hadn't happened. And right then he knew that if he married Katie he might be content, but he wouldn't be happy.

Would contentment be enough? The thought scraped over his mind like sandpaper. The answer scraped even harder: *No*. It wasn't enough.

Damn. His fiancée was missing and all he could do was stand there thinking about how he couldn't marry her.

Les moved to the sofa, where she promptly collapsed. Oh, God, she was a terrible, terrible person. Her best friend was missing and, five minutes ago, all she could think about was kissing Katie's fiancé. What kind of person did that? Les hugged herself against the building pain. Maybe a very panicked person, she told herself, hoping to relieve some of her guilt.

Joe was right. They hadn't done anything. Not on purpose, anyway. Seeing each other naked had been an accident. And being attracted to him was an accident as well. A huge fucking calamity, but an accident no less.

She heard Joe talking on the phone to the police. She toyed with the idea of leaving and going to stay at her parents' house. But what if Katie called? What if she needed her?

Closing her eyes, Les tried to think of the reasons Katie wasn't calling, reasons that meant she was okay. She'd had car trouble. She'd run into someone from high school and lost track of time. But neither of those reasons held water. Everything felt so . . . so fucked-up. And if Katie were here and heard Les say the f-word, she'd tell Les to save the f-word for only the f-word–deserving moments. In Katie's weird way of thinking, cussing wasn't a bad thing if the situation really warranted it. Les just prayed that this whole mess—Katie being missing, Les being attracted to Katie's fiancé—weren't going to be f-word worthy.

Katie sat on the floor beside the toilet and stared at Carl holding out one of Tabitha's cups, which he'd pulled from one of the boxes. The cup was filled with water. Sure, she'd mentioned she would kill for a drink of water but . . .

"I am *not* drinking that."

"It's clean, Red."

"Clean? It came out of a toilet."

"The back of a toilet. The sink isn't working."

"Back, front, it doesn't matter. A toilet is a toilet."

"Maybe a drink of water will help settle your stomach."

"I don't drink from toilets. I don't even like throwing up in toilets that aren't my own."

"Seriously, I've heard that the water from the back of the toilet is just like tap water. Look, I'll drink it." He started to take a sip.

She made a face. "At least now I won't want to kiss you anymore." Oh, God, had she said that aloud?

His widened eyes told her that yes . . . yes, she'd said that aloud.

"Fudge!" She gave her word choice a quick consideration and revised it. "Fuck!"

"Now it's f-word worthy, huh?" he asked.

She dropped her head between her knees and wished she could curl up into a ball and just die. Okay, considering her current situation, that she'd seen someone die, maybe she should be careful what she wished for.

"Are you sick with a bug or something?"

She didn't raise her head. "No." She spoke between her knees. "I told you earlier. It's just a nervous stomach."

"Wedding nerves?" he asked.

"Yeah," she said.

He chuckled and she somehow knew he was thinking about her flushing her ring. Something she tried not to think about.

But as soon as she got out of here, she knew she'd have to think about it. Even if she threw up constantly. Like it or not, she couldn't marry Joe until . . . until she knew it was the right thing to do.

And for the right reasons.

Chapter Thirteen

Where the hell was his son? Buck had gone from fretting to pacing in a little over three hours, and the damn poodle paced with him. A phone call to his elder son, Ben, had made Buck worry even more. Carl had never shown up at their place.

Buck gave his watch another glance. After midnight. That was it. He couldn't wait anymore. He had to stop thinking like a father and start thinking like a cop.

He went to the cabinet and found the yellow pages and looked under *J*. Buck remembered Carl saying he was going to talk to a lady about a case. That lady could be Tabitha Jones. And if Ms. Jones was listed, she was going to get a visit. Buck didn't care what time it was, not when his gut told him his son was ass-deep in trouble.

Les watched Joe pace across the living room. "That's it. I'm tired of doing nothing!"

Les had never agreed with anyone more. Doing nothing sucked. A crazy thought shot through her mind. She'd been doing nothing with her life for the last eighteen months. A year ago, she'd looked at her relocation to Boston as moving on, but now she saw it for what it had been: running away. And the only thing that sucked more than doing nothing, was running away.

Joe headed back into the kitchen.

"Where are you going?" she asked.

"I'm calling that wedding planner again. And if she doesn't answer, then I'm going over there. I think Katie has her card in the book. It has her address on it."

Les jumped from the sofa. "I'm going with you."

Red had finally fallen asleep. Carl lay there, his body throbbing with awareness—he was aware of how she smelled, aware of the soft strands of her hair that clung to his five o'clock shadow. Aware that he hadn't been this close to a woman in over a year. Aware that he, wearing a fuzzy pink scarf with glitter, was sporting a woody about the size of a two-by-four.

And he was also all too aware that a killer might try to come back and finish what he'd started earlier. No way in hell would Carl fall asleep and let the asshole get the jump on them.

The canine whimper sounded at the door again. Careful not to wake Red, Carl got off the cot and reached for the bag with the cakes.

He reached in, pulled off a little piece and, kneeling, he shoved the bit under the door. His mind went to his own prissy mongrel at home without his dinner, and he wondered how pissed Precious was right now.

The dog outside the door licked Carl's fingers clean.

"Now, go for somewhere warm to sleep," he whispered to the mutt. Standing up, he studied Red. Even wearing a ski jacket and covered with a thin sheet, that feminine form got his blood pumping.

"Thought you were going to arrest me if I gave him some cake," she said, her voice sleepy warm and so damn sexy it was painful. His gaze shot to her face; her eyelids were only half-opened.

"It was just to shut him up."

"And not because you might have a heart," she said, and rolled back onto her side. The sheet rolled with her and slipped to the other side. "You don't fool me, Carl Hades," she said.

He stared at her sweet butt encased in those light blue jeans. Closing his eyes, he sought the willpower to crawl back in that bed and *not* attempt to seduce her.

At least now I won't be tempted to kiss you. He heard her words from earlier, the first sign that the attraction hadn't been one-sided.

But for every reason his cock told him to go for it, his brain dumped out a whole mess of reasons why he'd regret it. And so would she. First, she belonged to another man—in theory, anyway. Carl didn't know what to make of the whole I-flushed-my-engagement-ring-down-the-toilet story, but it didn't bode well for a June wedding. Still, he had a thing about tapping someone else's well.

Second, there was something about Katie Ray herself. Something instinctively good. Something like the kind of women Carl had avoided for a long time, like a sharp poke in the eye.

He had thought that by staying away from Red's kind he could keep himself clear of emotional ties. Little had he known that even flawed women could needle their way into his heart.

Amy sure as hell had.

But then, Amy's flaw had ended up being the thing that attracted him to her. She needed rescuing. Needed saving from herself and her addiction to drugs. Without a doubt, he'd known that if Amy didn't get herself straightened out, she would die. So Carl had taken her in, protected her, and fallen so deeply in love with her that she'd blindsided him. Never in a million years had he expected to come home that day, six months after she'd been clean, to find her sitting on his sofa with her bags packed.

One look into her eyes, and he'd seen she was using

again. He'd still tried to keep her from leaving. Biting his pride back, he'd admitted he loved her and offered to make it official, marry her, have a couple of kids. He'd expected his proposal to win her over; instead she'd thrown it back in his face. *Stop trying to save me, Carl. I'm not your mother.*

No, Amy hadn't been anything like his mother, who'd spent her entire life taking care of others. But Red was.

She pulled the sheet around herself, telling Carl she was cold. Shaking off the past, he climbed back in bed with her, pulled the sheet around both of them, and shared his body warmth. But that heat was all he was sharing. Nobody was breaking his heart again.

Then Red rolled over. At first he thought she was awake, but when she pillowed her head on the edge of his shoulder, he knew better. If he pressed his lips to hers right now, if he slipped his hand up under that jacket and touched those sweet breasts, slipped his hand inside those jeans and showed her how well he knew his way around the female body, he suspected she might give in. But he wouldn't do that. Plain and simple, he didn't seduce women who didn't want to be seduced.

That was why Red's little statement about him using women was a hard one to swallow. When he was playing the field—before Amy—he'd never played games. Or better said, he'd made sure the women knew the rules to the game he was playing. Before he and the lady ever got to first base, he'd made his position clear: he wasn't looking for forever. If there was even the least bit of hesitation, Carl had walked away. He didn't even care how close they were to first base, or how much Mr. Wiggly had wanted to stay and hit a home run. Carl had never been one much on rules, but that one he followed.

Red snuggled closer. Carl couldn't stop his body from enjoying this. Not that there was a lot to enjoy. The ski jacket kept him from feeling the good parts. Ahh, but he'd felt her soft, full breasts earlier, and he knew they were there. C-cups, he'd bet. The kind that filled a man's hands. With a set like that, a woman didn't need a pretty face.

She had one, though. He glanced at Red's face. He counted five freckles across her nose. A few more on her cheeks. Odds were she hated her freckles, too.

He tilted his head to the side to see her neck. While the scarf she wore mostly covered it, and he didn't see freckles there, he knew she probably had those little brown speckles spread all over her sweet body.

What he wouldn't give to spend a lazy Sunday morning counting them, kissing them, making her realize how precious those little marks were to a man who'd had a hard-on for redheads since third grade.

The image of making love to her played like a film in his head, and because in his imagination no one walked away hurt, and because being hard as granite helped him stay awake, he pulled the pink scarf up over his ears, closed his eyes, and enjoyed the show playing on the back of his lids.

At the service station, Tabitha's killer filled the gas can and put it in his trunk. All he had to do was set the house on fire and leave.

As he drove down the back roads, he realized how close he was to his other brides. He'd left flowers yesterday. Beautiful carnations, pink and white. But maybe tomorrow he'd go back to see them. Maybe tomorrow he'd add Katie to his collection.

The laughing started in his head again. He rocked as he drove. Back and forth. Back. Forth.

Carl wasn't sure how long he'd lain there, Red's head on his shoulder, her hand curled on his stomach, but the show playing in his head had just moved from R-rated to XXX when something pulled him out of the fantasy. He listened. A low snarl, a growl: the cake-loving Baby by the door wasn't happy.

Sitting up, Carl held his breath. Baby's growl grew deeper. A serious kind of a growl. He shook Red by the shoulder.

"Wake up. You need to go to the bathroom."

She raised her head and blinked. "No, I don't."

The dog's growl grew more intense. "Yes, you do, Red. Come on. Don't argue. Move it!" He heard footsteps. "Now, damn it!"

Her eyes widened with alertness and her frightened gaze shot to the door. She threw off the sheet. "This time you're coming with me."

The footsteps grew closer. The dog yelped as if someone had kicked it. Carl grabbed Red by the arm and pulled her up and shoved her into the bathroom. He didn't have time to argue. "Lock the door. Now!"

As soon as he heard the bathroom door click shut, Carl heard some splattering noises in the hall, as if something was being poured. Then the smell of gasoline penetrated his senses. Instantly, he knew the plan. Jeezus, of all the ways he didn't want to go. This one came second only to being skinned alive.

"Damn it!" Carl yelled at the door. "Listen to me, you yellow-bellied coward, open the fucking door and fight me like a man."

"Don't have to," the voice came back.

Carl aimed his gun at the door and was very close to firing—even though he knew the bullet wouldn't penetrate the metal. His thoughts zipped to Red. About to get married and start the rest of her life. She deserved that. Damn, he wanted to be her hero.

The smell of gas grew thicker. A sense of doom filled his gut: they were trapped, and if the house went up in flames . . .

But damn him if he would give up. Not a quitter, he

yanked off his coat and stuffed it under the door, hoping to stop any of the gas from seeping inside. "Just unlock the door," he said. "Give us a chance." *And I promise, when I shoot you, I'll make sure it hurts!*

Carl could swear he heard another voice. Then more footsteps. Then running. "Talk to me!" No one answered.

The dog barked again. Then he heard someone call his name. "Carl?"

Carl recognized the voice instantly; relief came in a flood. "In here, Dad."

Shots exploded. Carl's gut turned inside out. He slammed his hand on the door. "Dad?!"

Katie bumped up against him. When the hell had she gotten out of the bathroom? His patience snapped. "Get back in there!" He shoved her toward the bathroom door. Of course, she didn't go. Women never listened.

"Who is it?" Panic hung in her voice. "What's that smell?"

"Son?" His father's voice again, and Carl breathed.

"There's gas everywhere, Dad. Be careful!"

The creak of the bar being removed from the door filled the silence. Carl held tight to his gun, and he pushed Red behind him.

The door pushed open; his dad appeared. Carl spotted the concern firing his dad's eyes. Then, just as quick, a look of relief filled his expression. "You gonna shoot me?" Humor was his dad's way of dealing with stress, or emotional issues.

Carl lowered his gun. "No, but I might kiss you." And Carl must have inherited a bit of his dad's coping methods.

"Now ain't that sweet." He gave Red a nod. "Buck Hades, ma'am."

Carl frowned. "How about we skip introductions." He gave Red's hand a squeeze and released it. "Ready?"

He looked back at his father, and they moved into the hall, guns held out, heads shifting left, then right. The light from the room they'd just left bounced off the wall and reflected in both directions.

"Which way did he go?" Carl asked.

His dad pointed toward the back of the house.

Carl nodded. "Red, go with my dad."

"Why don't you see to her?" his dad said, again serious. "I'll go after—"

"No." He looked over his shoulder at his dad, trying to communicate with his eyes that this wasn't negotiable. "Get her out of here," Carl said, and saw the panic on Red's face. He felt the overwhelming need to assure her. "And watch her." He grinned and touched his face. "She scratches like a girl."

"*No.* There's safety in groups." Katie grabbed Carl's arm, her tight hold sinking into the firm muscle of his forearm. "You might get hurt."

"Careful." Carl winked. "You'll make me believe you care."

She frowned. "Please, stay with us."

He saw concern brighten her eyes. "I'll be fine. Go."

"My son can take care of himself," his dad said, and reached out and took Red by the arm.

The older Hades, an aged version of Antonio Banderas, graying at his temples, gave her a gentle tug. Katie let go of Carl, but she didn't want to. What if the idiot who poured gas everywhere lit a match and Carl couldn't get out. What if Carl got shot like Tabitha? Katie's insides started shaking again as she watched him move down the dark hall, going deeper into the prison that was now doused with gas.

As she watched him disappear, fear curled inside her chest. "Why do men always do this?" she seethed.

Mr. Hades walked in the opposite direction, down the hall, into the darkness, and left her little choice but to follow. Well, she wasn't stupid. She didn't want to be alone.

"Do what?" Mr. Hades asked.

"Always think you know what's right," she snapped.

"That one's easy, ma'am," he said. "Because we're the inferior sex."

"You mean superior?" she asked. The darkness grew thicker, but she could still make him out.

"No, ma'am. Men may have been the first created, but it only makes sense that the Almighty did a better job the second go-round. We're the inferior sex, which explains why we always think we're right."

If fear hadn't run off with her sense of humor, she might have laughed. But the smell of gas flavored the air, and the man who'd taken care of her for the last twelve hours, the man who'd made her feel safe, who had cuddled with her, thrown up with her, was still back there.

She grabbed Mr. Hades by his arm. "Then why don't we go back and make Carl come with us? You're his father, make him—"

"Once my boy has made up his mind, there's no changing it. Stubborn as a mule, that one. Right now I really need you to calm down and—"

"But—"

He put a finger on her mouth. "Shh."

"But—"

"Quiet." His serious tone demanded obedience.

Katie clamped her mouth shut; then she heard the reason the senior Banderas wanted her hushed. Footsteps. Footsteps on the other side of the door. The door with the knob that he had his hand on and was at that exact moment turning.

He wasn't really going to open it, was he?

Oh, heck. He was.

Les jumped into Joe's car and they headed over to the wedding planner's place. After a twenty-minute drive that felt longer due to the silence, they pulled into a driveway.

"Crap!"

Les heard Joe's hand slam against the steering wheel as

she stared at the FOR SALE sign posted in front of the empty-looking home. But unwilling to give up, she got out and practically ran to the front porch. Something had to give. They had to find Katie.

Peering inside the window at the empty hall, she wanted to scream. Behind her, she heard Joe slam his car door. She moved to the next window and hoped she might see some sign that the house wasn't vacated—a small sign would do—a piece of furniture, a bathroom light left on.

The empty room brought on a wave of hopelessness.

Closing her eyes, she counted to ten and prayed that somehow, in some way, Katie would turn up and be okay. When she opened her eyes, she saw Joe on the front porch of the house next door.

He pounded on the door, his frustration ringing clear in the sound of his fists against the door. Wasn't it too late to wake up the neighbors? She checked her watch. Oh, hell, it was two A.M.

She heard voices and darted next door to join him. When she got there, Joe was raking his fingers through his hair. Bad sign.

"What?" she asked.

Curling his hand into a fist, Joe looked ready to fight. "He asked if I was the police. When I said no, he said he was calling them."

Les looked from Joe to the door. There were a lot of things she felt inept at. Unlike Katie, her knowledge of art ended at the finger-painting level. Unlike her brother, the accountant, she barely managed to balance her checkbook. But getting people to talk, to cough up information, that was Les's specialty. True, she'd given up investigative reporting to do restaurant reviews—food being another thing she knew. And since chefs were eager to hand over their specialties, she hadn't had to use her feminine wit or wiles, but Les felt confident she could still remember how to strut her stuff.

For Katie, she'd strut every bit of her stuff.

"How old was he?" She needed to know which persona to put forth: the I-could-be-your-daughter or the sexy bimbo.

Joe's brow puckered. "What?"

"How old did he look?" she asked again. "Come on, Joe. I shouldn't have to work to get the info out of you. Just him."

He shook his head. "Around my age. I guess."

"That old, huh?" She bent at the waist and tossed her hair over her head and gave it a few good shakes.

When she straightened up, Joe stared at her as if she'd lost her mind. "What're you doing?"

"Just step back." She pointed for him to move, and then she took off her jacket, tossed it to Joe, and gave her sweatshirt a few tugs to show her breasts to the best advantage.

Glancing down, Les suddenly realized Katie had been right about where her ten pounds had gone. Right to her boobs. Not bad. Funny how she hadn't realized it until now. Another symptom of running away, she supposed.

Adjusting her bra straps to give her the perfect lift, Les felt the cold seep through her clothes and go bone deep. She shivered and noted the icy weather had brought out her headlights. Which could work to her advantage, of course. After moistening her lips, she stepped up to the door and knocked.

"Sir," she said, in her best bimbo voice. "I know it's late, but could you please just answer a few questions?"

"Like that's going to work," Joe said behind her.

She shot him a quick glance. "Watch and learn." She knocked again. And for just a second, she felt the thrill of the old game. A thrill she hadn't expected to feel ever again.

After Mike died, Les had lost the joy of reporting. Basically, she had stopped enjoying life. But right now she felt alive and aware. Aware that she had breasts. Aware that she had a wow voice. Never mind it had said *wow* about a very unattainable man; what was important was that it wasn't completely broken. Yup, she felt alive. And, God, please let Katie be alive.

Alive and okay.

"Sir, I beg of you, please give me just a minute."

The curtain snapped back. "I already told—" His eyes widened with male appreciation.

"Hi." Les shot the man behind the glass a smile and leaned into the window. "Please, sir. Just a few questions. It's really, really important."

The curtain fluttered back into place.

"See," Joe said.

The door swung open and the man poked his head out, his gaze on her breasts. "Don't tell me, it's about Tabitha, right?"

Les's smiled faded a little. "How did you know?"

"Because a cop has already been here."

"A cop? What did he want?" Les asked.

"He just wanted to know where Ms. Jones moved to."

"Which is exactly what we need to know," Joe said.

The man frowned at Joe, and Les spoke up. "Please." And for good measure she smiled again.

Katie grabbed Mr. Hades by the elbow. "Maybe we shouldn't go in there."

"Stay behind me," he whispered back.

He opened the door and yelled out, "Hold it right there!"

Noise rang out, and Mr. Hades jumped in front of her. Noise. As in loud bangs. As in guns going off. As in bullets. As in bullets aimed at her.

Her mind flipped to the image of Tabitha falling to the white carpet and the blood spilling all over. Still holding her breath, Katie heard the creaking sound of a door opening, and light rushed into the room. Then the door shut.

"You okay?" he asked.

Okay? Had he not heard the bullets zinging around her? Her teeth chattered, and she felt herself slipping back into panic mode. "We shouldn't have come in here."

Her statement became even truer when she heard the thud of footsteps behind her.

Chapter Fourteen

"Police!" a voice yelled out. A familiar voice. A voice that was lying, because he wasn't really the police.

"It's us," Mr. Hades said.

"You okay?" Carl asked, his breathing labored as if he'd been running. A clicking sound filled the room, and then a bark.

"Fine," his dad said.

"Red?" Carl asked.

"Yeah," she managed to squeak out. She felt as if her lungs weren't taking in enough air.

"You doing okay?" he repeated.

Okay? Everyone kept asking her that. Were they idiots? Her panic state started naming all the reasons she wasn't okay.

Someone had shot at her.

Someone had poured gas all over the floors of the house where, until three minutes ago, she'd been locked inside.

Someone had killed her wedding planner.

Her engagement ring was joyriding down the sewer.

She had to pee.

And, oh yeah, she had to figure out if she should or shouldn't get married in two weeks. Her stomach roiled, and if she had anything in it, she would have lost it.

"I want to go home." Even to her ears, she sounded like a child, a very scared child about to have a tantrum if she didn't get her way. But she didn't care. If a serious tantrum would get her out of here, she'd throw a doozy.

"We're almost out," Carl's deep voice echoed, and just hearing him made her feel safer.

"He went out that door," the older Hades said.

"You two hang back a few minutes," Carl said.

Her mind turned, twisted, and she realized he was leaving her again. "Why don't we all hang back?"

"Gotta go, Red." The door squeaked open and Carl left, followed by the clicking paws of the dog.

Katie's knees wobbled and she felt her stomach twisting. "You ready?" Mr. Hades asked.

"For what?" Katie didn't hide her frustration.

"It's going to be okay." Buck sounded like his son.

"Carl said that about twelve hours ago, and it hasn't gotten okay yet. And as a matter of fact, it's just gotten worse."

He took her by the arm and forced her to move. "Let's go."

Light and heat greeted them as soon as they walked through the door. "Stay behind me." Mr. Hades kept his arm out, his gun extended. "Carl?" he called, moving in, and she followed in his shadow.

She had Carl's name on her lips to call out, too, when Carl and Baby—Tabitha's bichon frise; a white, poodle-looking canine—came hurrying down the hall. The hall with the white carpet. Katie suddenly realized where they were.

"Bastard got away," Carl growled. "I heard his car. And my fucking keys are in my coat pocket."

Mr. Hades cleared his throat. Katie stood on weak knees, her gaze fixed forward. From here, all she could see was a pair of legs. But she knew they were Tabitha's legs. And she knew if she moved just a little closer she'd see the blood. Tabitha's blood. Her head started buzzing. She pressed the tips of her thumbnails into her index fingers.

"What are you doing?" Carl asked his dad, but the conversation seemed far away.

"Calling for backup," Mr. Hades answered, his voice ringing even more distant. "I should have already done that."

One knee let go and Katie barely managed to keep standing. She leaned against the wall, the conversation happening around her registering like background noise, like a television left on after one dozed off to sleep.

"Give me a few minutes before you call this in," Carl said.

"For what?"

"To do my own look-around, so . . . Shit! Red?" This time his voice sounded less distant. "Don't look at her, Red."

"Too late," she mumbled, or maybe she didn't say it. She wasn't sure, because even her own voice sounded like static.

"You okay?" he asked.

Okay. Okay. Katie heard his voice echoing, but she couldn't seem to tear her eyes off the pair of legs. They were so still. Instantly, black spots popped into her vision like fireworks.

"Red?" Someone turned her around. Strong arms circled her. She leaned in and found the warm spot for her head on his chest.

"Breathe, Red. Breathe."

She inhaled the spicy scent and knew it was Carl holding her. Holding her against his chest, close, and amazingly she felt safe again. If he'd just keep holding her, she'd always be safe. And she wouldn't be lonely. Alone sucked. Alone hurt.

"Listen to me." His words played against her ear like soft music. "I need you to hold it together. Just a little longer."

"I'm fine," she managed to say, but didn't move. Moving, when her legs felt like rope, didn't sound like a good idea. Besides, she liked it here. Against him. *Safe.*

"You're not going to faint, are you?" he asked.

"I don't faint." Well, she had twice before, but those times didn't count. One involved alcohol—and yes, she'd sworn off tequila after that—and the other was at the funeral. But she was a Ray, and Rays were supposed to be strong. Remembering that, she forced herself to pull her head off his chest.

His arms dropped from around her. She glanced up. "I'm so sorry," she said.

"For what?"

"I lied." Then Katie fainted.

"Shit!" Carl caught her before she hit the carpet.

"Is she okay?" his father asked and closed his phone.

Moving out of the hall, Carl headed into the closest room—an office, from the look of things. And from the pile in the middle of the room that Baby ran to investigate, Katie had already been in here.

"Stop that," he yelled at the dog.

In the corner was one of those half-assed couches; he laid Red down, and then got on his knees beside her.

"Put her head between her knees," his father said.

Carl couldn't see trying to force Red into any awkward position. "Just see if you can find a bathroom and grab me a damp washcloth." He started unzipping Red's jacket and vaguely recalled doing this in his fantasies, but then he shoved those thoughts away.

"Come on, girl." He pulled her jacket off and tossed it over the mess on the carpet, then unwrapped her scarf. Leaning down, he whispered softly in her ear, "Red? Wake up."

Her eyelids fluttered open. She stared at him. Then she did the most amazing thing. She smiled.

God help him if it wasn't the most beautiful smile he'd

ever seen. It took everything he had not to close the half inch between their lips and taste her. He had a feeling she'd taste sweet and innocent—better than any woman he'd ever kissed.

"You okay?" He leaned back to avoid temptation, but couldn't resist brushing his fingers over her cheek. Skin, it was so damn soft, he'd never touched anything like it. Grabbing his hand, she pressed a warm kiss into his palm.

She blinked; her eyes widened as if she realized where she was and who she was looking at. Hell, maybe she'd even confused him for her fiancé—which would explain the sweet smile. Which would also explain the sweet kiss. *Now explain the surge of jealousy you feel toward the sensitive jerk.*

She dropped his hand. "Did I faint?"

"Don't worry. I told you, I like girly-girls."

His dad came hurrying back into the room. "Here."

Carl took the warm, damp cloth and started to wipe her forehead, but she took it and started pushing herself up.

"You should probably stay down for a minute." He got up, not trusting himself this close.

She closed her eyes for a minute, then sat the rest of the way up. "I'm fine."

Fine didn't begin to describe her. With the jacket off, her sweet body was open for viewing again. Breasts, curves. He tore his gaze off her. Baby bumped his leg with his nose. Carl ignored the dog, tried to ignore Red, and tried to think like a cop . . . or rather, a PI. If he was going to collect any information, now was the time, before the cavalry arrived. He knew his dad wouldn't give him but a few minutes.

He glanced around the room. An office. Thankfully, they'd ended up in the right place to search. His gaze moved back to Red. "Where does Tabitha keep her files?"

"Files?" She pressed the damp cloth to her forehead.

"On the weddings? She had to keep some kind of files."

She blinked her baby blues. "I think she did everything online."

"Son, we have to make the call." His dad's loyalty to the force rang in his tone—loyalty Carl no longer shared, and which was a bone of contention between him and all of the Hades family.

Carl hurried to the desk. "Five minutes," he bit out.

Fortunately, Tabitha was already signed in and had every file labeled and easy to identify. In a matter of minutes, he had her work files shooting to his e-mail. "Go for it," he told his dad, who held his phone out as if impatient.

His father called in the troops, then shot Carl a look. "They'll call your ass on the carpet for messing with her computer."

"Wouldn't be the first time," Carl snapped. "But they got my badge already. So I don't give a flying fuck."

His dad glanced at Red, then cut him a cold look. "Watch the language."

"I told him the same thing," Red muttered from the sofa.

Carl stared at his dad, then back to Red.

"No." He thumbed through Tabitha's desk. "You said the moment had to be f-word worthy. I vote this one f-word worthy."

She shifted, and his attention switched to her. Her long hair hung past her shoulders and clung to the soft mounds of breast. He should be looking at anything else, searching for clues. Something to help him catch this bastard. And he would catch him. That coward had been about to burn Red and him alive.

He started going through a few more of Tabitha's computer files. However, his gaze kept shooting back to the froufrou sofa and the damn froufrou woman sitting on it, looking as if she could use a good shoulder to lean on. And he happened to have two. One was sort of shot up, but she could still use it. Hell, when she'd leaned against him earlier, it'd felt so good that everything leading up to it had almost been worthwhile.

Sirens echoed in the distance and his dad spoke up. "Do me a favor before the police get here."

"What?" Carl forced his gaze away from Red.

"Take that pink scarf off. You look almost as fruity as Mr. Logan in that pink nightie." Buck laughed.

Carl snatched the scarf off. Baby, with her pink-painted nails, chose that moment to jump up onto Carl's lap.

"He said to take a left," Les insisted.

They had gotten lost and driven around for an eternity looking for the road in the dark. And like most living, breathing, penis-carrying specimens, Joe Lyon would rather have admitted to erectile dysfunction than to being lost. Asking for directions seemed to run right up there with castration. Only after she'd threatened to get out and find the address on foot did he find a twenty-four-hour food mart. *Les* asked for directions.

When Joe turned onto the correct street, Les's heart dropped. Police cars and ambulances were parked up and down the road, their lights flashing reds and blues into the night. She didn't wait for the car to come to a complete stop; she jumped out and ran up to the officer guarding the door. And when she spotted Katie's car parked to the right of the circular drive, her heart slammed against her rib cage.

"What happened?" She grabbed the officer by the arm and tried to move in front of him to see inside.

"Ma'am, you're going to have to step back." His tone held authority, but in her reporting days, Les had been accustomed to chewing up and spitting that out. "Anything for a story" had been the job's motto. Now, it was "Anything for Katie." And Les cared a hell of a lot more for Katie than she ever had for a story.

Joe came to a sudden stop beside her. "What happened?"

"Who are you?" The cop's gaze shot to Joe.

"Joe Lyon. We're looking for—"

With the officer's attention shifted, Les ran past him. If Katie was in there, she might need her. And except for the last year, there hadn't been a time she could remember that she and Katie hadn't been there for each other. From lost lunch money to missed birth control pills, from mono to funerals, they had faced life together.

"Ma'am!" the cop yelled behind her. "Stop!"

But it was too late; she'd already gotten far enough in to see the sheet-draped body and the blood-soaked carpet.

She came to an abrupt halt right inside the door. The cold air froze in her lungs and her feet could have been set in concrete, they were so locked in place. She couldn't breathe, couldn't tear her eyes off the red splotches on the white carpet.

The cop dragged her out. Another officer, dressed in plain clothes, came hurrying over. "Do you know Ms. Jones?" When Les didn't answer, he repeated the question.

Les couldn't answer. Images of Katie flashed in her head. Kindergarten, the first time they'd met, Katie wearing overalls, her hair in pigtails. Third grade, Katie punching a boy in the nose for calling Les names. Junior high, the two of them standing in front of a mirror stuffing their bras. College, both lying in the bed in their dorm room laughing their asses off as they talked about their unsuccessful attempts at performing oral sex.

Why those memories, those images, Les didn't know, but her mind clung to them because they were likely to be all she had left. Tears filled her eyes.

Joe rushed in, and Les became vaguely aware of him stepping between the officer and her—vaguely aware that she wanted to throw herself into his arms and weep like a baby.

"What happened?" Joe asked.

Les looked at him, but the words wouldn't come. Logic insisted she didn't know if the body under the sheet was Katie, but the panic clawing at her knew that there was a chance it was. And that chance opened up a chasm of pain.

"Sir, do you know Ms. Jones?" the older, plain-clothed gentleman asked Joe.

"Yes. Well, not me, but my fiancée. Tabitha Jones was planning our wedding."

"Is this your fiancée?" He pointed to Les.

"No," Joe said. "This is her friend." Then Joe's eyes widened. "That's my fiancée's car."

Another man spoke up. "What's her name?"

"Katie Ray." Joe looked at Les, saw her tears, and pulled her against him. Les buried her head against his shoulder and let even more tears fall.

"Miss Ray is okay," the cop said.

Les felt as if someone had removed their hand from around her throat and let her breathe again. She pulled away from Joe. "Where is she?" She swiped at her eyes.

"They took her to the police station to be questioned."

"Why?" Les and Joe asked at the same time.

"I can't explain. But if you'd like, I'm on my way over now and you can follow me. I'm sure they'll keep her for a while, but at least you'll be there for her when she's free to leave."

Katie stared at the man sitting across from her. Midthirties, and in some way he looked like . . . Antonio Banderas. Maybe it was a phase she was going through: simply everyone looked like Antonio to her. Ahh, but for her, this Antonio look-alike lacked the appeal that Carl Hades had.

This cop hadn't been rude, not really, but from the moment he'd walked into Tabitha's house, he'd separated her from Carl. It was as if he'd thought that the two of them talking would hurt the case. Well, it was a little late for that: she and Carl Hades had practically spent the night together.

She hadn't realized how much she'd grown attached to him until she'd seen them usher him out of the room. He'd glanced back at her and winked.

She'd almost cried. He'd been her rock for the last fourteen hours, and who wanted to lose her rock?

And thinking of rocks . . . She clenched her hands, remembering the diamond she'd flushed. Fighting off another wave of nausea, she met the cop's gaze and asked again to be allowed to use a phone.

She hadn't thought about calling anyone until after the police arrived. Of course, she'd had a lot on her plate. Realizing she'd been shot at and almost burned alive. Seeing Tabitha's legs.

Don't think about it. Breathe. She heard the voice inside her head, and it sounded a lot like Carl, her missing rock.

It had been after the cops had arrived and after they'd separated her from Carl and his dad that she'd remembered Les. When she'd asked to make a call, the cop had said they wanted to get her statement while it was fresh, that then she could call whomever she needed. And she really needed to call Les.

"Let's go over it one more time," the no-appeal Banderas sitting across the metal table said.

She went through it again. "And that's when you guys showed up." She'd recounted everything for the fifth time. Or at least everything she could remember. Some things didn't seem clear, like being chased by the man who'd shot Tabitha. She couldn't recall how she'd gotten to the back of the house. But she remembered being pushed against the wall, the gun at her ear.

And she remembered Carl—how he'd smelled. How he'd made her feel safe. How he'd made her laugh when laughing seemed impossible.

"Can I make that call now?" Her patience teetered on the edge.

"Are you sure you didn't see his face?"

"I'm sure." She felt uncomfortable under his brown gaze.

"You didn't recognize his voice?"

"No."

"Is there any way this man could have been there after you and not Ms. Jones?"

"I . . ." She hesitated. "No, they were arguing."

His eyebrow arched as if he was about to hit her with another question.

Katie leaned forward and spoke in a calm voice—calm, but with a tone that she used on patrons who tried to wheedle down the price of a piece of art that had no wheedling room.

"I realize you are doing your job, sir." She could only remember that his name was Ben, and first names didn't work well with this tone. "And I appreciate that. I'd really like to help you catch the guy, but I'm going to ask you one more time to bring me a phone. And if you don't do it, I'm going to walk out. I won't answer any more questions, and I won't be nice. And I really like being nice. But I'm running out of *nice*. You understand?"

He leaned back in his chair and almost smiled, then stood up. "One phone coming up, Red."

"Thank you," she said, and then the tail end of his sentence vibrated through her. *Red?* It wasn't a good vibration. Sure, the other Banderas look-alike had called her that, but oddly it hadn't bothered her then.

"My name is Katie," she said.

"Sorry. I think . . . someone referred to you as Red."

"I prefer Katie." She stiffened her backbone and wondered why she hadn't been more her assertive self from the start. It had to be stress. Because in normal circumstances, she wasn't the whimpering, tell-me-what-to-do-and-I'll-do-it type of female. Cooperative, yes. And she'd even admit that deep down she might be a marshmallow—but she did a good job of covering it up.

Had to. Life was hard. Just in the last year and a half, she'd taken on and won against the IRS when they'd audited her. She'd lived through losing her entire family. So she wasn't completely over it, but she hadn't cratered, and she would get through what happened tonight. She was a Ray, after all.

No question about it: Katie Ray, marshmallow on the inside and occasional fainter, was a survivor. She could take care of herself. Not that she wanted to. Bits and pieces of her conversation with Carl replayed in her mind. *Alone sucked. Alone hurt.*

Now all she had to do was to figure out if she was marrying Joe just so she wouldn't have to be alone.

Ben returned and held a phone in his hand. "Do you have someone who could stay with you, or somewhere you could stay?"

"Why?" she asked. "You think . . . think this guy will—"

"No, I don't. From what you told me, I don't think you're in any real danger, but being careful is never overrated."

"I'll be careful," she said. Rays were always careful.

He nodded, then put the phone down in front of her.

"Thank you." She dialed Les's cell phone number.

It rang twice. "Hello?" The urgency in Les's voice told Katie that her friend had been up worrying all night.

"It's me," Katie said, and for obvious reasons, marshmallowy reasons, her throat tightened.

"Oh, God, Katie. I've been worried sick about you."

"I'm so sorry. I didn't have my phone. And something terrible happened." She stopped to swallow. "I'm at the—"

"Police station. I know. I'm here. We're here."

"We?" Katie asked.

"Joe's with me."

Katie bit down on her lip. Good Lord, she hadn't even thought about calling Joe. Exactly what did that tell her?

"What happened?" Les asked. "All I know is that someone was killed. They don't think you did it, do they?

If they do, I swear, girl, I'll make some calls. I may have wasted a year of my life in Boston complaining about piecrusts, but I still have connections."

"Piecrusts are important," Katie said. "And I don't think I'm considered a suspect." Katie sensed Ben, sitting across from her, listening. "But we'll talk later. I think they're about to let me go." She looked up at Ben.

"Ten minutes," he said.

"Ten minutes," Katie repeated into the phone.

"Good. We're in the lobby waiting on you."

Katie hung up and looked at her naked left hand. What was she going to tell Joe? And why, why was she not thrilled about seeing him?

"Tell him the truth," she muttered.

"Tell who the truth?" the man sitting across from her asked.

She looked up. "Uh . . . it's about something else."

And right then she knew it was the right thing to do. She had to tell Joe everything. *Every*thing.

Chapter Fifteen

Les snapped her phone shut and shot Joe a quick look. "She'll be out in about ten minutes." Joe nodded, leaned back in his chair, and closed his eyes.

Les studied the worry lines creasing his brow. He cared about Katie. That much was apparent. Which meant he might make Katie a decent husband. By no means was Les completely ready to give him her blessing, though. Friends looked out for each other like that. But she'd admit, Joe Lyon appeared to be a decent man.

Les dropped the phone back into her purse. Funny, how quickly things could be put in their proper mental places. For example, how unimportant her silly attraction to Joe became when she'd thought it was Katie under the bloody sheet. How insignificant it was that they'd seen each other naked. And the kiss that almost . . . but, seriously, never happened. It was simply brought on by the night's stress. Nope, none of that mattered right now. It was so trivial. Les doubted Katie even needed to know about it. All that mattered was that Katie was alive. Les's best friend was going to walk through those doors, and together they would make more silly memories. They would laugh at each other's insecurities, talk about their mistakes, listen to each other whine about PMS and bad sexual experiences, and be best friends forever.

And if marrying Joe made Katie happy, Les would be there to toss confetti in the air.

Joe stood up. "I'm going to find a restroom."

As Les watched him walk away, she noticed one little problem with the Katie-didn't-need-to-know-about-it plan: the scratch marks running down Joe's face.

Okay, so she'd have to tell Katie about that. But the wow voice thing? That was . . . trivial. Not important. At all.

Carl waited with his dad. Ben had rung their dad's cell phone to let them know that Red would be out in about ten minutes. Carl, having endured his own interrogation, had been relieved to know Ben would be the one to question Katie.

Oh, sure, he knew his brother wouldn't spare her any of the grueling questions or stop short of making her repeat the story a hundred times. It was police procedure. He'd done it himself and had seen it work. But Ben knew when to call it quits. And Ben, like himself, had inherited the gentleman gene and wouldn't cross the line with a woman.

Red deserved that much. She'd been through enough. He recalled her embarrassment at passing out. But considering what she'd endured in the last fourteen hours— witnessing a murder, being chased by the murderer, being held at gunpoint and locked in a room with a stranger— Katie Ray had spunk. He'd seen men cave faster. Which was why he wanted to make sure she was okay.

Stopping off at the bathroom, he kept telling himself that seeing Red through the ordeal fell under his job description. As he washed his hands, he glanced up at his reflection. For the past hour, his old co-workers, even his brother, had given him a ribbing over the scratches.

Who wants to take his shirt off and see if he has 'em there?

They'd had fun, all right. At his and Red's expense. He could take the abuse, but he hoped she didn't get wind of it.

A man walked over from the urinals and turned the water on at the sink next to Carl. Carl looked at the man's reflection. On his cheek he wore four scratches, identical to Carl's. A laugh jumped out of Carl's mouth before he could stop it.

The man grinned at the mirror. "Long story," he said.

"Mine, too." Carl touched his cheek. "You know, normally, I might think you were a son of a bitch and deserved those scratches, but I can't think that right now."

"Isn't that the truth," the stranger answered.

"Women," Carl said, and ran his hand over the four marks. Then he grinned. "Mine was worth it. Yours?"

The man's gaze glazed over for a second, as if remembering something. "Yeah." Then he tossed some cold water on his face.

Carl turned and walked out.

After visiting with his dad a minute, Carl went to the waiting room to wait for Katie. He hoped she'd feel up to grabbing a bite to eat. The idea that he shouldn't offer flittered through his mind, but he rejected it. It was just a meal. It wouldn't lead to anything. No, Red was totally safe . . . because she was off-limits. Even if he wasn't avoiding women, he avoided her kind. The marrying kind.

The waiting room held a crowd of chattering people. The police station was like Vegas: it never closed down. His gaze caught on the blonde sitting with the dark-haired man from the bathroom.

Carl moved to the other side of the room for coffee. He noticed the body language of the couple. Not overly friendly. Then the man cut the blonde a glance when she wasn't looking. Male appreciation darkened his eyes.

As Carl poured his coffee, he checked the blonde out for himself. Pretty, but not as appealing as Red.

Carl's focus shifted to the man's back, and just like his co-workers, he wondered if the man had matching scratches across his back. Had they done the bump and grind? Carl recalled the look in the man's eyes when he'd asked if it had been worth it. Yeah, the guy had probably sampled his assaulter. Lucky bastard.

The door opened from the back of the room. Carl's gaze shot up. Red walked out. Emotion swelled in his chest when he saw the unshed tears glistening in her eyes. If Ben had been too hard on her, he'd answer for it.

He'd taken one step forward before the man sitting with the blonde shot up. And Red, never looking at Carl, ran into the man's arms.

The coffee in his hand nearly slipped. The hot liquid spilled from the cup and burned his fingers. He watched as Red pillowed her head on the man's shoulder and, just like that, Carl knew this was Mr. Metro-Sensitive.

Carl had been an idiot not to realize that Red would have called him. This was Red's fiancé. Pulling the cup to his lips, he sipped at his coffee. The bitter, hot taste matched the feelings crowding his chest. Feelings that didn't make a damn bit of sense. Emotions he had no right to feel.

Setting the cup down, he cut across the room to escape. He walked out the door, passing his dad, who studied him with his all-knowing gaze.

Katie felt people's eyes on her, and she removed herself from Joe's embrace and fought the emotion tightening her throat. "Let's move out of here," she said.

Joe led them out into a hall. Once they'd left the curious stares of the strangers in the waiting room, Les grabbed her and she and Katie held each other even longer than Katie had held Joe. "My God, what happened?" Les asked.

Katie let her arms drop from around Les and gave the two-minute version of events.

Les grabbed Katie's hands when she was through. "You must be a bundle of nerves."

"I've had less stressful days." Katie tried to smile, but her ability to make light of the situation failed her now.

"Let's get you home." Joe started moving toward the exit.

Katie took a step, then looked back. Hope swelled in her chest that Antonio Banderas would magically appear. That he would have waited for her to . . . to what, exactly?

He wasn't there. Her chest filled with emotion. She really needed . . . needed to say thank you. Or had she said it?

You don't need to say thank you, Red. I'm just doing my job, she remembered him telling her.

"Did you leave something?" Les asked.

My rock. "No."

Joe's hand pressed against the small of her back.

For a brief second, she relived the moment when he'd pulled her into his arms in the waiting room. He'd held her close. Tight. She'd buried her face in his shoulder. When she'd breathed in his scent, she found it warm, comforting. Like Joe always smelled. But it wasn't safe.

"Are you sure? Where's your purse and stuff?" Joe asked.

"It . . . it's in my car. And my car's at . . . Tabitha's." Her throat tightened. "The police said I could get my car after they checked it out. They also said I should be careful . . . and not to stay alone."

"You won't be alone," Les said.

"It's going to be okay," Joe said.

Katie turned to Joe. "I . . ." She stared at the scratches down Joe's cheek. Was she imagining things?

She blinked. "What happened?"

"I happened," Les said.

Katie glanced back at Les. "Huh?"

"It was a misunderstanding," Joe said.

Katie looked from Joe to Les. "What kind of . . . ?"

"We saw each other at the bar," Les said. "But I didn't know who he was. I went back to your place. Joe was looking for you too, he let himself in, and I thought he'd followed me. Then a limb in your backyard snapped and broke the window and . . ."

Katie tried to soak in what Les was saying; it was hard because Les talked fast. She always talked fast when nervous. Then again, maybe Katie was just thinking ultraslowly.

"I'm so sorry," she said. "I didn't tell you that you were both joining me at the bar because I didn't want you to have a hundred and one questions prepared to ask Joe." She looked at her fiancé. And why hadn't she told *him*?

"I didn't tell you because . . . we've hardly talked these past few weeks." And why was that? The questions she needed to ask formed in her head. Lots of questions.

"I'm sorry," both Les and Joe said at the same time.

Shaking off questions that would be better asked and answered later, she took a deep breath. "I should have told you." Then she focused on Joe's face again.

"Does it look that bad?" he asked.

"No, it's just . . . weird."

"Weird, how?" Les asked, her voice sounding tense.

"Remember the PI I told you was with me?"

"Yeah," Les answered.

"Well, I . . . I scratched him, too."

"But you said he was the good guy," Les said.

"He was really nice. I . . . scratched him before I knew who he was."

All of a sudden, talking to them about Carl felt awkward. And leaving without saying good-bye to Carl felt even more awkward. "Should I check and see if we can go get my car now?"

Joe ran a hand over her shoulder. "I'll call and have someone drive me there to pick it up tomorrow."

"Thanks," she said, and couldn't think of another reason for her to turn around and look for Carl.

"Here, why don't you take this." Joe took off his jacket. "You should wear it—it's cold out there." He helped her slip on his jacket and then said, "I think I ran into him."

"Ran into who?" Katie asked.

"The man you scratched."

Katie's heart picked up speed. "You saw Carl?" She turned around, hungry for the sight of him. "Where?"

"He was in the bathroom. We saw each other and noticed each other's faces." Joe put his hand on her back, then pulled away, and started moving them toward the door.

Katie pulled his jacket close and tried to understand how she felt about Carl seeing Joe. She snuggled into Joe's jacket, hoping to find the warmth in it that she'd found from a certain brown leather coat. Not there. No warmth. No safe feeling. She stopped walking, wanting a minute to think. To think about leaving Carl. To think about what she needed to tell Joe.

Katie looked up at her fiancé. Kind eyes. Caring eyes. Why didn't he make her feel those same things Carl did?

He gave her arm a squeeze. "I'm glad you're okay."

She nodded but couldn't speak. She loved Joe. Didn't she?

Her heart pounded and she knew. Yes, she loved Joe. She just wasn't sure if it was the right kind of love.

"You okay?" Les asked, standing to her left.

"I am." *I think*. And she realized she needed to think before she spoke to Joe. Needed to know the right way to express her doubts without being too brash. Joe deserved that.

As she stepped out the door, she looked back one more time. The air carried a chill so intense it hurt to breathe. Darkness clung to the sky, but to her right, dawn fought for its own space, and some gold fingers of light spread across the horizon. As they got to Joe's car, he opened the doors for her and Les. Les slid into the back and Katie crawled into the front.

Joe settled behind the wheel and then reached over and

took her hand in his. Her left hand. The hand devoid of the ring he gave her.

She met his gaze and forgot about not being brash. "I flushed my engagement ring down the toilet."

"You did what?" he spat out.

"And it may not have been an accident."

The music clicked off and woke him up. Tabitha's killer continued the humming in his head, though. *Here comes the bride. All dressed in white.* He rolled over and stared up at the ceiling. The smell of gas still clung to his skin. His breath caught when he remembered how badly he'd screwed up.

He sat upright, bounced back and forth against the headboard, and pulled his photo album from the bedside table. On the first page, he saw Maria's picture in the paper. Her wedding announcement to another man, less than six months after their own announcement had been printed. In the photograph, she had worn a big smile. And he knew she'd been laughing at him. Laughing as she'd laughed at the church. The way everyone at the church had laughed.

Still bouncing back and forth, he flipped the page and stared at the images of his brides without their smiles. Beside them was the picture he'd clipped from the newspaper last week. KATIE RAY AND JOE LYON ANNOUNCE THEIR ENGAGEMENT . . .

She was smiling in the picture. Just as Maria had smiled. But not for long, he promised himself. Katie Ray wouldn't be smiling for long.

He set the album down and pulled a rose from a vase of flowers. Soon he'd bring Katie Ray flowers just as he'd brought the others their flowers.

"No fucking way!" Carl scowled at his dad. "Just take the bitch with you." Carl stood up from his computer, where for the last hour he'd been going through Tabitha's e-mailed files.

After leaving the precinct, his dad had dropped Carl off at his car. Carl came straight home and left his dad to visit with his old cronies at the crime scene. But now his dad was here, with company in tow.

"I'm serious," Carl said again. "Get her out of here."

His dad frowned. "She likes you."

"Well, I don't like her." Carl pointed to the door. "Keep her for yourself."

"I can't have pets at my place." His dad put Ms. Jones's dog on the floor. The prissy mongrel, tail spinning, ran up to Carl.

"They were going to take her to a shelter," his dad said.

Carl stared away from the dog. "Then let them."

"It's just for a few days." He moved into the living room. "I'm sure some relative of Ms. Jones will come claim her."

The dog ran circles around Carl's leg, then rose up on her back legs, placing her front paws with pink-painted nails on Carl's knee as if pleading with him to change his mind.

"Damn!" Carl grumbled.

Precious hauled ass into the room, his bark box turned on. The two dogs stood a foot apart from each other, growling and sniffing the air.

"See? They won't get along. You have to take her."

"Bullshit, give them some time. They'll be the best of buds."

Carl shook his head. "No! It's bad enough I get stuck with one sissy dog, but I'll be damned if I'll get stuck with two."

His dad shrugged. "I don't know. You looked comfortable in that pink scarf this morning."

"Real funny." Carl walked around the dogs as they made circles around the coffee table, each trying to sniff the other's ass.

"Is that coffee I smell?" his old man asked.

"Yeah. I just made a pot. But you're taking that dog

with you when you go." Carl went to the kitchen. His dad followed and grabbed his cup from the dishwasher.

"I figured you'd be sawing logs by now."

Steam rose from Carl's coffee. "Ahh, so you were going to just sneak the dog in and leave, weren't you?"

His dad didn't try to pretend. "Seemed like a good plan."

"Well, it didn't work." Carl brought the cup up to his lips. He should have been sleeping, but he'd spent every second in bed remembering how soft Red had felt, how she'd fit against him, and how bitter it had felt seeing her fit all that softness up against Mr. Metro. Finally, Carl gave up trying to sleep and started reading through Tabitha's files.

His dad focused on Carl's desk. "CSI is checking the computer. They'll know you snagged those files."

Cup held to his lips, Carl looked at his dad through a trail of steam. "They have their job, and I have mine."

"I hope she cut you a check before she checked out."

"It's not about money. It's personal. I take personal offense when someone tries to use me as kindling."

Glancing back at the painting resting on his mantel, Carl frowned. He remembered Katie's look when he'd told her he'd bought a painting done by an elephant. And now the painting had taunted him since he'd come home. He couldn't forget how Red had looked when she'd talked about painting. No disrespect for the dead, but her parents had been assholes to rob her of her dreams.

His dad grabbed the coffeepot and filled his cup. "Did you find anything in her files?"

"Just some names to look at."

"You do know Ms. Jones made a police report last week about her missing brides." Steam rose from his dad's cup.

"Yeah, I got that much when I talked to her on the phone."

His dad blew on the coffee. "They blew her off."

Carl leaned against the counter. "Yeah, she said they did."

"They're going to be talking out their asses trying to make up for it, too."

Carl studied his dad. "What do you mean?"

"A body was found about an hour ago. A woman. Rumor has it she was one of the missing brides."

Carl set his cup down. "I was hoping Ms. Jones was wrong about the brides."

"Doesn't look that way," Buck said. "What all did she tell you on the phone?"

"Just that she thought someone was killing her brides-to-be. She said she thought it was one of four people, but she never got around to saying who. I got the impression it was someone connected to the weddings. Ah, shit."

"What?" his dad asked, noticing Carl's mood shift.

"The freak could be after Red next." He let out a pound of oxygen.

His dad's eyebrow shot up. "Red's getting married? Whoa. I thought . . . I mean the way you two—"

"Yeah, she's getting married."

"But . . . she wasn't wearing a ring."

Carl grabbed his coffee. "She flushed it down the john."

His dad's lips twitched into a smile. "They had a fight."

"Supposedly, it was an accident."

"Doesn't sound like an accident."

"I know." Carl burned his tongue on the coffee. His dad continued to study him.

"What are you going to do?"

"I'm going to make sure Ben talks to her," Carl said. "Then I'm going to catch the bastard."

"Why don't *you* talk to her?" His dad's tone spoke volumes.

"That's Ben's job," Carl snarled.

"They won't offer her around-the-clock protection."

"Neither will I." He'd had one night of around-the-clock with her and wasn't sure he could handle another. "Besides, she doesn't need me. She has her fiancé to take care of her." The image of Mr. Metro and her together stabbed at his mind.

His dad's left brow arched. "I thought you two bonded."

"We were locked in a room together. We had to bond."

A grin widened his dad's mouth. "How close of a bond?"

"Not that close. She's not like that." Carl made sure the look he shot his dad had a warning stamped all over it.

Buck Hades seldom paid heed to warnings. "You should go see her. Perhaps she'll realize the real reason she flushed the ring and maybe you two can hook up."

"Stop it." Carl held up his hand.

His old man wrinkled his forehead. "I just think—"

"Stop thinking. It gets your ass in a crack every time."

His dad shrugged as if letting it drop. They stood across from each other, each leaning against the counter, sipping coffee.

Carl's thoughts zipped back to Red. Had Ben warned her about being in danger? He needed to talk to Ben.

Eyeing his dad he asked, "Have they released the name of the bride?"

"Not yet," his dad said.

Would Ben give Carl the name? Like his dad, Carl's brother played by the rules and believed in the system. Of course, the system hadn't ever let them down, not the way it had him.

"Carl?" His dad's brow creased. From the look on Buck's face, Carl surmised they were back on the subject of Red.

"She's getting married, Dad. So drop it."

"It's not about Red." His dad grimaced.

"Then what?" he asked, not liking his dad's expression.

"You were wrong." His dad pulled his cup to his lips.

"Wrong about what?"

"The dogs are getting along . . . just fine." Buck motioned to the living room.

Carl turned around. "Ah, fuck!" And yes. This was definitely f-word worthy. It was also what was going on.

"Yup," his father said. "I think that's what you call it."

"This is your fault." He pointed at his dad.

"Yup. I'll take the hit on this one." His old man eyed Carl over his coffee cup. "But you're going to forgive me."

"And what makes you so damn certain of that?" Carl snarled.

"Because I saved your ass this morning."

Carl gritted his teeth. "There is that."

Both of them stood and watched the dogs go at it. Carl finally laughed. "At least now I know he's not queer."

Les walked into Katie's study, where Joe had just finished nailing a board over the broken window. "Katie's asleep. I talked her into taking a sleeping pill."

Joe placed the hammer on the side of the desk. It teetered on the edge, then fell and clattered against the floor. Joe's frown, along with the way he raked his hand through his hair, told her he was on his last nerve. They all were. But Katie won the Worst Night award.

"Hell of a night." Joe picked up the hammer.

"I was just thinking that myself."

Tired lines were etched around his still-bloodshot eyes, and exhaustion echoed in his tone. Leaning against the desk, Les watched his Adam's apple go up and down.

The crease between his eyebrows deepened. "We need to tell Katie about the shower and the 911 call. It's not as if—"

"Anything happened," Les finished for him. "I know." She picked up a heart-shaped marble paperweight from Katie's desk. The rock felt cold and heavy in her hands, sort of how her own heart felt lately. She held the stone tight.

He studied her. "Knowing Katie, she'll laugh," he said.

Les forced a smile on her lips. "It is kind of funny when you step back from it." Her smile became genuine.

"You looked pretty stunned when you stepped into the shower." She palmed the cold paperweight tighter. It felt a little warmer.

They shared a grin. He stuck his hands into his jeans, then pulled them out. "I've got to run by work for a bit. My plan is to grab a few hours of sleep. Then I'll go get some glass to replace the window. I'll be back sometime this afternoon, and I'll see what I can do about getting Katie's car back."

"That's fine. I'm sure she'll sleep most of the day." Les smoothed her fingers over the heart-shaped rock.

His gaze moved over her. "You look exhausted. You should try to get some rest also."

"I will." Their gazes met and held, and the humor she'd seen in his eyes seconds earlier faded into something different.

He shifted. The heater moaned as it tried to kick on. "Is the ring what you weren't telling me about earlier?"

Les hesitated, then decided she had nothing to hide. "Yeah."

"Was she really going to buy another one?"

"Yeah," Les answered.

Katie had told Joe the truth. Les had sat in the backseat feeling like a third wheel and secretly admiring Katie for being honest. And admiring Joe. You had to respect a man who could hear that his fiancée had flushed his eight-thousand-dollar ring down the toilet and not get angry.

But then Katie had continued: "And the bad part, Joe, is that I'm not sure if it was an accident."

Les had seen Joe's shoulders tighten, and the only thing he said was, "I'm sure you're tired right now."

Then the car had gone silent.

In the silence, Les had remembered she'd been the one to earlier accuse Katie of having motives for flushing the ring. *Nothing like feeling responsible for creating your best friend's problems.*

Katie's heater groaned again, bringing Les back to the moment. She clutched the heart-shaped paperweight.

Joe stared at the ceiling. "Do you think she meant to flush the ring?"

Les swallowed. "Don't blame Katie. I was the one who said maybe she'd done it on purpose. She said she loved you and I . . . I planted the doubt there."

"Why?" he asked.

She gave his question a quick thought. "I was concerned that maybe she was getting married just to replace her family. But now I'm not sure if maybe I wasn't just . . ." The word jealous didn't seem appropriate.

"Just what?"

"Envious." That word came a little easier, but she stared at the wall. "Envious that she could move past everything, and I couldn't." She felt him looking at her and she glanced back.

He frowned. "Katie said you and her brother were close. Soul mates, she called it. Losing someone can't be easy."

She set the paperweight back on the table. "It isn't."

But this conversation wasn't about her. "Katie's not thinking straight. Tomorrow you guys will go pick out another ring."

His jaw clenched. "I don't think that would be wise."

"What?" Had she heard him right? No, she couldn't have.

He closed his eyes, and when he opened them he met her gaze head-on. "Katie's not the only one having second thoughts, Les."

No, this couldn't be happening. "It's called cold feet. It's normal."

He ran his hand through his hair and didn't stop until he squeezed the back of his neck. "I almost kissed you."

Hearing him say it aloud gave her an emotional jolt. "But you didn't."

"I wanted to," he admitted.

"But you didn't," she repeated, and before she used her hands to strangle him, or herself—yup, she blamed herself for this, too—she grabbed the heart-shaped paperweight again.

"Katie deserves someone who . . . wouldn't want to kiss someone else a few weeks before the wedding."

Les didn't know if she could argue with that, but she had to try, because no way in hell was she going to let this happen when it was her fault. She couldn't, wouldn't, hurt Katie.

"It was stress. Our emotions were out of whack. You can't make this decision based on something that didn't even happen."

"What about right now?" he asked. "What if I'm still wanting to kiss you? Is it just wacky emotions? Or could it be a sign that maybe Katie was right to flush the engagement ring?"

Chapter Sixteen

"Don't say that." Les dropped the piece of cold stone back on the desk. "Oh, God. *What* have I done?"

"This isn't your fault. I'm the one engaged here."

As if that excused her. "Engaged to my best friend, and I—"

"You didn't do *anything*." He took one step to the door.

"Neither did you." She had to fix this. *Now*. Right now. He turned around. "But I wanted to do something."

So did I, Les thought, but she didn't dare say it. Then, grasping at straws, she started talking. "Look, all men are dogs. They'll hump anything. What's important is that you didn't go hump crazy." Okay, so her grasping-at-straws talk wasn't up to par. She grabbed him by the arm and started down the hall toward Katie's room. He put on the brakes.

"What are you doing?" He came to a complete stop.

"You two are going to kiss and make up. Right now. I'd rather eat worms than think I did anything to hurt Katie."

He pulled away. When she reached for him again, he held up his hand. "Stop it, Les. Katie and I don't need to kiss and make up. What we need is to be honest with each other."

Les shook her head. "I refuse to be the reason—"

"Whoa." He glared at her. "It's not *just* you. I've been second-guessing what I felt for three weeks now. You were just the straw that broke the camel's back."

Straw? "Well, I don't like being straw."

"I'm sorry." He pinched the bridge of his nose between two fingers. "I shouldn't have said anything. Frankly, it's not even about you. It's about Katie and me." Then he took off.

Oh, gawd! Les watched him leave. What had she done? And how the hell was she going to fix it?

Carl stepped up to the front door and knocked. After his dad left, Carl had gone through Tabitha's files again and typed a report and made two copies. If he was going to wheedle information and a few favors out of Ben, it would help if he had a bargaining chip. Info for info. Most of it could be found on Ms. Jones's computer, but Carl knew how slow Computer Forensics was at combing through files.

The door opened, and Ben junior stood there wearing his Zorro costume and carrying his sword. Carl yanked out an imaginary sword and challenged his nephew to a duel. "To the death!"

Benny, grin in place, started swinging. They fought their way into the living room, dodging moving boxes and making battle grunts and moans and imaginary sword-slamming noises.

"No roughhousing," his sister-in-law's voice rang out.

"But Mom, were fighting to the death," Benny whined.

"Not in the house you're not," Tami said from the kitchen. "And go finish unpacking your toys and put them away."

Carl swung his nephew up in his arms. "Princess Tami has requested a truce, but we'll continue this fight another day."

Benny patted Carl's pocket and whispered, "Got any worms?"

Carl glanced toward the kitchen in time to see the all-hearing Tami frown. "You promise to brush your teeth."

"Promise," Benny said.

Carl put Ben down and handed him the bag he'd bought. Then, as his nephew ran to hide his stash, Carl went to face the music from Princess Tami—same song and dance every time.

"You're taking him to the dentist, and when they find cavities you will feel like scum."

Carl gave his sister-in-law a hug. "I'm his uncle. I should be allowed to spoil him."

"Not with candy." She thumped him on his chest before she looked up and frowned. "Heard you had a bad night."

"Piece of cake," he lied.

"Ben said you'd been in a catfight. He didn't tell me the cat won." She chuckled. "Hungry?"

"Hungry? My stomach's sucking on my backbone." Remembering why he hadn't eaten reminded him why he'd come. "Is Ben here?"

"He just got out of the shower. How about I heat over some of last night's spaghetti—that you didn't show up for."

"Spaghetti?" His mouth watered. "I swear, if my brother is stupid enough to leave you, I'm marrying you."

"And who says I'd take you," Tami shot back. "I know your reputation with the ladies."

He followed Tami to the kitchen and dropped into a chair.

"Are you hitting on my wife again?" Ben walked in, wearing jeans and a towel hung around his bare shoulders.

"Yeah. But it's your own damn fault," Carl said. "You should've married someone ugly who couldn't cook."

Ben grabbed himself a soda from the fridge, kissed his pretty wife on her neck, then shot Carl a look. "And here I thought you'd have a certain redhead on your mind."

"Funny you should mention her." Carl reached into his coat pocket and laid out the folded papers, his bargaining chip.

His brother pulled on the towel around his neck. "Why do I get a bad feeling in my gut?"

"Probably just gas." Carl chuckled.

Ben turned a chair around and straddled it. "What's up?"

"I thought we might help each other out."

"And how's that?" Ben stared at the papers.

"The Jones case. You scratch my back, I scratch yours."

"Stan said you were holding back in your statement."

Carl scratched his jaw. "Well, Stan's a smart cop."

Ben shook his head. "Tabitha Jones is dead. She's not your client anymore, so let us take care of it."

"I like the scratch idea better." Carl crossed his arms. As Tami set a plate of spaghetti in front of him, he inhaled the scent of tomato, onion, and garlic. "I love you," he told her.

She smiled. "Eat before you pass out."

He picked up the fork and Ben reached for the papers. "Not so fast," Carl mouthed around some pasta and snatched his bargaining chip out of Ben's reach. "Do we have a deal?"

"What is it you want?"

"A rundown on the names I give you. A few answers." He wrapped more pasta around his fork. "But mostly, check on Red, make sure she knows this is serious. Make sure, okay?"

Ben eyed him. "Why can't you check on her?"

He swirled his fork some more to catch noodles. Then he grabbed a piece of French bread that magically appeared on the table. God, he really did love his sister-in-law—loved all women who could cook. "That's not my job."

"Red's not your job, but neither is catching this guy."

"True, but you know how I feel about people who try

to burn me alive." Carl dipped the bread in the sauce and savored it.

"Yeah, that always did piss you off, didn't it?" Ben let out a deep breath and chuckled.

"Then it's a deal?" Carl picked up another piece of bread.

Ben's brows pinched. "You haven't said what you've got yet."

"I've got a list of suspects."

Ben scowled. "And you knew this when you talked to Stan?"

Carl used a paper napkin to clean sauce from his chin. "Not really." He forked another bite of pasta into his mouth.

Ben studied him. "Should I ask where you got this info?"

"I wish you wouldn't." *Not when I know you're going to chew my ass out later.*

"Okay, but you know there's lines I won't cross."

"I respect lines," he lied, knowing lines were the reason he'd quit the force. The reason he'd taken a bullet. Carl ate the last bite of pasta. "Who was it you found? Beth Hill or Susie Langs?"

Ben's expression hardened. "How did you get the victim's name? It hasn't been released."

"There were two canceled weddings in Ms. Jones's files." Carl set his fork down. "Where was the body found?"

"In a patch of woods in Northwest Houston." His brother paused. "So you think Susie is dead, too?"

Carl frowned. "I'd give those woods a good hard look."

"Damn, I hate looking for sick fuckers," Ben said.

"And he's really sick." Carl paused. "And here's the thing: All the people who were lined up to work on the weddings—the florist, the DJ, the cake maker, the photographer—they were all working on those two weddings. And they're all men."

Ben's frown deepened. "So you think it's one of them."

"That's what I'm betting on. Ms. Jones hinted it was someone working with her. And Red said that Tabitha and the shooter had dialogue."

"She told me about that." Ben ran a hand over his jaw. "So I do background checks on all of them."

"And you share that info with me," Carl said.

Ben's brow creased, and he twisted the towel around his neck. "What about other weddings? Other brides? Are any of the men on the list working with other brides now?"

"Two. I called them and made it clear that they weren't to contact *anyone* working on their weddings until they talked to you."

"And Red's one of them?" Ben asked.

"No." Carl didn't mind letting his relief show. "None of the men are listed as working on her wedding. But what would it hurt for you to just talk to her? Tell her to be careful."

"And that, brother, brings me back to my original question. If you care that much, why aren't you talking to her?"

Carl dropped his fork. "I told you, that's not my job."

Tami set a slice of pie in front of Carl and pressed a kiss on her husband's bare shoulder.

Carl flashed Tami a smile. "You've got to keep that woman," he said, as the flaky crust and sweet apples melted in his mouth.

Ben watched his wife walk out of the room. "I am. Because, let me tell you, her talents don't stop in the kitchen."

Carl laughed, and for a second he wanted this: home cooking, home loving. Then reality struck, and he knew better. But his mind flashed to an image of Red. Could she cook?

He handed the papers to Ben. "Go see Red today." The pie melted on his lips.

"I can't today." Ben rose from the chair.

"We had a deal." The pie lost its flavor.

"I said I'd check on her. But if what you say is true, I have two other brides I should take care of first."

"Damn, Ben. How long would it take to stop by and see her?"

"I'll go, but I'm not promising it'll be today. And if that's not good enough, go see her yourself."

"Well, it just looks like I'll have to, don't it?" He dropped his fork at the same time Ben's cell phone rang.

"Yeah?" Ben answered, and a look of disgust filled his eyes. "I'm on my way." Ben snapped the phone closed.

"What?" Carl asked.

"You were right," Ben said. "They uncovered another body. This one's wearing a wedding gown." He snatched up Ben's papers. "This is getting uglier and uglier."

Tabitha's killer slowed down, then stopped when he saw the police cars parked on the side of the road. He hadn't intended to get out, just drive by. He usually drove by once a day. Why were the police here? Were they going to take the bodies away? *No!* They belonged to him. They were his brides. He wasn't ready to give them up yet.

He gripped the steering wheel. The tap at his window made him swing around.

The cop motioned for him to roll down his window. He inhaled, once, twice. Then he did what the officer bade him do. *Normal. Act normal.*

"You'll have to turn around, the road's closed." The cop visually searched the car, as if looking for something.

"What happened?" he forced himself to ask, because normal people would ask. And he worked really hard at pretending to be normal. Even before Maria, as a kid, he'd hated it when people looked at him as weird, when they made fun of him or treated him like a freak. He couldn't help it if he wasn't normal.

As he got older, he'd learned to hide it. People had stopped laughing. Or at least they had until the wedding.

"Police investigation," the cop said, confirming his fears.

He managed to keep a normal expression on his face. Nodding, he turned the car around. They were taking his brides away. He would have to do without them.

He waited until he got far enough away that the officer couldn't see him before he started rocking against the car seat. Back. Forth. If someone saw him they would laugh. They had always laughed before he'd learned to control it. Now he only did it in private. Pulling off to a side street, he let himself rock faster. Harder.

Back. Forth. Back. Forth.

After a few minutes, the need to feel the rhythm lessened. He would get more brides. Find a new place to keep them. He started humming. Music helped. He knew all the wedding songs. So he hummed. Then he envisioned Katie Ray dressed in white. She was going to make a beautiful bride. But it would have to be soon. Maybe he could drive by her house now just to see her.

"Katie." Someone whispered her name.

Katie forced her eyes open and stared at a puffy-eyed and sleepy Les staring down at her. She smiled, then rolled back over.

"Katie, some guy's here, and he says he needs to speak to you. He's being insistent about it. Do you want me to tell him to come back later?"

Pushing away the cobwebs of sleep, Katie rose up on her elbow. "Who is it? What's his name?"

"His name?" Les repeated in her drowsy voice. "He didn't give me his name. And I didn't ask."

Chapter Seventeen

Katie sat straight up, the cobwebs gone. "Carl Hades? Was it Hades? Does he look like Antonio Banderas?"

Les dropped down on the edge of the bed and yawned into her hands. "Now that you mention it, he does."

Katie's heart took up speed racing, but it had no place to go, so it just ran laps around her chest. She jackknifed out of bed, started for the door, stubbed her toe, then glanced down at Papa Smurf smiling up at her from the front of her nightshirt. What was wrong with this picture? Okay, "Smurfwear" didn't feel like the proper attire for this situation.

Question Number One popped into her head: What *is* this situation?

"Oh, boy," Katie muttered and bunched up her hair.

"Do you want me to tell him to come back later?"

"No!" She met Les's eyes. "I just need . . . a minute." Her mind *would* start functioning. Right? Carl was here.

Question Number Two: Why was her heart doing marathons?

"Clothes." She pointed to her closet. She grabbed her hair again. "Ponytail." She pressed a hand to her mouth, sniffed, and frowned. "Gotta brush teeth."

Les squinted at her. "Katie? Are you awake?"

"Yes." Katie scurried to her closet and tossed out a pair of jeans and a pair of khakis, followed by a green sweater and tan blouse. Darting back into the room, she held each piece of clothing up and eyed Les. "This one? Or this one?"

Les blinked. "Green sweater. Dark jeans."

"Oh, you're so good at this." She tugged Papa Smurf over her head and tossed him on the bed, then ran to grab a bra.

Les continued to stare. "I'll tell him you're coming."

Three minutes later, dressed, ponytailed, and minus most of the peach fuzz on her teeth, she stepped out into the hall. She saw him from behind. And heavens, he looked good. Tall, sturdy, and the nicest butt she could ever recall seeing.

Stop! Oh, gawd! Why was she checking out his butt?

Because you're interested in his butt.

Okay, physically she was attracted to Carl. She could handle that. She wasn't a prude. But neither was she the type to be stopped dead in her tracks by a man's butt. Especially when she was supposed to be engaged to someone else's butt. *Supposed to be?*

Her heart skipped a beat as she remembered what she'd told Joe. *I'm not sure if flushing the engagement ring was an accident or not.* Was Joe here now? Her gaze shot around the room.

No Joe.

Katie had planned to get home and finish that discussion, but by then she couldn't think in sentences, much less talk in them. Then Les had persuaded her to take a sleeping pill, and—

Her attention refocused on Carl's backside and instantly Katie wanted to run. Run back to the bedroom, bury her head under the covers. Hide. Hide from what Carl Hades made her feel. Hide from what Joe Lyon didn't make her feel. Oh, yeah, that sounded like a plan. She had her foot poised to turn when, just like that, like a film going off in her head, she saw Tabitha being shot. Panic curled in her belly.

"Here she is," Les said.

Carl started to swing around, and Katie's desire to hide did a complete turnover. Utterly complete. She remembered how he made her feel safe. How he smelled. How he'd made her feel so alive even while she'd been facing death.

He hadn't completely turned around before she threw herself into his arms. And boy, was that a mistake.

But it was one of those too-late-to-stop mistakes. Like the moment when your hand pushes the car door closed behind you, you hear the lock click, and your brain shouts *Keys!* When your mind yells *Don't*, but something has already said *Do*, and the brain refuses recalls.

Yep. The man she'd Velcroed herself against wasn't Carl Hades.

Katie's first thought was, *At least this mistake has a nice butt.*

Her second thought was, *Nice butt or not, I could have just worn Papa Smurf.* Impressing strangers wasn't too necessary.

Her third thought was that she really needed to peel herself off him, but her fourth thought was just to stay right where she was. Because as soon as she un-Velcroed herself, she'd have to face this stranger with the nice butt.

"Miss Ray?" Said stranger dropped his hands from around her. Obviously, he'd felt compelled to return her embrace. That, or he'd felt the need to protect himself. "Are you okay?"

There was that word again: *okay*. Why was it that people chose the most inopportune times to ask that question?

She stepped back and stared. Not a stranger. She knew him. Her mind searched through identifying data. Her brain finally spat out the answer. The cop who'd interviewed her.

"Miss Ray?" He appeared concerned—as in the are-you-nuts kind of concerned.

She couldn't recall his name. Nor could she recall thinking he had a nice butt earlier at the station. Funny, how you missed things like that.

"I'm Detective Ben Hades. We met this morning?" The fact he felt inclined to remind her of their meeting confirmed that he thought she might be a good candidate for a padded cell.

"I remember you," she said. "I don't hug just anyone." Okay, she wished she hadn't said that. What was wrong with her?

Sleeping pill.

Yes. She could blame this all on the sleeping pill, and she'd started to do just that when he grinned and her mind spun off in another direction.

She stared at his smile. So familiar. Her brain started playing connect-the-dots. "Hades? Your name is Hades?"

"Yes. Ben Hades. I'm the one you spoke to this morning."

"I remember," she said. "I just didn't catch your name this morning. Are you related to—"

"Yes." His eyes widened as if he'd figured it out. "Carl's my brother. I guess we sort of look alike . . . from behind."

"Yes, you both have nice . . ." She caught herself before she fell into that one. But, quick, she needed a replacement word.

"Thank you." He grinned as if he'd finished her thought.

Her face flushed. Definitely, the sleeping pill.

Silence threatened. "And your father. You all look alike. Not that I . . . checked out his backside." *Yup! Sleeping pill.*

He chuckled. "That's right, you met my father, too. You just need to meet my wife, my son, cat, and dog, and you'll know the whole family."

His words triggered an image, a family image. "What about Precious?"

Ben Hades laughed for real this time. The deep-timbred sound brought on memories of another laugh. Her heart filled with an ache. How could she miss someone she barely knew?

"I can't believe he told you about Precious. Did you know my wife has to take it in to be groomed because Carl's too embarrassed? But she gets them to put bows in the dog's hair just to tick Carl off."

Katie smiled and found she liked Mr. Ben Hades more now than she had this morning. "Please sit down."

"Why don't I fix us some coffee?" Les offered.

Katie had forgotten Les was there. "I'm sorry. This is my friend Les Grayson."

"We introduced ourselves." Ben glanced at Les. "I'll take a rain check on the coffee." He gazed back at Katie. "I came by to tell you . . . to remind you again to take precautions."

"Has something else happened?" she and Les asked at the same time.

Ben stuffed his hands into the pockets of his blue Dockers. "You witnessed a murder. While we don't have any reason to think you might be in immediate danger, it's best if you're cautious."

A chill worked its way through Katie. "You . . . you think he might come after me?"

"I didn't say that. I just think being careful is wise."

Ben left soon after saying that, and Katie and Les locked the doors, made coffee, and sat in the kitchen in an awkward silence.

"Did Joe go to work?" Katie inhaled the scent of her coffee.

"He said he was going in for a while, but he'd be by later."

And I have to figure out what I'm going to say to him.

Les shifted in her chair. "You know, we could both go

and stay at my brother's," she said. "Or a hotel. It could be like a vacation: order room service, buy some romance novels, and—"

"Ben didn't say I had to leave." Katie peered at the steam rising from her cup. "And we *did* lock the doors."

"Yeah, but who wants to stay somewhere where a murderer may or may not come looking for you?"

Emotionally, Katie flinched. If this had happened a few days ago, she would have suggested they stay at Joe's place. Sweet, handsome, wonderful Joe. "Oh, God." She dropped her elbows on the table and moaned. "Everything is so fucked-up."

"*Fucked*-up?" Les asked. "You mean, you deem this f-word worthy? Now I'm really getting scared, girlfriend."

Katie looked at Les and just said what was eating at her: "I can't marry Joe."

Les's green eyes grew round. "Okay, it's f-word worthy." She dropped her head on the table and gave it a thump.

Katie studied the top of her friend's head. "I just—"

Les snapped back up. "No. I can't let you do this. I'm the one who put this stupid notion in your head. I'm the one who said you flushed the ring on purpose. And . . ."

"And what?" Katie asked.

"And I'm an idiot. You don't need to listen to me."

"But I always listen to you." Katie half grinned.

"Well, you shouldn't." Les jumped up from her chair and paced.

"Hey, I'm not feeling this way because . . . because of anything you said."

Les swung around. "Are you sure? Absolutely sure?"

"Yes. I mean, it's true that what you said made me start thinking, but the questions were already there. You were just the straw that broke the camel's back."

Les made a face. "Again with the straw! I don't fucking want to be the straw! I *can't* be the straw." She stared at Katie. "You can't do this."

Katie swallowed a gulp of uncertainty. "So you think I should marry Joe?"

"Yes. No! I mean, it's not important what I think. What's important is what *you* think. You told me you loved him."

Katie blinked. "Yes, and I do. I mean . . . I think I do." She pressed a hand to her stomach. "But I want to throw up every time I think about him."

"Okay, but like you said earlier, you throw up before every big event in your life. You're a nervous puker."

Katie stared down at her coffee, fighting the nausea and recalling the sympathy puker with whom she'd spent last night. "Maybe I don't really love Joe." The nausea increased. "No, that's not true," she confessed. "I do love Joe. I do."

"Good, then that's solved." Les let out a big sigh.

"I just don't love him in the right way," Katie finished.

Les's shoulders slumped. "Maybe it's just cold feet."

Katie stared at her coffee. And the tiniest bit of doubt rose in her like steam from her cup. "Did you have cold feet?"

"Me?" Les asked, as if she didn't understand the question.

"Yes. When you were engaged to Mike. Did you ever think you were making a mistake?"

Les plopped down in her chair and reached up to touch her chest. "No. I couldn't wait to marry Mike." She spoke while looking down at her coffee. "Without him beside me, I didn't feel whole or complete. It was as if I needed him to breathe." Les looked up. "You don't feel that way with Joe?"

"No." She forced herself to admit the truth. "It feels comfortable. But I don't stop feeling lonely." She frowned. "Even the sex is . . . ho-hum." She shook her head. "It's crazy, Les. Joe's a sexy guy. Great body and he does everything right. His techniques are on the mark. Not too fast, not too slow, and yet . . ."

Les stared. "You've never had the big O?"

"Of course I've . . ." She blinked. "Okay, I've faked it some. A lot." She hated admitting it, but this was Les she was talking to. "Most of the time."

Katie paused. "I keep waiting to hear the voice go off in my head. The one that says, 'yes.' You know that voice?"

Les glanced away. "Yeah, I know that voice."

Katie hesitated. "I have comfortable. I have sweet. But no pizzazz, and I don't think it's his fault. It's me."

"How could it be your fault?" Les asked.

"I . . . Until last night, I thought I was broken."

"What happened last night?" Les's eyes widened. "You slept with that man?"

"No. Okay, I slept with him but we didn't *do* anything. It was cold and there was just one cot and nothing happened."

"But . . . ?" Les asked.

Katie swallowed. "He smelled so good and felt so good."

"And?" Les asked.

"That's it. That's all that happened."

"Wait. You feel guilty because you noticed he felt and smelled good?"

Katie fought the urge to go at her lip again. "I wanted to do something. There were all sorts of bells going off." She sighed. "I might have been freezing my ass off, but I was so hot. If I hadn't been engaged to Joe, I swear, Les, I would have screwed that man every which way to Sunday."

Les's eyes lit up. "That's why you practically attacked Mr. Hades. His brother is the guy you spent the night with, right?"

Katie nodded. "Guilty."

"Why, Katie Ray." Les grinned. "You little slut."

Katie moaned. "I'm a terrible person, aren't I?"

Les rolled her eyes. "You couldn't be a terrible person

if you graduated with a master's degree in it." She paused. "But decent people feel guilty about wanting things, even when they didn't do anything but want." Her gaze became somber. "However, this means you *do* care enough about Joe to feel guilty. So maybe you do love him."

"Do you really think this is just cold feet?" Katie asked.

"I don't know. And don't ask me to tell you what to do."

Katie half grinned. "You've been telling me what to do since I was in kindergarten."

Les smiled, but her expression was forced.

Katie rose to get a coffee refill and was hit with a very ugly thought. "Can you imagine what my parents would say about me calling off a wedding?"

Les huffed. "Fuck it, Katie. When are you going to stop trying to live up to their standards?"

Katie went back and dropped back into her chair. "Probably never," she admitted. "But I'm going to have to talk to him."

"To who? Joe or the Hades guy?"

Katie looked up. "Joe, of course. At the very least, I need to tell him how I feel."

One of Les's eyebrows rose. "And what about Hades?"

Katie visualized Carl, all perfect six feet–plus of him. "Remember Trey Poke?"

Les grinned. "I haven't thought about him in years. Yum."

"Remember the vow we made to each other?" Katie asked.

"To never be one of his pathetic 'Poked' conquests." Les giggled.

"Well, Carl Hades makes Trey look like Pee-wee Herman. He's a hundred percent bad boy. Hates marriage, afraid of commitment. All he wants is a sperm bank with legs."

"That may be the case, but let's be honest. If Trey had cast either of us a mere look, we'd both have taken that train to Brokenheartsville so fast we'd never hear the whistle blow."

"Maybe," Katie admitted. "But we're older and wiser now."

"And as boring as a sugar-free, nonfat, plain-vanilla latte." Les sighed. "Didn't you just tell me he rang your bell? Maybe life's too short not to listen to the bells because . . . Oh, hell, what am I saying? Don't listen to me."

Katie started to answer, but the ringing of another bell—the doorbell—interrupted her.

Les looked toward the living room. "You don't think a murderer would ring a doorbell, do you?"

Chapter Eighteen

"Don't you dare open that door!" Les called from behind her.

"It's a florist delivery guy." Katie looked over her shoulder at Les wielding a brass lamp in her hands like a weapon.

"And how can you be sure?"

"Because, Sherlock, he's wearing a uniform with 'Florist' written on it, and he's got flowers."

"Yeah, and how many *Law & Order* episodes have you seen where the guy delivering the flowers is the murderer?"

Katie's hand paused on the lock. "Okay, you have a point."

The lock in the door clicked. Clicked like being-unlocked clicked. Clicked, like a murdering florist delivery guy on the other side was unlocking the door.

"Fudge," Katie said and jumped back.

"No. *Fuck*," Les screeched.

The door pushed open and a brass lamp went flying through the air.

Joe, flowers in tow, ducked in the nick of time, losing a few daisies in the process. The lamp clattered against the wall. "What the hell?" he asked.

"You . . . you surprised us," Katie said.

"Imagine how I felt." He glanced at the lamp.

"A cop came and said we should be careful," Katie explained.

"And throwing lamps is careful?" He shrugged, and Katie saw him mentally release his frustration. Joe was good at that, letting things just roll off him. But he was also good at avoiding. And he'd avoided her for the past month. No longer.

"Here." He held the flowers out to Katie. "I got these from the delivery guy."

"Thanks." Katie took the vase, expecting Joe to say he'd sent them. Which was going to make her feel like the slimy stuff you clean out of the bathtub drain, because she was about to have a serious heart-to-heart with him.

"From you?" she asked, trying not to sound unhappy.

"Not me."

"Then who . . ." *Carl?*

Hope filled her chest. She plucked the card from the plastic fork. Then she called herself a fool. Carl Hades didn't seem like the flower-sending kind of guy. And if he was, the fact that he hadn't waited around to speak to her at the police station meant he wasn't interested in her in the send-flowers kind of way.

Not that it would have made a difference. Katie hadn't liked the idea of winding up on the Poked List in high school any more than she liked the idea now. Bells or no bells. She wasn't anyone's sperm bank.

"Who're they from?" Joe asked.

Aware that she stood staring at a bunch of daisies and yellow roses thinking about one man, while another—her fiancé—stood a foot away, made her concerns feel less manageable. She opened the card and read the note.

"It's from the florist. The one I hired before Tabitha insisted I hire a different one. They're congratulating me. Us."

"That's nice." But Joe didn't sound as if he meant it.

She met Joe's eyes. "We need to talk."

Joe's gaze shot to Les. Katie cleared her throat to draw Joe's attention. She wouldn't let him avoid her anymore. And he had to listen to her, really listen.

And just like that, she knew what she had to do.

Dropping the flowers on Les, she took Joe's arm. "Come on."

She marched him down the hall, into her bedroom, and past the bed, yanked open her closet door, and motioned him inside.

"What?" he asked.

"After you."

"In the closet?" His expression flatlined.

"Yes."

"Why?" He looked at her a little strangely.

"Because." Because she could still recall how talking in the dark with Carl Hades had made it so easy to listen, easy to hear the truth. And right now, she and Joe needed to have a truthful conversation that involved a lot of listening.

"Katie? Are you okay?"

"No! I'm not okay." She gave him a hearty nudge into the closet, stepped in behind him, and shut the door.

The bell on the door jingled as Carl stepped into the shop. The mixture of floral scents teased his senses with a vague memory. Inhaling, he moved behind a guy at the counter who talked to the female attendant about the type of flowers to send the woman he'd spent the night with.

"Well," the attendant asked, "what message would you like the flowers to send?"

Thanks for a good lay, Carl thought to himself, but keeping his opinion and smile to himself, he moved back a few feet and pretended to be interested in some bouquets.

It wasn't that he had anything against the idea of

sending flowers. His brother had probably seduced Tami with roses, candy, and all the other romantic gestures. But considering that Carl's involvement with women was never meant to lead anywhere, he'd never put that much effort into the sentimental side of romance.

Hearing the two people still talking behind him, he stared again at all the flowers. Most were common varieties—roses, carnations, the kinds of flowers even men could identify—but there was one . . . For some unexplainable reason, he thought of Red, of having a bouquet delivered. Had Mr. Metro sent her flowers?

Right then, he knew what the flower's scent reminded him of. Red's perfume.

All day, his mind had teased him with images of her: her smile when she'd first woken up from passing out, the pattern of the freckles across her nose. And, oh yeah, the one he'd enjoyed the most, her standing frozen, staring wide-eyed at the enormous vibrator in her hands. Yup! Definitely his favorite.

"Can I help you, sir?" a female voice asked.

Carl turned around and chased the image of Red from his head. "Yes. I wanted to speak with the owner. Jack Edwards?"

At first, Carl had decided to wait and get the background checks before doing the face-to-face interviews, but patience had never been his game. Who knew how long it would be before his brother got the information back? Especially with two more crime scenes to comb through.

"Mr. Edwards went to make some deliveries. I don't think he's planning on returning today. Is there something I can do?"

"No." Carl frowned. "But if you could have him give me a call at his earliest convenience, I'd be grateful." This made the third name on his list of four that he'd visited who hadn't been around: the cake maker, the DJ, and now the florist.

He handed the woman his card and turned to leave. Three down and one to go. He planned to stop by the photographer and—

"Private investigator?" the woman's voice piped up.

Carl glanced back. "Yes, ma'am."

From her expression, he could see she was more than a little curious. "And what is this about?"

He smiled. "A wedding."

"Then I should be able to help you. I'm the one who sets up Mr. Edwards's weddings. He hates doing them."

And why would that be? "I appreciate it, but I'd rather speak to Mr. Edwards myself."

Joe fumbled around the closet until he found the light switch. He stared at Katie standing by the door. Her long hair was pulled back into a ponytail, her blue eyes honest, caring.

"Please cut it off," she whispered.

He had the word *no* on the tip of his tongue, but then he met her gaze. So pleading.

So sweet.

So Katie.

Why couldn't he love her as she deserved to be loved? What the hell was wrong with him?

She reached over and hit the switch.

"Leave it off, Joe."

His question changed. What the hell was wrong with her? Why did she have him in the closet with the lights off?

The darkness pooled around him. "Katie, what's going on?"

"Sit down, Joe."

"There's shoes everywhere," he said, and wondered if she was suffering from some kind of postpanic attack.

"Just push them away and sit down."

He shoved the shoes aside and found a spot. "Are you going to explain what we're doing in here?"

"We need to talk," she said.

"Talking is fine, but you do know you brought me into a closet, right?"

"I know." She paused. "Last night when I was locked in the dark, I discovered you're forced to listen when you can't see. I need you to listen, Joe. Really listen."

"Are you saying I don't listen?" Of course she was. He'd avoided listening and speaking to her for weeks.

"Yeah, that's what I'm saying. But it may not be just you."

"I'm so sorry, Katie." He heard the guilt in his voice.

"For what?" she asked, as if she heard more in his statement.

For not loving you enough, for lusting after your best friend, for having to call off the wedding. "For not listening."

Coward.

He had to tell her. "I'm sorry for everything." The silence hung in the dark like the clothes hanging over his head. The tiny room smelled like Katie's perfume.

"What are you not telling me, Joe?"

He'd spent all morning searching for the right words, but there wasn't a good way. "I don't know how to say this. You're so damn perfect, Katie. Google the Internet for the perfect wife and I swear, your picture will come up. You're sweet, caring, sexy, but . . ."

"But what, Joe?" she asked.

Leaving the florist, Carl noticed the temperature had risen nearly twenty degrees. Houston was back to feeling like Houston. Carl looked up at the blue sky as he hit the clicker and unlocked his car. He'd just gotten behind the wheel when his phone rang.

"Yeah?"

"Carl Hades?" the voice asked.

"You got him."

"This is Will Reed, with Reed's DJ. Your card and a note was taped to my door. You needed something?"

The man sounded nervous. "Yes. I was hoping to meet with you to discuss a wedding." There was silence. "Mr. Reed?"

"I'm sorry. Your card said 'private investigator.' I thought it was about something else."

"I get that a lot." Carl focused on the man's voice, hoping he might recognize it as being the man who'd tried to burn him and Red alive. "Everyone has something to hide." He tried to sound light.

"I guess," Reed said, still sounding cautious. Too cautious.

"Are you home now? Can I swing by?"

"I'm busy cutting CDs. Why don't you check out my Web site? If you're interested, we can talk later."

In the background, Carl heard music, wedding music. If he pushed Mr. Reed for answers too quickly, the guy might get suspicious. Maybe even as suspicious as Carl felt. "I'd really like to talk to you today."

"Can't do it. But tomorrow would be fine. Around three?"

Maybe by then Carl would have his background info, but damn, he didn't like waiting. "I guess I'll have to be patient."

"And feel free to bring your bride with you. Brides are generally the ones with the most input on music."

Carl's suspicion deepened. "She's working out of town, so I'm stuck doing all the women's work."

"Fine. I'll see you tomorrow then."

"I'll be there." Carl hung up and grabbed a notepad from his glove box. He wrote down the time beside Mr. Will Reed's number and address. Then he dialed his brother.

"Hades," his brother answered.

"How soon can you get background checks?"

"Maybe by tomorrow. Maybe next year," Ben said.

"That bad, huh?"

"He's a sick bastard. Visits the bodies. Leaves flowers."

Carl glanced up at the florist's shop. "I really need those background checks, Ben."

"But what?" Katie asked when Joe stopped talking. Waiting for him to answer, she tried to lean back, only to feel something in her way. She reached around and realized what it was. Her old paintings. She'd forgotten they were in here.

"I love you. I do."

Joe's words brought her head up. Then she recognized a hesitation in his tone. "But?"

"You're perfect. But I can't marry you."

He couldn't? Had he really said that?

He continued, "I know this creates huge problems. And it's embarrassing as hell. And I'll take all the blame, Katie."

He would? She envisioned her parents glancing down from the afterlife saying *Thank you, God. The Ray name is saved.* Relief trickled over her. She could hold her head high. It was easier being the victim of a canceled wedding than the villain.

She could hear Joe breathing and sensed the guilt he felt. She finally spoke. "I'm not perfect." She could almost hear her parents gasp. "I'm a lousy cook, remember?"

He chuckled. "Okay, I'll give you that one."

The silence returned. "And I can't paint."

She ran her fingers over one of the canvases, over the thick smears of acrylic. She felt the loss of her dreams in the brush strokes, just as she felt the loss of her dream of making her own family to replace the one that had been so unjustly yanked away from her. *Alone sucks. Alone hurts.*

Tears threatened. She stiffened her spine. She'd survive.

"I didn't know you painted," Joe said.

It seemed odd she'd told Carl Hades, a stranger, something about herself that she hadn't told Joe. "I suck at it."

"I'm sorry," he said again, and she knew he wasn't talking about her lack of artistic talent.

"I'm really not perfect, Joe." Her parents had wanted her to be, but she wasn't.

"You're close enough," he said.

"No." She took a deep breath. "I'm so imperfect that I'm sitting here wondering if I can live with myself if I let you take all the blame for canceling the wedding. The truth is that I brought you in here to tell you the same thing. I love you, but I don't love you in the right way." The darkness went silent.

"How did you figure it out?" he asked. When she didn't answer, he prompted, "Katie?"

"Do you really want to know?" She didn't think he would. After her talk with Les, she realized what her first clue had been.

"Yes?"

"The sex well, it . . ."

"It what?"

"Sucked. Well, not that I . . ." How was she going to get out of this one?

"Okay, that hurt." There was a bit of tease in his voice.

"It's not your fault. There just wasn't any pizzazz."

"And that doesn't help." He shuffled around, then let go a deep gulp of air. "But I know what you mean. I sort of kept waiting for it to get better, too. Not that it was your fault."

She got quiet, glad he understood. "I'd started questioning my feelings earlier, then Les picked up on my doubt. She's always been good at that. Seeing things in me. But last night . . ." She didn't know why she felt the need to confess, but she did. "When I was with Carl Hades. I felt pizzazz with him."

A hush fell on them. "What are you saying, Katie?"

"Nothing happened," she clarified. "But I felt things. And now I feel terrible." She shut up, and the silence thickened again.

"You shouldn't feel bad," he finally said. "We're human."

"We?" The word meant something. "It happened to you, too?"

His pause answered before he did. "I didn't mean for it to happen. And like with you, nothing really happened."

"But you wanted it to?" she asked, feeling her guilt ease.

"Yeah," he confessed.

"Some girl at your office?" she asked, not really knowing why, but wanting to know.

"No."

"Someone I know?"

"Is it important?" he asked, his tone edgy.

"No, but *I* told *you*." She remembered his neighbor. The woman was always flirting with Joe. "Oh, gawd! It's—"

"Katie, I swear. Les didn't have a thing to do with it."

Carl continued to talk to Ben while staring at the florist's shop. "Did you see Red?"

"Ahh, now there's an interesting topic," Ben answered.

"Why?" Carl started his car and pulled into traffic.

"She literally threw herself at me."

Carl's grip on the phone tightened. "She did not."

"I haven't held a woman, other than Tami, that close in years. She's a nice package."

"Don't shit me. She's not that kind of girl," Carl snarled.

"Who's shitting you? She was all over me," Ben said.

"You're lying," Carl accused. "She's engaged. And even if she wasn't, she's not the type to—"

Ben's laughter spilled out of the phone. "I knew it. You fell for her. My no-good sorry-ass brother finally fell for a good girl. That's why you won't go to see her, isn't it? You're scared shitless, aren't you?"

"You're talking out your ass." He pulled out onto the street, ready to hang up when Ben continued.

"Truth is—Red *did* throw herself at me. But only because she thought I was you."

His brother obviously wasn't finished having fun. "Right."

"Seriously. She threw herself in my arms. When she realized her mistake, she got this nice shade of red. About the same color as her hair. You always had a thing for redheads. Nevertheless, I think she's missing your ass something terribly."

Just like that, Carl was hit with an aching need to see Katie Ray. And damn it, he missed her, too.

"You should go see her, Carl. No kidding," Ben said.

Carl inhaled. "Maybe I will." *Maybe?*

It was Les? Katie couldn't believe . . . "I was thinking it was your neighbor."

"Nothing happened," Joe said with urgency in his tone. "We met briefly at the bar. Then I came here. I thought it was you in the shower."

Katie digested what he said and remembered . . . "No! You didn't climb naked into the shower with her, did you?"

"She beat the shit out of me. Called 911."

Part of her wanted to laugh. Part of her still couldn't believe it. More silence crawled into the closet while she absorbed the facts. Why hadn't Les told her?

"Nothing happened." His voice vibrated with frustration.

"I believe you." Katie rested her head on her knees and found herself reaching for one of the paintings.

"How do we do this?" he finally spoke.

"Do what?" It wasn't like Les to keep things from her.

"Call off the wedding. Maybe your wedding planner could help . . . Oh. Never mind."

"Don't worry; I forget every few minutes, too." She paused. "I guess we need to get our wedding RSVPs and call everyone."

"This sucks," he mumbled.

"Majorly," she said. "We have the gifts to return, too."

"I'm really sorry, Katie."

She knew he meant it. Joe wouldn't hurt anyone intentionally. And then the thought of never again seeing sweet, handsome, good Joe brought a pain to her chest.

"Joe, this sounds totally cliché, but do you think we could remain friends?"

"I'd like that." The dark silence no longer felt so wrong.

Katie traced her fingers again over one of the paintings and wondered which it was. The ocean scene? The flowers?

"Ah, shit," he said. "I just realized I gotta tell my mom."

"Do you want me to go with you?" Katie liked Joe's mom. Yeah, she was a tad domineering with Joe, but compared to her own parents, Joe's mom didn't really seem so bad.

"Nah, I'll handle it. Do you think tomorrow night is soon enough to start calling people?"

"Yes. At lunch tomorrow I'll contact everyone I hired to help with the wedding." Of course, Katie didn't know whom she'd hired, since Tabitha had changed things.

"I know this is difficult," Joe said.

"On both of us." Her thoughts shot back to how embarrassed her parents would have been if they'd been alive. Rays didn't back out of things at the last minute.

"We'll live through this," Joe said, as if reading her mind. *Live through it.* Live? The image of Tabitha falling to the carpet hit again. Katie's breath hitched. She dropped her head on her knees. "I sure as heck hope so."

Joe must have read her mind, because he spoke all too fast. "Why don't you come stay at my place?"

Katie let the thought run around her head. Then she remembered Ben Hades saying, *We don't have a reason to believe you are in immediate danger.* Logic chased away the beginning spasms of fear.

Plus, staying with Joe would be awkward to the max.

"Les is here. And we might go stay at a hotel. We'll be fine," she said.

Now, all she had to do was believe it.

Chapter Nineteen

Carl had run his three miles, showered, and had just finished shaving when he heard his dad.

"Son?"

He frowned at his image in the mirror. He really needed to get his key back. "In here."

His dad appeared at the door of the bathroom. "Morning."

"Morning." Splashing on aftershave, he grimaced when the liquid hit the scratches. He eyed the marks. Red had got him good, not that he blamed her.

"You made coffee?" his dad asked as he headed down the hall.

"Yup." Wearing only boxers, Carl went to stand in front of the open closet. What did one wear to an art gallery?

A pair of khaki pants caught his eye. He tossed them on the bed. His light blue oxford shirt would work. Then he spotted another shirt tucked in the back. Way back. The shirt Tami had given him last year for Christmas. She'd sworn it would look great on him. *Oh, what the hell.*

Five minutes later, he stepped out of his bedroom, clean, combed, and ready. His dad sat at the kitchen table, his nose in the business section of the *Houston Chronicle*.

The newspaper lowered. "Why are you fancied up?"

"Paying a visit to the suspects in the Jones case."

"And you gotta dress up to do that?"

"I thought I'd stop by the gallery where Red works." Carl had told himself it meant nothing. Common courtesy.

His dad continued to stare. "Since when do you fancy pink?"

"It's light red." Carl grabbed his cup and went to fill it.

"Which is another way of saying pink."

"Tami gave it to me." Moving back to the table, Carl settled into a chair. "Besides, women aren't into macho anymore." He had that from a good source. A source that had kept him awake half the night fighting his own stiffy while his dog got lucky. That was just plain wrong.

"What are women into now?"

"Metro men." Carl picked up the sports section.

"A man who takes the bus?"

"No. It's a man who's not afraid to wear . . . light red."

His dad laughed. "You gonna take her out to lunch?"

"No. I'm just popping in to check on her."

"Take her some flowers," his old man said.

Carl snapped open the sports section and ducked behind it. "Don't make something out of this. I'm just being courteous."

"Right," his dad mumbled and then, "Women like flowers."

Carl ignored his dad. Besides, he already had a gift for Red.

The tap of claws echoed around the table. Precious came to greet Carl's dad, gave Carl's feet a bump with his nose, then went back to Baby. So, his poodle preferred chasing tail to his feet? Carl couldn't say he blamed the dog, but being second fiddle didn't feel good. *Second fiddle.* He remembered seeing Red with her fiancé.

His dad eyed the dogs. "Where's those doggy panties I got?"

"Precious ripped them off of her. I tried keeping them in separate rooms. They both howled nonstop for hours."

"Love is the air. Can't fight it."

"And I'm going to let you tell that to Ms. Jones's next of kin when they come to pick her up." Carl raised the paper, then lowered it. "Which reminds me. Do you know when that will be? Has someone been contacted?"

His dad pulled the paper up, shielding himself from Carl's view.

Carl pushed the paper down. "What gives, Dad?"

"Detective James told Tabitha's cousin about the dog and she said she couldn't take her."

Carl shot the white puffball of a dog a look. "She *has* to take her."

"She said to give it to a shelter."

Carl gritted his teeth. "Fine. You take her to a shelter."

"Me?" Buck asked.

"You brought her here. You handle it."

Baby let out a pathetic bark as if she understood. "I can't keep you," Carl muttered, but refused to look at her.

"She's not big," his dad said. "And Precious likes her."

Carl cut his dad a cold stare. "*You* are taking her to the shelter. I mean it, when I get back, this dog will not be here." He eyed his watch. His appointment with Mel Grimes, the photographer, was at ten.

"Shouldn't one of us be following around Mr. Johnson?"

Shit. He'd forgotten all about the Johnson case. And Mondays were when Johnson's wife suspected him of meeting with some other woman. "Yeah. Follow Mr. Johnson." Carl knew he'd be sorry for bringing his father into another case, but he didn't see what choice he had. "Take my cameras. But be careful."

"I'm always careful." His dad reached down to pet Baby.

"And you *still* have to handle the dog situation," Carl said.

"Okay, but you know they'll put her down, don't you?"

"She's a pedigree," Carl snapped. "Someone will want her."

"Just like you do, huh?"

"Don't put this on me. I told you I didn't want that dog."

"Yeah, yeah!" His old man brought the newspaper back up. "What time should I start trailing Mr. Johnson?"

"The wife said he doesn't leave the house until noon."

For the next ten minutes they drank coffee and read the morning news in silence. "Son?" His dad set the paper down.

"Yeah?" Carl thumbed through the other sections, looking for the comics.

"I . . . I, uh, needed to talk to you about something."

"I'm not keeping the dog, Dad."

"It's not that." His tone sent up warning flags. Carl recalled his dad had gone in for a physical last week and was supposed to be getting his results back. Carl's gut tightened.

"Test results?"

"Test results?" his father repeated. "Oh, you mean from the doctor. Hell, no. I got those back Friday. I'm fit as a fiddle."

Relief came instantly. As much as his old man drove Carl crazy, he knew losing him would cost him more than he wanted to admit. "Good." He grinned. "So, what's up?"

His dad palmed his coffee cup—a sure sign of nervousness. "I asked Jessie to marry me last weekend."

Carl leaned back in his chair. "You're joking, right?"

"I'm tired of being run out of her bed every night. She doesn't believe in living with a man, and I respect that."

"You're sixty-six. You shouldn't be in her bed every night."

"You think my wingwanger don't work?"

"Dad, I don't give a rat's ass if your pecker works or not. I'm talking about . . ." Hell, what was he talking about? "I just think it's late in the game to be . . . to get yourself hitched to some woman."

"It's not some woman. It's Jessie. I love her."

"Then love her. But why screw it up by getting married?"

"Because when people love each other, they get married."

"What about Mom?" The moment the words stepped off his lips, Carl regretted them.

"She's been dead sixteen years," his dad said.

Carl inhaled. "Oh, screw it. I don't know why we're talking about this. You're not going to listen to me." But the idea felt wrong. "Marry Jessie. Adopt a kid with her. It's not up to me." He shot up from his chair.

"I'd really like your blessing."

Carl stopped. "Blessing? Have you told Ben about this?"

"Yes."

"And didn't he tell you that you were an idiot?"

Buck folded his hands together on top of the paper. "Actually, Ben and Tami are thrilled for me."

"Well, that's great," Carl said. "Do what you want. You don't need my damn blessing." He grabbed his coat and the package for Red and left.

Joe had taken the day off from work, something he hadn't done in ages. But since he wasn't going on a honeymoon, he could afford some downtime. Not that telling his mom about the wedding cancellation fell into the category of downtime.

Much as Joe hated admitting it, last week's visit to his mom's cardiologist confirmed his worst fears. She was a conniving manipulator who didn't have anything that closely resembled a heart condition. All her medical woes were crap, a ploy to pull at his sympathy strings—to encourage him to rush the wedding. She'd been pushing for him to marry for years.

Not that he blamed her for the wedding fiasco. He'd proposed to Katie before his mom had even known about it. But the fact that she'd lied to him about her health ticked him off.

Of course, not enough for him to confront her about it. Face it, he was thirty-four years old and afraid of his mommy. But hey, Mildred Lyon was no ordinary woman. With one cut from her eyes, she made him feel thirteen and guilty of something.

Katie had assured him that his mom was just lonely. Katie also insisted his devotion to her was a sign of a caring son. But letting his mother get away with lying was too much. Yes. So what was he going to do about it?

Courage wavering, he walked into her apartment. "Mom?"

She didn't answer. Was probably next door. He went to the kitchen and grabbed a soda. While debating if he wanted a sandwich, he heard a noise from the bedroom.

"Mom?" Imagining her fallen out on the floor, he went running into the bedroom. And . . . Well, fuck! He swung around. But, too late. The image was tattooed onto his memory. Not those temporary tattoos, either. Permanent.

"Joe!" his mom screamed.

He heard a loud thump against the wall and prayed it had been her bedmate and not her. And it would have been a hell of a lot better if the bedmate had been a real person. But to see his mom, naked, enjoying a battery-operated boyfriend—well, that basically was just too damn much.

He stood in the hall, trying to decide what to do. His mom scrambling around behind him told him that she hadn't fallen to her death. He raked ten fingers through his hair. "Shit."

"Joey. I . . . I . . . You should have never seen that."

"For once, we're in total agreement on something." Right then, Joe called the games over. No more placating his mom.

He swung around, relieved to find her in a robe. "I came by to tell you that the wedding has been called off."

His mom pressed a hand to her heart. "But—"

"*Don't* say anything." He pointed at the bed. "Any

woman who can do what I saw isn't suffering from a weak heart."

She blushed, but still had the audacity to send him her don't-talk-to-me-that-way look. But her look held zero power, not after seeing . . . Oh, damn, he wished he could forget.

"I love you, Mom. I do. And I'll be here for you, but what I saw proves that you need to get your *own* life. Maybe even a *real* boyfriend. And you need to stop interfering with, meddling in, and trying to run my life."

Joe stepped out, but not before snatching the phone book from under the coffee table. Something about standing up to his mom empowered him, and while he might be an idiot, there was one other woman he wanted to see.

In his car, he looked under *G* to see how many Graysons were listed in North Piper. Les wouldn't want to see him, but damn it, there were some things that just needed to be said.

Chapter Twenty

Katie had worked four hours and gotten one hour of work done. Her mind kept juggling problems.

Ball one: Tabitha's demise and those reoccurring images. Katie worried about what had happened to the woman's dog.

Ball two: Carl Hades. She wondered why she missed him.

Ball three: Joe and his confrontation with his mom. She worried about Joe and his mom's relationship.

Ball four . . . Katie grabbed her cell phone and replayed Les's message from the night Tabitha was murdered. *I'll tell you about this really hot guy I met at the restaurant.* Katie had a sneaking suspicion she now knew why Les hadn't mentioned the shower scene: Joe Lyon hadn't been the only one lusting in Katie's shower.

Ball four was the one giving her the most problems at the moment. If confronted, Les would deny everything and probably run back to Boston. Yup. Les, who excelled at telling everyone else how they felt, sucked at admitting her own feelings.

Or was Katie making more out of this than she should? Did it mean anything that Les was physically attracted to Joe? Part of Katie wanted to say no, but then Katie knew that Les hadn't been attracted to anyone since Mike's death.

Katie tried envisioning the results of such attraction. What if Joe and Les actually got together as a couple? How would that make her feel? Sitting back in her chair, she dug deep in her mental junk drawer seeking answers, thinking she'd find some sort of resentment. But, nope. It wasn't there. And wasn't that a confirmation that she and Joe were totally, completely, wrong for each other?

"Katie?" Lola said.

"Yes?" Katie looked up at the office door and to Lola, the gallery owner and one of the main exhibiting artists. Instead of seeing Lola, the image of Tabitha with blood pouring over her white suit played across Katie's mind. Her stomach clenched.

"Katie?" Lola said again.

Katie shook off the sudden queasiness. "I'm sorry. You were saying?"

"There's a guy here to see you." Lola glanced down the hall, then back to her. "*Bien bonito.*" She kissed her fingers.

"Ben Hades?" Katie refused to hope otherwise. Ben had probably gotten her message. And honestly, that's the only reason she'd called him earlier: about Tabitha's dog. Not to ask about Carl.

Lola grinned. "I was so enamored, I didn't catch his name."

Katie stood. "He's married, Lola."

"Should have known. He's marked by his woman already." Lola ran her nails down her cheek.

Katie flopped back down in her chair. "Oh, fudge."

"*Chica*, after the week you've had, you deserve to say 'fuck.'"

"True," Katie agreed. Planting her hands firmly on her desk, she squared her shoulders. She could do this. But whether she could do this without making a fool of herself was anyone's guess.

Giving her ponytail a tug, she moistened her lips, then stood. Now, if she could just get her feet to move.

Looking at Lola, who swore she was part witch, Katie reached out and gripped her hand. "Give me some of your mojo, Lola."

"What kind of magic you need?"

"The willpower kind. Lots of willpower." She would not throw herself at Carl Hades—even newly single, she would not end up on his Poked List.

Carl walked around the room studying the art hanging on the walls. Seriously, the elephant in Mexico had more talent. And after looking at these, why didn't Red think she could paint? He rolled his shoulders and tried to release his tension.

It had been a hell of a morning. First his dad's announcement. *Marriage?* What had gotten into the old man? Then Ben hadn't gotten the background info, and to top it off the photographer, Mel Grimes, in spite of their appointment, hadn't been home. That got Mr. Grimes on Carl's look-at-closer list. Grimes didn't know it, but it wasn't a good list to be on.

Hoping the morning wouldn't be a total waste, he'd driven by the florist's shop, only to find that the owner, Mr. Jack Edwards, hadn't been in, either. Today at three, Carl had the appointment with the DJ, and had managed to make a five o'clock with the cake maker, Todd Sweet. He hoped Ben got the info back before then. Going in with some knowledge under his belt was always best.

Carl heard footsteps and swung around. The moment he saw her, the ground shifted beneath his feet. He'd experienced one earthquake in his life while visiting California, and he hadn't felt as unbalanced then as he did right now.

Katie stopped about four feet in front of him. *She's an engaged woman.* The four words swam around his head. His gaze shot to her left hand, to see if she'd gotten a new ring yet. When it wasn't there, he let his gaze move over her. Her hair was up—a shame, he loved it down. But the pale green business suit traced her body with precision. The scooped top, a lighter green, gave a hint of cleavage, and the skirt, just snug enough to make a man drool, came midthigh. And it was just high enough to make it difficult to decide on where to focus: cleavage or legs.

Carl knew right then that any man shopping here hadn't come for the paintings but the sculptured art of Red's body.

"You clean up nice," he said.

She's an engaged woman, he reminded himself again.

Yeah, but it didn't mean a damn thing if she didn't wear a ring.

"So do you." She grinned.

That soft, sexy smile of hers hit him right between his legs, and his loose-fitting khakis suddenly weren't so loose anymore.

Her smile widened. "I like you in pink. It matches your scarf from the other night."

"It's light red. And besides, I heard metro men aren't afraid to get in touch with their feminine side."

"So you're going metro, huh?" she asked.

Holy hell, she was gorgeous. "I'm trying it on for size." Their gazes met and held. "You know," he went on, "I'm a little disappointed."

"About what?" She twisted her high heels into the carpet.

"My brother bragged about the greeting you gave him, and I don't even get a handshake." He wasn't sure why he said that, maybe because he liked teasing her, or maybe because he'd been disappointed when she hadn't touched him. His body ached to feel her, to get close enough to see if she wore the same perfume, to get close enough to see the spray of freckles across her nose.

"He told you about that, did he?" Color rose in her face.

Damn, she was pretty when she blushed. "Just in passing." *She's an engaged woman.* "So, this is where you work?"

"This is it." She waved her arms around, which made her blouse pull tighter across her breasts.

His gaze caught the clock on the wall. He'd told himself he wouldn't do this, but . . . "Want to grab some lunch with me?" Her expression prepared him for disappointment. He hated disappointment. "Don't break my heart, Red."

She blinked. "I seriously doubt I could break your heart."

And yet the idea didn't seem so far-fetched to him.

She fidgeted. "I planned to run some errands—"

"I saw the diner right next door. A quick lunch. Say yes."

She hesitated. "Lunch," she said.

"Just lunch," he said, because that's how she'd seemed to mean it. While that's exactly what he'd told himself this was, just lunch, he suddenly found the idea depressing as hell.

Les turned the page of the photo album, feeling the nostalgia curl up inside her chest. Mike's handsome face smiled up at her. Amazingly, the pain was almost bearable now. Realizing it seemed too quiet in the living room, Les went to check.

Good thing, too.

"*No*, Mimi." Les took the lipstick from her grandma's hand.

Her mother had asked Les to Mimi-sit today. It had seemed like a small thing, but Les had learned that Mimi's condition had worsened since she'd left for Boston. Before, Mimi would sit in front of the TV for hours and be content. Now she was all hands, either pulling her clothes off or finding something to get into.

Les wondered how her mom did it. A tickle of uncertainty wiggled in her chest. Another incentive to move back home. This morning, Les had actually called her old boss at the paper. He'd been excited to hear from her, and the first thing out of his mouth was, "If you're calling for a job, it's yours."

She hadn't been calling for a job, but his offer had her thinking. Was it time? Time to move back and stop running away?

Les grinned at the painted clown smile on her grandma's lips. Down deep, it hurt to see her grandmother like this, but on another level, Les was glad that Mimi, unlike so many other stroke victims, was a happy victim. Mimi smiled constantly and seemed pleased to be alive. Not bad for her age.

"Let's go to the bathroom, and I'll wash your face."

"Love my shoes," Mimi said, and held up one foot.

Les smiled, recalling her mom saying Mimi had refused to take the shoes off last night. "I'm glad you like them."

Mimi started unbuttoning her blouse.

"It's not bedtime," Les said.

The doorbell chimed and Les went to get it, picking up the bag of oranges her mom said to give to the neighbor who would be by around lunch. Les picked up the bag with a note taped to the top and opened the door. "Big, and good enough to squeeze," Les read the note before looking up. Her heart stuttered.

"Thank you, I think." Joe Lyon grinned.

Les dropped the bag of fruit. "I thought you were—"

"So, I'm not good enough to squeeze?" He tucked his hands into his jeans pockets.

Panic slammed into Les's chest. At first, she didn't exactly understand the feeling, but it quickly became apparent. Something about Joe had changed—something subtle but scary.

"What are you doing here?" she asked.

"Like my new shoes," came Mimi's voice from the living room.

"Just a second," Les said, and ran back to the living room. Mimi sat in front of the TV, one foot extended in front of her. When Les turned back around, Joe was right behind her. And darn if he didn't look good enough to squeeze.

Wow.

He wore a blue sweater, the same color as his eyes, and hanging loose over the sweater was a black jacket. His jeans, faded as if they were his favorite pair, showcased his waist and legs. His dark hair looked a little tousled, as if he'd been running his fingers through it.

Les remembered how attentive he'd been to Katie last night. He'd replaced her window and had had a friend drive with him to retrieve her car. He'd even followed Katie and her to the hotel, where she and Katie had stayed the night.

Good, sweet, handsome Joe. How many times had she heard Katie describe him that way? Katie was an idiot to let him go. How could Katie not feel pizzazz for the man?

"You need something?" Les asked, unable to think straight.

"Yeah. I do." His tone was husky, full of innuendo.

What kind of innuendo? She glanced up. Their eyes met.

"We need to talk," Joe said.

Chapter Twenty-one

Don't tell him about canceling the wedding. Those seven words were Katie's mantra as they walked to the diner. Carl opened the door for her and, when she walked past, she brushed against his arm. The brief touch sent currents of emotion shooting through her. She looked up and his expression told her he'd felt the fireworks, too.

She took off for her regular table. His footsteps echoed behind her and, in her mind, she heard him say *Breathe, Red.* Following the advice, she took a big swallow of oxygen and lowered herself into a chair. He took the seat next to her. His leg brushed hers under the table, sending more emotional currents racing up her thigh and settling in the pit of her abdomen.

She felt him staring at her, so she picked up the menu and studied it as if she didn't already know everything on it, as if she didn't order the same thing every time she visited.

"What's good here?" he asked.

"The salads are good." Remembering their macho conversation, she eyed him over the menu and smiled. "The quiches are great, too. But real men don't eat quiche, do they?"

He chuckled. "I can eat quiche." Their gazes lingered a bit too long. His smile faded. "How are you, Red?"

Don't tell him about canceling the wedding. If she could get through this lunch, then he'd leave, and she'd probably never see him again. And that's what she wanted. Right?

Wrong. But she was a Ray. And Rays didn't do stupid things. They didn't go after things they knew they couldn't have. Failure wasn't an option in the Ray family. And if she went after Carl Hades, she would fail. Fail miserably. He wasn't the forever kind of man.

"I'm fine." She refocused on dressing selections.

"No flashbacks? You're not replaying things in your head?"

The menu almost slipped from her hands. "How did you know?"

He leaned in and she caught his scent. "It's normal. When you see something traumatic, it happens."

She reached down to the mismatched silverware on her cloth napkin. The knife had a rose engraved on the handle and the fork had little daisies. "You must have had that happen a lot when you worked for the police."

"A bit. You may need to see someone. Talk."

She blinked. "Did *you* see someone?"

"The Force made us see a counselor when something happened."

"What did they do for you?" She moved the fork away from the knife, because the two looked too different to be in one setting.

"Not a damn thing." He chuckled. "But they claimed talking about it helped. Mostly, I think it just takes some time."

"Good. Because I don't like the idea of . . . of being someone's lab rat." Rays also didn't go to shrinks.

The waitress came by. Katie ordered her usual: a fried chicken filet over a green salad, and nonfat ranch dressing. She figured one balanced out the other. Carl ordered a sandwich and the quiche.

Katie snickered when the waitress left. "You didn't have to order it."

"I have a point to prove. I can wear"—he looked down at his shirt, frowned—"pink, and I can eat quiche."

She laughed. He stared. She stopped laughing.

"Damn, you're beautiful when you laugh."

She pulled her napkin from the table and placed it in her lap. The silence seemed heavy, and she studied the silverware so she didn't have to look at him.

"Something wrong with your fork?" he asked.

She looked up. "They don't match."

"Do they have to?" He glanced at his own silverware.

"It doesn't matter. I just noticed, is all."

"Are you a perfectionist, Katie Ray?"

That comment won him what Les famously called Katie's eye roll. "Not about silverware. At home I use plastic forks and eat out of paper plates because I forget to run the dishwasher. When you live alone you . . ." She hesitated. *Alone hurt. Alone sucked.*

The silence seemed to rain down on them again. "Tell me more," he said.

"More?" She picked up the iced tea the waitress had left her.

"More about yourself."

Don't tell him about canceling the wedding.

But, oh goodness, she wanted to tell him. Tell him that she wasn't engaged anymore, to let him know that if he was interested in her then she was interested in him. But that couldn't happen. He was a playboy; she was a girl who wanted to get married so badly she'd almost married someone she loved like a brother. A man so much like her brother that—

That thought brought her back to Les and Joe. Was that why Les liked Joe? Because he was so much like Mike?

She remembered Carl's question. "I'm just me."

"And what does *me* do for fun?"

She almost said paint. But she didn't paint anymore. "I watch TV, go to see chick flicks, read. Oh, I volunteer at the hospital once a month."

"Hospital?" He sipped his tea. "What do you do there?"

"I rock premature and sick babies."

His eyes widened. "Rock babies?"

"The nurses don't have time to do it. So they get people to volunteer. It's easy. And it kind of makes me feel good."

"Sounds like a worthy cause." He let out a deep breath. "Sounds like what I expected you to do."

"What do you mean by that?"

"Just that you are the rocking-babies kind of girl."

The waitress brought their food. And the conversation turned to the quiche as Carl forked a big mouthful into his lips.

"See, I can eat quiche." He polished off every last bite. Then he asked, "So, what do you watch on TV?"

She leaned back in her chair. "A little of everything."

"Like?" He picked up his sandwich.

"Reruns of *Sex and the City*. *Law & Order*. And . . ." She grinned, realizing her eclectic taste. "And *Brady Bunch* reruns."

He chuckled. "Now, there's a mix."

"What about you?" She forked a piece of chicken and lettuce. The fork had daisies and, oddly, it still bothered her.

"Reruns mostly, just like you. *Law & Order*. *Fear Factor*. Oh, and *Two and a Half Men*."

"I could have guessed." She grinned. "Favorite movie?"

He took a drink of his tea and thought about it. "I have several. *Die Hard*. *Alien*. And I laughed my a . . . butt off at *40-Year-Old Virgin*."

"It was funny," she admitted. "Joe and I rented the video."

"Really?" He set his sandwich down. She didn't miss his expression.

Don't tell him about canceling the wedding.

The silence held. "What're your hobbies?" she asked.

"I jog for exercise. And do PI work."

"What kind of PI cases do you get?" She took a bite.

He grinned. "Not always the ones I'd like to get."

"You get a lot of cheating spouses cases?" she asked.

He nodded. "Last Saturday I got shot at by a man wearing a black thong and a pink nightie."

Katie laughed. "What did you do to make him shoot at you?"

Carl grinned. "He caught me taking his picture while he was entertaining some other freak he'd met on the Internet." Carl held up one hand. "Which I justified doing because his wife needed to prove to the judge that the husband wasn't the father of the year he was claiming to be."

"And because she paid you," she said.

"Yeah. There's that reason, too." He rolled his shoulder and reached back to rub it. "Actually, I've had a few good cases. I caught a pedophile a couple months ago. And I'm getting more and more corporate security–type jobs."

"You like doing this more than being a cop?" she asked, remembering he'd never told her why he'd quit the police force. She almost asked, but realized the less she knew about him the better. Today's lunch was it. Good-bye.

"There are things I miss about carrying a badge, but overall, yeah, I like working for myself."

The waitress came and took their plates and left the check. Katie tried to pay, but Carl refused to let her.

"Thanks for lunch." She glanced at her watch. "I should . . . be getting back."

He looked at her as if he knew this was good-bye, too.

Don't tell him about canceling the wedding.

Standing, Katie glanced back at the silverware still on the table. Like the fork and knife, she and Carl didn't match. Didn't belong together.

They left the diner, silently walking to the entrance of the gallery. *Don't tell him about canceling the wedding.* She turned to say good-bye.

"I . . ." She swallowed. "I guess this is good-bye."

He reached out and touched a strand of her hair that had escaped the ponytail. "Do you really want it to be good-bye, Red?"

Les forced herself to met Joe's eyes. "What do you need to talk to me about?"

"Time to go to bed," Mimi called out.

Les swung around. Mimi was removing her blouse.

Les looked back at Joe. "I need to get her down for a nap."

"No problem," he said.

She breathed a sigh of relief and motioned toward the door. He didn't move.

"I'll wait right here."

Les blinked. Behind her she heard Mimi shifting. Probably half-undressed. "Fine." She swung around and closed Mimi's blouse and helped her to the bedroom.

Five minutes later, Les walked back into the living room to find Joe sitting on the sofa. For some crazy reason, she didn't want to sit beside him.

"I need a soda. Want anything?" She headed for the kitchen.

Joe followed her. "A Coke would be nice."

Les headed straight for the fridge and pulled out one diet drink and one regular. For some reason, she didn't think Joe would drink diet. Mike hadn't.

He took the Coke from her. Their hands touched briefly, and she almost jerked back.

"Was that your grandmother?" he asked.

Les nodded. "Yeah."

"What is it? Alzheimer's?"

Les held the cold soda can close. "Stroke."

"I'm sorry. It must be hard."

"I'm sure it is on my mom. But Mimi seems happy."

His gaze moved around. "Is this the house you grew up in?"

"Yeah." Nervous, she asked, "What is it you need, Joe?"

He hesitated as if he was searching for a topic. "I told Katie about the shower."

Les felt the blood run from her face. "Why?"

"It was the right thing to do."

Okay, Les had known she'd have to tell Katie, but . . .

Joe's gaze went to the table—no, not the table, but the photo album opened to an eight-by-ten of her and Mike. Before she could react, he'd moved over to get a closer look. "You and Katie's brother?" He sat down.

Air, still flavored from this morning's bacon, hitched in Les's lungs. She wanted to grab the album away, but she knew how silly that would look. "Yes." She walked over and dropped into a chair.

He turned the page and studied the pictures, images that had made up her and Mike's life together. Les gritted her teeth.

"You two looked happy." He turned another page.

"We were." And that's all she could take. She reached over and closed the album. "Sorry," she said. "It's just—"

"You don't have to explain." The kitchen became so quiet the refrigerator's motor sounded loud. He finally spoke. "Did Katie say anything to you about our talk?"

"I know the wedding is off."

He inhaled. "I told her the truth, Les."

"You mean about the shower?" She studied him.

"That . . . and the fact that I've got a thing for you."

Carl waited for Katie to answer him. She didn't. Instead, she turned to the door.

"Wait," he said. "I have something for you. It's in my car," he added when she turned back. "Sort of . . . a gift."

"A gift?" She looked panicked at the idea.

"It's not much." He met her eyes again. She's an engaged woman, he reminded himself. He walked to his car parked a few feet away and pulled out the manila-wrapped package.

A drop of rain fell as he made his way back to her. She opened the door to the gallery and held it open for him. They ducked inside.

The Latina who'd greeted him the first time popped her head out of a room from the back.

"It's just me." Katie set her purse behind the register.

Carl followed her and handed her his gift. "It's not much."

She placed the gift on the counter. With a lot more care than he'd taken wrapping the dang thing, she removed the paper.

She stared at it. When she looked up, he felt foolish. Foolish for giving it to her. "It's the elephant painting. The one I told you about."

She smiled, and again his gut ached from wanting things he couldn't have. *She's an engaged woman.* And even if she weren't, Katie Ray wasn't . . . she wasn't his type.

He felt the need to explain. "I'm not saying it's any good. Hell, I wouldn't know good art if it came up and bit my . . . I just thought maybe it would remind you that if an elephant can do this, then so can you."

Her eyes widened. She looked down at the painting and when she raised her head back up, she had tears in her eyes. One of those tears rolled down her cheek. Carl had no idea what he'd done to make her cry.

She brushed a tear away. "I canceled the wedding."

"Oh, gawd!" Les dropped her forehead on the table and gave one good thud. She counted to ten before she raised her head. "Why in all of hell's glory did you tell Katie that?"

He raked a hand through his hair. "We both agreed we needed to tell her."

"I agreed to tell about the shower. I didn't, *did not*, agree to tell her that we were attracted to each other."

"I didn't mean to tell—" Joe stopped talking. His eyebrow arched up. "We? You said 'we.' *We* are attracted to each other."

"No!" she lied. Out-and-out lied. But no way in hell would she admit it.

"You're attracted to me?" he asked. "I thought so."

She dropped her head back on the table.

Joe's laugh a second later had her raising her head.

"How can you laugh about this? It's not funny."

His smile faded. "I know."

"No, you don't know. Katie's my best friend and this is so fucking wrong!"

He leaned forward. "It's not our fault."

"And you think that makes a difference?" she asked.

His Adam's apple went up and down. "Actually, it does make me feel better. Especially now that the wedding is off."

"Well, I'm just thrilled you feel better, but I have news for you. It doesn't make it right."

He turned the soda can in his hands. "It's not as if Katie and I broke up because of this. We both agreed we were wrong—"

"Wrong. Now there's a word for you. As in *this*—this you-and-I thing—is wrong." She shook her head. "Wrong."

"Why? Why is it so wrong?"

"Why? Are you *dense*?"

"No." He frowned. "However, I have had a bad, very bad day, and my brain might not be functioning at normal level. So why don't you explain it to me."

"You were engaged to my best friend. Does that ring a bell?"

He leaned back. "So, because I was involved with Katie, you can't be involved with me?"

"You're finally catching on." She popped up from the chair and went to toss her drink in the garbage.

From behind, she heard him. "You don't lie worth a shit."

She swung around. Joe had the photo album in his hands again.

"It isn't about Katie. *This* is why you won't get involved with me."

Carl stared at Red, and her words bounced around his skull. *"I canceled the wedding."*

"Why?" Oh, hell, did he even care why? She wasn't engaged anymore. The air suddenly tasted sweeter.

"Because you were right," she answered.

"Right about what?" He stared at her.

"About the reasons I was getting married. About me flushing my ring. I don't love Joe. No, I *do* love Joe, but I love Joe like I love Mike."

"Who's Mike?" he asked.

"He is . . . was my brother." She gripped her hands together. "He was in the car accident."

"You lost your brother in the accident, too? Damn!"

She nodded. "Yeah. Damn."

He felt guilty for standing there feeling overjoyed while talking to her about her deceased family. And that's when it hit. His world shifted again and he remembered his own grieving experience. His mother. Amy. Right then all the reasons he'd stayed away from women like Katie came rushing back. Reasons that had nothing to do with her being engaged or free. Letting himself get close to Katie Ray could only end in some serious hurt.

She continued talking. "I don't know how you feel about me, but . . ." Her tongue came out to swipe across her bottom lip.

He pressed a finger to her mouth. Desire shot through him so quick, so fast, his breath lodged in his lungs. Whatever it cost him later, the pleasure he would experience now would be worth it. He moved his hand from her lips to touch a strand of hair hanging down beside her ear. *Soft. Silky.*

"I think you know how I feel, Red."

She smiled that sweet, innocent smile of hers. And that's when it hit him again. He might be willing to pay the price, but was she? Was she expecting more than he could offer?

"Are you sure you want to pursue this?" he asked. "Think about it. You rock babies. You watch *The Brady Bunch*." She was so out of his league. Just the type he avoided.

"What do you mean?" she asked.

He had to be honest. She had to know what she was getting into if she pursued their attraction. Letting out a deep sigh, trying not to watch her tongue make another pass over her lips, he forced himself to say it. "I want you. I want all of you. But I don't plan to be *The Brady Bunch*. I've never even watched the damn show."

She blinked, and he could see her mind working—as if asking herself if she could play by his rules.

He ran his finger over her lips again. "I don't make promises I don't plan to keep. I don't even pretend to make them. But please make my day, Red. Tell me you're interested in what I can offer. Tell me that today, now, will be enough."

Joe let Les take the photo album from him. "I think you should leave," she said.

He stood up, made it almost to the kitchen door before he thought, *What the hell.* He swung around. "And will that solve anything, Les? If I walk out of here, are you going to stop feeling so damn guilty?"

"I don't feel guilty." Her green eyes shot fire at him.

"Bull. It's all over your face. You don't want to feel anything for me because in some insane way, feeling something for me means what you felt for Katie's brother didn't mean anything."

Her chin snapped up. And all Joe could think about was how sexy she was when she got mad.

"Jeezus! When did you get your shrink license, Mr. Lyon?"

"I don't need a license, Les. I saw you naked. Naked except for a dead man's engagement ring around your neck."

She closed her eyes. "Please go."

"You think I haven't noticed that every time I get close to you, you reach up for that damn ring? I'm not blind."

Her eyes opened, angrier now than when she'd shut them. "Maybe I'm still connected to Mike. But even if I wasn't, I couldn't do this. Do you know how awkward it would be?"

"We could deal with awkward. Awkward would fade."

She shook her head. Her blonde wispy hair shimmered around her shoulders and his fingers itched to touch it. To touch her. To know every inch of her body. He wanted to chase away the pain she felt at having lost Katie's brother. He wanted to see her smiling at him the way she'd been smiling at the man in those pictures.

She reached for her ring; then as if she realized what she was doing, she stopped. "I would rather die than hurt Katie."

He gripped his hand to keep from reaching out to her. "Katie and I are over. How would it hurt her? I'll bet if you asked Katie—"

"Oh, please! Katie would never admit to being hurt about anything if there's a chance that it would hurt someone else." She stormed across the room. "Katie gives up a Saturday a month to rock babies. She'd sacrifice her own happiness for anyone she loves. She wanted to be an artist all her fucking life, and what happens? Her parents tell her it doesn't make them happy, and poof, suddenly, Katie stops painting."

"And that was wrong?" Joe baited her.

"Of course it's wrong."

"Then how is this between us any different, Les?

You're refusing to explore something that we should explore because you're afraid of hurting Katie."

"You're twisting this all around," she snapped.

"I'm not twisting anything. What if you and I were meant to be together? What if we miss out on something because—"

A banging noise came from the other room. Les did a complete mental shift. She remembered Mimi and took off.

No Mimi in the living room. Then the noise came again. Les swung around and watched as the wind caught the open door and banged it against the wall. And there, there beside the open door, was Mimi's sweater. "No, no, no."

"What's wrong?" Joe asked.

Les didn't answer; she took off in a dead run down the hall to Mimi's bedroom and prayed, prayed with everything she had, that Mimi was still in bed.

No Grandma.

"No!" Then she flew back out the hall and ran outside. Her gaze zipped left and right. Her heart pounded. "Mimi?" Tears clouded Les's vision when there wasn't a wrinkled, smiling old lady wearing pink shoes anywhere in sight.

Joe came up behind her. "Make sure she's not in the house. Then we'll drive around. She can't have gotten too far."

Panic swirled in Les's head. "I should call the police."

"We'll call on my cell. But first, check the house."

Carl stared at Red while indecision played across her face. "I want this," she whispered.

Music to his ears. His heart commenced beating again. That's all he needed. The green light. The taste of victory lay sweet on his tongue. But he longed to taste her instead. How long before he had her naked in his arms—in his bed. Would she come with him now?

"But . . ." She reached up and toyed with his shirt collar. "You're right. It would be a mistake."

"I didn't say it would be a mistake."

Her smile broke his heart. "No, you didn't. I guess I came to that conclusion all by myself."

And he had to respect that. He did. He told himself to go, but instead he leaned down and did the one thing he had to do before he walked away. One taste. That's all he wanted.

He kissed her.

He meant it to be a quick kiss, just enough so when he dreamed of her, he'd know her taste. But quick got lost when she melted against him like warm butter, when her mouth opened and invited his tongue to explore. Quick didn't exist when her sweet body burrowed even closer.

Close enough that he felt her tight nipples against his chest, close enough that the throbbing ache between his legs was cradled against her abdomen.

But not close enough.

He dropped his hand to the curve of her ass. Wanting to touch skin, he caught the material of her skirt and raised it.

His fingers brushed against her silk panties, but he wanted what lay softer beneath her underwear. He found the elastic band of her panties where her bottom met the back of her thigh. He slipped his fingers inside. Her bare ass was so soft, so—

"Ah, *Dios*!" The voice was like a knee to the balls.

Carl jumped back so fast Katie nearly fell. He caught her by her forearm while she yanked her skirt down.

"Pretend I was never here." The Latina took off.

He looked back at Katie, embarrassment flaming on her cheeks. She brushed his hand from her arm and took a step back.

That small step said it all. Nothing had changed. The kiss, the hottest damn kiss he'd ever experienced, hadn't made a difference in her decision. He turned to leave. To walk away.

"Carl?"

Her voice stopped him. He swung around. Hope built in his chest so fast his lungs ached. "Come home with me, Red."

Katie shook her head. "I can't. I just wanted to say . . . thank you. For the painting. I'll cherish it. More than you'll ever know."

He nodded. Then, before he embarrassed himself by begging, before he pulled her back into his arms and made love to her right there in the middle of the fucking gallery, in the middle of fucking daylight, before he made that big fucking mistake, he walked away.

Chapter Twenty-two

Les talked to the police while Joe drove; her gaze zipped from one side of the street to the other. Panic bit into her chest and hung there. Before they'd left, she'd run to her mom's neighbor and got her to stay at the house just in case Mimi came back or someone called.

"She couldn't have been gone more than twenty minutes," she told the police. "I thought she was taking a nap."

"We'll have someone out looking in the area," the officer said.

Les folded the phone closed and bit down on her lip until she tasted blood. How could she have done this? How could she have let it happen?

Fear hit her again. Fear that Mimi was hurt, or worse. A moan leaked from her lips.

Joe reached over and took her hand. "We'll find her."

Les's first instinct was to jerk away, to blame him, but she couldn't do it. She'd been the one in charge. She'd been the one on Mimi duty and had failed.

Joe turned around and started down another street. Then he slammed on his brakes. "I saw her!"

"Where?"

"Down that side street."

Les reached for the door.

"No, let me turn around."

"Thank you, God!" Les bounced around in her seat, wanting, needing to see Mimi herself, to know she was okay.

Joe made the turn and pulled up to the curb, and Les saw her. Her heart gave a jolt. Les jumped out of the car and ran over to where another lady sat in her car talking to her grandma. Her very naked grandma. Les didn't care that her grandma was naked, didn't care that other cars were pulling off to the side and honking their horns. She ran over and pulled Mimi into a hug. "Are you okay?"

Suddenly, Joe was there stripping off his coat. "Let's put this on," he told Mimi in a calm voice that didn't match the situation.

Mimi smiled at him. "Like my new shoes," she said.

"Yes," Joe said. "They are very pretty."

Les turned to the lady who was obviously trying to help before they showed up. "Thank you," she said.

"I'm assuming she belongs to you." The lady smiled.

"Yes." Les brushed the tears from her face.

When she turned back to Joe and Mimi, she saw he had yanked off his sweater and, with the care one would take with a baby, he carefully tied it around Mimi's waist to cover her bottom half.

"Let's get her in the car," he said, and took Mimi's hand.

"Yes." Les bit down on her lip and started for the car. "Do you think we should take her to the hospital? Just to make sure she's okay?"

Joe looked back at Mimi. "She looks fine, but I'll be more than happy to drive you there."

Les gave her grandma another once-over. "Are you okay, Mimi?" Mimi just smiled.

Les looked back at Joe. "Let's take her back to the house. Mom should be home soon, and I'll see if she thinks we should take her in." As she took another step, she saw her grandmother's clothes on the side of the road, and she went to grab them.

Rising up, Les watched as a naked-from-the-waist-up Joe helped her grandma, covered with a man's coat and sweater, get into his car. Her heart did a strange wiggle. In her mind, she heard Katie saying, *The first time I met Joe, I thought, "Wow, Les would totally love this man."*

Katie had been right.

Fighting that crazy thought, Les hurried to his car.

After several deep breaths, Katie stepped into Lola's office. "I'm sorry, that was so unprofessional." *So un-Ray-like.*

Lola grinned. "This isn't a church, *chica.*"

"It's not a motel, either." Katie dropped into the chair across from Lola's desk. Her tears threatened to fall.

"Art inspires passion. Too bad he's married," Lola said.

A wave of shame ran through Katie. "He's not married. I thought it was his brother when I said that."

Lola raised her hand, her bracelets jingling. "Then why stop?"

"Because he's not right for me."

Laughter twinkled in her boss's dark eyes. "From what I saw, he looked pretty right for you."

"He's a playboy."

Lola leaned in. "Then play with him."

Katie's words came from the heart: "I wish I was made like that. But I'm not. It has to mean something, or I just can't give myself to it." But she almost had, hadn't she?

"Then tame the playboy. Make it mean something."

Katie cut Lola a doubtful look. "Did he look tamable to you?"

Lola chuckled and raised a dark brow. "You have a point."

Pulling at her hair, Katie frowned. "I hate to ask this, but . . . would it be too much if I left for the day?"

Lola looked at her. "You should have never come to

work today with everything that happened. Go. And take tomorrow, too."

Katie started to argue—Rays didn't skip out on work—then she decided maybe this Ray deserved it. Just once. "Thank you."

Carl drove two blocks away and pulled into a parking lot. He sat in his car, counted to fifty, and waited for the ache in his chest and in his dick to fade. Not even as a randy teen had he wanted a woman this bad. But holy hell, he had to get past this. Get past her.

But, wait. It wasn't just her. It was the damn fact that he hadn't allowed himself to be with a woman for almost a year.

He snatched his cell phone from his coat pocket. This problem could be fixed. He tried to remember Peggy's last name. "Peggy Little." Peggy was safe. Divorced, two kids. She'd ruled out marriage, ruled out full-time relationships, but loved occasional sex. Why hadn't he called her already?

He couldn't remember her number. He could dial information. She was listed. One call, and he'd have her number. One call to her and he was as good as laid. Peggy liked sex. Peggy loved hot sex. He was two calls away from being laid. So why the hell wasn't he dialing?

His phone rang. He stared at the caller ID. *Ben.* Snapping open the phone, he asked, "You got those background checks yet?"

Ben ignored the question. "How'd your date go?" Their dad must have blabbed.

"None of your damned business."

"What crawled up your ass and put you in such a good mood?"

"You did. What's this crap about you giving Dad your blessing to get hitched?"

"Why wouldn't I? Jessie's great."

Carl gripped the phone. "He's in his sixties."

"Give it up, Carl. Dad deserves to be happy. Mom's been dead for sixteen years. And he did nothing the first eight but raise us. He loves Jessie and deserves to be happy."

Carl frowned and gave up trying to reason with unreasonable people. "Have you got information on the list of names?"

"That's why I'm calling."

"Anything interesting?" Carl shifted.

"Yeah," Ben said. "Problem is that none of them is lily white. Mel Grimes, the photographer . . . he had a problem with prescription drugs a few years back. Jack Edwards, our florist, he has a thing about beating up girlfriends. Todd Sweet did seven years for robbing a . . . of all things, a bakery. His real name isn't Sweet. And Will Reed—this one is interesting. No trouble in the last five years, but earlier, he had a weakness for setting fires."

"And where there's smoke, there's fire," Carl said, remembering how close he and Red had been to being toast.

"Could be," Ben said. A pause lingered. "Dad said you were paying these guys a visit today. Don't go messing with my case."

"I'm telling them I'm getting married. Just feeling them out for vibes."

"Well, guys like this don't like their vibes checked. I really wish you'd leave this to us," Ben said.

"I used to be one of the 'us,' remember? I can take care of myself."

"And you got the scars to prove it, too," Ben said.

"You're just jealous that I've been shot and you haven't."

"Yeah. That's what I want, to catch a bullet so I can prove I'm a real man." Ben sighed. "You said you heard this guy's voice. Do you think you could recognize it?"

"I've thought about that. But he said three words to

me. I've spoken to a couple of the suspects on the phone and didn't get anything. But who knows, maybe I'll get lucky in person."

"Lucky?" Ben paused. "You're a pain in my ass, but my kid and wife love you. Don't rely on luck. Be careful."

Katie got in her car and just sat there. She had originally planned to go to the hotel she and Les stayed at last night, to crawl under the covers and have herself a pity cry. And it was such a pity, too. She couldn't ever remember feeling . . . so turned on. Oh, she'd heard people talk about being desperate with desire, lost with lust, hot to trot, but honestly, she'd just thought they'd been exaggerating.

Sure, she enjoyed sex. Not so much with Joe, but before Joe. She'd even had one or two experiences she considered great. But she'd never, ever, been so caught up in one kiss that she'd let a man pull up her skirt and stick his hands in her panties in the middle of the day, in the middle of a public place, with her boss less than ten feet away.

Rays didn't do that.

But Rays didn't crater, either. So she picked herself up by the heels of her Nine West shoes and made a new plan. No hiding under the covers. She had a wedding to cancel and deposit checks to get back.

Talking about money was something she could control. Unlike the bizarre got-you-by-the-throat sexual attraction she'd felt earlier with Carl. That was not controllable. Besides, staying busy kept her from cratering.

She could do it on the phone, but face-to-face contact upped her chances of getting her money back. Not that she would be in financial woes if she didn't, but Rays were money wise and this was the wise thing to do. Especially after deciding to pay Joe back for the engagement ring she'd flushed down the john.

So she pulled out her wedding book where she kept

everyone's info and headed first to see Todd Sweet, the cake baker.

Carl stood on the porch. Mel Grimes, the photographer, opened the door on the third knock. He looked half-asleep. Carl recalled the information about the man having had a prescription drug problem. His green eyes were bloodshot. He wore navy Dockers and a white shirt, but the clothes looked crumpled, as if he'd slept in them.

"Can I help you?" Good ol' Mel didn't look happy.

But neither was Carl. "I'm Carl Hades. We had an appointment at ten and you weren't here."

Grimes frowned. "I thought that appointment was tomorrow."

"Not according to my notes." Carl pulled out his pad.

Grimes stepped back. "Come in. I'll give you one of my portfolios." He motioned Carl into the office right off the entryway. Hanging on the walls were all sorts of photography—family portraits, some wildlife shots, a couple of artsy shots of trees, even a couple of nudes. None were of brides.

"Looks as if you'll shoot anything." *Pun intended.*

Grimes settled behind a desk and pulled open a file cabinet. "I photograph what catches my eye."

"And brides catch your eye?" Carl studied his reaction.

"Not really, but I have to make a living." Grimes grinned. "Not that I'm not good at shooting weddings." He pulled out a folder and pushed it over toward Carl. "Here are some samples of my wedding shots. My prices are listed in the back. Take it with you. Show it to your fiancée."

Carl listened to the man speak and tried to remember the man's voice at Ms. Jones's house. No bells were ringing, but who could tell.

"I will." *His fiancée.* Why did a vision of Red fill his head? He gazed at the nude of a brunette. Peggy, the single mom who liked sex, was a brunette. He could call her when he left. Set up a date, get Red out of his system.

"I sell prints, if you're interested," Grimes said, as if noting Carl's lingering gaze. "I had a show last year." Grimes went on for about five minutes talking about his photography. In spite of Carl's initial reaction, Grimes was coming off normal enough.

Flipping open the folder, Carl studied the images. Normal wedding shots. "Can we come back and talk to you later?"

"Sure." Grimes stood up as if eager to get rid of him.

Carl stood. Grimes followed him to the door.

"Aren't you the one who left a card? You're a PI, right?"

"That's me." Carl cut him another look, trying to read him.

"If you ever need to hire a photographer to get images of people doing what people shouldn't be doing, I'd be interested." Grimes grinned.

"I generally do my own. But I'll remember you," Carl said.

"Do that, and call me if your girl likes my work."

Carl got in his car. Resting his folder on the steering wheel, he jotted down some notes. *First impression, not so good. Second impression . . . normal guy.*

Carl always trusted his first impression.

Les sat at the doctor's office between her mom and Mimi. Her mom flipped through a magazine. Mimi pulled at the loose strings on her sweater. Les clutched her hands.

"I'm so sorry, Mom," Les blurted.

Mom put down the magazine. "I've already told you, it's not your fault. And I'm sure she's fine. Look at her, we're only here to be on the safe side."

"I know, but I can't believe I let it happen."

Her mom reached over Les and stopped Mimi from pulling a hole in her sweater. Then she looked to Les.

"Sweetie, she got away from me about three weeks ago. Luckily, she'd only gotten as far as Mr. Gomez's house. But"—she smiled—"he had a rude awakening walking into his kitchen and finding your grandma sitting naked at his table."

Les grinned, then sighed. "How do you do this every-day?"

Mom frowned. "It's not easy, but sometimes life doesn't offer us choices." Her smile returned. "Let's forget worrying about that and tell me about this friend of Katie's who helped you with Mimi. Is he in Katie's wedding? Is he . . . cute?"

Les hesitated, trying to think how to explain it to her mom.

"Oh, I forgot," Mom said. "You got a call from someone who needed to talk to Katie about the wedding. He said he got your number from Katie's file. He tried to reach her at her house. I told him you two girls were staying at the hotel for a mental vacation." She picked up a new magazine.

Les remembered the cop's warning. "Who was it?"

"I'm not sure, but it was someone about the wedding."

"Did you tell him what hotel?"

"No, but I gave him the hotel's number. Why?"

"Nothing." Les looked at her watch and decided to call Katie and tell her about the call before she got off work.

Ten minutes later, and with a half hour to kill before his appointment with the DJ, Carl drove back to try the florist again. He spotted a man loading flowers in his car. Hoping it was Edwards, Carl walked over.

"Mr. Edwards?"

The man didn't turn around, but he answered, "Yeah?"

Pay dirt. "I'm Carl Hades. I've been calling you."

He still didn't turn around. "And I think my assistant offered to help you, too."

"I like to talk to the person I'm hiring."

"Sarah does the weddings." The man, early forties, wearing a shirt advertising his florist shop, finally turned around.

"But you're the . . . owner." Carl noticed the scratches down his neck, not quite as obvious as his own, but they appeared to have come from the same animal: a woman. An angry or scared woman. Maybe one about to be shot?

"Something wrong?" Mr. Edwards asked.

"Just that we both seem to have gotten into a little cat-fight, if you know what I mean." Carl touched his own scratches.

"Yeah." Edwards swung back around and put another vase of flowers in a box in the backseat of his SUV.

Carl made a mental note to ask Ben if CSI had recovered any skin from under Tabitha's fingernails. "Can you give me a few minutes to discuss prices for a wedding?"

"Sarah will be happy to help you with that. I've turned all my weddings over to her. I've dealt with my last bride."

Carl decided to go one more step. "But Tabitha Jones recommended *you*, not Sarah."

Edwards turned around. "Was Tabitha Jones your planner?"

"Yes."

"Well, you'd better go looking for someone else."

Carl played it dumb. "Why?"

"She was murdered. It was on the news last night."

"Really? Do they know who did it?"

"The news didn't say." He showed no sign of remorse for Tabitha's demise. "Consider yourself lucky," he said.

"You didn't think she was good at what she did?"

The man picked up another vase of flowers and turned away. "Sometimes people get what they deserve."

"She deserved to be murdered?" Carl's tone became more official, coplike.

Edwards cut him a quick glance as if recognizing the change. "Look, talk to Sarah. Or don't. It's up to you. But

I don't have time to chitchat." He got in his SUV and drove off.

"I think I will talk to her," Carl muttered, mentally putting Mr. Edwards on the top of the suspect list.

Glancing at his watch, Carl decided he'd have to come back and visit Sarah later. He got in his own car to head to the DJ, but before he drove off, his phone rang. He checked to see the incoming number.

"Hey, Dad. Mr. Johnson being a bad boy again?"

"Not yet. I took the dog in. Sad story. They said she had three weeks to get a home. Then she's history."

Carl frowned. "She'll find a home. She's a purebred."

"Nope. They said purebreds were harder to place because people assume there's something wrong with them. Especially with her pregnant."

"Pregnant? How the hell can she be pregnant so damn fast?"

"Didn't we have that talk when you were thirteen?"

"Funny. I meant, how could they know she was pregnant?"

"She probably has that glow about her. Anyway, there's no need to worry about her being pregnant. They're going to abort the babies. Can't have no mix breeds."

"You had to find the worst shelter to leave her at." Carl rubbed his shoulder, and he knew he was going to regret this. "Fuck it. Go back and get her."

"I'm glad you feel that way. 'Cause when she tried to follow me out, I took her back to your place." Buck cleared his throat. "Here comes Mr. Johnson, I gotta go." Then he hung up.

Carl slung his phone down. He'd bet a hundred bucks his dad never took Baby anywhere. Then, remembering his conversation with Mr. Edwards, he dialed his brother's cell.

Todd Sweet wasn't in. So Katie drove to the home office of Will Reed, the DJ. She knocked. Before anyone answered,

Katie heard the music playing inside. The music reminded her of . . . what? Oh yeah, the strange phone calls she'd gotten.

The door opened and a thirtyish, dark-haired man stood in front of her. Katie extended her hand. "Mr. Reed? I'm Katie Ray. We've spoken on the phone and I e-mailed you. It's about—"

He took her hand in his. "Your wedding?" He smiled. "Why is it the most beautiful ones are always getting married?"

She released his hand and noticed his gaze shifted to her scoop-necked blouse. Fidgeting with her purse, she fought the urge to adjust her neckline. While the look Carl had given her earlier had been ten times more suggestive, this man's attention struck a nerve. Carl—well, he struck different nerves. Good nerves. The music changed tunes.

"I tried to call you today," he said. "Left a message."

"You did?" Katie asked.

"Yes. Tabitha e-mailed that you'd decided to go with someone else. I wanted to check, since I'd already gotten a deposit."

"Actually, that's what I've come to discuss," Katie said, trying not to react to the mention of Tabitha's name.

"Come on in." Mr. Reed stepped back. "I'm just cutting another music video for one of my brides."

"He has scratches," Carl told Ben. "I got a sense of bad blood between them." Carl frowned when his brother's laugh came through the line. "What?"

"It's just funny that you'd point out his scratches, considering your own face." He sighed. "But if it makes you feel better, I had Mr. Edwards in this morning. We're looking at him. However, he came in voluntarily."

Carl turned onto Mr. Reed's street. "Look hard at him."

"Where are you at now?" Ben asked.

"On my way to see the DJ."

"Then I must be right behind you."

"I don't need big brother taking care of me, you know?"

"I never said you did. My schedule cleared up and I decided to check a few of these people out today."

"Right." Carl didn't buy it. He almost got pissed, then realized that if he knew Ben was out interviewing a suspected serial killer, he'd want to watch his back, too. "Let me visit him first, you show up later."

"I'll park up the street, but don't take too long, I need to see if CSI has anything back on Tabitha's body. Plus, some patrols just brought in Sweet, our cake maker, for questioning."

"He came in willingly, too?" Carl asked.

"Not really. But his license sticker was expired."

"Convenient," Carl said.

"Not for him. Anyway, I'd like to get back there before they let him go." Ben paused. "Didn't you say you visited the photographer? What was your take on him?"

Carl parked in front of Reed's house. "At first he . . ." His gaze slammed into the car in the driveway. "Fuck." His gut clutched. "What is Red's license plate number?"

"I have it in my files, but not on me. Why?"

"There's a car here like hers. I gotta go!"

"Wait on me!" Ben said. "I'm two minutes behind you."

"Can't." Carl traded his phone for his gun.

He darted to the Honda, hoping to see something that would tell him he was wrong—a pack of Pampers, a messy interior—anything that told him that this wasn't Katie's car. Instead, his gaze lit on the passenger seat. Or rather what was sitting on it. The elephant painting.

Chapter Twenty-three

Images of Red flashed in Carl's mind. Her smile. The way that strand of red hair kept falling against her cheek during lunch. Then his mind flipped to the images Ben had described of the mutilated corpses they'd pulled out of the woods.

"Damn!" Adrenaline shot through him and he bolted to the porch. His mind searched for the right approach. He reached to knock. Images of a knife being held at Red's throat rained down on him. His hand went to the knob, twisted. The door was unlocked. An invitation.

He stood on the porch for a second, listening. Music. Churchy music. But no voices.

With his foot, he inched open the door. Listened harder. Nothing but music. He slipped inside, his gaze moving left. Right. Why was Red here? She wasn't using this DJ service.

The entryway dumped him into a living room. Voices mingled with the music. He followed the voices.

He heard sirens outside, growing nearer. His brother.

Gun held out, Carl moved down the hall. A man stepped out of a door. "Freeze!" Carl growled.

The man bounced back against the wall. "What the fuck?"

"Red?" Carl called.

A squeak, as if someone rose from a chair that needed a good oiling, sounded from the other room. Katie Ray appeared at the door—alive, unharmed, perfect. Her blue eyes rounded when she saw the gun pointing at Mr. Reed.

"Police!" Ben's voice rang out. "Drop your weapons!"

"In here," Carl yelled.

Ben turned the corner, his gaze zipping from one person to the other. "What happened?"

"I'd like to know that myself," Reed stated.

Carl's attention zipped back to Red. "Are you okay?"

His brother spoke up. "Did Mr. Reed threaten you in any way, Miss Ray?"

"No," she managed to say.

Carl left Ben to talk to Mr. Reed, and he motioned for Red to follow him. He got her outside before he let go of the burning question. "What the hell are you doing here?"

She stiffened. "I . . . What are *you* doing here?"

"Answer me." He rolled his shoulder; the tension had his muscles in knots.

She blinked those blue eyes at him. "I came to see if I could get my deposit back."

"Deposit? Tabitha's files showed you used a different DJ."

"Not originally," Red said. "I'd hired Will Reed. Tabitha went crazy and changed everything that last day."

"Everything?" He gave his left shoulder another squeeze. "Who else were you working with?" When she didn't answer, he started ticking off names. "Jack Edwards with The Red Rose?"

She nodded.

Damn. "Todd Sweet?"

She nodded.

Double damn. "Grimes Photography?"

She nodded again. "Why is that important?"

"Fuck!" he said.

"Is this really f-word worthy?" she snapped.

"Yeah. It really is."

Ben walked up, a frown so deeply grooved in his face it looked permanent. "He's agreed to forget this whole thing happened. But you'd better God damn pray that this guy isn't our man, because I can guarantee you that if he is, this will come back and bite us in the ass."

"Oh, God!" Red said. "Do you think he killed Tabitha?"

Ben looked at Carl. "I thought you said she wasn't working with any of our names?"

"Ms. Jones changed things, but she was originally with them all."

"What's going on?" Red insisted.

Ben frowned and looked at Red, then back to Carl. "You'd better tell her."

"*Somebody* tell me," Red insisted.

Carl held up his hand. "Follow me to the Starbucks on the corner, and we'll talk."

She didn't look happy about the temporary delay, but she finally took off to the car.

"You screwed up!" Ben snapped as soon as Red was out of hearing.

Yeah, he had. He shouldn't have kissed her. Touched her. Carl's gaze stayed focused on Red's hips swaying toward her silver Honda. The memory of slipping his fingers inside the back of her panties, touching the softest skin known to mankind, had a stiffy coming on again.

"Get your eyes off her ass," Ben snapped. "I'm talking to you. Did you have to go in like Rambo?"

"I thought he had Red, doing God only knew what. I didn't—"

"Do you realize the trouble I'm going to be in if I have to arrest him later on? Illegal entry . . ." Ben ticked off all the rules he'd broken.

"If he's our man, we'll find a way around it," Carl said.

"Isn't that why you quit the Force, because trying to get around the rules got you and others shot?"

Carl took a step closer to his brother. Ben might be older, but Carl had never backed down from a fight. "I made this situation hard for you. For that, I'm sorry. But don't throw that other shit in my face. Because I can fucking guarantee you, if you'd been in my shoes, you'd have done the same thing I did."

"There are rules," Ben ranted. "Rules exist for a reason."

"Yeah, and how many criminals walk the fucking streets because those rules work more in their favor than ours?"

"It still doesn't give us—"

"I'm not part of that 'us' anymore. I don't have to walk that line. And I didn't ask you to babysit me today."

Red's silver Honda, backing out of the driveway, brought an end to the heated conversation. Carl took off for his car.

She met him at the door of Starbucks, and they walked in together. "What is this about?" she asked. He almost rested his hand on her lower back. But touching her could be dangerous.

The coffee's aroma filled his nose, and he resented the way that it chased away Red's scent. Still trying to figure out how to tell her without scaring her half to death, Carl moved to the counter.

"Let's order first." He needed something to cut the edge off his frustrations—both the sexual ones and the problems with Ben.

Red set her coffee down, dropped in a chair, and gazed up at him. "Okay, spill it."

Carl's cell phone rang and he held up a finger asking for one more minute. "Hades," he answered, and stared down at her. The view offered him more cleavage. His breath hitched.

"It's me," Ben said. "I didn't mean to drag up the past."

"Yeah." Carl accepted his brother's apology and tried not to focus on Red's cleavage. "Ditto about causing you trouble."

There was a pause. "Look, I didn't mention this earlier because it didn't seem important, but now it might be."

"What?" His gaze shifted from the soft mounds of flesh to a loose strand of hair resting on Red's cheek. His fingers itched to touch it. Oh hell, he wanted to touch those breasts, too.

"You know we had to run a background check on Red."

"And?" Carl wasn't going to believe anything bad had come up on Katie. She rocked babies. Watched *The Brady Bunch* and *Sex and the City*. His gaze shot back to the cleavage.

"We stumbled over the fact that a 911 call was made from her residence the night of the shooting. One of her friends made the call. It was written up as a possible break-in. I spoke with the uniforms who covered it. They found a broken window and something was said about a back door being found open. But there were some downed tree limbs from the storm beside the window and it was questionable if it was the storm or something else."

"And you're thinking something else." Carl watched Red sipping her brew but listening. The thought of someone hurting her the way they hurt those other women brought out every manly instinct he had: hero, gentleman, not-so-gentleman. Instincts that led him to one conclusion. He wasn't going to let anything happen to her. Right then, protecting her became his top priority.

"It looks suspicious," Ben said, drawing Carl's attention back to the phone call. "I've got men going out to talk to the photographer. I'll let you know if something turns up."

"Yeah," Carl said.

"Another thing," Ben added. "We talked to the family

of the victims found in the woods. Both women had started getting prank calls. Something about the caller playing music. Ask Red about that. If she's gotten any, let me know ASAP."

"I will." Carl cut his phone off and met her eyes. She didn't look happy. He knew he was part of that unhappiness. He'd admit the whole gallery scene had been over the top, and maybe he had broken a few rules. But as Ben had pointed out back there on Will Reed's lawn, Carl had always sucked at following the rules.

"That was Ben," he said.

She set her coffee down. "What's going on?"

Sitting down, he shouldered back in his chair, tried to find a pretty way to say it—but one didn't exist. "We think the guy who shot Tabitha also killed two other women. The other women were both . . . engaged."

Her face went white. "And their wedding planner was—"

"Tabitha. I'm afraid so." He palmed his hot cup.

A wrinkle appeared between her eyebrows and she ran a hand over her chest. "Was it the women found in the woods?"

He wanted to touch her, assure her he wasn't going to let anything happen to her, but he just nodded.

"And you think . . ." Her face paled another notch. "You think this . . . this guy is coming after me?"

This was where it got tricky. "There's a possibility."

Her blue eyes stood out against all the soft white skin. "And Will Reed? You think he might be that guy?"

He reached for her hand. "Could be."

"Oh, fuck!" She pulled away.

He agreed this was definitely f-word worthy. He waited for her to sip her coffee before he asked, "Have you been getting prank calls? Maybe where you hear music?"

The look on her face told him the answer before she spoke. "I just got another one. Just a few minutes ago."

"It's okay." He grabbed her hand and this time held on. After the first jolt of emotion, touching her felt so damn right.

Katie's cell phone rang. Before he could tell her how to deal with the call, she'd apparently come up with an alternate plan: flinging her purse across Starbucks.

Carl jumped up, grabbed the purse, snatched out her cell phone, then walked over and showed her the number displayed on the front. "Recognize it?"

She shook her head. Her pale color grew chalkier. He leaned down and whispered in her ear. "Breathe, Red. All I want you to do is say hello. Got that?"

She nodded, and he opened the phone and put it to her mouth.

"Hello," she managed.

He passed a hand over her cheek and winked at her. Pulling the phone to his ear, he waited for a voice. Or for music. "This is Hank Links at Piper Hotel," the voice said. "I hate to have to call you like this, but . . . but I'm afraid there's been a break-in in your room."

Break-in? "Hello," Carl snapped. "This is a friend of Miss Ray's. Was anyone apprehended?"

"No, I'm afraid a maid found . . . found someone in there. He knocked her down and ran out."

"Can she describe him?"

"I don't know."

"When did this happen?" If this just happened, it couldn't have been Will Reed.

"This morning. I apologize about just now getting to you."

Carl gritted his teeth. "Did you call the police?"

"Well, we weren't sure anything was missing and so—"

"And so you didn't want it going on public record!" He knew how hotels worked. "Is the maid still there?"

"Yes."

"Keep her there. We're on our way." He hung up.

Red looked up. "What now?"

"Someone broke into your hotel room."

Panic hit her eyes. "Les wasn't there, was she?"

"I don't think so." He handed her the phone. "Call her to be sure."

Katie sat in the hotel office, feeling numb inside. Les hadn't been there. And neither was the maid by the time they'd arrived. It seemed apparent the maid was an illegal, and talking to the police made her nervous.

The call to Les on the way to the hotel had been cut very short because Les was in the exam room with the doctor and her grandma. When Katie asked if everything was okay, the only thing Les said was that she'd call Katie back as soon as possible.

Katie watched Carl verbally stretch the hotel manager on the rack, and decided Carl made a better friend than enemy. Before the fiasco ended, he'd called Ben. After they questioned everyone at the hotel, they took her into one of the back meeting rooms and, from the way Ben looked at her, she knew he was about to interrogate her again. Not that she minded, but she really just wanted to go somewhere and throw up.

The television hanging from the wall blared, and at that moment a news flash came on. A woman reporter appeared in front of a patch of woods. "Two bodies were found here, and from our sources we're told we may have a serial killer on our hands. While the police are yet to confirm these findings, we have spoken with Robert Barton, the man who found the bodies while hiking. According to Barton, both bodies were women, both, we're told, were brutally stabbed—"

"Damn it!" Ben snapped. "I told Barton he wasn't to talk to anyone. He pulled out his cell phone and started punching in numbers.

The TV went black. Carl held the remote control. "No use watching that." He stared at her, concern filling his eyes.

Not that she gave his concern much thought. She stared back at the television screen and the reporter's words echoed in her head.

Brutally. *Brutally.* Katie leaned back in her seat. Ben hung up the phone and she stared at the two of them. Two men who looked like Antonio Banderas shouldn't be a bad thing, but she wished someone would tell that to her stomach.

"Breathe, Red," Carl said, studying her.

She inhaled and looked around for a bathroom. Spotting one, she slapped her hand over her mouth and took off.

"Ah, shit!" Carl said behind her.

She barely made it. Seconds later, leaning against the stall, some tissues pulled from her purse, and trying to talk herself out of a good, long, hard, gut-wrenching cry, she heard the bathroom door swish open. She flushed the toilet.

"Red?"

"I'm fine," she sputtered. "Go away." She heard water running. The stall door pushed open.

"Here." Standing outside the cubical, Carl pressed some damp paper towels into her hands.

Meeting his gaze, she saw the green tint to his skin. "You should leave before you start throwing up."

"Aren't you finished?" His frown deepened.

"I think so."

"Then I'm safe. It's the sound that does me in."

She pressed the paper towels to her face. He inched closer and pushed a strand of hair from her cheek. His simple touch sent currents of emotion to her chest and those tears she'd talked herself out of shedding suddenly flooded to her eyes. Before she knew how it happened, she had her head pillowed on his chest and he held her. The feelings, the emotions—they weren't anything like those at the gallery. This wasn't sexual; it was different.

His spicy smell and his touch surrounded her, and

right there, in a woman's bathroom, he made her feel safe again.

She took a deep breath and pulled back. "I must have really done something bad in a past life, huh?"

"Why would you say that?" He touched her cheek.

"Because for the past year and a half, the universe seems to be screwing with me."

"You want me to kick the universe's ass?" He smiled.

"Do you think you could take it on?" She smiled back.

"Piece of cake." He glided a hand over her shoulder.

Emotion filled her chest and she pulled back. "Thanks." They stood there staring. It felt right. She wasn't alone.

Finally, he spoke. "I'm sorry, but Ben has a few questions."

Tabitha's killer paced and rubbed his temple where the throbbing had grown worse. Had he messed up? Were they laughing at him now because they knew he'd done it?

No. He'd done good. Mostly good. He'd only gotten anxious once or twice. But he felt certain they thought he was normal.

Or did they?

He went to his window to peer out. Were they watching him? Waiting for him to screw up? He began to rock.

He shouldn't have gone to the hotel. That had been a mistake. Mistakes would lead them to him. But he needed . . . needed to slow down the laughter. He needed a bride. Needed to hear her beg, the way Maria should have begged for him to forgive her. He needed to stop the laughing.

If he could visit them, he'd feel better. But they'd taken them away. He leaned against the wall and began to move. Back. Forth. Back. Forth.

Rocking was bad. He shouldn't keep rocking. How many times had his mother told him that? *Don't rock. Don't rock. People will laugh at you.* She was right. People would laugh. They would see he wasn't normal. Then his mother would send him back to the hospital. He stopped rocking.

Music. Music helped. He ran back to his bedroom and hit the recorder. "The Wedding March" sang in his ears. He pulled out his photo album and looked at his brides. Then he turned the page and stared at Katie Ray's wedding announcement. He couldn't let her marry another man. She was his.

A nap. Katie longed for a nap. After going over the phone calls again and again, after telling both Ben and Carl about every contact she'd had with anyone who had anything to do with the wedding, and after repeating one more time the names of those who had known she'd been staying at the hotel, Katie dropped her head on her arms and listened to the sound of blood pounding in her ears.

"You okay, Red?" Carl asked. She raised her head.

"Are you sure there's nothing else?" Ben asked her. "No contact with any of the wedding people?"

"I've told you everything," she said, but then . . . "Wait. The flowers."

"What flowers?" Ben and Carl said at the same time.

Katie told them about the flowers the florist had sent, and they made her go over it, and over it.

Finally, Carl interrupted. "I think we're done now."

They all stood, and Ben gave her a nod. "You realize you can't stay at this hotel anymore, don't you?"

Katie grabbed her purse. "I'll find somewhere else."

She noticed the look Ben shot Carl. She didn't know what it meant, but she could tell they'd just mentally communicated.

Carl ushered her outside. He touched her waist as they walked. The sexual awareness from his touch tickled her mind, but Katie didn't fuss; she was too busy trying to wrap her mind around the fact that a serial killer had her on his wish list. Panic buzzed in her head. It wasn't as bad as what she'd felt from seeing Tabitha get shot, but it was close.

She slipped into his car. He folded himself into the driver seat and looked at her. "You're staying with me for a while."

Okay, the buzzing began to ebb. While she could remember the safe feeling he offered her, the memory of the gallery scene sent those safe emotions right out the window.

She shook her head. "I don't think that's a good idea."

He ran his hands over the steering wheel. "Why?"

Had he forgotten they had practically had sex in the gallery? Okay, maybe he didn't see that as a bad thing. "I'll find someplace else to stay."

"Is this because of the kiss?" he asked.

"Oh, it's not the kiss," she snapped. "It was your fingers in my panties. In public. At my work. While my boss watched. That is the problem." She folded her arms over her chest.

"Look, I'll admit I was probably wrong to have raised your skirt like that."

"Probably?" She squinted at him.

He gripped the steering wheel. "Why is it women focus on one word? I said I was sorry."

"Jeez, I totally missed that part."

"Okay, I said I was wrong. Isn't it the same thing?"

"You said you were *probably* wrong," she corrected.

He stared at the car ceiling as if in frustration. "Do you have somewhere else you could go?"

"Yes," she lied and started brainstorming, because . . .

"Where?"

Because she knew he was going to ask her that. She mentally searched for options. Joe? No. That would be too awkward. Les's parents? No, they had Mimi living there, which was why Les was planning on staying with her. Lola? Lola lived over the gallery in the efficiency apartment and had Allen, and occasionally Marco, popping in for quickies. Another hotel? Considering the killer had found her at one of those, the idea—

"We're adults, Red." Her time was obviously up.

"Really? We didn't behave like it back at the gallery."

Both his eyebrows arched over his soft brown eyes. "*We?* Are you actually taking part of the blame here?"

"I never said I didn't share in the responsibility. But I didn't stick my hand in your underwear, either."

"Probably a good thing," he mumbled.

"Yeah. *Probably.*" Silence filled the parked car.

"Look," he said. "I have an extra bedroom and—"

"You can honestly tell me that *you* won't . . . that *we* won't do anything."

"I can honestly tell you that if you tell me no, I'll accept it."

"But you're not above trying?" she asked.

"Probably not." He grinned at her. "But hey, we've been together for almost two hours since the gallery and we've managed to keep our clothes on."

But she'd thought about getting naked with him. Both before and after she'd found out she had a psycho killer after her. Now how bad was that? If learning she was next to be brutally murdered wasn't enough to douse the flames of desire, what would?

Throwing up.

In the bathroom it hadn't been sexual. It had been tender, caring . . . and on some level those emotions scared her more.

"Let's be logical," he said.

Okay, she'd give logic a shot. And logically, if she agreed to go and stay at his place, she knew what would happen. She'd end up on the Carl Hades Poked List.

Oh, and how had he so logically put it back at the gallery? He didn't intend to watch *The Brady Bunch*? Sure, she had to give him a point for honesty. But honesty didn't make a big whopping difference in the big picture. Because all the things she valued—a family, a home— mattered zilch in the world of Carl Hades.

"Come on, Red. Nothing will happen unless we let it." All the teasing had faded from his eyes. "This guy isn't playing around. He's serious." Pause. "Just for a few days."

She gripped her hands together. "I need to think about it."

He let go of a deep gulp of air. "Are you saying that you'd rather risk being killed than risk having sex with me?"

"That's what I'm trying to figure out."

Frowning, he started the car.

Chapter Twenty-four

Katie had a hunch she was the first woman who hadn't leaped tall buildings for the chance to leave a wet spot in Carl's bed. Mostly because when he parked beside her car back at Starbucks ten minutes later, he hadn't stopped looking stunned. Sighing, she mentally went over it one more time. If she stayed at his house, she'd probably have sex with him, but if she went out on her own, a psycho might track her down and kill her.

She weighed her options. Sex. Wonderful sex. Or being murdered. Brutally murdered. Okay, she wasn't stupid. She knew one had a lot more going for it than the other, but . . .

It was just that sex for sex's sake, with zero pretenses that it could lead anywhere, was wrong. It was just . . . well, it was so un-Ray-like.

Not that her parents had raised an idiot, either. It had only taken her one-tenth of a second to conclude she'd be going home with him. The other nine minutes, fifty-nine and nine-tenths of a second she'd spent thinking about it were for fun. She loved the look of total disbelief on his face.

"Only for a few days," she said. "And I'll need to get some things at my place first." She studied him again.

He smiled. The scratches she'd given him were fading. Again, she was hit by how much he looked like Antonio Banderas, how attracted she was to him. Not that this was just a physical attraction. She liked him, inside and out.

And right then, Katie knew that if she didn't proceed with caution, she'd leave behind more than a wet spot when she crawled out of his bed. She'd be leaving her heart.

She had just pulled out of the parking lot to pick up some of her things from her house when her cell phone rang. The thought that it might be the killer made her want to toss the cell out the window; then she forced herself to look at the caller ID. Just Les.

"Hi." Katie hoped she sounded normal. Normal versus a woman who'd just found out she was being stalked by a serial killer. Then a sprinkle of guilt hit her for having forgotten about her best friend's grandma. "How's Mimi?"

"She's okay." Stress clung to Les's voice.

"What happened? She didn't have another stroke, did she?"

"No. She . . . Oh, Katie, I was watching her and she got away. We found her walking down Megan Drive. Naked."

"Oh, my," Katie said. "I'm sure it wasn't your fault."

"Yes, it was," Les said. "The doctor went ahead and had her X-rayed to make sure she hadn't fallen, but she's fine."

"Thank God." Katie knew how much Les loved her grandma. There was a silence; then Les spoke. "Katie, I'm thinking about getting my ticket moved up and heading back to Boston."

"Why?" Katie asked.

"I'm just not . . . I can't handle being home."

"Because of Mike?" Katie felt Les's pain. Some days she missed her family too much to be alive.

Another pause, then Les finally answered. "Probably."

Probably, again. Right then, Katie remembered the whole Joe and Les issue. She almost blurted out that if Les was attracted to Joe then she should explore it. But knowing Les, she would deny it. Best to broach that subject in person.

"Please don't leave. I need you," Katie said. "I—"

"Oh, shit. I forgot. You aren't at the hotel yet, are you? Please tell me you aren't there."

Reacting to the panic in Les's voice, Katie stopped at a red light a little fast. "No, why?"

"It's probably nothing, but someone who said he needed to speak with you about the wedding called my house this morning. Mom told him where we were. I'm sure it's nothing, but it weirded me out after what that cop said about being cautious."

Chills tap-danced up Katie's spine. A deep breath later, she told Les everything. Well, she didn't tell her about having almost had sex with Carl in the middle of the gallery, but she told her friend about the elephant painting—which brought on more dangerous feelings than the almost-sex episode.

Katie looked in her rearview mirror to see the elephant-painting giver following her in his car. Then she told Les about the break-in at the hotel, about how the cops thought the man who'd shot Tabitha was the same one who'd killed the two women on the news. "And they think he's after me now."

"Why do they think that?" Panic radiated from Les's voice.

"I've been getting calls and someone just plays music."

"Oh my God! He called your house three times that night you were missing!"

Great. All Katie needed was more proof that the psycho was after her. Forcing herself to continue, she told Les about how Ben thought someone *had* broken into the house and that it hadn't been just the storm that broke the window.

Silence echoed across the line. Les's whispered words finally came. "Joe showing up saved my life."

Fear crowded Katie's chest. Then it faded as an idea began to take shape. "Guess you owe him, huh?"

"Yeah," Les said. "So, are we going to change hotels?"

More ideas formed in Katie's mind. It was a long shot, but if she could pull this off, maybe, just maybe, she could force Les into facing things head-on instead of always running away.

"Actually, Les. I have a big, *big* favor to ask."

"Why do I not like your tone?" Les's voice echoed. Les always picked up on tones.

"I'm going to go stay with Carl for a few days."

Hear-a-pin-drop silence came over the line.

"Les?"

"Yeah, I'm just trying to figure out what I'm supposed to say to that. Tell you to go for it, or talk you out of it."

Katie changed lanes. "Didn't you just tell me last night that life was too short not to listen to bells?"

"Are you sure about this, Katie?" Les asked.

"No," she admitted. "But I'm going to do it anyway."

"Are you going to sleep with him?" Les hung the question out there.

"Probably." *Probably.* Now Katie had said it. Funny, how little she'd used that word in her past. It just wasn't a Ray-like word. Rays didn't believe in probably. They set a course of action and made it happen. And if whatever they were after didn't seem attainable, Rays didn't go after it. Because failing wasn't an option.

Sometimes, Katie was certain she'd been adopted.

"Okay," Les snapped. "Who are you, and where have you hidden my best friend? Because the Katie Ray I know would never think of sleeping with a man she barely knows."

"I know him. I mean . . . I don't *know* him. But I do. Know what I mean?"

"Oh, hell yeah, that made perfect sense." Les laughed, but it stopped abruptly. "Maybe you should think about this first."

"I have thought about it, Les. I'm safer with him. And you're safer not staying with me." Katie had another near panic attack when she thought about how she'd feel if something happened to her friend. "Can you stay with your brother?"

"Yeah. But . . . I might as well go back to Boston."

"No! I need you," Katie pleaded, and turned down her street.

"But if you're staying with Antonio, you don't need me."

Katie hesitated, decided to jump in headfirst and hope her plan worked. "I need you to help Joe."

Silence filled the line. "Help Joe do what?"

"Help Joe cancel the wedding. I obviously can't do it."

"Joe's a big boy. He can handle that by himself." Les's voice sounded tight.

"That's not fair and you know it."

"What does fair have to do with it?" Les snapped.

"Fine. Don't help." Katie hated resorting to the manipulation skills her parents had used on her. But hey, they worked. "I hardly ever ask you to do anything. How many times have I been there for you? Covered for you with your parents? Helped you study? How many nights in college did I sleep on the sofa so you and Paul Bakley could do the wild thing? I even pretended like I didn't hear you two going at it. Over and over again. And I ask one thing. One thing."

"Okay. Stop! I'll help Joe."

Katie smiled. "Thanks. Do you have his cell number?"

"Yeah, he gave it to me today."

"Today?" Katie smiled again, and knew Les hadn't

realized what she'd said. Good for Joe. "Then call him. We were supposed to meet tonight and start making calls. And then there's all the gifts at his place that need to be returned. Oh, ask him how his talk went with his mom. She's sort of hard to handle sometimes, so I know he's upset about it."

Les moaned. "You are *so* going to owe me. And if you ever bring up me banging Paul Bakley again, I'm divorcing you."

"Agreed." Katie parked in her driveway. The sight of her cozy patio home had always brought out a sense of pride, but knowing the killer had been here changed that cozy feeling.

"And what am I supposed to tell Joe about you?" Les asked.

Katie looked up and saw Carl sauntering over to her car. All six feet and more of him, a brown-eyed devil in khaki pants and a pink button-down, he was moving toward her with a slow, sexy gait. Their gazes held and he winked. The air in her lungs caught.

I'm probably going to have sex with him. Probably.

"Tell him . . . tell him the truth. I think he'll understand."

"It's not as impressive as your place." Carl watched Red glance around his small one-story starter home in a suburb west of Houston. Was she doing the same kind of thing he'd done at her place, when he'd looked for clues to help him figure out who Katie Ray really was? Her place was neat, feminine, cozy, and homey. All words he'd use to describe Katie herself. She even had those scented candles that his sister-in-law loved. One room smelled like apples, the next like flowers. Her bedroom smelled like her, though. And on the hallway walls, Katie had nothing but photographs of her family.

While she'd packed her things, he'd taken the time to look at those images. He'd found himself hurting for all she'd lost. A whole family. Gone. He could only imagine how much she'd grieved. Or how much she still grieved.

"This is nice." Katie's voice brought Carl to the present. She leaned in to look at his L-shaped kitchen, then she glanced back at his living room with an adjoining dining room.

Carl watched her gaze move from item to item, his sixty-four-inch television, his old leather sofa—which had seen better days but was more comfortable than any couch he'd tried to replace it with—to his dad's old, scarred desk, which Carl had placed in the corner of the living room so he could use the third bedroom as a weight room. Then her focus cut to the swimsuit calendar hanging over the desk.

He wondered what she assumed about him by looking at his things. Compared to her place, his home came off as cold and unfeeling. Is that how she saw him—cold, a little scarred, and maybe even a little lonely? He reached up to rub his shoulder, hating the fact that his home did indeed reflect his life right now, hating the fact that he cared how she viewed him and his home. He'd never cared what other women thought.

"Here, let me take your things." He reached for her bags, but she pulled them back when his hand touched hers.

"Just show me where."

He turned the corner to show her to his room, flinching when he spotted his unmade bed. Not that it should have surprised him; he hadn't expected it to make itself. In fact, he couldn't remember the last time he'd made it. But he could still hear his mother ragging him to do it.

His frown deepened when he saw the dirty socks lying next to the Victoria's Secret catalog on the nightstand. Oh yeah, he was looking really good now.

"Isn't this your room?" she asked.

"I'll sleep in the guest room," he said, but honestly, did she really believe they wouldn't be sleeping together? In spite of what she might or might not think of his home, the sexual energy between them flowed so hot it could melt concrete.

Back in the car when she'd been weighing the options of having sex with him or getting murdered—which ticked him off royally, by the way—he'd come within a hair of promising her nothing would happen. But he'd caught himself just in time. He didn't make promises he couldn't keep. While he'd never pressure her to have sex with him, he sure as hell wouldn't get in the way of its spontaneously happening. And considering the sparks flying between them, a spontaneous explosion had pretty much been written in stone.

She eyed his bed with skepticism.

He frowned. "The sheets are clean."

"It's not that. It's . . . I'm not running you out of your bed." She U-turned, but stopped short at the door. "*Oh!*"

What now? Had he left his underwear out? He moved in. "Damn!"

"Is that . . . Tabitha's dog, Baby?"

"Yup." There in the entrance of the extra bedroom were Baby and Precious. Precious had ripped off another pair of Baby's panties. They weren't standing there cute-like with their tails wagging. They were going at it like . . . like a couple of dogs.

"And that's Precious?" She chuckled. "Your big, manly dog?"

"Yup. But hey, he's looking pretty good in the manly department right now." He chuckled and moved closer. So close the smell of Red's hair filled his nose. He ached to encircle her waist with his hands and pull her against him.

"You took Tabitha's dog?"

Her voice came out soft. As soft as her lips looked when the words left them. He opened his mouth to blame all this on his dad, but something that looked like admiration passed over her expression. "Yeah, sort of."

"You really are a marshmallow, aren't you?"

"Is that a good thing?" he asked.

"Yeah." Her smile widened with admiration. "It's good."

"Then I'm a marshmallow." He took her small suitcase and set it against the wall. They could fight about where she'd sleep later. After the spontaneous explosion.

"Why don't we let them have their privacy?" He gave her a little push out of the hallway before the temptation to pull her back to his bed overtook him.

She started moving, then stopped. "I would kind of like to get out of these clothes."

He'd kind of like to get her out of those clothes, too. Holding his breath, he motioned back to the bathroom off the hall. "It's all yours."

Patience, he told himself.

As soon as she disappeared into the bathroom, he shut the door to the extra bedroom so the dogs wouldn't make another embarrassing appearance. Then he ran to his bedroom, grabbed up his dirty socks and the Victoria's Secret magazine, and hid them under his bed. Trying to think of anything else his mother would have griped about, he ran to the master bathroom, gave the toilet a few swipes with a brush, and lowered the lid. After washing his hands and gargling with some mouthwash, he headed back to the living room. He started to turn on the television and decided instead to go for music. He found the easy-rock station and set it to low. Looking around, he realized his palms were sweating.

Holy hell. He was acting like some pimple-faced teenager about to get his first piece of ass!

It's your first in a long time. Yeah, that had to be it.

And he'd been up-front with her. He'd told her he wasn't into *The Brady Bunch*. He had the green light. So, why the nerves?

Inhaling, pushing the negative thoughts away, he went to the kitchen to see what he had to offer her to drink. Two beers. Was that bottle of red wine still in the cabinet?

He found the wine, dusted it off, and set it out with two glasses. They didn't match. Tomorrow, he'd buy another set. Then he found the neighborhood phone book, which listed the restaurants that delivered.

He heard her footsteps. His heart took a tumble when he turned around. She'd let her hair down and it hung loose around her shoulders. The formfitting jeans she wore did more for her body, and more for his, than the skirt had. Her top, a long-sleeved gray T-shirt, clung to her breasts and told him he'd been wrong: her breasts weren't just amazing, they were fucking fantastic.

"Is something wrong?" she asked.

"No." He glanced at the phone book he held in front of his zipper. A good place for it, considering his dick liked her T-shirt, too. "I was deciding who to call for dinner. Chinese? Italian? It's your call."

"No quiche?" she teased.

"Hey, I ate my quiche."

She grinned. "Okay, no more quiche jokes. I guess I can't tease you about wearing pink either, huh?"

"Nope. I think this might be my favorite shirt now. And I now have two sissy dogs. I can almost say I like them."

She grinned. "You definitely get points for taking in Tabitha's dog."

And what did points get him? His body needed to know.

She glanced at the phone book. At least, he hoped it was the book and not what he had going on behind the yellow pages.

"I'm easy. Most anything will pass these lips."

Okay, that didn't help. He fought back the desire to suggest they skip dinner. "Chinese it is, then."

* * *

Les knocked on Joe's door. Flurries of uncertainty swirled in her stomach. She'd called Joe and told him about Katie asking her to help him cancel the wedding. He hadn't even asked why Katie wasn't going to come.

So, would someone please explain this to her?

It didn't make a freaking bit of sense. How in the hell could two people be planning to get married one day and both be interested in other people three days later?

Because they were never in love. They couldn't have been in love. Mike had been dead for a year and a half, and the idea of being attracted to someone else felt like trying to walk with rocks in her shoes.

Joe opened the door. His hair hung a little darker, like it was still wet. He wore jeans, a navy T-shirt, and a smile. "Come in." He motioned her into his well-decorated, contemporary-style condo. Lots of dark wood and chrome.

"Thanks." She walked in, feeling those imaginary rocks in her shoes, and caught a whiff of his clean, masculine scent.

When she pulled off her jacket, Joe's eyes widened as he took in her dress. She'd worn it just for him, so the fact that he noticed seemed appropriate. Back in Boston, she'd had her own apparel for such an occasion. But she'd packed in a hurry and hadn't thought she'd need any special outfits.

So she'd borrowed one. The dress could be described as a typical tent dress, A-line from the neck down. The color was a bright kelly green, with huge orange pumpkins on it. It was in Les's opinion the ugliest piece of clothing she'd ever been unfortunate enough to lay eyes on. Though she supposed it looked wonderful on Mimi.

Hence, it was perfect to wear to Joe's. The last—the very last—thing she wanted was for him to think she'd come here out of some sort of perverted interest in him. She was here because Katie had begged her. Here, because

Katie had reminded her of how she'd forced her to sleep on a futon that was about as comfortable as a bed of nails while she and Paul Bakley had noisy, sweaty sex in the only bedroom.

Of all the bad mistakes in Les's life, Paul was up there on top. Really great noisy, sweaty sex—but a huge mistake nonetheless. And his wife had agreed. Not that Les had known he had a wife until she'd shown up during one bout of noisy, sweaty sex.

Ugh! Les hated cheaters. Even when they were great in bed. Instantly, the memory of what hot sex had felt like tickled her mind. She hit the delete button on that tickle and faced Joe. Head held high and wearing pumpkins, she was ready to help Joe Lyon call off his wedding.

"So, what do you think we should do first?" she asked. "Give me the list of names and I'll start calling. I figure we don't need to explain it. Short and sweet. Something like, 'The wedding's off. Don't show up. If you've sent a gift already, it will be returned to your store for a credit to your account, or we will mail it back to you.' Does that sound okay?"

He hadn't stopped staring at her dress.

"Joe?"

Finally, he raised his eyes and started laughing.

"What?" she asked.

"It's not going to work. But I give you an A for effort."

"I don't have a clue what you're talking about," she lied.

"Right." He laughed again. "You want a beer? I need one right now." He laughed his way to the adjoining kitchen.

Okay, maybe the dress was a bit of overkill, but hell, it wasn't that funny. She caught a glimpse of herself in a framed mirror. Okay, so it was way over-the-top, but it still wasn't that funny.

She walked into his kitchen. He handed her a beer and shook his head but couldn't wipe the grin from his face.

"I'm sorry," he said. "But that dress looks like a bad imitation of a really ugly Halloween tablecloth."

Les really didn't mean to do it, but his description fit the dress to a T and she laughed.

When the humor faded, they both sat down, and using their cell phones called the wedding guests and offered apologies for the cancellation of the grand event. Joe ordered pizza, and they both drank two beers. They talked between the calls, laughed about Mimi's streaking tendencies, and it was, in Les's opinion, the most fun she'd had with a man in eighteen months.

And that was downright scary.

Katie and Carl had kicked back on his worn leather sofa, eaten fried rice and cashew chicken, and talked. After two glasses of wine, and having been joined on the sofa by two dogs, one wearing a pair of panties, Katie actually began to relax.

"Are you aware that Hades means—"

"God of the underworld and ruler of the dead?" he said, grinning. "When I was ten, I thought it was pretty cool."

She chuckled.

"More wine?" He picked up the bottle.

Katie ran her hand down Baby's back as Tabitha's dog sat in her lap. "You trying to get me drunk?"

He grinned. "Would it help?"

"Not unless you want us both to be in the bathroom fighting over the throne."

He set the bottle down. "You've officially been cut off."

She grinned. Amazingly, the evening had passed without any awkward silences. They'd talked about personal things, too. But she still had a few questions.

"What's your favorite memory of your mom?" she asked.

His brows rose as if this question pushed the limits. Then he shrugged. "You'll think I'm terrible."

"No, I won't," she insisted.

He took in a deep mouthful of air. "The last time her cancer came back . . . my dad had already missed a lot of work. Ben was in college. I sort of took over taking care of her." He grinned, but Katie saw a sad shadow in his smile. "Chemo . . . made her sick." He hesitated. "She'd take the john and I'd take a bucket. We'd throw up and then laugh our asses off because . . . I don't know, it just seemed funny. I think I got to know my mom while sitting on the bathroom floor."

Emotion tickled her throat. "Why would I think that was terrible?"

He shrugged. "It just shouldn't have been a good memory."

She felt tempted to reach over and hug him. "You took a bad situation and made it meaningful."

He let go of another gasp of air. "What about you?" he asked. "What's your favorite memory of your family?"

She grinned. "Every Easter, Mom would give us kites and we would go to Lakeview Park. Once, my dad couldn't get the kite to fly. Of course, he refused to quit until he finally got it up. But he was so focused on keeping it up that he walked right off a pier and into the lake. We were all laughing. Easters were always the most perfect days."

He smiled, and she noticed he'd scooted closer and started playing with her hair.

She almost asked him about his leaving the police force, but she spotted two framed pictures on the television. Curious, she set the dog down from her lap and went to check them out. One of them was of a young boy. She looked back at Carl still on the sofa, his poodle on the floor with his head on Carl's feet and Tabitha's dog already settling in his lap. "Your nephew?"

"Yeah. How did you know?"

"Ben mentioned he had a son." She glanced back at the image. "He looks like you two."

"There's a small chance he might outgrow it," Carl said.

She picked up the other photograph, a picture of a younger-looking Carl and an older woman. *His mom.* "She was beautiful."

"Yeah, she was," he said.

She considered what Carl must have felt being fifteen and watching his mother die slowly from cancer. "It must have been hard losing her."

"Not compared to what you went through."

She looked back. "I don't know. I think it might be worse, knowing someone is dying. Then there are times I would give anything to have had a chance to say good-bye."

Suddenly he was behind her, wrapping his arms around her middle. "You are one tough cookie, Katie Ray."

"Not really." She leaned back into him. So solid. So warm. "I fake it mostly. I'm really a marshmallow."

A big marshmallow about to end up on someone's Poked List.

"Could have fooled me." His arms tugged her closer. His five o'clock shadow came against the side of her face, his scent surrounding her. Spicy. Male.

She closed her eyes. This was where *probably* ended and she decided which side of the fence she fell on. Sex. No sex.

His lips brushed her ear. "I want to make love to you."

Okay, the man didn't beat around the bush!

"I want to feel you against me. No clothes. Nothing but skin. Your skin . . . against my skin."

Okay, she'd read about verbal foreplay. Read how it could melt a woman to jelly. And yup. She had jelly to go with her marshmallow interior.

"I want to touch you, Red. I want to taste you."

Her breath caught when she realized that verbal

foreplay wasn't his only specialty. His hands were on the move. Up, up over her ribs, to . . . oh, boy . . . her breasts.

Stop him now or forever hold your peace.

Too late. He was there. Both hands. Both breasts.

Chapter Twenty-five

Katie held her breath.

"I want to taste you," he said. "Right here." He teased her nipples. Her breasts felt instantly fuller, heavier. Her mind created the visual image of his lips on her naked flesh. She exhaled. Oh, yes, she wanted that. Pleasure rushed through her. Liquid heat pooled low in her abdomen, anticipation of what was to come. And if she'd had any question as to what that would be, she could feel the hardness between his legs pressed against her lower back.

One of his hands inched downward, sliding over her abdomen, past her belly button. "And here," he whispered. "I want to lick and taste every inch of you. But I really want to taste you . . ." His fingers slipped inside the front of her jeans, down, over her belly, under her panties, "Right here." He found her most sensitive spot and her knees almost gave out. "I want to make you come with my tongue, at least once. Maybe twice."

A moist, wet kiss moved across her ear. "What do you want, Red? Tell me what you want."

She opened her eyes and stared at the dishes on the coffee table. Her knees wobbled. "I want . . . to help you wash dishes."

She felt him flinch, and he pulled his hand out of her panties.

Embarrassment swept through her. What had possessed her to say that? *I didn't mean it*, she almost blurted. *Life's too short not to listen to bells.* Les's words echoed in her head.

She turned around and met his eyes, which were filled with disappointment. Right then, she'd have given anything to take her words back. To trade them for something suave and seductive. *I want to taste you, too.* Or, *What are you waiting for? Taste me.*

"I'm sorry," he said, his voice husky. "I thought . . ."

You thought right, she wanted say. Where was the rewind button? Couldn't she have a do-over? Okay, she knew do-overs weren't real, but maybe . . .

"Washing dishes can be fun," she said in her best sultry voice. Then she didn't have a clue why she did it, or what possessed her to do it, or what she planned to do next, but she reached down and pulled her T-shirt off. Holding it with the tips of her fingers for a second, she then tossed it into the middle of the floor. "You want to wash or dry?"

His eyes rounded as his gaze whispered over her low-cut bra, or rather what was falling out of her bra. He swallowed, his Adam's apple dancing up and down. She had the crazy urge to adjust her bra, but then, he seemed to go for the bulging-out look. *Deep breath.*

"I'll dry." Never taking his eyes off her, he tugged his own shirt over his head.

She watched him. Watched his chest become open for viewing. And what a view. Antonio Banderas had nothing on Carl Hades. His skin shone golden and a soft spray of dark hair spanned across his chest. The spray, silky soft in appearance, tapered down his flat abdomen, thinned into a sexy trail, and disappeared into his khakis.

He tossed his shirt on the floor with hers. Leaning back on the heels of his shoes, he studied her as if daring her to remove another piece of clothing. The temptation was there, but why play by his rules? This was her game. She called the shots.

And yes, she planned on making them up as she went along. She grabbed the dishes off the coffee table and cruised to the kitchen. Her hair moved against her bare back as she walked. She looked over her shoulder and almost laughed at his dumbfounded expression.

"Coming?" she asked in her best sultry voice.

"Try and stop me." He followed.

She set the dishes on the counter and started filling the sink with water. He edged in and traced a finger over her bra strap as if to remove it. Goose bumps rose from the sweet seduction of his touch. She fought against falling under his spell and letting him take charge. No, she wanted to tease, to cast a spell of her own.

"Dishes first." She brushed his touch away.

"Dishes?" he repeated, as his focus stayed on her exposed cleavage.

She became so aware of his gaze that her nipples grew harder against the satin of her bra. Turning to the sink, she squirted some soap into the water, then held out her hand. "Sponge?"

He opened a drawer and held it out. "What do I get for it?"

She took the sponge and decided he might need a reward. She dropped it in the sink and leaned down, offering him a good view of her breasts as she removed her shoes. Rising up, she tossed the white leather Keds into the dining room. *Thump. Thump.*

His brow arched as if he now understood the game. And if he'd just explain it to her, she'd feel better. Faking it was hard. But fun, she had to admit.

He removed his shoes, and one by one, tossed them beside hers. With each *thud* of a shoe, her heart thudded with it. Okay, it was time to come up with a game plan. How in hell was she going to make washing dishes a sexual game? Or maybe he would just keep staring at her boobs and not care?

She reached into the warm water and drew out a plate. Slowly, she moved the sponge over it, caressing the plate like a lover. His gaze shifted from the dish to her breasts. Raw desire flashed in his eyes. It actually seemed to be working. Her hope flared.

He moved closer. She passed him the dish. For a minute, he just stood there, plate in hand, his gaze locked on her breasts spilling out of her bra. His chest rose with his breaths.

"You rinse, dry, and put away," she said.

He pulled the nozzle out of the side of the sink, halfway sprayed the plate, then set it in the dish drainer. Licking his lips, he looked back at her with expectation. *Another reward*, his gaze demanded.

She considered it. Slowly, she unzipped her jeans, let him get a glance at her white lace panties, and turned back to the sink.

"Not fair," he mumbled, but he lowered his own zipper.

She faced him. "My game. My rules. Besides, you didn't finish the job. I said you rinse, dry, and put away."

"I'm not much of a rules player," he said, his voice husky.

"That's a shame." She sighed in feigned disappointment.

"But I could learn." He grabbed a towel from another drawer, swiped the dish, and stored it in the cabinet. Turning back to her, he leaned against the counter—waiting.

She didn't move.

"Done," he said, his eyes traveling to her unzipped jeans as if hinting at the particular piece of clothing he wanted removed.

She reached down, touched the bare skin where the jeans lay open; then, smiling, she leaned down and removed one sock and tossed it into the living room with their shoes.

"Tease." He released a deep gasp of air, then he stood on one leg to remove one of his socks and toss it beside hers.

Enjoying this more than she'd thought possible, she slipped her hand inside the warm water and picked up the second plate. She ran the sponge over it with slow precision. Once. Twice. Three times.

He leaned close, feigning interest in the dish. "I think it's clean." His bare shoulder brushed up against her arm. Skin to skin, and it felt wonderful. So wonderful, her breath caught.

He must have noticed, because he leaned in to kiss her.

She ducked away just before his lips met hers. If he kissed her now as he'd kissed her at the gallery, this would end. And she was enjoying the game too much.

"Dishes first." She looked from the plate to him. "You, Mr. Hades, need to work on your patience."

"Yeah, I've always had a problem with that," he said.

She held the dish up and studied it one more time before handing it off.

He pulled the nozzle out, rinsed, picked up the towel, dried, and had the dish in the cabinet in seconds. Turning, he folded his arms over his bare chest. His right eyebrow arched as if demanding she pay up. His gaze went back to her open zipper, where she knew he could see her panties. He really wanted her pants off.

"You work fast," she whispered.

"You work slow," he countered. "You're killing me, Red."

And she wasn't finished yet. First, she toyed with her bra strap, slipping her finger under it and watching his eyes widen. Then, sending him her best sultry look, she leaned over and took off her other sock.

He groaned, but his second sock hit the pile of clothes at almost the same time hers did. "You do know I have a dishwasher, right?"

Smiling, she pulled a spoon from the soapy water. She scrubbed it, rinsed it off, and then wrapped her hand around it suggestively. Feeling braver, she pressed it to her lips and slipped it inside her mouth, bringing it out slowly, then taking it back in.

He gripped the edge of the sink. "You'll pay for this."

She dipped the spoon in the soapy water again and set it in the empty sink. He let go of the counter, shot a spray of water at the utensil, and dropped it in the drainer.

Clicking her tongue, she eyed the spoon. "You have a bad habit of not finishing what you start."

His eyes tightened. "I think it's you that's a little slow in the finishing department."

"My game. My rules," she whispered seductively, and reached out and ran her wet hand down his chest, then pulled back and pointed to the spoon.

He snatched up the spoon, dried it, and put it away. Then he looked back to her. "Pay up."

She tried to decide what came next. The bra, or the pants. Wanting to tease him, she slowly reached back to unhook her bra. She looked at him, his attention riveted on the front of her chest, waiting for her bra to fall.

Pulling her arms back around, she slid her palms down her abdomen all the way to the edge of her panties. Then as if she had all day, she pushed the jeans open a little more. His gaze zeroed in on every move.

Smiling at the anticipation on his face, she wiggled the denim over her hips, careful not to take the silk white panties with them. Bending at the waist, she stepped out of the jeans, stood, and with a flick of her wrist, she added them to the pile of socks and shoes.

His gaze moved over her with a slowness that had her heart hammering. Meeting her eyes, he held up a finger and motioned for her to turn around. Her pulse raced, and more heat pooled between her legs. Trying really hard not to blush, she did a slow turn for him.

Facing him again, she saw the heat in his eyes as they whispered down and up her body again. Finally, after he'd taken in every inch of her, he reached and pushed his khakis over his hips.

She watched his cotton, blue and white–striped boxers become exposed. But it was the heavy bulge in the front of the boxers that had her heart racing. She considered running a finger over the length of him. But she knew they had a few dishes left, and if she touched him now, the game would be over.

He stepped out of his pants, and they went flying through the air. The khakis landed right on top of her light blue denims. And something about the pile of clothes heaped together, as if they belonged together, made warmth fill her chest.

She looked back at him wearing only his boxers. Remembering what he'd done to her, she motioned for him to turn.

Not blinking an eye, he began a slow circle. "Meet your expectations?" he asked at half turn.

She inhaled as her gaze followed the contours of his tight butt, and when he came around, she noticed the size of the bulge had grown behind the soft cotton material.

She blinked. "You'll do."

"Ouch. Now that was uncalled for." He grabbed for her.

She held up a hand. "The dishes aren't done."

His tongue passed over his mouth, reminding her: *And I want to taste you here.* The ache between her legs grew. She yearned to be touched. And yes, to be tasted. She almost gave in, called the game over, when the sound of a door being opened and then closed chased all the wonderful, sexual bliss right out the window.

The dogs barked.

"Son? I brought your cameras back. Caught ol' man Johnson doing exactly what his wife thought he was doing."

Carl wearing only boxers and a hard-on, tore out of the kitchen. "Got some good shots, too," Carl's dad said.

"Stop right there!" Carl's voice boomed.

Joe offered Les another beer, but she turned it down. He knew she would. Twice in the last ten minutes he'd seen her reach to her chest to touch the ring. He'd love to personally remove that damn chain, but he didn't dare. Frankly, he was surprised she'd even agreed to come over here tonight. Almost as surprised as he was at himself for going over to her house today.

Honestly, what were the chances of something actually working out here? His situation reeked of rebound. People would talk and accusations would fly. Never mind that he hadn't loved Katie in the right way.

And Les's situation—well, it was just a damn waste that she preferred to hang on to the dead man than live in the present.

She looked up, and he knew her words before she said them. "I should be going."

He nodded. "I understand." No, he didn't understand, but it wasn't his place to question it, either. Well, at least not again. He'd had his say today in Les's kitchen.

She stood and gazed down at her dress. When she looked up, she smiled. And damn if her smile didn't reach down into his gut and pull out a wad of courage. Screw the odds against them. Screw what people would think.

"Then I'll see you tomorrow," he said.

"Tomorrow?" she asked.

"To return the gifts. I just assumed you'd help me."

She blinked, indecision played in her eyes. "I guess I can."

He grinned. "I can't wait to see what you wear."

Her smile widened. "I promise, I'll dress normal."

Their gaze held—one of those moments that usually led to someplace better. Then she touched that damn ring.

"Does that mean you won't wear a dead man's ring

around your neck? Because that ring offends me a lot more than that damn ugly dress." He hadn't meant to say it—or maybe he had.

Her green eyes shot fire at him. He almost apologized, but he realized maybe this was what Les needed, needed to get mad, needed for someone to force her to see the obvious.

Her chin shot up. "How dare you judge me when you and Katie are the fucked-up ones. I mean, look at this. You're coming on to me, and Katie's off sleeping with some PI she just met."

"Katie's doing what?" He took a second to digest what Les had said, and another second to realize it didn't hurt near as much as it should have. Heck, it hardly hurt at all. "At least we're living, Les. At least we're not afraid—"

"I'm not afraid." Tears, angry tears, filled her eyes.

"Prove it. Take the ring off. Take it off right now. Or let me take it off." He went to pull the necklace when—

She slapped him. His cheek stung like hell. Joe touched his face, not sure what shocked him more: her hitting him or his instant hard-on.

Jeezus! Where the hell did this little perverted side of him pipe up from? Maybe it was just left over from their naked bathroom struggle. Maybe it was because one of her pumpkins, the one over her right breast, kept winking at him. He met her gaze. "Do you feel better?"

"No!" She slapped him again. "Why did you have to be at that bar?"

He had a real woody going on right now.

She raised her hand as if to hit him again. "You flirted with me. You rubbed the back of my hand with your thumb."

Her palm came at him. He caught her wrist. "If you hit me again, I'm going to kiss you, and it probably won't stop with a kiss. I'm not joking," he warned. "As fucked-up as this sounds, I'm totally turned on by a girl wearing a pumpkin tablecloth and slapping the shit out of me."

He let her go, praying she'd do it, praying she'd test him. She did.

Her hand struck, stung like hell, and he had her in his arms before her palm left his cheek. He backed her up against the wall and kissed her. It was a hot, opened-mouthed kind of kiss. The kind that didn't stop with just lips and tongue. And thank God, he wasn't the only one participating. They were going down. And fast. His dick got harder.

Before he knew what was happening, Les had her hands inside his shirt, yanking at his belt and then his pants. When she slung his belt across the room, he grabbed the hem of her hideously ugly dress and pulled it over her head.

She stood there, breathing hard, wearing the red underwear he'd seen on Katie's bed. He wanted to look, but she slammed him back against the wall and started kissing him again.

Then came the voice, telling him this was wrong. He might have listened, too, if Les hadn't slipped her hand in his pants.

Lost in the feel of her hand sliding over his cock, he unhooked her bra and the flimsy fabric dropped between them. Stepping out of his jeans, now pushed around his ankles, he walked her to the sofa where he fell on top of her. He held her wrists and she ground her pelvis against his dick. Pulling those pink nipples into his mouth, he tasted heaven. Then he felt the ring burrowing a hole in his chest.

He started to pull the damn thing off himself, but he knew he couldn't do that. She had to do it. It had to be her choice.

Or could he ignore it?

He couldn't ignore it. He shot off the sofa. "Take it off, Les. Take the ring off."

She looked at him, so damn sexy, and he wanted her, wanted to yank those red panties off and . . . He couldn't.

"Take it off," he said through gritted teeth. "Take it off, or get your tablecloth back on and leave."

Katie's gaze searched for anything to use as cover. She eyed the heap of clothes in the dining room, but didn't know if she could be seen if she tried to grab them. Swinging around, she pulled open the pantry door and hid behind it. Hid, as in tried to become one with the cans of pork and beans.

"What's wrong?" Carl's dad's voice echoed.

"Not a damn thing," Carl said. "Just go."

"What's going . . ." His dad's voice faded. Had he seen all the clothes on the floor?

"Good-bye, Dad."

Carl's voice reeked of frustration. Katie moved farther into the pantry. She heard a door being opened and then shut. Had Buck gone?

Footsteps echoed. "I am so sorry," Carl said.

She stayed behind the pantry door, but stuck her head out.

Carl appeared at the kitchen entrance. "He's gone."

She nodded, and knew her face and probably the top half of her body were the same color as the cans of tomatoes. Another curse of being fair-skinned.

He tilted his head to the side, as if to see around the door. "Come out, Red." His voice didn't hold any of the remnants of frustration he'd used on his dad. Nope, Carl's tone went straight back to playful. He motioned to the sink. "We got dishes to finish."

She worry-nipped her lip. "Did he know someone was here?"

Humor danced in his eyes as he glanced at the front of his boxers. "He might have figured it out."

"Oh," she moaned, and ducked behind the door again.

"Red?"

She peered at him from the side of the door. He crooked his finger at her to move away from it.

"Do you think he knew it was me?" She would call herself a fool for playing such a stupid game, but right then, the heat in Carl's eyes reminded her how much fun it had been.

"Does it matter?" He motioned for her to come out again and gave her a soft, sexy smile. Then he pulled her from behind the pantry door and backed her up against the sink.

Kissing her softly, he whispered, "Do we finish the dishes or leave them for later?" His arms came around her.

The heat of his body met hers, the feel of his hard sex upon her belly, and she was aching to call the game over. Almost. She turned and dropped her hands in the water.

He moved closer, dipping his hand beneath the floating suds and curling his fingers around hers. "Let me help you." He pulled the last and only fork from the water, squirted it with the sprayer, dried it, and dropped it in the drawer. With a look of triumph lighting his brown eyes, he turned to her. "Pay up."

"Are you sure there's no more dishes? Where's *your* fork?" she teased, hoping to draw this out a few more minutes—just until she found her nerve. She had a hunch she'd probably left it in the pantry.

"My fork's already in the drawer." He eyed her panties, then her bra. "Come on, Red."

Okay, she couldn't stop now. She reached back to unhook her bra. As soon as she released it, she remembered all the things she'd have liked to change about her body. The freckles. The way her right breast seemed to be a little larger than the left. And her butt always seemed a little big.

The bra slipped off her shoulders, caught on her nipples, whispered down her arms, then fluttered to the tile floor.

Carl's breath deepened as he looked at her naked breasts.

"Do you have any idea how angry I am with myself right now?" he asked.

The urge to cover herself hit strong. She fought it. And held her arms to her sides and let him look. "Why?"

"I can't begin to count the number of women I've turned down who offered to help with the dishes."

His teasing calmed her, and she grinned. "See the advantages of being metro?"

"Well, I'm all metro now. Doing dishes. Eating quiche. Wearing pink. Two prissy dogs." He hooked his thumbs inside the elastic band of his boxers and slid them off.

His sex, hard, and slightly larger than she was accustomed to, bounced upward. Embarrassed by his nudity even when he wasn't, she raised her eyes.

"Would you like me to turn around?"

She did, but was too abashed to say so. "That's okay."

He stepped closer and pulled out the sink stopper. "Dishes are done. But we still have one article of clothing left." His hand, still damp with dishwater, moved down her abdomen and toyed with the top of her panties. "Can I have the pleasure of removing them? Or is this against your rules?"

All her gumption seemed to have been sucked down the drain with the water. "I think you left your fork in the living room."

He kissed her softly on the mouth, then knelt in front of her. His lips found her belly button. He ran a finger over the silk and lace of her panties. Then he caught the elastic of her panties, beside her crotch, and slid his finger inside. She jumped when his finger slipped between the folds of her sex.

"You're so wet. Lean against the counter, Red." He looked up when she didn't move instantly. "Now, you play by my rules."

She started to suggest they go to the bedroom, but something about his voice, his demanding tone, made her want to obey. He was the master. She his . . . sex slave. Fantasies arose. A yearning spiraled between her legs and she leaned back.

"Spread your legs a little wider."

She slid her foot to the left. He pulled her panties to the side. She felt his breath on her sex. Heat rushed to her cheeks, but she stayed where she was. His finger brushed over her again, fireworks of pleasure shooting deep in her abdomen. Her knees buckled. She would have fallen if he hadn't stood up and caught her.

Then holding her up, his lips met hers. "Breathe, Red."

Chapter Twenty-six

Katie inhaled. The scent of her sex lay on his mouth, so close to hers. A fire of want and need pulsed between her legs. A fire Carl Hades had started, a fire only he could put out.

"Can we take this to the bedroom?" he asked. "Or do you have more chores for us? And believe me, sweetheart, I'm not complaining."

"Bedroom." She pressed her hands to his chest and watched as her fingers moved over the hard wall of muscle. She stopped when she came to an ugly scar on his left shoulder that she hadn't noticed until now. Meeting his eyes, she sensed the pain he must have felt. Leaning in, she pressed her lips to the angry mark.

He leaned down and picked her up; she wrapped her legs around him, and they moved into his bedroom.

He laid her on his bed, opened a drawer on the bedside table, and dropped some foil packages beside the lamp. Then, totally naked, totally gorgeous, he stretched out beside her.

"What happened here?" She touched his scar.

"Bullet," he answered, and passed his finger over her nipple.

"Did it hurt?" She moaned at the feel of his touch.

"Let's not talk about that. I need to know what I can do for you that will blow your mind, Red."

Feeling braver, she reached down and wrapped her hand around his long, hard shaft. "Can you think of a place this might go?"

He pulled his hot, smooth sex from her fist. "There's one little problem with that."

"Problem?"

"Ahh, Red. The moment I'm inside you, I'm going to blow. It's going to be as embarrassing as hell, but there isn't a damn thing I can do about it." His touch lowered, and he slipped his fingers inside her panties. "So here's my plan." He passed his finger over her, and Katie raised her hips to meet his touch.

"You're so wet." He slipped the panties down her legs. He leaned on his elbow to look at her. "And finally naked."

"What's the plan?" she asked, wanting to feel him inside her. She brushed her fingers down his chest, and then lower. She wrapped her hand around his throbbing shaft and moved her fist up and down.

"I can't take it." He pulled back and hissed. "Here's the deal. I'm going to help you cross over, then I'm going to climb on top and come right behind you. And I can guarantee you, I'm not going to last five seconds."

She wasn't sure she could last five seconds, either. "But—"

"Let me finish. In five minutes, maybe not even that long, we'll do it again. And then I promise, I'll give it to you as hard and as long as you want it."

He kissed her, then—moist kisses that slowly moved from her lips to her breasts. He ran his tongue around her nipple, sucking, then he began traveling downward, kissing her, inch by inch.

He kissed her stomach, her navel, and the sides of each of her thighs. Then he was between her legs. Where he'd said he really wanted to taste. Where she really wanted him to taste.

He spread her thighs farther apart. "You're beautiful everywhere." He slipped one finger inside. She jutted up her hips and the pleasure that had been building all night, or maybe since she'd cuddled up on the cot with him in the dark, came in waves. Oh yes, she'd wanted this since she'd first laid eyes on him.

His tongue moved slowly over her sex, once, twice. She shattered. And it was she who was embarrassed when she couldn't control the moans escaping her throat.

"Looks like you enjoyed doing the dishes as much as I did." He snatched a condom, and before she realized it, he'd positioned himself between her legs.

He brushed her hair from her face. "Just remember, I already apologized for this." He entered her in one hard thrust and there was a second of nothing but rightness. Him. Her.

He moved in and then out. Her body made room for him. She waited for his next thrust and she moved with him. In. Out.

"Wrap your legs around me!" He gritted out the words.

She did. He pumped into her again. Deeper. The length of him stretched her, filled her to the navel. Her breath caught. Another orgasm beckoned, her hips rose, but his body hardened. The noise escaping his lips was primal. She smiled at the realization he'd been right; she hadn't crossed over this time.

"I'm sorry," he ground out, and rolled them on their sides. "I knew that was going to happen."

"And then," Les swiped at her tear-streaked cheeks, "he said I either had to take the necklace off or leave."

Les knew she should shut up, that some things weren't meant to be shared, but if she didn't tell someone, she would explode. "I almost took it off. I swear, I almost did it and then . . ." Another wave of tears flooded her eyes. "Then I jumped off the sofa, got dressed and ran out. A big part of me didn't want to leave, but because I loved Mike . . . Why the fuck did he have to die?"

Les buried her face in her hands. Then she felt a gentle touch on her shoulder. She peered through her fingers at the concerned face of her listener.

"I like my new shoes," Mimi said, but then with the tenderness of a loving grandma, she pulled Les into her arms, and as Les cried on her grandma's shoulder, she wondered if Mimi didn't somehow understand more than she could communicate.

The music clicking off woke him up. Opening his eyes, Tabitha's killer realized his headache had faded. Now maybe he could think clearer, focus on what he needed to do.

Rolling over, he spotted his photo album on the bedside table. And panicked.

If the cops came back and saw his album, they would know. He sat up so fast, he felt a little dizzy. His eyes darted to the closet, the closet where he'd hidden the gun he'd used on Tabitha and the knife he used on his brides.

He had to hide them. If the cops came back, if they searched his house, they would know he wasn't normal. And they would send him back to the hospital.

The headache returned and started to drum harder. No! He couldn't let the pain come back. Couldn't let the laughter start again. *Focus.* He had to think of how he was going to stop the police from knowing it was him.

He started rocking, but not too hard. Rocking helped. He was a smart man. Even the doctors had told his mom. People with his condition were gifted. He could do this. He'd find a way that people wouldn't know he'd done this.

Rolling out of bed, he found a pillowcase and dropped the gun, the knife, and his photo album inside. He would find a place to hide them. Hide them really well.

* * *

Carl woke up when Katie's naked warmth snuggled up to his side. Having slept alone for so long, not counting dogs, the slightest movement woke him up. Not that they'd been asleep long. He'd made love to her two more times after his embarrassing Johnny-come-quickly episode.

As for that, he knew the episode wasn't *all* his fault. Her X-rated dish game had done him in. He'd been lucky he hadn't shot his wad when she'd given the spoon a blow job.

She stirred, her hair caught in his chin stubble, and her breasts brushed against his side. His dick swelled and he wondered if she could handle another go at it. Three times, and he still felt desperate to be inside her.

Maybe it was because he hadn't had any in so long. No, truth was she was the best piece of ass he'd ever had. *Piece of ass.* The words rang crude in his head. She'd been so much more than . . . than that. She was . . . Brushing her hair back, the sight of her sweet face had his lungs calling in for a sick day. She was not a piece of ass, she was . . . so damn innocent.

Emotion—deep, intense, and soul shattering—took the place of oxygen in his lungs. What the hell had he done?

Fuck. Shit.

Sunday night, when they'd been locked in that room, he'd told himself this could not happen. That it had MISTAKE stamped all over it in huge block letters. And yet, he'd done it anyway. He'd let the organ between his legs convince him that as long as he'd gotten the green light from her, he could proceed with a clear conscience.

Well, where the hell was his clear conscience now?

Fuck. Shit.

He gripped his shoulder. Hadn't failing Amy been bad enough? At least Amy's life had been screwed up before she'd met him. But Katie . . . Katie was the type of woman that men should never fail. And he would fail her, because that was just what he did. He'd failed his mother. He'd failed Amy.

He closed his eyes. Katie watched *The Brady Bunch* and rocked sick babies. The framed pictures of her family flashed in his head. She'd lost everyone she loved. So innocent, and he'd barged into her life and took some of that innocence away. And for what? What was he going to do for her?

Oh sure, he wanted to protect her. But he'd also wanted to fuck her. And he had. He'd fucked Katie over really good.

He groaned. What the hell had he done?

Katie rolled over and blinked at the sun streaming in the window. Her eyes shot open. For a second, she didn't know where she was, then the tinge of soreness between her legs brought it all back. Deliciously back.

She smiled into the spray of sun, and wanting to study him sleeping, she rolled over, and . . . No Carl.

She sat up. The sheet slipped down her breasts. She recalled telling Carl she was getting her gown; he'd refused to let her go. *I want you naked all night*, he'd insisted. But ahh, now she had a little problem: her clothes were in the hall bathroom.

The smell of coffee reached her nose. She swung her feet over the bed. Tiptoeing into the master bath, she spotted her clothes from last night neatly folded on the bathroom counter. And tossed in the corner of the floor were his khakis and pink shirt.

The memory of their clothes piled together on the dining room floor flooded her mind. There was something almost disturbing at the sight of them now. Hers, folded and neat, separate from his. She had the oddest desire to throw hers over with his, to rejoin them. Then another plan hit.

She donned Carl's pink shirt. Let him see that she didn't mind wearing pink, either.

Searching, she found some toothpaste and a comb. She gave her hair a few passes, and finger-brushed her teeth— no, she wouldn't use a guy's toothbrush until she slept over at least three times; it was a rule she and Les had devised—then she tiptoed into the living room. Empty living room.

She moved to the kitchen, and her heart gave a squeeze when she saw him. Wearing Dockers and a white button- down, his back to her, he poured himself a cup of coffee. Tiptoeing in, she cupped his bottom and whispered, "Need help washing dishes?"

She felt him tense. Then she heard someone be- hind her.

"That's my husband's ass you've got your hands on."

Katie jumped back, and Ben Hades swung around. Katie swung to face his wife. "I . . . I thought—"

The woman, with short brown hair and soft green eyes, started laughing. "Don't worry, I've pinched Carl's ass more times than I can count."

"A subject I don't care to talk about," Ben Hades piped up.

Katie swung back to Ben and quickly reached up to close another button on Carl's pink shirt. "I . . ."

"Their asses aren't identical." His wife walked over. "Turn around," she told her husband. He did, and she ran her hand down his bottom.

"If you'll notice, Ben has fuller cheeks here." She pat- ted her husband's tush. "Carl's butt is thinner and more tapered."

"Are you done playing with my ass?" Ben looked back.

His wife laughed. "I'm Tami."

Katie managed to smile. Ahh, but on the inside, she was still dying. "I think I'll go—" She backed up and nearly tripped over the two dogs. Her face burned with embarrassment as she ran into the hall bathroom.

Ten minutes later, dressed and nose powdered, she planted herself on the toilet, stared at the door, and waited. Waited for Carl to appear, laughing about her mistake, and offering to help her make a better impression on his sister-in-law.

A knock came at the door. Thank God. She pulled it open.

Ben's wife stood there, smile in place. "You okay?"

Katie took a deep breath. "I'm just trying to pull myself together after making an idiot out of myself by grabbing your husband's ass."

Tami chuckled. "Seriously, I've pinched Carl's butt more times than I can count."

The warmth in Tami's expression took Katie's humiliation level down a notch. "Speaking of Carl, is . . . is he here?"

Tami's expression tightened. "Uh . . . he had to head out. He asked us to come by. Ben needs you to look at some mug shots and then . . . I'm supposed to drop you off at his dad's."

"His dad's?" Had that question sounded as unsettled as Katie felt?

Tami's brow furrowed. "Yeah."

"I see." She didn't see.

Katie fought back the rising emotion in her chest. Disappointment. Maybe even a little anger. Sure, she understood he had to work, but would it have been too much to ask for a simple good-bye, a *see you later and thanks for screwing me three times last night*? Okay, maybe she was overreacting. Maybe he'd tried to wake her. That had to be it, right?

"Do you need some coffee?" Tami asked.

"I'm fine," she lied when she saw the look on the woman's face. Pity? Why would Carl's sister-in-law pity her?

Sitting across from Ben again in the same room she'd sat in before brought back a lot of things for Katie to worry about. Things other than a missing lover or the unexplainable pity in his sister-in-law's eyes.

Duh, she'd been so busy having sex, she'd forgotten that she had a serial killer after her.

Ben spread some pictures in front of her. "Do you recognize the guy who delivered the flowers to your house the other day?"

Katie studied the images. "I think it's this guy. But I only saw him through the peephole. Joe could probably tell you."

"Joe?" Ben asked.

"My fiancé." Katie blushed. "Ex-fiancé." Did Ben know she'd been engaged? Oh, hell.

Much to Ben's credit, he didn't smirk or seem to judge her. But should she be judging herself?

Ben passed a notepad over to her. "We'll need his contact information."

Katie wrote it down, then glanced at the photographs. "I thought you guys were thinking the DJ, Will Reed, was the one."

Ben frowned. "We're looking at four suspects."

"All the guys working on the wedding?" she asked.

He nodded. "Is there anything you can remember about any of them that may help us?"

Katie sighed. "I never met any of them, except the DJ the other day. I either hired them over the phone or dealt with assistants. At the florist, I was working with . . . I think her name was Sarah. And I only met Todd Sweet's assistant."

Then Katie remembered her initial reaction to Will Reed, the DJ, when she showed up at his house yesterday. "This may be nothing, but I kind of got the creeps from the DJ when I was there. He made some flirty remark and the music he was playing made me think about the phone calls I'd received with the music."

"We're looking at him real close." Ben glanced at

Katie's purse hanging on the chair. "We're going to have to confiscate your phone. Just in case someone calls."

Feeling as if the conversation was winding down, she asked, "Tami mentioned something about my going over to your dad's place. Do you think . . . I mean, do I really need to do that?"

Ben leaned back in his chair. "If I said no, my brother would kill me." He sighed. "Carl's determined to keep you safe. And he was adamant about you going to Dad's."

Katie didn't know what to say, so she didn't say anything. But the questions ran like kittens chasing butterflies in her mind. Did that mean he cared? Did it mean he would be at his dad's when she got there? Did it excuse him for not . . . not at least kissing her good-bye this morning?

"And honestly," Ben continued. "I think it would be best. Besides, my dad is looking forward to seeing you."

Tami met Katie in the hall. Ben had insisted Katie ride with her to the police station in case the killer knew her car. "I'm sorry you had to wait," Katie said.

"It was nothing." Tami held up a romance novel. "I brought my book. I hope my husband wasn't too hard on you?"

"No." Katie smiled. "Ben seems like a nice guy. And in spite of how it looked this morning, I'm not interested in him."

Tami laughed and dropped her book into her purse. "I have orders to take you to Dad's house. However, I've got to pick up Ben junior from school, and thought we could grab a bite to eat."

"Sounds great. I'm sorry for . . . messing up your day."

"Actually, it's nice to get out of the house. We just moved, and all I've done is pack or unpack for weeks."

They went first to pick up Ben junior from kindergarten. Katie was able to spot him right away. She probably would even have been able to pick him out if she hadn't seen his photograph.

"He really looks like his dad and uncle," she said as the boy carrying a Batman backpack came running toward the car.

"And he's just like his dad." Pride rang in Tami's voice.

Ben junior, aka Benny, crawled into the backseat, chattering so fast Katie could hardly understand.

"Calm down," his mom said. "And say hello to Miss Katie. She's . . . a friend of Uncle Carl."

Benny buckled himself in, then looked over at her. "Are you my uncle's new girlfriend?"

Okay, nothing like being put on the spot by a five-year-old.

"Benny, it's not polite to . . . to ask questions."

"Sorry." Benny bounced in his seat. "Amy used to be his girlfriend. I used to catch them kissing all the time. But she left and when he went to find her he got shot."

"Benny." Warning rang in Tami's voice.

Katie glanced at Tami, wishing she'd explain. But no explanation came.

Tami rolled her eyes. "Kids."

Over lunch, Katie and Tami discussed safe topics— Katie's job, Tami's new house—while Benny played in the restaurant's indoor playground.

"So, do your parents live in town?" Tami asked.

Katie picked up her tea. She hated explaining it and went for the short version. "My parents have passed away."

"Oh," Tami said. "They have you late in life?"

Katie relented and told the long version. The pity in Tami's expression reminded Katie of a similar look this morning.

"I'm sorry," Tami said, and then came the dreaded silence.

Katie bit her lip to keep from asking if there was something Tami wasn't telling her about Carl. Maybe even ask her about Carl's old girlfriend, and about his getting shot. But those things Carl needed to tell her. Right?

If he chose to tell her. Or maybe he wouldn't. Like he hadn't chosen to say good-bye this morning. Every few minutes, Katie reminded herself that she'd entered into this fling with Carl knowing it wouldn't last.

However, Katie didn't know how to do flings. She'd had four serious boyfriends in her life, and they had all started out the way normal relationships should: two people getting to know each other, learning about each other's lives, learning to care about each other, and then falling into bed. Katie wondered where she might find some information on the proper etiquette for flings. Maybe in flings, men weren't expected to speak to their lovers on the morning after.

Katie felt her face flush with both embarrassment and—okay, she'd admit it—anger. At the police station, she'd expected Carl to call. Just to say hello or something.

"I'm sorry I brought your parents up," Tami said.

Realizing Tammy was reading something into Katie's silence, she looked back at Ben. "He's so cute."

"You want kids?" Tami began stacking the dishes.

"Two." Katie spoke on automatic. "A boy and a girl. Two years apart. In a house with green shutters, out in the suburbs."

"And a white picket fence." Tami laughed.

Katie grinned. It hit her again, how mismatched she and Carl were. Everything she wanted, Carl called crazy.

Tami's phone rang and she glanced at Katie as she spoke. Katie's stomach clenched, and in spite of her last thought having been that her night with Carl had been a big, huge mistake, the idea that it might be him had her heart singing with joy.

"I stopped off to get Benny." Tami frowned. "We're having lunch. I didn't know I had to get permission." Tami hung up.

Katie waited for her to say the call had been from Ben.

Because if it had been Carl, he would have asked to speak to her, right? Tami didn't offer the information, so Katie put her head on the chopping block and asked, "Ben?"

The look of pity jumped back into Tami's eyes again. "Carl. He's pissed that I didn't take you straight to Dad's."

Was he waiting for her? "Is he there?"

Tami blinked. "No. He said he'd spoken with Dad."

Thirty minutes later, they knocked on Mr. Hades' apartment door. Mr. Hades answered with what Katie thought of as a come-on-in smile.

"Come on in," he said.

Had she called the situation right or what? Now, if she could just figure out what name to call his son. Oh, a few were coming to mind. But Rays didn't use that kind of language. Unless it was really worthy. And she hadn't yet figured out if this was worthy.

"*Mi casa es su casa,*" Hades senior said. Then he picked up Benny and gave him a whirl. "How's my favorite grandson?"

"I'm your only grandson." Benny laughed.

"Dang, you're smart." Mr. Hades turned back to Katie. "Put your things in the extra bedroom. I changed the sheets."

Sheets? Did that mean . . . *Deep breath.* So, she wasn't here just for the afternoon? Which meant Carl didn't want her staying at his place. He was . . . dumping her. Katie tried not to react to the pain slicing at her heart. Tried. But from the way Tami looked at her, Katie figured she'd failed miserably.

"She didn't bring her things, Dad," Tami said, frowning.

"We can run and get them later. Or Carl can bring them by."

Carl was really dumping her. Welcome to the one-night-stand club. Or better said, welcome to the Poked List, a voice whispered in her head. Maybe the situation was worthy of some bad language, after all.

Why had he done this? Had she said something, done something wrong last night? Of course, how was she to know? She didn't know the fling rules—the let-me-screw-you-a-few-times-and-that's-all-I-want rules. Oh, God, she'd been such a fool.

"Nice place." Katie pretended to look around. Then her gaze caught on all the framed pictures of Carl and his brother. His face, his gorgeous fucking face stared at her. Just like that, she knew she couldn't do this. Couldn't stay here.

She faced Tami. "I really need to get back to my car."

Carl pulled into the florist's parking lot. Today, he'd gone to talk to Mr. Sweet at Sweet's Bakery and hadn't found him home. He'd interviewed Mr. Sweet's neighbors and got the usual *he's a nice, quiet neighbor* crap.

He'd also spoken to the neighbors of the photographer, Mel Grimes, who'd been equally glowing. Maybe too glowing. Which upped Carl's suspicion of the photographer. According to the old lady who lived next door to Grimes, the guy never brought home women and never dated.

Carl remembered the nude photographs displayed on the man's wall. Something told him that the man who'd taken those pictures had a sexual interest in women. And if he had a sexual interest in women, why didn't he date? Then again, Carl had himself gone thirteen months without dating. Maybe Grimes had his reasons.

Next Carl had paid a visit to Will Reed's neighbors, and they'd had less than glorious things to say about the DJ. Supposedly, he was loud, always bringing home different girls, and had the neighborhood association on his ass for running a business out of his home. Nevertheless, none of the information made him more likely to be a serial killer.

But then Carl walked into his neighbor's yard and peeped over the fence. And he'd be damned if he didn't see a few gas cans sitting beside the garage. It might not be enough to get a warrant, but it gave Carl a reason to look at the guy a little harder.

The neighbors of Edwards, the florist with the attitude, were thrilled to share their opinions. Apparently, before he'd gotten his last divorce, he'd banged up his ex-wife. While domestic violence tendencies didn't necessarily go hand in hand with serial killing, Carl's gut said that here was their guy.

And that's why he was at the florist's. He'd made an appointment with Mr. Edwards's assistant.

As he got out of his GTO, his brother's official sedan pulled into the lot. Carl hurried over to him.

"Is your cell phone broke?" He'd left three messages wanting to know if Katie had been able to identify Mr. Edwards. "What happened this morning?"

Ben clicked the lock on his car. "Katie picked out Mr. Edwards, but then said she wasn't sure. I've got Joe Lyon coming in to see if he can give us a positive ID."

Carl flinched at the mention of Joe Lyon's name. Last night he'd wanted to ask Katie how the man had taken the news of being dumped. But talking about her ex didn't blend with having sex. Not that Carl had forgotten how Lyon had eyed the blonde at the police station the morning Red and he were questioned. And after spending last night with Red, Carl didn't get how any man would cheat on her. When you had the best, why look further?

Then, to complicate his already-complicated emotions, the idea of her having slept with Lyon, of possibly washing dishes with that guy, had put Carl in a dandy of a mood.

"How was Katie?" Carl's chest spasmed just saying her name.

Ben frowned. "You should have told us that she didn't know you were sending her to Dad's. Tami's going to shoot your ass."

Carl squeezed his aching shoulder. "I deserve to be shot. I screwed up. I . . . I slept with her."

Ben leaned against his car. "Well, from the way she grabbed my ass this morning, I'd say it was a mutual decision."

Carl frowned. "What?"

"I'm telling you, she's got a thing for me." Ben laughed. "Seems our butts are almost identical—so said my wife right after she caught Red feeling me up in the kitchen."

Carl didn't see the humor. He could imagine how Katie felt when she woke up and he hadn't been there. But wasn't it best to stop it now? "I don't have a fucking clue why I let it happen."

Ben grinned. "Oh, I could tell you that. She's hot."

Carl eyed his brother's smile. "And you're married."

"Married but not dead. Not that I would trade in Tami, mind you. I'm just saying I know why you went for it."

"It was wrong. Katie's not like that. I was a fucking bastard to . . . to let it happen."

"So you decided to be a bigger bastard and leave without telling her, and then to dump her on Dad without telling her."

"I'm going to speak to her. I just . . . I didn't know what to say. I figure I'll see her at Dad's tonight."

"And tell her what?" Ben asked.

"Tell her the truth. That I'm no good for her."

"And why are you not good for her?" Ben crossed his arms.

"You know who I am."

"I know that you got your heart broken a year ago. That you got yourself shot trying to protect Amy even after she left your ass. So, are you telling me you still love Amy?"

"No!" And it was true. He didn't love Amy, not anymore.

"So what's so bad about dating Red?"

Carl squeezed his shoulder again. "I told you, she's not my type. For God's sake, she watches *The Brady Bunch*. She's the marrying kind, the I-want-a-couple-of-kids kind."

"And you didn't ask Amy to marry you?"

Carl stared at his brother. "How did you know about that?"

"You told me that night you got drunk off your ass."

Carl shook his head. "The point is that I should have never gotten involved with Amy. But Katie's . . . she's innocent. She's not the kind you screw and walk away from."

"Then why walk away?" Ben arched an eyebrow.

"Because I'd end up hurting her. I'm not a total bastard."

"What? You don't think you can keep your dick in your pants?"

"No, that's not it," Carl answered.

"Then what is it? What is it with you and decent women? Are you so afraid of marriage that you only date unfit gals? But, wait, even that didn't work, because you fell for Amy, even when . . . when she wasn't the marrying kind."

"I'm not afraid. I'm selfish." And in some ways it was the truth. "I like making myself happy, not worrying about making someone else happy." Being emotionally responsible for someone was a bad thing, especially when you sucked at it.

Ben's arms remained crossed. "You know what Tami says? She says your commitment problems go back to Mom. I'm beginning to think she's right."

Carl ground his teeth. "And when did your wife get her shrink license?"

"She's pretty good at reading people." Ben looked at Carl as if he was trying to do some reading himself. "It wasn't your fault. Mom made the choice. She was tired of suffering. And if I'd been the one who'd found out, and she asked me not to tell? Hey, I'd have done the same thing you did. It would have killed me inside, too. But I'd have done it."

Carl refused to shovel through the past. "Well, why don't I just pull out my checkbook and pay for this little session."

"Just don't say I didn't try." Ben shoved away from the car and waved toward the florist's shop. "You want to do this together?"

"Isn't that against your rules?" Carl bit back.

"Get your ass off your shoulders, brother," Ben snapped.

Chapter Twenty-seven

"Please, take me back to my car," Katie told Tami, and tried not to let any emotion show on her face. "I just realized I can stay with a friend. I shouldn't be burdening any of you."

"It's not a burden," Mr. Hades tossed into the conversation.

Tami studied her as if downloading everything from Katie's mind. "Dad, watch Benny, Katie and I are going to take a walk."

"Sorry," Mr. Hades said, "but considering someone might be after her, I think a walk is out of the question. Now, if you want to go sit out on my patio, make yourself at home."

Tami walked to the sliding glass doors. "Katie?"

Katie could hear the conversation already, *You slept with my brother-in-law without even knowing him, so stop being surprised that he isn't living up to your standards. Stop acting as if he's broken your heart.*

Well, Katie didn't need Tami telling her what she already knew. What she needed was a ride back to her car. Yup, the sooner she forgot that man, the better she'd be. But since Carl's sister-in-law seemed pretty stubborn, Katie stiffened her backbone and stepped outside.

Tami pulled out the two chairs at the patio table. Katie sank down into one and fought the urge to bang her head against the table the way Les did when she got frustrated.

"Let me start with saying I love Carl. And—"

Katie held her hand. "I'm not blaming Carl for anything. It's my fault. I know that."

"Your fault?" Tami made a face. "It's your fault that my brother-in-law is being a total scumbag asshole?" She touched Katie's arm. "Sorry, but this one isn't on your head. Carl is in such deep doo-doo with me right now, he'll never eat another one of my pies as long as he lives. And the next time he comes over with his dirty laundry, I'm washing his boxers in the detergent that gives both him and his brother the worst case of jock itch known to mankind."

Tears came to Katie's eyes, and she tried really hard not to let them fall, but one got past her.

Tami huffed. "His balls will be peeling for a week."

Maybe it was the peeling-balls statement that did it, but suddenly Katie didn't need to cry. She laughed. "Thanks."

"No thanks needed. But here's what I do need." The woman leaned her arms on the table. "Don't put yourself in danger because Carl's an ass. The only thing I know is you are somehow connected to those two women who were found in the woods yesterday. I don't know details, but I know my husband. And when he comes home and spends half the night in his son's room, it's because he's seen something so ugly that nothing short of watching an innocent child sleep will help."

Tami inhaled. "Dad and Ben, and even my asshole of a brother-in-law, excel at taking care of people. Don't go."

Katie folded her hands together. While she ached to escape Carl, the image of Ben watching little Benny sleep filled her head. "I wish I knew what I'd done to get . . . banished."

"Look, I'd say you didn't do anything. From the get-go,

you had Carl tied in knots. He came over the day after you two were locked up. He made Ben promise to make sure you were safe. And when Ben asked him why he couldn't go, he got all huffy and said, 'It's not my job.'"

"But it wasn't his job," Katie said.

"No, but if it wasn't his job, why was he so worried about you? And Ben told me that Carl got worked up when Ben joked with him about you throwing yourself at him the day he went to see you."

Katie blushed. "I thought he was Carl that time, too."

"Oh, I know. The moment I saw your face when you realized you had a hold of my husband's ass, I stopped worrying." Tami smiled. "What I'm saying is I think Carl cares about you. That's why he's being an ass. Not that it excuses him. And God forbid I tell you to forgive him, or give him another chance, but the best punishment would be for you to stay and make the dirtbag pay. I'll bet fifty bucks that he can't stay away from you."

Taking a breath, Katie asked the question. "Did Carl ask you to bring me back here so he wouldn't have to deal with me?"

"All he told Ben was that . . . that he didn't think your staying at his place was a good idea. For us to bring you here. We thought you knew about the changes until we got there."

Carl really was dumping her. Welcome to the Poked List!

"But you can't put yourself in danger because—"

Katie held up her palm. "I'll stay." Probably not for the reasons Tami thought. The idea of Carl paying didn't appeal to her. Okay, it did. He'd been an ass. And revenge could be sweet. But that wasn't the reason she was agreeing to stay. It was what Tami said about Ben spending hours watching his son. She sure as heck didn't want to be the next reason Ben Hades or any cop spent hours staring at an innocent child trying to forget how her body had been mutilated.

Now, if she could just convince herself that her heart hadn't already been handed the same fate.

Carl and Ben walked into the florist's shop and Carl asked for Sarah. The clerk said she'd be right with them. As they waited, Ben started looking around. "Maybe I'll buy Tami some flowers."

Carl walked over to the cooler with his brother; the red flowers from the other day caught his eye.

"Can I help you?"

He and Ben turned to Edwards's assistant.

"Hi again." Sarah led them to her office. When Carl introduced Ben as his brother, she appeared surprised. "Normally the grooms or the groomsmen don't care about the flowers."

Ben looked at him and flashed his badge. "Actually, ma'am, we need to ask a few questions about your boss."

The woman didn't look all that surprised. "About what?"

Carl sat down in one of the flimsy metal chairs. "Do you know if there were any bad feelings between Mr. Edwards and Tabitha Jones, the wedding planner?"

The woman paled. "Is this about her murder?"

"Please just answer the question." Ben stared at her dead-on.

"I . . . A few months ago, they were seeing each other."

Ben's eyes widened, and Carl could tell that Edwards hadn't mentioned this in his interview. "Did it end badly?" Ben asked.

"I . . . wouldn't know." Sarah gulped.

Carl leaned in. "Is it customary for you to send flowers to the bride and groom a few weeks before the wedding?"

"You mean, from the florist?"

"Yes," Carl added. "Just as a congratulations."

She blinked. "We've . . . never done that."

Ben and Carl exchanged a knowing glance. "So, the florist didn't send Katie Ray flowers Monday evening?"

The woman's brows arched. "You mean the Ray–Lyon wedding?"

"Yes." Carl's gut tightened at hearing Katie's name associated with the man who'd been supposed to marry her.

Sarah appeared confused. "You must be mistaken. Ms. Jones notified us last Saturday that we wouldn't be doing that wedding. I've already canceled the orders on those flowers."

Someone called to Sarah from the front, and she excused herself. Ben took out his cell phone and punched in a few digits.

"It's Hades," he said. "Has Joe Lyon been in to make an ID on the photos yet?" Pause. "Great." A smile twisted his lips, and he hung up. "He picked Edwards out. I think we got him."

"You can let go anytime." Katie pulled out of Les's embrace. Les had stopped by Mr. Hades' place unannounced.

"I'm sorry," she said. "But when I called your cell and Ben Hades said you were with a bodyguard, it really sank in. My best friend has a serial killer after her."

"Sucks, doesn't it?" Katie admitted.

"I'll say." Les looked around Hades senior's apartment. "Then he made me swear I wouldn't tell anyone where you're staying. Especially my mom, since Mr. Hades said that's how the creep found our hotel room. I'm so sorry, I never dreamed that—"

"It's fine," Katie said. And that was a big fat lie. Since Tami left, Katie had battled the war of tears. Every few minutes she'd get a flashback of how totally unbelievable last night had been. And it wasn't the sex.

Okay, it was *also* the sex. But it was other stuff, too. How they'd laughed, teased, and how, as long as Carl had been around, she'd felt safe. With him not being around anymore, she hadn't felt safe all afternoon. She'd started again having those flashbacks of Tabitha getting shot.

Yep. Her mind kept flipping from flashbacks of great sex to a bloody Tabitha. Now, wasn't that a combination?

Katie led Les into the extra bedroom and they plopped their butts down on the bed the way girlfriends do when it's time to talk about serious stuff.

Les studied her. "You're chewing your lip. What happened?"

Katie fell back and stared at the ceiling. "I fucked up."

Les dropped back beside her. "Just so I'm clear. You said 'fucked,' not 'fudged'?"

"It's f-word worthy. I slept with him."

"And now you realize you still love Joe?" Les asked.

Katie twisted to look at her. "No!"

Les looked relieved. "Then why is it f-word worthy?"

Katie didn't answer.

Les sat up. "He sucked in bed, huh?"

"No. It was . . . okay." Katie gritted her teeth. She could not lie. "Oh, Les, he was *so* amazing. Curl you toes, dig your heels into the mattress amazing."

Les giggled, then grew serious. "You had great sex with a hunky man who's trying to protect you, and yet you still look as if someone ran over your pet rock? What am I missing?"

"Because he is such a dickhead," Katie said.

"Ouch. You never say 'dickhead.' This must be really bad."

Katie snatched a bed pillow and hugged it. "He left this morning without a word. Not a thank-you or even 'I've got your number and I'll call you.'"

"Ouch."

Katie bit down on her lip. "And when I woke up, his brother and sister-in-law were there with orders to bring me here. Apparently he doesn't want me to stay at his house anymore."

"Dickhead!" Les snapped.

"I know." A wave of heartache washed over Katie. "So

tell me why it hurts so much? I shouldn't miss a dick-head."

"The leg humpers are the ones who hurt us the most. Remember Paul who you so inappropriately reminded me of earlier?"

Katie nodded. "Paul was definitely a dickhead."

Les sighed. "And it seems they are the best in bed, too."

Katie's eyes widened. "Les Grayson, shame on you. Are you saying Paul was better than my brother?"

Guilt shadowed Les's face. "Not better. Just different."

Although Katie didn't think Les realized it, this was the first time since Mike's death that she had mentioned anything about an old boyfriend. Which meant maybe Les was moving on. Maybe? Then Les touched her ring under her shirt.

Katie pulled Les's hand away. "It's time to let him go."

Les's eyes grew moist. "I loved him so much, but I think what's going on in my head right now isn't just about letting him go. I'm afraid. I'm so afraid of falling in love and then losing it again. I couldn't live through losing someone else." She blinked and another tear escaped.

Katie took Les's hand in hers. "You're just confused. Because Les Grayson, the girl who went skinny-dipping in the Guataloupe River, who snuck boys up into our dorm room, who tells Boston chefs that their fried chicken just isn't southern enough, why, that Les Grayson isn't afraid of anything."

Les sniffled and chuckled at the same time. Then she got all serious looking. "I know that Joe told you that . . ."

"That you two are attracted to each other," Katie finished.

Les's brow puckered. "I swear, Katie, when I first laid eyes on him at the bar, I didn't know who he was and it was like . . . *wow*. And when I found out who he was, I nearly croaked."

Katie sighed. "Les, please listen to me. Honestly, I've

dug deep inside of myself looking for maybe just a tiny bit of resentment, but it's not there. There's not a good reason why . . . why you and Joe couldn't see where it leads."

"I don't think that would be a good idea," Les said.

"Why not?" Katie asked.

"So many reasons," Les said; then she dropped back onto the bed. "What are you going to do about Dickhead?"

"Forget him," Katie said. "I hate being on the Poked List."

Les rolled over. "Do you love him?"

"Love? You're joking, right?" Silence reigned, and then the truth started bubbling to the surface. "When I'm with him, I feel safe, and this is going to sound so corny, but it's like he gets me, like he sees inside me. Remember what I told you about him giving me the elephant painting? I barely knew the guy and yet he somehow sensed how important painting was to me. And he can just look at me and know when I'm feeling panicked. He says to me, 'Breathe, Red.' And every time he's said that, he's been right on target."

Katie hugged the pillow closer. "And he makes me laugh and . . . I've always had to work at being a Ray. I never felt good enough, or poised enough, or pretty enough, or witty enough. But when I'm with Carl, I feel all those things."

She closed her eyes. "Oh, God, Les. I think I am this close to falling in love with a dickhead."

They both just sat there for a long minute, before Les asked again. "So, what are you going to do about Dickhead?"

Katie sat up, still hugging the pillow. "If I see him again, I'm going to kick his ass."

Les laughed. "I trained you well."

Baby and Precious greeted Carl with affection at the door. He knelt and gave them both a few pats. Then, standing, he stared at the sofa. He envisioned Red there.

He needed a beer. He stepped into the kitchen, and damn if he didn't see Katie in there, too. Peering at him from behind the pantry door, embarrassed because his dad interrupted . . . He gazed at the sink and got a hard-on. *Shit.* He grabbed a beer.

Being a masochist, he went to his bedroom, stared at the rumpled sheets. Visions flashed—of how she'd looked sitting on top of him, riding him, of how she'd tasted between her thighs, of how tight she'd been when . . . He inhaled. Her musky scent still hung in the air.

He went and sat down at the dining room table, the only place her memory didn't cling. Then his mind created the image of the clothes piled on the dining room floor. Hers. His. Together.

He reached back and squeezed his shoulder, remembering how he'd wanted to buy some of those red flowers for Katie. The case would be wrapped up soon. Maybe it would be okay to just spend these days with her, enjoy it for a few more days. Wrong. Best to cut it off now. Besides, after the MIA stunt he'd pulled this morning, his chances of getting back in her good graces were nil.

So let her have her anger. Ending things in anger was better than sad good-byes. He sipped his beer.

Baby scratched his leg. He moved his chair back so she could jump up on his lap. Then Precious curled up at his feet. He didn't need a woman. He had two prissy dogs. And beer.

He sucked down another cold swig. Red deserved to hear him tell her that she was too good for him. And knowing women the way he did, she probably deserved the opportunity to tell him what an asshole he'd been. Besides, he had to take her things over, anyway.

A little while later, he used his key and let himself into his dad's apartment. When he made it past the entryway, he saw his dad settled in the usual easy chair, reading. His old man lowered the newspaper.

"I figured you'd show up sooner or later." The paper rattled as his dad went back to reading.

Stepping farther into room, Carl searched for Katie. In spite of knowing it would be a huge punch in the gut, he was starved to see her—to look, not touch.

"Is she in the extra bedroom?" He rubbed his shoulder. Then he set the bag with her things beside the sofa.

"Nope." His dad didn't look up.

"Bathroom?" Carl asked.

"Nope."

Carl tensed. "Damn it! You didn't let her leave, did you?"

The paper rattled again. "She's outside on the patio."

He took a deep breath. Wiped his sweaty palms on the back of his jeans and took a few steps toward the sliding glass door.

"I wouldn't go out there," his dad said coolly.

Carl swallowed. "She's pissed, huh?"

"Probably. But that's not why you shouldn't go out there."

Carl looked away from the heavy blinds covering the door to his dad. "Why shouldn't I go out there?"

"She's got company."

"Company?" Carl remembered Ben telling him he'd given Dad's address to Katie's friend, Les. Rotating his shoulder, Carl went and sat on the sofa. He wondered again if Les was the blonde at the police station the other night. "Is she a blonde?"

"Is who a blonde?"

"Katie's friend, Les?"

"Oh. Yeah, she's blonde. She visited this afternoon, too."

"Too?" Carl asked.

"Yup." The newspaper didn't budge.

Carl's gaze shot to the glass doors. "Who's here now?"

"Her fiancé."

Chapter Twenty-eight

Katie stared at Joe. When Ben had called and said Joe was looking for her, she'd told Ben to give him the address. It felt a little strange seeing Joe after she'd slept with Carl so soon after their breakup, but she did want to remain Joe's friend. And to do that they both had to accept that there would be other people in each of their lives.

Katie had already concluded that she didn't have an issue with it, but she didn't know about Joe.

"I just wanted to check on you," he said. He looked back toward the door leading into the apartment.

"I'm fine," she lied. Mr. Hades had treated Joe like something that needed to be cleaned off the bottom of his shoe, and Katie pretty much knew why. He was looking out for his son's interests. Not that he should; his son wasn't interested in her. All he'd wanted was a night of sex, and he'd gotten it, too. The pain of that settled into her heart and threatened to hang around like a bad case of stomach flu.

"You know, if you wanted to come to my place, you could, right? And I mean . . . just as a friend."

She smiled. "I know." And right after she'd discovered Carl had dumped her, she'd almost decided to do that.

But she didn't want to mess up any chance there might be for Les and Joe.

"Did you tell your mom?" Katie hugged her sweater tighter.

Joe raked a hand through his hair. "Don't ask about that."

"Bad, huh?" Katie frowned.

Joe laughed. "I'll say."

"Oh, Joe, she's just lonely and you're all she has."

"Which is why I told her she needs to get a life," he said.

Katie couldn't argue with that.

Joe looked back at the patio doors. "I thought you were staying with the PI? Why're you here, with his father?"

Katie tried not to react. "I think this is best."

"Something go wrong?" Joe asked.

Glancing away, she answered, "Sort of."

"I'm sorry," he replied, and sincerity rang in his voice.

She looked at him and decided now was the best time to bring up the next topic. "I talked to Les."

He literally flinched. "She told you about last night?"

Katie remembered Les baring her soul before she left. "A little."

Guilt flashed in his eyes. "I'm sorry."

She held up her hand. "Joe, I'm not upset . . . really. I just wanted you to know that Les is vulnerable right now. Give her some time."

He studied her. "You really don't have an issue with this?"

She smiled. "You want to hear something crazy?"

He rolled his eyes. "As if things could get any crazier?"

"In a way, I think I picked you out for Les."

His eyes widened. "You did what?"

"I know this sounds nuts. But you're just like my brother."

He laughed. "Well, that explains why the sex wasn't good."

She laughed, too. "Seriously, you're totally Les's type."

His smile faded. "She doesn't seem to think so."

"Give her time." Katie stood up and went to hug him.

Carl sat on the sofa, trying to figure out why the hell he should care if Red was with Joe Lyon when . . . when he and Red were over. He couldn't wrap his mind around it. Then, unable to take it any longer, he bounced up from the sofa.

"She's with Joe Lyon? Out there. Right now?"

"Yep." His father turned the page and Carl could swear he heard the man chuckle.

"She broke up with him." Carl's gaze shot from the door to his dad. "He's not her fiancé anymore."

The *Chronicle* lowered, and his dad eyed him over the sports page. "Break up. Make up. You know how you young kids are."

"They made up?" Carl's heart fisted. She'd done the dishes with him. They'd made love. How could she go back to Joe?

Not that he'd exactly given her any reason not to, but still.

"I'm guessing," his dad said. "She was happy to see him."

"She was?" Carl took two steps to the door.

"I wouldn't go out there, son."

"The guy doesn't deserve her." Carl swung around and finally found a good reason why Katie couldn't get back with Joe Lyon. "That bastard was cheating on her. And I think with her friend—that Les chick."

"Well, I'm sure a woman like Red knows how to handle that."

Carl went to the blinds and pulled them back. And damn it to hell, Red stood there with Lyon, and that asshole had his hands all over her.

"Oh, shit." Joe saw the man glaring at him from the other side of the glass and he dropped his arms from around

Katie. It had been a simple good-bye hug. But from the look in Carl Hades' eyes, the man didn't think it was that simple.

"I think we've got company," he told Katie.

She looked up, and a world of hurt filled her eyes. The thought that someone had hurt her stirred some uncomfortable feelings in Joe's gut. Not jealousy, but the need to protect her from any asshole.

Joe shot another glance at the PI and saw jealousy in the man's eyes. Joe knew some men were jealous just to be macho, but some men were jealous because they really cared.

The door jerked open and the PI stepped out. He held himself like a man who knew how to fight and didn't mind doing it. Joe wasn't a fighter, but he swung damn hard if swung at.

Katie must have read the same thing in her new boyfriend's mood, because she jumped between them. Her gaze went from Joe to Hades. "I think you two have met before," Katie said.

"At the police station." Joe nodded, willing to take the first step toward clearing the tension.

Obviously not amenable to this, Hades crossed his arms over his chest. "How did you know Katie was here?"

Joe squared his shoulders. "Your brother."

That news didn't seem to land so well with Hades. But at least some of his cockiness seemed to fade. Joe looked at Katie. "I should be going. If you need me, call."

"She won't be needing you," Carl said.

"Excuse me?" Katie bit out, and Joe nearly laughed at what he saw in her eyes. Katie had never looked at him like that—with anger and passion. But damn him if Les hadn't.

Then Joe looked to Hades and saw the same intensity in his eyes. Something told Joe that this man cared about Katie. Something also told him that, if given the right circumstances, these two might stand a chance. But what had the jerk done to hurt her?

Joe looked the man in the eyes. "If Katie needs me, I'll be here." He didn't budge, not even when Hades stepped closer.

Hades senior suddenly stepped through the doorway as if he'd felt the tension brewing all the way inside. He put a warning touch on his son's shoulder.

Joe took it a step further and gave Katie a quick kiss on her cheek. He didn't like the idea of swapping fists with Hades, but a man who knew he had some competition was less likely to behave like an ass. Then, before Hades got a chance for retaliation, Joe left. Buck saw him to the door.

Katie felt anger burn in her belly. How dare he come out here and throw his machismo around as if he had some claim on her after passing her off like a bad gift? She crossed her hands over her chest and told herself to breathe before Carl said it first.

"What the fuck is going on?" Carl flung the question at her.

"I'm wondering that myself," she snapped.

"Is the wedding back on? You taking that asshole back?"

"Joe Lyon has never been an ass. Unlike some people."

Carl's jaw tightened. "Maybe you should ask him about his feelings for your best friend before you say that!"

Katie wasn't sure how Carl had gotten this information, but it didn't matter. "At least he . . . watches *The Brady Bunch*."

She saw her verbal jab hit right where she wanted it to: below the belt.

"You're going to marry him?" The words came out in a growl.

The truth escaped her. "No. But why do you even care? I gave you what you wanted. We're done." Unable to control the ache in her chest, she darted around him and went inside. His dad frowned when he saw her come in.

Carl followed her inside. "We're not through talking."

"Yes, we are." She didn't look back as she went into the kitchen and found her purse. She had nothing else to say to him. But she did have something to give him. It had taken her almost an hour to get the information out of Mr. Hades, but he'd finally relented and given her Carl's rates.

"Come back outside," Carl ordered, and motioned to the door.

She didn't reply. Instead, she yanked open her purse, pulled out the check she'd written, and met him at the door. She slapped the check into his hand. "This should cover it."

"Cover what?" he snarled.

"Your fees. I don't think I should have to pay you for the time we were locked together at Tabitha's because that wasn't my fault. But I paid you from yesterday at lunch until now. Your dad gave me your going rate. Which I must say is a bit pricey."

He glared at the check. "My rates for what?"

"For working my case. Isn't that what you do—private investigations? Protect people. Solve their problems."

"God damn, Katie, we had sex!"

"Oh, do I need to pay you for that, too?"

"Fuck!" He ripped the check in half. "You never hired me."

"So true," she snapped. "But just in case you're wondering, I *am* firing you. I'm no longer your problem, got that?"

"If you think I'm going to let you leave here and risk that some SOB could get to you, then you better think again."

She moved in. "I'm firing *you*. But I've hired your dad."

Carl looked mad enough to chew nails into staples. "He works for me."

"Not on this case, he doesn't. And just for the record, if

I chose to leave here, I could walk out that door and there wouldn't be a damn thing you could do about it. But believe it or not, as much as your presence annoys me right now, you are not worth risking my life for."

She started down the hall to her assigned bedroom, but then something had her turning around. Her throat tightened. "By the way, thanks for a wonderful time last night."

She slammed the door and heard Hades senior say, "Well, that went better than I expected."

An hour later, Carl leaned his head against the bedroom door. *By the way, thanks for a wonderful time last night.* Nothing she'd said to him tonight stung more than that. Because in her words, he'd heard exactly how much he'd hurt her. Damn! He really was a no-good piece of shit.

"Katie, please open the door and let's talk," he said *again*. She hadn't said one word since she'd gone in there.

"I'm not leaving until we talk," he added.

"Mr. Hades?" Katie called out rather loudly. From her voice and tone, Carl knew she wasn't addressing him.

"Yes," his dad called from the next room, where he'd returned to his paper. Who knew the *Chronicle* was so interesting?

"Do you work for me or not?"

"Yes, ma'am. That I do."

"Then stop the dickhead at my door from harassing me."

Carl's old man coughed to cover his laugh.

"Stay out of it, Dad," Carl warned when his dad appeared.

"Well, son, I might have been able to do that if you hadn't gotten me knee-deep in it by doing something stupid. So leave the lady alone." Then his dad motioned him away.

Carl relented and followed his dad into the living room. "Let her simmer down," his dad whispered. "I've seen your mom and even Jessie that mad, and they got over it in time. But don't stop trying. If you don't try, they get madder."

Carl went and fell back on the sofa where he pushed his palms into his eye sockets. He couldn't think straight. He needed to talk to her and yet didn't have a clue what he needed to say. He'd come here prepared to give her up. But seeing her in the arms of Joe Lyon had changed everything.

Yet, it hadn't changed anything. He sucked at relationships. He failed people. He still couldn't promise Katie anything, because he didn't make promises he couldn't keep. And a woman like Katie deserved promises. But damn it! He still had to get her to talk to him. He had to tell her . . . He still fucking didn't know what he had to tell her, but it must be important, because he was hurting like hell.

Katie woke up to a headache, puffy eyes, and an even puffier bladder. She rolled over to look at the clock. Three A.M. She'd cried herself to sleep around midnight, convinced that in spite of it being totally illogical, she'd somehow managed to fall in love with a man she'd known for only a few days—a man whose interest in her was purely sexual. A man who after one night of sex had sent her away. Well, she'd never excelled at sex.

But if the sex sucked that bad, why had he been jealous of Joe? And why had he begged her to open the door. Oh hell, why ask why? The point was that it had been a mistake.

God knew she could deal with a broken heart. That was the thing about surviving really sucky tragedies like losing your whole family: it made you realize you could survive anything.

Getting up to go to the bathroom, she stopped at the door and listened. She wondered if he was still there. He'd sworn he wasn't leaving, but why should she believe him?

She cracked open her door and peered into the hall. Empty. What did she expect? That he'd still be waiting? Not likely.

She started for the bathroom, but paused by the living room. Had he slept on his dad's couch? She tiptoed in just enough to see the sofa. The empty sofa. Feeling silly for caring, she hotfooted it into the bathroom to relieve herself.

She flipped on the light and turned to glare at herself in the mirror. *Hammered shit* came to mind when she saw her red eyes and blotchy face. Amazingly, she still looked better on the outside than she felt on the inside. She pulled her hair from her face. "You're an idiot," she whispered to her reflection.

Letting out a sigh, she pulled her silk nightshirt up, her panties down, and plopped her bottom on the toilet. She'd just got a healthy stream going when the shower curtain swept back. And she saw him. In the bathtub. His legs were bent at the knees, head bent at a weird angle. But his eyes were on her.

Crap!

His focus shifted to her spread legs. She slammed her thighs together and yanked at the toilet paper roll for a few squares. But before she could give herself a one-swipe wipe, he'd climbed out of the tub and had the door blocked. She hit the flusher and popped up.

She glared at him. "Let me by."

He shook his head. "Not until you listen to me."

"I don't care to hear anything you have to say.

"I was an asshole. A piece of shit."

She nodded. "Go on."

"See? I do have something to say you want to hear."

He leaned against the bathroom counter. She eyed the space between him and the door and made a run for it.

He snagged her around her waist and they fell against the wall. One of them must have hit the light switch, because darkness fell. Sweet darkness. Katie's breath hitched.

"Kind of brings back memories, doesn't it?" he asked, and drew her a little closer.

"Bad memories," she lied, and tried to pull away, but he held her. She heard the bathroom door shut. "What are you doing?"

"I just want to talk to you." His hand moved over her hip. That wasn't talking.

"Why were you sleeping in the bathtub?" She reached back to stop him from touching her, and in doing so she brushed her breasts across his chest. Pleasure shot through her, up and down and all over her body. Her nipples became instantly tight. She heard him inhale and knew he'd felt them.

"I wasn't sleeping," he said. "I was waiting for you."

"In the bathtub?"

"I thought about the floor in the hall, but knew you'd see me and shut the door. I thought about the sofa, but I knew you'd hear me coming and run back in the bedroom. I considered just standing in the bathroom, but you might have made it back to the bedroom before I caught you. Then it occurred to me that if I caught you on the pot, you were too much of a lady to run before you wiped." He chuckled. "And I was right, too."

"I see no humor in that," she snapped.

"I guess it's a man thing." He almost grinned.

She tried to pull away again, but his arm tightened. Not too tight. She knew all she'd have to do was yell out for Mr. Hades and he would rescue her. And Carl had to know that, too. Which meant, he knew she wanted to be here. To be in his arms, against his chest, in the dark.

"You hurt me," she said, fighting the intimacy of the darkness that surrounded them.

"I know. And I'm really, really sorry." He pressed his lips to her temple. It was a sweet kiss. A simple kiss. A test to see if she might let him do it again. "I don't have a good excuse either. Except I was . . . I was scared."

She listened and knew he'd spoken the truth. His hand

slid down her back to the curve of her bottom. His slow touch moving over the silk felt like a warm breath on her bare skin.

"Scared of what?" she asked.

"Of you. You scare me, Red."

"How do I scare you?" She sighed when his fingers started slowly inching up under her nightshirt, touching bare skin.

"In every way there is. The way you make me feel. The way I get instantly hard when I look at you." He jutted out his pelvis just to let her see what he meant. "The way your smile makes me melt inside. The way I don't mind wearing pink or eating quiche that really tastes like crap, the way I wish I had matching wineglasses to serve you in. The way I felt tonight when I saw you in another man's arms." He kissed her neck. "Tell me you're not going back to Joe."

"I'm not." She moved her head back to give him better access. His lips trailed a path down her throat as his palm made an upward sweep to her naked breasts.

"Got any bathroom chores we can do?" he asked.

She ran her hand over the bulge behind his zipper.

"Oh, yes, touch me, Red." He unzipped his pants and eased her hand inside. She wrapped her fingers around him, the pulsing heat of him making her want him inside her right then. She tightened her fist around him and said as much.

His mouth covered hers. His hand moved from her breasts to between her thighs. He slipped two fingers inside her. Then, before she knew what had happened, he'd picked her up and was carrying her down the hall.

He laid her on the bed and pulled at her nightshirt. The silk whispered up and over her body. Then he shucked off his pants and shirt and came down on top of her. His penis probed between her legs. He jutted his hips out an inch, just an inch, and the round tip of him entered her, but then he pulled out. He kept teasing her, giving her only the slightest bit of him, then taking it away.

"I want all of you." She jutted her hips and took every inch of him inside her. Then she wrapped her legs around him and began to move for him, with him. And they rode the hot wave of passion together. The words *I love you* lay on her tongue. She barely managed to hold them back as the pleasure exploded.

She knew the moment he came because his body became a rock of tight muscle. He fell to the side of her, their bodies still joined. Then his body tensed again, his muscles turned hard.

"Shit! Fuck!" He rolled off her so fast, Katie gasped.

Chapter Twenty-nine

"What?" she asked.

"I didn't use a condom." He sat up, put his feet on the floor, and dropped his face into his palms. "This is why you scare me, Red. I can't think! I fucking never forget to use a condom."

Katie froze. His language, his tone. Like an eraser, it wiped away all the wonderful and left the naked truth.

"Are you on anything?" he bit out, not even looking at her.

The naked truth. If she got pregnant he'd feel obligated to marry her, or at the least to act as a father.

Katie pulled her knees up to her chest. She recalled the mismatched daisy knife and rose fork during their lunch at the diner. Carl Hades and Katie Ray were just like that restaurant's cutlery; they didn't belong together.

"I'm on the pill." The ache in her chest doubled. "But pregnancy isn't the only thing we need to be worried about."

He looked over his shoulder. "I'm clean."

"As if you had a blood test just last week." Right then, she saw the bedroom door was standing wide open. They had made love in his father's house with the door open. Embarrassment had her yanking a blanket to cover herself.

"No, like I had a blood test since I've been with anyone."

She waved toward the door. "You've got to go."

His gaze shot to the door. "Shit!" He scrambled out of bed and closed it.

"Leave, Carl. Please, leave." She rolled over, not wanting him to see her tears—and she really needed to cry. She stared at the wall, feeling the knot grow in her throat. She heard him breathing. Not moving.

The bed shifted as he slipped in beside her. "I did it again, didn't I? I acted like a bastard." He touched her shoulder and his touch sent shards of pain to her heart.

"This isn't going to work, Carl. You know that," she managed to say, but the words came out with the sound of pain.

He pressed his face into her hair and wrapped his arms around her middle. "And that's the biggest reason you scare me," he whispered into her ear. "I'll hurt you, and I can't stand that thought." He got up. She heard him gathering his clothes.

She heard him move for the door. His footsteps stopped.

"Did Ben tell you that we think we got the guy?" he asked.

Got what guy? Then she remembered. Odd, how easy it was to forget one was being hunted by a serial killer. "No."

"You should be able to go home soon."

"Good." She closed her eyes and realized what he was saying. That soon they'd be out of each other's lives.

He walked out, and Katie buried her face into the pillow and cried. It didn't help when she told herself she'd be okay because she'd survived losing her entire family. She knew that. She was just so damn tired of losing people she loved.

The next morning, Carl stood behind his brother.

"You fucking can't do this!" Edwards growled.

"Yes, we fucking can." Ben pushed his way inside Edwards's home and shoved the copy of the search warrant in his face. Ben had done Carl the big favor of letting him come along, with threats that if Carl said or did anything, he'd send him packing. Or arrest him.

So, biting his tongue, Carl stood back. He watched his old peers tear through Edwards's place searching for evidence—any piece of evidence would do. Anything that would help put the creep away. Anything to make sure he never laid a finger on Red.

Carl watched Edwards pace back and forth like an angry child. Carl's hands itched to get involved. His fist itched to teach Edwards a few lessons.

Carl hadn't seen the victims, but from the disrespectful way his old peers tossed Edwards's things, all of the guys here had. The thought that Edwards wanted to hurt Red in that way had acid pooling in the pit of Carl's stomach.

Someone bumped into a table, sending a lamp crashing to the floor. Edwards took a defensive step toward the officer, and Carl and two other officers swung around, all hoping he'd do it: give them a reason to go at him.

Edwards, not as stupid as he was pissed off, stopped.

For the next hour, Carl watched the SOB pace. Back. Forth. He watched him bite back threats, but what Carl didn't see him do was get worried. Not once. And that worried Carl. Someone yelled out something from the bedroom. Carl moved in to hear, but didn't catch it. Ben walked out, the frustration etched on his face telling Carl that whatever they'd found, it wasn't enough.

"Just some photos that prove Edwards and Jones were acquainted." Ben's disappointed expression explained more than his words had.

Carl reached back and rubbed his shoulder and shot Edwards another glance. "He's not worried, Ben. Either he's already gotten rid of the evidence or he doesn't have a reason to worry."

"He lied to us about his relationship with Tabitha. We

can put him at Katie's house. He has to be our man, damn it!"

"I want to believe it, too," Carl said.

"But you don't?" Ben snapped.

Someone in the garage let out a victory whoop, then Carl watched as a young homicide detective came strutting out. Hanging from his gloved finger was a 9 mm Smith & Wesson, just the type of gun suspected of killing Tabitha Jones.

Carl had never been so happy to be wrong in his whole life.

That afternoon, Carl stood behind the mirrored glass as Ben questioned Edwards. They had their man. So why was it that Carl still didn't feel satisfied? Could it be that he just wasn't ready for it to be over? Because Katie would leave his dad's apartment, leave Carl's life forever?

Edwards pounded his fist on the table. "That's not my gun! Yes, I was fucking her. She'd fuck anyone." The man's lawyer put a hand on his shoulder to calm him, but he knocked it off. There was no calming Edwards.

Ben spoke up. "And you just decided to lie to us about your relationship when I questioned you the first time?"

"If I'd told you I was seeing her—"

"And you lied to us about the flowers you took to Miss Ray."

"I explained that. I knew Tabitha had been the one to fire me. I thought I'd send the bride-to-be flowers, hoping she'd change her mind and show Tabitha . . ."

Carl stood there and listened to the man protest his innocence.

Ten minutes later, Ben left the room. "He's not giving it up," he said.

"Maybe he hasn't got anything to give," Carl answered.

Ben cut him a sharp look. "We got the fucking gun. What do you want—a video of him doing the killings?"

Carl shook his head. "Something doesn't feel right."

"Well, it will feel a lot better as soon we get the green light to arrest his ass."

"What are you waiting for?" Carl asked.

"DA wants to make sure the gun is a match."

"So you're going to let him walk out of here? What if he goes after Red?"

"Oh, now you think he did it!" Ben frowned. "We don't have a choice, Carl. Until this is resolved, just make sure she stays with Dad."

"I'll probably see you guys tomorrow," Carl said, and walked out his dad's door.

Probably. Katie watched him go and pulled the hot cocoa to her lips. The last week had passed, each day much like the other. Les would come over in the afternoon and they'd rent chick flicks and make Mr. Hades watch them. Afterward, he would make her and Les play poker with him. "Girl time for boy time," he bargained.

After poker, she and Les would crash on the bed and talk. Katie told Les about the whole bathtub and sex fiasco, and about what seemed to be their mutual agreement not to pursue things. Les insisted they were throwing in the towel way too soon. But when Katie asked about her plans with Joe, Les said only that she wasn't ready, and the talk ended.

In the mornings, Tami would stop by and they would all sit around laughing and telling Ben-and-Carl stories. Little Ben and Katie had bonded. She taught him how to make paper airplanes and they would hold competitions. Katie even got good at pretending she wasn't hurting.

Carl had stopped by every day, too—short visits, as if he couldn't stand to stay away. Yet when he got there, he couldn't stand to stay. He was always nice; he never got too close. Sometimes she'd catch him studying her as if he wanted to say something, but he never said it. And neither did she.

And she knew that was best. But sometimes being in

the same room with him and not being close enough to inhale his scent, to touch him, was pure torture. She told herself to stop thinking about what she didn't have and just be glad she got to see him at all. Because come next week, if they arrested Jack Edwards, she'd probably never see Carl Hades again. Probably. It was a word she hated but was getting used to.

"You okay?" Mr. Hades studied her, and when he sat down, his weight jarred the sofa and her cocoa almost spilled.

"Fine." She sipped from her cup, barely tasting the sweetness.

He reached over and patted her arm. "You two are breaking this old man's heart."

Katie smiled. "Please, we both know you don't have a heart to break."

They laughed, and he hugged her. Then Katie parked her cocoa in the kitchen sink and went to her bedroom and cried.

Carl didn't come over again for the next three days, and crying herself to sleep became a ritual. She would eventually get over him. Probably.

The next Wednesday at lunch, Mr. Hades announced he had a hot date with Jessie, whom Katie had met several times, and he asked if Katie minded going to Carl's for the evening.

Katie minded. Carl obviously didn't want to see her, and afraid Mr. Hades might ask Carl to come here, she improvised. She called Tami and asked if she and Benny would babysit her. Of course Tami had agreed, but only if Katie would help her with some decorating ideas.

"So, you think yellow paint?" Tami pointed to the living room wall.

"Mom?" Benny, dropped off from the car pool, came running into the house and tossed his backpack on the sofa. When Benny saw Katie, he broke out into a big little-boy smile and ran over and hugged her. Katie's heart did a big-girl squeeze when his arms went around her neck.

"Can we make airplanes?" he squealed.

"You betcha!" Katie said.

He pulled back and looked at her. "I like you a lot better than Amy. I'm glad Amy left Uncle Carl."

Katie's heart did another squeeze. "Well, I like you better than any other little boy." And right then it hit her, she'd not only fallen in love with Carl, she'd fallen for his family, too.

Benny scrunched up his face. "I'm not little. I'm five."

"Oh, I forgot." She stared into his soft brown eyes, so much like his uncle's. For just a second she wondered, if Carl and she had created a child, would it have looked like Benny?

Tami piped up. "Why don't you go work at your computer on the spelling game while Katie and I cook dinner?"

"But we're going to make airplanes," Benny whined.

"You can make airplanes after dinner," Tami said. "Go."

Benny whimpered but obeyed. As Katie followed Tami into the kitchen, she felt obliged to say, "I'll do anything you ask, but I have to warn you, I seriously suck at cooking."

"Not at my type of cooking you won't," Tami said.

"Please! I've heard nothing but praise about your cooking since I've been staying at your father-in-law's place. Your pies, your homemade breads, your homemade pasta sauces."

Tami grinned. "Which is why I must have you swear on . . . on a stack of cookbooks that what happens in my kitchen, stays in my kitchen." She pulled out a cookbook from one of the shelves and slammed it on the kitchen table. "Come on."

Smirking, Katie put her hand down on the book. "I solemnly swear on a stack of cookbooks."

"Good. Now that we got that covered, look in the pantry, way back in the back, and pull out the bottled spaghetti sauce."

Katie laughed. "You've got to be kidding."

"I kid you not, girlfriend! You see, when I was dating Ben, they had been eating their dad's cooking, which was so bad that they thought the canned beanie weenies I served were gourmet." Tami pulled out a pot from under the cabinet. "Anyway, the praise felt so good I actually took cooking lessons."

"Ahh, so you can cook?" Katie found the sauce that really was hidden way in the back of the cupboard.

"Well, let's say I managed to put together a few meals. You'd have thought those Hades men died and went to heaven." She filled the pot with water. "But as much as I loved all their praise, I learned some truth about myself. I hate cooking." Laughing, Tami put the water on to boil. "So, I started experimenting with what you might call quick-fix meals. And frankly, dear, I found Ragu can make as good a sauce as I can. And the day I found out that Mr. Dough Boy made a pie crust better than mine, I practically"—she lowered her voice—"offered him a blow job." She grinned. "Grab me the cherry pie filling from the bottom shelf."

"You are such a phony," Katie teased.

"Remember, you've sworn on a stack of cookbooks."

A few minutes later, as Katie made the salad, Tami shot her an unsure glance. "You know Benny was right, don't you?"

Katie looked up. "Right about what?" Her gaze caught on the family photo hanging over the phone. The image of the three of them, Ben, Tami, and Benny, sitting on a blanket at some park, drew Katie's eye. She wanted that. Family.

"You're much better than Amy."

Katie and Tami hadn't spoken about Carl or the problematic relationship, and Katie had decided that it was best. She didn't want to pull his family into their issues.

"So, Ragu is as good as homemade, huh?" Katie focused on the tomato sauce and not on the unanswered remark hanging heavy in the air.

"I've seen the way he looks at you," Tami said.

"Looks can be deceiving." Jumping subjects again, she asked, "So, Ben really doesn't know you use canned sauce?"

Tami didn't go for the ploy. "He's not a bad guy, Katie. He was hurt. First by his mom and then by Amy."

"His mom?" Okay, now it was Katie plowing right into a subject. "I thought . . . he seemed to love her a lot."

"He did. She had cancer. The treatments worked in the beginning, but it came back, twice. The last time it was really bad. My father-in-law, he . . . he's stubborn, really stubborn, and he just wouldn't accept that it couldn't be fixed. He signed her up for all these last-ditch efforts. And she was tired."

Katie's heart ached for Carl and all the Hades men. "Damn!"

Tami continued. "Carl found out that his mother had stopped her treatments. She was seeing some holistic doctor instead. And she made Carl promise not to tell his dad and brother." Tami stirred the pasta. "She died about a month later. Ben said that Carl broke down at the funeral. He told his dad that it was his fault because he'd known she'd stopped the treatments." Tami sighed. "He was fifteen. I think he really believed he'd killed her."

Emotion tightened Katie's chest. "It wasn't his fault."

"I know. I guess that's why I have a soft spot for Carl. It's as if he's a wounded animal or something." Tami frowned. "Ben said that after his mom died, Carl changed."

"How do you mean?" Katie asked, but she knew all about the changes one goes through when someone you love dies.

"Don't get me wrong, he's a womanizer. Or he was until

Amy. There hasn't been anyone since her. But before . . . Ever heard that country-western song, "I Like My Women on the Trashy Side?" I swear it was written for Carl. Ben claimed Carl went after the loose women because he thought he wouldn't fall in love."

"Well, that makes me feel real good," Katie said.

Grinning, Tami added, "Not you. Ben jokes that the only reason you caught his eye was because you two were locked in a room together and he couldn't run when the lights came on and he saw you weren't a tramp."

"Thanks," Katie said. "I think."

From the other room, Katie heard Benny squeal. Tami looked at the door and guilt lit her face. "Don't thank me yet. I . . . I should warn you. Carl's coming for dinner. I'm pretty certain that's him now."

Katie glanced at the back door.

"Don't do it," Tami said. "I'll trip you if you try!"

Chapter Thirty

Katie watched Tami grab the sauce jar and push it down in the trash. "Please don't be mad. And remember, you swore on cookbooks not to tell my secrets."

Katie closed her eyes, then heard the happy voices.

"To the death!" Benny squealed.

"Prepare to meet your maker," a familiar voice said. Katie's heart clutched at Carl's husky, playful tone. "And the winner gets to eat *all* the worms."

"No horseplaying in my house," Tami yelled from the door. "And no worms before dinner."

Katie leaned into the counter, feeling wave upon wave of emotion. "Does he know I'm here?" she asked in a hushed tone.

Tami grimaced. "I . . . may have forgotten to mention it."

Footsteps drew near. Katie prepared herself to see him.

"Something smells good." Carl stepped inside the kitchen and hugged Tami. He was mid-hug when Katie caught his eye. One look at his unhappy expression and her stomach lurched. It took everything she had to keep from running to the bathroom and throwing up.

Ben arrived home shortly thereafter. Dinner went off

without a hitch . . . except the one in Katie's throat the whole time that kept her from eating. Carl hardly looked at her. God knew, he hadn't said three words. Even Benny noticed.

"Are you mad at Katie?" Benny asked, and twirled his pasta around his fork.

"No." Carl flinched, though.

"Then how come you and Amy used to kiss and stuff? And you haven't kissed Katie. And you keep looking at her . . . all sad and all."

Carl's gaze shot to her; then he looked at Tami as if begging for assistance.

Tami complied. "Benny, I think you're done with dinner."

"Dinner was great," Katie said, hoping to cut the tension.

"It always is when Tami cooks." Ben dropped his fork.

"It was good," Carl added, and sipped his tea.

"I'm glad you liked it so much." Tami smiled. "I hope you won't mind helping Katie wash the dishes."

Carl choked on his drink. "Dishes?"

Katie would have smiled if her heart weren't busy breaking.

Five minutes later, they were alone in the kitchen. Carl moved in beside her. "Does Tami know about your dish game?"

"God, no!" Katie squirted soap into the water and kept her gaze on the bubbles, and not on his wide shoulders encased in a blue shirt, or at the shadow of hurt in his eyes.

"I didn't think so," he said.

She sensed him studying her and fought the urge to reach over and touch him.

"You didn't know I'd be here either, did you?" Annoyance hung in his tone.

"No." Katie watched the foamy suds growing.

"They don't have a damn right to get in the middle of this."

Katie looked up. "They love you." His brown eyes met hers and held. Looking at him hurt, but her heart invited a little more pain to come inside. "Right or wrong, they're trying to help. That's what family does."

He reached back and rubbed his shoulder. "But—"

"No buts, Carl. They love you." She watched his fingers massage the muscle. She ached to do it for him. To soothe him. "Does it hurt because you were shot?"

"I'm okay." He pulled his hand away.

She picked up a plate and started washing.

His gaze whispered over her, and she tried not to do anything that could be considered seductive or teasing, but every move her hand made felt sexual, and she remembered it all: doing the dishes with him. Okay, she really needed a new topic.

"How did you get shot?" When he didn't answer, she glanced over to see him frown. "Forget I asked."

He let out a deep breath. "I thought they would have already told you all my dirty secrets."

Shaking her head, she swallowed the emotion. "They haven't told me about that."

He hesitated. "There was a drug dealer who made it a habit of going after ex-users who were trying to go clean. He got someone I cared about using again. So I went after him."

She rinsed a plate and put it into the drain. "Amy?"

He nodded. "Yeah."

"You say that like it was a bad thing."

Another pause hung. "I talked my partner into going with me. We walked in on a drug deal. It got ugly. My partner got hit in the leg. I took one in the shoulder." He picked up the plate and dried it. "I fired back. Turned out the shooter was only seventeen and a judge's nephew."

She squeezed the dishcloth. "Did he—"

"Die? No. But he's got a pretty bad limp and will remember me the rest of his life." Carl blinked. "I shouldn't have been there. I nearly got my partner killed."

Emotion filled Carl's eyes, and she wanted to help, to touch him. To hold him. She couldn't.

"I'm sorry," she said. "Maybe you shouldn't have gone, but I understand. You went because you cared about someone."

He stared at her and then found a towel and dried the plate. "We didn't have a search warrant. They threw the book at me and my partner. Neither of us were let go, but they made it difficult to stay."

"Is that when you went to work for yourself?"

"Yeah." He searched in the cabinets until he found where the plate went. When he turned around, he smiled. "Don't suppose I'll get a piece of clothing for that dish, huh?"

Even as much as she hurt, she grinned. "Probably not."

He stepped closer and touched her cheek. "You have no idea how much I wish . . ." His words faded.

"Wish what?" She fought the desire to lean into him, to be the one to grant him any wish his heart desired.

He sighed. "Oh, Red, I don't watch *The Brady Bunch*. I'm not the type who makes promises." He leaned in and pressed his chin to her temple. "And you're the kind of girl who needs them, aren't you?"

Katie's gaze caught on the photo of Ben, Tami, and little Benny. A fun day at the park with the family, such a simple thing, but something she wanted. Like Easters with her family.

"Yes," she said, and pulled away. "I need promises."

Les came bouncing into Mr. Hades' apartment two days later as Katie packed her things. "I heard they arrested him."

"We're waiting to hear that he's being held, and if so . . . I'm free to leave." Katie faked a smile. Losing the Hades family wouldn't be easy.

"I'll bet you are so relieved," Les said.

"It will be nice to get back to my life," she lied. Truth?

Her life sucked. Alone sucked. Alone hurt. And she didn't even have Joe anymore. "I talked to Lola today and she's really happy I'm coming back."

"It's good to be needed." Still smiling, Les dropped down on the sofa and Katie noticed a particular gleam.

"What's up, Miss Cheery?" Katie asked.

"I've got some news." Les rubbed her hands together.

"You and Joe?" Katie's hope soared even though she'd spoken to Joe last night and he hadn't mentioned Les.

"No," Les said.

"Why not?" Katie asked.

Les did her eye roll. "Hey, I'm taking baby steps here. Can't you at least be happy with what I did do?"

"What did you do?" Hoping, Katie's gaze went to the tan turtleneck Les wore. But Katie could see the shape of the ring behind the shirt.

"I just got my old job back at the paper."

Katie squealed and hugged her. "You're moving back? Yes! Do you have any idea how happy that makes me?"

Les grinned. "Me, too. But I've agreed to give a four-week notice at the *Boston Globe*. Help them train someone. I already booked my flight for next Monday."

"A whole month?" Katie whimpered.

"Yeah," Les said. "But it'll be good. I need the time to get my head on straight."

"You mean about Joe?" Katie asked.

"Joe and other things." Les sat up and stared at the painting Katie had set on the coffee table. "Did you do this?"

Katie laughed. "No, an elephant did it."

Les's eyes widened. "This is the famous elephant painting?"

"Yeah. It's actually not that bad." Katie looked away from the piece of art. "Are you going to at least go say 'bye to Joe?"

"I went by last night, but he wasn't there. I was going to call him, but I hate saying good-bye over a phone."

"He keeps a key under the planter beside the door," Katie offered. "If he's not home, just go in and wait."

Les nodded, then looked back at the painting. "You should start painting again."

It was Katie's time to share her own good news. "I am. I made that promise to myself. I'm going to do it and I don't care if I suck at it."

Katie and Mr. Hades were watching *Oprah* that afternoon when the phone rang.

"Hello," he answered. "Good!" He looked at Katie, then lowered his voice. "You're not going to come by?" He frowned. "Fine. I'll tell her."

Getting the gist of the conversation, Katie felt a knot rise in her throat. It was over. She could leave. And Carl wasn't going to say good-bye.

Mr. Hades hung up. "It was the same gun. Edwards is being held without bail."

Katie stood up, not wanting it to be a long good-bye. "Looks as if you're finally going to get me out of your hair." She tried real hard not to let the sting in her throat sound in her voice, or to let it climb up her sinuses and make her cry. But of course she failed.

"Oh, girly, don't you tear up on me!" He pulled her against him. "I'm not sure if you want to hear this or not, but I personally think my son is the biggest fool known to mankind."

Katie pulled back before her mascara smeared on his shirt. "I left the check on the table," she said.

"No!" Mr. Hades bellowed. "I mean it now. You aren't paying me one dime."

Katie patted his arm. "Yes, I am. And if you don't like to think of it as payment, then think of it as a wedding gift. Take Jessie somewhere really nice on her honeymoon."

He squeezed her hand. "You'll be at the wedding, right?"

"We'll see," Katie said, unwilling to lie. But the truth

was, the sooner she let go of this family, the better-off everyone would be.

Katie went to get her bag, then kissed Mr. Hades' cheek. "Jessie is one lucky woman."

Carl stood in the back of the courtroom and watched them lead a very upset Jack Edwards away. But Carl wasn't happy. He had wanted to hear the man say he'd done it. He wanted the niggling doubt in his gut to fade. Reaching back to rub his shoulder, he told himself this feeling was about losing Red and not because he believed Edwards was innocent.

Ben walked over. "Did you call her yet?"

"I told Dad to tell her."

Ben frowned. "And you're not going to go see her?"

"A clean break is best," he said, but the words cut deep.

Ben shook his head. "You are the biggest damn fool I've ever known." He walked away.

Carl left the courthouse and got in his car. He didn't start it, though. He sat there and thought about losing Katie forever. "Shit. Fuck!"

And yes, Red, this is f-word worthy. He grabbed his phone and hit redial. "Don't let her go yet. I'm coming over."

"Well, you're just about ten fucking minutes too late! But you know where she lives, right?"

Carl snapped his phone shut. He knew where she lived, but what the hell was he going to say when he got there? He needed that answer before he could go to her. Leaning his head back, he fought the ache that threatened to consume him and tried to find the answer.

"You'll make a beautiful bride." Tabitha's killer sat down at his desk and looked at the brunette sitting across from him. She looked around his office.

"It looks as if you photograph other things besides weddings."

Her eyes were brown, like Maria's. His heart thumped

against his breastbone, and he tried to find the willpower to send her away, to tell her to go hire someone else.

He had to stop. He'd heard the police had arrested a suspect. And he knew who it was, too. He was really proud of himself for pulling it off. He might not be normal, but he was smart.

"I shoot what catches my eye. But I have samples of my wedding photography." He pulled out one of his portfolios. "Take it with you. My prices are in the back. If you like what you see, call me."

She smiled. Was she laughing at him? He let himself rock back once, twice.

"Okay." She stared at him. Had he rocked too much?

"I'll call you," she said.

"You do that." He walked her to the door.

She had black hair like Maria's. Black hair.

But she wasn't his bride yet. If he took a bride, he had to get the one on his list. The one that got away. The one whose picture taunted him, laughed at him. Katie Ray.

He watched the brunette leave and then went to his desk and pulled out the one thing he'd let himself keep: the wedding announcement of Katie's wedding. It was supposed to happen next week. And he still had her deposit check. Would she call him now that Edwards had been arrested? Should he call her?

Maybe he would just drive by her house. Just drive by it the way he used to drive by the woods where his brides were. Just drive by. He started to rock. Back. Forth.

The next morning, Katie forced herself out of bed, leaving Les curled up on the other side. They'd fallen asleep watching a movie. Or at least Les had. Sleep hadn't come easy for Katie. She kept thinking about Carl. She'd even thought about Benny. Was the kid going to miss her? Would Mr. Hades? Odd, how she'd grown to love that man, a surrogate father of sorts. Although he wasn't really anything like her father.

Katie pushed herself out of the bed, but glanced back longingly at the warm covers. Then she shook off the urge. She was a Ray, and Rays didn't sleep in when they had work to do.

She'd called Lola yesterday and told her she'd be back in on Monday. Lola, being Lola, had agreed. The work Katie needed to do didn't involve the gallery, but it did involve art. Today, Katie was going to the art store, buying canvases and paint, and she was going to do it. She was going to paint.

Fifteen minutes later, showered and dressed, she gave Les a quick shake. "I'm off to the art store. Are you going to be here when I get back?"

Les rose up on her elbow, looking early-morning puffy. "I promised Mom I'd come over. I'm not sure when I'll be back."

"Go see Joe while you're out." Katie started for the door.

"Go see Carl while you're out." Les rolled back over.

Just hearing his name had pain gnawing at her ankles. She ignored it. It would go away. Eventually. Just like the fierce grief of losing her family had faded. She just needed to keep going. Rays always kept going.

Katie got almost to her car, then went back and grabbed her wedding book. If she didn't take too long at the art store, she might go see if she could get her deposits back.

He drove by the house but didn't let himself stop. He couldn't stop. He couldn't take her. Not now. It was too soon. Too soon. Too soon.

His head started throbbing. He was almost out of pain medicine. Would the doctor give him more?

Then he heard it. Distantly, but he heard it. Laughing. No, he couldn't handle the laughing now. It had to go away.

He pulled over and parked. And let himself rock. Her house was down the street. Maybe he would walk by. Just walk by. Maybe peek in her window. Maybe seeing her would be enough to stop the headache from coming back and keep the laughter away.

Katie spent hours at the art store, debating between cherry red and apple red paint. Things like that were important to an artist. And she was an artist. Maybe not a great artist, but if an elephant could do it, then . . . Her heart went straight to Carl, and then went straight to pain.

Afterward, she stopped by the gallery and had a late lunch with Lola. In spite of the constant ache lodged inside her soul, it felt good to be busy.

After lunch, Katie sort of mentioned to Lola her desire to be an artist. Okay, it was more like a blurted confession. "I'm an artist. Please, don't fire me."

"Fire you, *chica*? Did you honestly think I didn't know?"

"Well, yes. Seeing as I never told you," Katie said.

"Ah, *Dios*, only an artist can understand art like you do. I figured you'd come out of the closet someday."

"But I suck at it, Lola. I had a few shows and—"

"Painting is like sex." Lola compared everything to sex. She loved sex. "Sometimes it is great. And sometimes it is all about faking it and avoiding the wet spot. You show me some of your work, and I will show you your talent."

"What if all I do is fake it and avoid the wet spots?"

"You keep faking it until it's real," Lola said.

They hugged, and before Katie left the gallery, she tried to call Les. The call went to her answering machine. "Hi, Les," Katie said. "Just thought I'd remind you to go see Joe."

On the way home, Katie almost stopped by Grimes Photography, but at the last minute she decided to go home and start painting. She turned on her car's heater. While it wasn't that cold, the chill in the air reminded Katie of another cold day. A day she'd been locked in the dark with a man who had stolen her heart.

It also looked as if another storm had its claws into

Houston. Why else would it be almost dark at three in the afternoon?

When she pulled in front of her home, the lights beckoned from her windows—and not a warm beckoning, either. *Relax*, she told herself, *Les must already be here*—and thought, *Good*, not wanting to face an empty house. Knowing the killer had been in her house ruined the warm, cozy feeling of coming home.

Katie walked into the entryway and called Les's name. Nothing. No answer. The central heat kicked on and groaned. That was it, tomorrow she was calling someone out to fix it.

"Les?" She stepped into the living room. Nothing. Katie took off to her bedroom. She stood in the door looking at the unmade bed. Normally Les at least pulled the covers up.

Katie picked up her bedroom phone. The beeping told her she had messages. But she dialed Les's cell again.

It rang. Then Katie heard the ring in her house. She walked into the bathroom, and on the floor, beside a wet towel, was Les's cell phone. Why would Les leave her phone on the floor?

Katie swirled around. "Les?"

She got no response, so she hung up and dialed to get her messages, hoping one was from Les. One hangup. Then Katie's heart skipped a beat when right before it disconnected she could swear she heard music. Wedding music. But that couldn't be. They'd caught the killer. So, she pushed that crazy thought away.

The next message sang in Katie's ear. "Hey," Les said. "I know I left your place a mess. Woke up late, left my phone, and have just barely avoided being fingerprinted and tossed in the slammer. I'll explain later."

Chapter Thirty-one

Buck Hades walked into his son's house. The flicker of the TV lit up the dark space, and the sound of feminine squeals bounced around the room. "Carl?" The room went dark and silent.

Buck cut the corner and saw his son sitting on the sofa, in the dark with two dogs, the remote in his hand. Buck glanced at the TV fading from just being switched off.

"What're you watching?" Buck asked.

"Nothing." Carl's reply came too fast, and his look took Buck back twenty years to when he'd first caught his son watching porn. Buck hit the light switch. On the table were a couple of open DVD cases. Buck frowned. It wasn't the porn that bothered Buck, it was the misery stamped all over his son's expression.

"You make about as much sense as a perfumed fart," Buck said. "You've got a sexy, sweet woman who's half-crazy for you, and you'd rather watch porn than have the real thing."

Buck tossed the white envelope in his son's lap. "That's my wedding announcement. And like it or not, I expect you to be there." He started out.

"Dad?" His son's deep voice stopped Buck.

"Yeah?" He looked back.

"If this wedding is what you want, I'm happy for you."

Buck let out a deep breath. "That means a lot, son. Now, what about Katie? What are you going to do about her? You're an idiot to let her go."

"I'm trying to figure that out right now."

Buck cut his eyes back to the dark television. "Well, I don't think watching skin flicks is going to do it."

Les walked up to Joe's door and popped one of the breath mints that had almost gotten her carted off to jail into her mouth. Then again, it may have been the hemorrhoid pads that had really ticked the cops off. As she knocked, her heart hammered in her chest.

Her heart had been hammering all day. First, when she'd woken up an hour late to meet her mom and Mimi to go shopping. And again, when she'd almost been arrested leaving Wal-Mart because Mimi had managed to drop a pack of breath mints, hemorrhoid-soothing Tucks pads, and some vaginal lubricant with warming qualities in Les's purse while security guards watched.

Nevertheless, here Les was, to say good-bye to Joe—to say, *Can you give me a month to get my head screwed on right and then maybe we can enjoy the vaginal lubricant my grandma picked up for me?*

She knocked again. No answer. "Well, fudge." Maybe it just wasn't meant to be. She turned to leave when she spotted the flowerpot and recalled Katie telling her about the key. The idea of being there when Joe walked in didn't appeal to her, but maybe she could just go in and write him a note. A note was better than trying to say this on the phone.

Unlocking the door, she dropped her purse on the sofa. The sofa where she'd almost had wild, wonderful sex with Joe.

She looked around for a pen and paper. Did Joe have an office? She started down the hall when . . .

"Oh, damn!" The shower was going.

She swung around, grabbed her purse, and had colored herself gone when her heart started hammering again.

What was she doing? Running?

Les Grayson didn't run. Not anymore. Isn't that what she'd promised herself?

Catching her breath, she dropped her purse back on the sofa. She'd wait. Wait until he got out to talk to him. Yeah. Wait.

She sat down on the sofa. The memory of his mouth on her breasts had her tightening her thighs. Then another memory made a grand entrance: Joe stepping into the shower. Naked. Wonderfully naked.

The idea hit. It was crazy. Didn't make a bit of sense. Which was why she wasn't going to do it. So, why was she stripping off her blouse?

She kicked off her shoes before she got to the hall. Her bra fluttered down at his bedroom door, her pink panties slipped off her thighs as she arrived at the bathroom. She peeked in, and behind the shower curtain she could see his shadow. Her heart did a lap around her chest cavity.

Reaching up, she pulled the chain over her head and laid it on the bathroom counter. Right then, she felt more naked than she had in eighteen months. She almost turned around and ran. But she heard Joe whistle. The man whistled while he showered? What else did he do? She wanted to discover all the little things about him. Did he sleep on his side or his back? Did he drink juice in the mornings? Or just coffee?

She counted to three, then tiptoed to the shower. Pulling the curtain back, she peered inside. He had his back to her, shampoo in his dark hair. Her attention followed a stream of soapy water down his back to his well-shaped ass. His tight, sexy ass.

"Do you mind some company?" She stepped inside.

"Shit!" He swung around. Shampoo-laden suds ran

down his face and into his eyes. He froze. The steam rose around them.

His gaze whispered down her body—over her breasts, down to the blond patch of curls between her legs, then swept past her thighs and didn't stop until he studied her toenails.

Pink. She'd painted her toenails pink last night.

His gaze snapped back up to her chest. For a second, she took that to mean he was a breast man. But then she knew what he was looking for. Only, it wasn't there. She'd left it on the counter.

His gaze shot to her eyes, then back to her chest. Okay, maybe he was a breast man.

"We gotta stop meeting like this," he said.

"I can leave," she whispered, feeling a tad unsure and sort of hurt that he hadn't already touched her.

"Now would that be any fun?" He ran a finger over one of her already-tightened nipples.

Definitely a breast man.

"No, it wouldn't be fun." She sighed at the desire his touch aroused in her.

"Then how about you stay." He stepped forward and the spray of water hit her square in the face. He chuckled and she heard him turn around to adjust the showerhead. Her gaze moved down to his naked bottom again. Okay, she'd admit it, her favorite part of a man's body was his butt.

He turned around. And it wasn't his tight tush she now admired. His sex was already hard, thick, and pointing upward. And good heavens, if there wasn't more of that than she needed.

He moved in closer. "Are you really here, or am I dreaming this? Because I've pictured this a hundred times in my mind."

"Pictured what?" she asked.

He smiled. "Pictured you. Naked. In the shower."

"Fighting you. Squirting shampoo in your eyes," she teased.

Pushing a lock of hair from her cheek, he pressed his lips to her temple. "Okay, I'll admit it, that turned me on."

She pressed her hand on his wet, soapy chest. Slowly, she inched it downward until she held his velvety erection in her fist. She stroked him. Measured him. Savored his heat, the power of the hardness. And his deep sounds of pleasure told her he liked it.

His hands cupped her breasts. "You look good wet."

She stroked him again. "And I thought I might have to wear the Halloween tablecloth and slap you to get you in the mood."

"You're going to use that against me, aren't you?"

"Yep." She passed her thumb over his throbbing tip.

"Then let me show you what I'm going to use against you," he said with a moan.

He caught her around the bottom, swooped her off her feet, and pushed her against the shower wall. With one adjustment, his hard shaft found the spot between her legs. He held her. Moving his hips ever so slightly, the round tip of his sex probed inside the folds of hers, teasing, testing.

"You get the picture?" he asked in a tight voice.

"I'm just wondering what you're waiting for," she baited.

He jutted his hips up and, in one solid stroke, he filled her.

She gasped. The sudden invasion almost hurt. Almost.

"You okay?" His forehead pressed against hers.

"Oh, yeah." Her body stretched around him. "I'm going back to Boston day after tomorrow," she gritted out. She felt him tense. "Only for a month. Then I'm moving back for good."

He drew out and pushed back in. "I'll come out on the weekends."

They began to move faster. She almost told him they

should use the time apart to think, to figure out if this was real, but he felt so good inside her, and she knew she wouldn't be able to go without this for a month. And damn, it already felt so real. "Okay."

After Les called to say she wouldn't be coming back tonight, Katie got all her paints out. She was even kind of glad Les wouldn't be coming home. Tonight, she would paint. She thought about Les and Joe together. Recalled the wispiness in Les's voice when she'd said, "I'm going to stay over at Joe's."

A tickle of something unpleasant touched Katie's heart. Jealousy? Yes, jealousy. Not because of Joe, but because she wanted that for herself—wanted that with Carl. She pushed the thought away. Because she was a Ray, and Rays didn't sit around pining over what they couldn't have.

When she realized she hadn't bought anything to mix the paint in, she went to her kitchen and found an old cast-iron frying pan and took it back to her study. Then, setting up her easel, she leaned the blank canvas on it and studied it. She didn't have a clue what to paint.

She ran back into her living room and found a glass vase with one red silk flower. As she started out, she spotted the elephant painting she'd placed on her mantel. She grabbed it for inspiration. "If an elephant can do it, so can I," she said, remembering Carl telling her that.

As she set up a still-life display, her thoughts went back to Carl. Would it have killed him to say good-bye? She reached for a brush, and her vision grew cloudy with tears. Okay, maybe this Ray did pine over what she couldn't have.

He leaned against the window and watched her paint. Watched her cry as she dabbed paint on the canvas. He loved it when they cried. His need to see her had driven him here tonight. He wouldn't take her now. It was too soon. Too soon.

But seeing her helped. Knowing she was waiting for

him. If he squinted his eyes just so, he could pretend her hair was black. Pretend she was Maria.

He remembered. *Do you, Maria, take this man . . .* She'd laughed. Laughed. Then everyone was laughing. Generally, there was only one way to stop the laughing. He needed to take his bride.

Friday morning, Carl sat up. He'd chosen to watch the DVDs on the sofa because his bed still smelled like Red. Every few hours he'd nod off, but then he'd force himself to watch. Truth was, there wasn't enough action to keep him interested. But he watched anyway. He had three more DVDs to go.

Taking a deep breath, he dropped his face into his hands. Precious barked at the back door, wanting out.

What the hell was he going to do? He missed Red so much, drawing air into his lungs hurt. He got up, let both Precious and Baby outside, and went back to the sofa and hit *play*. He watched the blonde's face appear on the screen. Then three other blondes flashed. Then came the redhead. The music started.

He heard his front door open. He snatched up the remote and cut the TV off.

"Hey." Ben walked into the living room and studied him holding the remote. Then his brother's gaze went to the empty beer bottles.

"Dad's right. You're watching porn and crying in your beer."

Carl leaned back. "Did you come all this way just to give me a ration of shit, or do you need something?"

"No, I came all this way to check on you." He dropped into a chair. "You going to be okay?"

"Yeah." Carl set the remote on the coffee table.

His brother reached for it, but Carl moved quicker and snatched it away.

"Hey, I just thought we'd have a male-bonding experience," Ben said.

"How about let's not," Carl said.

"Why the fuck don't you just call her?" Ben's cell phone rang and he answered it. "Hades. Yeah."

After a long pause, Carl's brother's eyes shot to him. The look on Ben's face set off all kinds of alarms. Carl had only seen that look once, the night Ben had met him at the hospital door and told him his mother had already passed.

Carl shot to his feet. "What is it?"

Carl, with Dr. Pope, stepped into the cold, anesthetic-smelling room. The morgue held no color; everything seemed to be either white or chrome. He waited for the flood of emotion to hit him, but it was as if he'd received a shot of novocaine in his heart. The organ lay behind his chest bone, big, fat, and numb, and he wanted to claw at it as one might chew at one's lip to make sure it was still there.

The body lay out on the metal table, a white sheet covering it, but he could still make out the feminine form. Then he saw it. The only damn color in the room. A strand of red hair hung over the back of the table. Even it looked dead.

He had loved her. He hadn't wanted to, but he had.

Dr. Pope moved to the other side of the table. "Such a waste." He pulled the sheet down. "Is it her?"

Carl forced himself to look at her face. "Yeah. Her name is Amy Bentley."

"Looks like it's a clear-cut OD. Needle marks in the arms tell the story. We'll know more when the tox screens come in."

Carl closed his eyes. His heart started feeling again. Not love, but regret. And guilt.

"You know," Dr. Pope spoke, "if I had fifty bucks for every OD victim I've seen, I'd be a rich man. Why do they do it to themselves?"

Do it to themselves. Carl forced himself to look at Amy,

her face so still, so devoid of expression or emotion. So dead.

Right then he remembered begging her not to leave. To stay. To let him help her. She'd refused. He recalled her parting words: *Stop trying to save me, Carl. I'm not your mother.*

He looked again at the track marks running up her arm and something about seeing them, about seeing the ugly truth, brought some clarity. This wasn't his fault. Amy had made her choice.

She had. Not him. It wasn't his fault. Something started to shift inside him. Then the last bit of numbness faded to just a big pit of understanding, and then some old pains. Right then he heard Amy's words again. *I'm not your mother.*

Had he wanted to save Amy because he couldn't save his mom? Was that why he couldn't take a chance on Red—because he was afraid he couldn't save her, either?

Katie's doorbell rang. She put down her paintbrush and eyed the painting of a single red rose in a glass vase. Then she looked at the rose and vase on the table. Something wasn't right. But what? Then she saw the problem. The problem was that she sucked at painting.

The doorbell rang again. She walked out of the study. A quick glance through the peephole brought a moan to her lips. She'd called Lola this morning and asked if she could stop by. But now? Did she want to hear Lola tell her she wasn't an artist?

Katie opened the door. "I've changed my mind. Good-bye."

Lola pushed her way inside. "It can't be so bad."

"But I think it is," Katie said.

"I'm not believing. I think you have talent. And I know these things, remember?"

Katie sighed and led her to the study where Lola stared, really stared, at Katie's work.

"Well, *chica*, you are a smart girl."

"Smart?" Hope flared inside Katie.

"You are right, the painting sucks."

"See, I told you," Katie said, and in the back of her mind she could hear her parents saying, *I told you so*.

"Not that you don't have talent."

"Just don't give up my day job, huh?" A knot crowded Katie's tonsils. It shouldn't have hurt this bad, but somehow this was the last dream she'd held on to.

"It's as if you are trying to make it perfect. Art, like life, is not perfect." Lola pointed to the vase and rose. "You paint a perfect silk rose. You paint it almost as perfect and artificial as it looks. Why not take a picture?"

Katie wanted to curl up in a ball and cry.

"You need to paint what you feel, not try to make it perfect. Perfect is boring. Art needs passion. Take a risk."

Katie studied Lola. "I'm a Ray. We either make things perfect or we don't make them."

Lola shot her a disgruntled look. "Then I would say that Rays lead a very disappointing life. Perfection is a myth. People who hunger for it die hungry. Look at your work, Katie. Your talent shines, but you are trying to force it to be what you think others will want to see. Follow your heart, paint what you feel. Do you not know what you feel?"

Katie heard Lola, but she was no longer thinking about her art. Was this what she'd done with Carl? Gave up on them because . . . because he wasn't her version of perfection?

Oh, fuck. Yep, she'd said *fuck* again. She'd given up on Carl because he didn't meet her standards. She had a stupid picture in her head of what life was supposed to be. Two kids, the suburbs. And when he didn't fit into her nice neat little perfect dream she'd rejected him. Rejected him because . . . because it would have meant taking a chance.

She looked back at Lola. "You're right. Life isn't perfect.

And right now I would love to sit down and visit with you, but I've got to fix the big picture in my life."

Lola smiled. "Does it have anything to do with a sexy PI?"

"You bet your sweet bottom it does. Can you give me some more of your mojo?" Katie laughed as she walked Lola to the door and for the first time in . . . a long time, she felt happy.

"What kind of magic you need?"

"The kick-ass kind," Katie said.

Carl walked into his brother's office.

Ben looked up from his desk. "Hey. You okay?"

"Yeah. I think I am." He sat on the edge of the desk. He picked up a pen, turned it in his hands, and met his brother's questioning eyes again. "The other day, you said if you'd been in my shoes with Mom, you'd have done the same thing."

Ben's eyes widened at the unexpected conversation. "Yeah, and I meant it, too."

Carl pulled the top of the pen off, then recapped it. "I should have told Dad, but she believed the new doctor was going to make a difference." He closed his eyes for a second. "She kept telling me, 'Love will make it all okay.'" He shook his head. "Now it seems stupid. I mean, I know love can't really heal. But at fifteen I thought anything was possible."

Ben leaned back in his chair. "Mom wanted to spend her last days without being used as a guinea pig. Without being sicker than the cancer was making her. So, in a way, love did make it better. Her last month was easier."

"I know that. I think I knew it then, too. But when she died I . . ." He felt his throat tighten.

Ben leaned his elbows on the desk. "Cancer killed her, Carl, not you." He paused. "Tami's right, isn't she? Mom and . . . even Amy, it's the reason you let Red get away, isn't it?"

"I wanted to save Amy. Maybe because I couldn't save Mom. And I tried. Today, seeing her . . . it made me realize she made her choice, not me. But how do I stop being afraid?"

"Afraid of what?" Ben asked.

"Afraid I . . . afraid I can't save the next person I love. Afraid of losing someone else." His chest tightened.

Ben leaned his elbows on his desk. "I think about it sometimes. About something happening to Tami or Benny. Talk about a kicked-in-the-nuts kind of pain." He sighed. "But even if something did happen, I wouldn't trade what I have now. It's life." Ben studied him. "You love Red, don't you?"

"I do." Carl tossed the pen back onto the desk. Ben leaned in and his elbow nudged a folder, from which a few contents slipped. Carl's gaze caught a nude photograph among the typed notes. A very artsy nude photograph.

"What's that?"

"Copies of the pictures we found at Edwards's place. Ms. Jones wasn't bad looking for forty." Ben laughed. "Though I doubt she'd compare to what you were watching this morning."

Carl ignored Ben, his mind churning. "Did you talk to Mel Grimes, the photographer, about his relationship with Ms. Jones?"

Ben's brow puckered. "Why?"

"Because I saw pictures almost exactly like that at his house. He shoots nudes. And I think he took this."

"I interviewed Grimes," Ben said. "He said he and Tabitha had a professional relationship and nothing more."

"Did you get anything on Grimes's background check?"

"Some stuff came in yesterday, but we haven't looked at it."

"Let's look." Carl didn't like what his gut told him.

Ben rolled his eyes. "We got the guy, Carl. Relax."

"What would it hurt to look at the info?" Carl growled.

Ben left to get the file. Carl pulled out his cell phone

and dialed Red's number. He had so many things he wanted to say to her that didn't involve the case, but keeping her alive came first. The phone rang and then went to the recorder. He dialed her cell phone. It went to voice mail.

His gut continued to churn his morning coffee. He told himself Red was probably at work. That she was okay. Then Ben walked back into the office and the look on his face told him nothing was okay. "What?"

"The guy has a long list of mental illnesses. He was in and out of institutions the first twenty-two years of his life."

"Fuck." Carl called the gallery. A receptionist answered and said Katie wasn't there.

Lola left, and Katie started shedding clothes as she went to the bathroom. Her phone rang, but she ignored it. Whoever it was would leave a message. She had a list of to-dos:

Shower.

Find something sexy to wear.

Dress in something sexy.

Go see Carl and have him remove something sexy.

Maybe, talk him into doing some dishes, too.

Tell Carl she no longer needed promises. She just wanted to be with him. For today and as many tomorrows as she could have.

She turned the shower on and stepped into the soft spray. One minute later—the important parts clean—she went to work on her makeup. Minimal makeup. She had just finished drying her hair when she heard a noise.

She stuck her head out of the bathroom. "Uh, Les?"

Then she heard the sound of glass breaking.

"Les, please tell me you just broke a glass or something."

Chapter Thirty-two

When Les didn't answer, Katie grabbed her robe. "Les?" She stepped into her bedroom. Still nothing.

Pulling her robe around her, she walked out into the hall. As she passed her study, she saw the easel on the ground. And her still-wet painting lay facedown on the carpet. Not the biggest loss in the world, but . . . She knelt to pick it up, and when she did, a pair of man's shoes came into her peripheral vision, and those shoes were attached to a pair of legs.

She looked up. Connected to the legs was a stranger's torso, and connected to his torso was a face. A face she didn't recognize. "Who . . . are you?"

He stared at her with cold green eyes. Eyes so cruel Katie pretty much guessed he wasn't there to try and sell her candy bars for a Little League team, or to ask if she had clothes to donate to some charity.

He pulled his hand from behind his back. And in that hand he held her best butcher knife. Panic arrived in waves. Time stood still and her brain started chewing on bits of information.

Bit Number One: The creep hadn't even brought his own weapon, but had planned to borrow hers.

Bit Number Two: Did it fucking matter what he used to kill her?

Bit Number Three: Today just wasn't a good day to die. She had her to-do list already made, and it included getting sexy and getting laid. Dying wasn't on that list. Rays always followed the list!

Bit Number Four: She was going to throw up.

He grabbed her arm and yanked her to her feet. "I saw your picture in the paper. You were laughing at me, weren't you? And you thought you fooled me at Tabitha's that night, didn't you?"

The answer to both questions was obviously no, but sadly Katie didn't feel a reply would do any good.

He held the knife in front of her face. "Tell me you're sorry."

She reached back to the art table holding her supplies, reached back until she found what she wanted.

"I'm sorry," she said, but that was a big, fat fucking lie. She wasn't one bit sorry.

With everything Katie had, she hit him with the cast-iron frying pan, splattering him with paint in the process. The knife dropped from his hand, but because she'd seen too many scary movies where someone should have hit the bad guy again, she did it. She hit him again. He collapsed facedown on her carpet and, uncontrollably, her stomach lurched and she threw up all over him. She let out a scream that could have curdled cream and took off at a dead run.

Frying pan still clutched in her fist, she ran down the hall, swerved around the corner, just in time to see her front door swing open.

Lola's kick-ass mojo must have really worked, because Katie didn't stop to think about what she was doing. She'd be damned if she let anyone take her down. The skillet started swinging.

One man ducked one way. And the other . . . "Red!"

Hearing the voice, she let go of the weapon midswing.

It Frisbeed across the living room. She heard glass shattering, then she heard the voice again. Right then, she felt herself falling. Rays didn't usually faint, but this one sure did.

Then she felt someone grab her. Someone that smelled a little spicy. Someone that made her feel safe. "Carl?" Her rock.

"Are you okay?"

Okay? Okay? Okay. The words echoed in her head.

"He was going to kill me," she managed to say, and then her own words echoed in her head.

"Where is he?" Ben asked, in a voice that sounded as if he yelled—or maybe he didn't yell, maybe it was an echo. She pointed down the hall, feeling dizzy, seeing black spots float before her eyes.

Carl leaned her against the wall and took off with his brother. Katie's knees folded and she slid down the wall to the floor. Her teeth started chattering.

The next thing she knew, Carl was lifting her up and moving her to her bedroom. As they walked past the study, she saw Ben standing over a crumpled form, a crumpled form that had come at her with her own butcher knife.

Then a new thought exploded in her head. Had she killed a man with the cast-iron skillet? Rays were so not murderers. "Is he . . . is he . . . ?" She couldn't say the word.

"No," Carl said. He forced her to keep moving until he had her in the bedroom. He kept walking her until he sat her down on the bed. Then he took her face in his hands and studied her. "Red? Did he hurt you? Did he . . . touch you?"

She understood what he asked. "He didn't rape me." She immediately started shaking and her teeth started rattling.

He held her against him and then helped her get dressed. She'd had so many plans for the day and they had included being naked with him, but not like this. Not like this.

Before Katie was completely dressed, sirens started wailing and a few minutes later her house was wall-to-wall cops. Katie watched them buzz around her place and she couldn't think straight; everything seemed to pass in a blur. At least she recognized what was happening this time. The shaking, the jitters. This was shock. But she would get over it, because she was a Ray.

And because she had her rock.

At least for now, anyway.

Les showed up and sat on the sofa with her. Carl came over to introduce himself, and Les shot him a go-to-hell look. "So you're the dickhead, huh?"

Carl didn't flinch. "That would be me." He walked away.

Katie and Les watched as ambulance drivers wheeled Mel Grimes away. The creep tugged at the restraints and screamed about everyone laughing at him.

"You kicked a serial killer's ass!" Les said for the tenth time, and gave Katie's arm a squeeze.

She still felt numb inside. "It was Lola's mojo."

Ben walked over, smiling. "I personally like the fact that you puked on him."

"Oh, that's priceless," said Les.

"I didn't mean to," Katie said, not really seeing the humor.

"You feel up to answering some questions at the station?" Ben asked.

Katie met his eyes. "Haven't we done this enough?"

He helped her up. "Just my job, Red. I mean, Katie."

Katie promised to call Les as soon as she was released, then rode with Ben and Carl to the police department. Carl sat in the backseat beside her. He pulled her into his shoulder. She wanted to tell him that she didn't need perfect, but the timing didn't feel right. Nothing felt right yet.

When they arrived at the police station, Mr. Hades waited in the parking lot. As she stepped out of the car, he came hurrying over to her and pulled her against his solid frame. For some reason, she chose that moment to completely fall apart. She sobbed into his shirt, then she sobbed some more, and he held her, held her as her father might have held her, if he'd been alive.

When Ben led Katie away to get her statement, Carl looked at his dad. Carl had never believed he'd be jealous of his own old man, but when Katie had clung to the elder Hades as he'd wanted her to cling to him, he'd felt the green emotion gnaw at his backbone.

Red had needed someone, and that someone hadn't been him. Sure, he didn't deserve to be her hero. He'd been an ass, but—

A terrible thought hit him. What if it was too late for him to turn things around? What if Katie wouldn't forgive him?

No, he couldn't accept that. He had to show her . . . show her that . . . that he really wanted to change. That he planned on changing.

Carl jumped up, then swung around. "Call Ben and tell him not to let her out until I get back. Thirty minutes tops."

"Where the hell are you going?" his dad bellowed.

"I've got to get something at my house."

"Get what?"

"Something for Red. Something I have to show her."

Carl shot out the door and then came running back in. Before he asked, his dad tossed him his car keys.

He rushed home to get the one thing that might convince Red he could change.

Thirty minutes later, Carl came storming back in. "She's not out yet?"

His dad shook his head. Carl dropped his bag in the

chair. Too antsy to sit down, he paced around the waiting room.

Suddenly his dad was beside him, with the bag in his hand. These aren't the ones you were watching yesterday?" Buck asked.

Carl could have sworn he heard Ben's voice, and he kept his eyes on the door, waiting for Red.

"Son, are these the videos you were watching yesterday?" Buck asked, more forcefully this time.

"Yeah," Carl muttered.

The door swung open and Red was there.

Carl snagged the bag from his dad. His dad grabbed the bag back. "You can't give these to her."

That got Carl's attention. "Why the hell not?"

Buck looked worried. "Damn, son! Katie's not some . . . she's a good girl," he added, lowering his voice.

"I know that." Carl pulled on the bag.

His dad pulled back.

"Let go," Carl growled.

"No. You're gonna ruin it."

"I'm not going to ruin it!" Carl shot Red another glance and literally yanked the bag from his dad's hands.

"Oh hell," Buck said, and held up his arms in fury. "You can't give a woman porn! I thought I raised you right."

Katie stepped into the waiting room, praying Carl would be there. When her gaze lit on him, she suddenly felt her world might be okay. She'd stopped shaking, mostly.

After exchanging words with his dad, which looked almost confrontational, Carl marched over to her and, in front of everyone, he pulled her into his arms.

"I'm so glad you're here." She pulled back.

"We need to talk," they said at the same time.

She decided to go first. "Today I painted a rose and it sucked. It wasn't totally sucky, but even Lola agreed, it pretty much sucked. She said that it was because I was trying to make everything perfect. She's right. I wanted to meet up to what everyone expected of me, and I thought . . ."

Carl leaned in. "Red. *Breathe*."

She did. Once. But she really wanted to say this before he said something like good-bye. "Lola said—"

"Red?" He put a finger over her lips. "If you're about to tell me that you don't think this will work or call me a dickhead, not that I don't realize I've been one, but well, first, please let me . . ." He paused as if the words wouldn't come. "I . . . I got you something. Or I got me something, but you should see it."

He held up a plastic bag.

"Don't do it!" Mr. Hades yelled out from the other side of the room.

She glanced at Carl's dad and shook her head. Then she focused back on Carl and his bag. She didn't want gifts. "Carl, I don't want—"

He kissed her again to shut her up. "Red, please, open up the bag."

She did. Tucked inside were DVDs. She looked up him.

He spoke before she could ask. "It's *The Brady Bunch*. I got all they had."

Katie looked into the bag and her vision fogged with tears. Crying in public was so un-Ray-like, but she decided it was time for her to make some new Ray guidelines.

"I've watched all of them but three."

She pressed her palm against his chest. "You really watched them?"

"All night. And the thing is, I can do this. The whole *Brady Bunch* thing. I'm 100 percent positive I'm going to screw up along the way. So I figure, I'll probably be spending a lot of nights waiting for you in the bathtub. But . . . I want to wash dishes with you for . . . for forever. I want to fly kites with you every Easter, and when you need a shoulder to cry on . . ." He reached over and rubbed his shoulder. "I want that shoulder to be mine. I know one of mine is shot up, but it feels so much better when you're against it."

She wrapped her arms around his neck. Lola was wrong. Perfection wasn't a myth. Maybe it came rough around the edges, but Carl Hades was perfect . . . well, perfect for her. "I think I'm *probably* in love with you, Carl Hades."

His brow pinched. "Probably? What's this *probably* shit?"

She smiled. "Let me rephrase that. I love you, Carl Hades."

"Much better." He kissed her, and it wasn't the kind of kiss a Ray accepted in public, but it was just the kind of kiss Katie wanted to get, publicly and privately, for the rest of her life. And there was no probably about that, either.

☐ **YES!**

Sign me up for the Love Spell Book Club and send my FREE BOOKS! If I choose to stay in the club, I will pay only $8.50* each month, a savings of $6.48!

NAME: _____

ADDRESS: _____

TELEPHONE: _____

EMAIL: _____

☐ I want to pay by credit card.

☐ **VISA**   ☐ **MasterCard.**   ☐ **DISCOVER**

ACCOUNT #: _____

EXPIRATION DATE: _____

SIGNATURE: _____

Mail this page along with $2.00 shipping and handling to:
Love Spell Book Club
PO Box 6640
Wayne, PA 19087
Or fax (must include credit card information) to:
610-995-9274

You can also sign up online at **www.dorchesterpub.com**.